Futuristic Romance

Love in another time, another place.

BOLD SEDUCTION

"Aayshen?" Laura said worriedly. His face was flushed, the wineglass poised in midair. It had never occured to her that he might not react the same to alcohol. Her anxious voice rose half an octave. "Are you all right?"

"I'm very fine," he said. He gave her a long smoldering look and brushed a hand along her ankle.

"No, Aayshen." She drew a shuddering breath, then gently pushed his hand away. "I don't want you to touch me, and I don't want you to poke around in my head, either."

Confusion darkened his opaque eyes. Ever since that first night she had welcomed the touch of his mind and hands. "Laura...."

She rose on her knees and faced him, a slow, sensuous smile playing over her shadowed features. "Tonight is different...special." Her eyes, dark with expectation, caught and held his. "Don't move, don't talk, don't even think," she whispered. "All I want you to do is feel."

He was completely bewildered now. "I don't—"

"Shh." She lifted a finger to his lips to belay any questions. "You're about to learn what the word seduction means, Aayshen Rahs."

Not Quite Paradise

JAN ZIMLICH

LOVE SPELL   NEW YORK CITY

LOVE SPELL®

September 1995

Published by

Dorchester Publishing Co., Inc.
276 Fifth Avenue
New York, NY 10001

The name "Love Spell" and its logo are trademarks of Dorchester Publishing Co., Inc.

Printed in the United States of America.

*For my family, especially my mother,
Helen McBride Nelson, who always wanted a book
dedicated to her—not quite what you expected is it?*

Prologue

Sunset was just a memory now, a vague waking dream of pastel shades textured with the grays of twilight. A still, heavy darkness had settled over the sloping levee and the ancient water oaks that rimmed the muddy banks of the Pascagoula River. The sunset hues had yielded to the deepening night, and the cold white light of a thousand stars glittered in the Mississippi sky.

No wind moved through the weathered gray oaks, and the only sounds were the furtive rustlings of an occasional night creature foraging through the marsh and scrub. Even the river was quiet. Slick and brackish brown, the water slid past without sound as it curled southward on its slow journey to the Gulf of Mexico.

Atop the crest of the levee, Laura Malek pillowed her head in her arms and gazed up at the distant stars arching across the winter sky. She sighed deeply, enjoying the sight, the dearth of sound, the peaceful landscape. This was her favorite place, hers and Bryan's, their special place.

"Star light, star bright, first star . . ." The childish voice hesitated.

Laura smiled in the darkness and wrapped an arm around her young son, snuggling him close against her side. Saw grass prickled her back through the old quilt spread beneath them. "First star I see tonight," she prodded gently.

Bryan Malek fixed his gaze on the brightest star and squeezed his lids closed. "I wish I may, I wish I might, have the wish I wish tonight."

Her fingers twined through his blond-red hair. "Don't tell me what you wished or it won't come true," she said.

"I won't." The five-year-old opened his eyes and gave his mother a swift, probing glance. "What about you, Mom? Did you make a wish?"

"What for?" Laura smiled again and hugged him closer. "I already have you, and Grampa. I don't want or need anything else." A sudden wistful expression stole across her heart-shaped face. Was that true? Really true?

Bryan turned his attention back to the stars. He lifted a stubby finger and pointed to a tiny circle of light shimmering in the blackened sky. His star. "Which one is that, Mom?"

She lifted her gaze heavenward and followed the direction of his finger. Luckily it was one she knew. "Polaris." Other stars in the constellation were only dim pinpoints. "It's called the North Star because sailors use it for navigation." A sliver of moonlight found its way through a tree, bathing the quiet river in its silvery glow. "No matter where he is, if a sailor can see that star, he can find his way home again."

Polaris shone steadily, a solitary beacon lighting the way through a vast black sea. They watched the sky in silence for long minutes.

"Mom?" Bryan said finally. "Isn't space kind of like a sea?"

Her fingers moved through his hair again. "Sort of, I guess."

The child was quiet for a few seconds, considering. The inky blackness stretched in every direction, as far as he could see. "You think there are sailors out there? Maybe they use the North Star to find their way home, too."

"I don't know." An uncertain frown rippled across her forehead. Laura stared at the sky and glittering stars, wondering herself. "Maybe."

Chapter One

In the darkness beyond the viewport, the cloud-mottled planet swelled in size, a shimmering circle of blue turning through the cold black silence of the cosmic night. Aayshen Rahs sat very still, transfixed by the vivid jewel-toned blue of the planet's vast seas, the deep greens and reddish browns of its cloud-streaked landmasses, colors so vibrant and intense they made his eyes ache. The sight was breathtaking, and alien to everything he knew.

As the shuttle streaked closer, the small blue planet continued to grow, expanding in size until it almost filled visible space. Aayshen stared out the viewport in silence, fascinated by a delicate swirl of clouds sweeping across a sunlit sea. The old legends about water planets were many and galaxy-wide, tales of liquid seas stretching from horizon to horizon, of exotic worlds where life was not a scientific oddity. He shook his head slowly and flexed the knotted muscles in his back. This was no legend, no tale told to wide-eyed children. This was real.

"So much water . . ." Aayshen whispered to himself.

Beside him, the shuttle's Kri technician stirred, his slanted yellow eyes fixed on the planet turning slowly in the darkness. "Yes. It seems unfair somehow, don't you think, Commander?"

Aayshen nodded, feeling a twinge of envy himself. "No one ever said that the Fates were fair, Drallondryn." War. Misery. Death. He had learned long ago that the universe was cold and unrelenting.

Drallondryn sighed in agreement and keyed a command into the shuttle's sensor array. "Beginning preliminary scans of the planet's surface."

"This is an inhabited world, Technician," Aayshen warned him. "Keep your sensor sweep to a minimum. We're here to do a quiet planetary survey, not broadcast our presence on every wavelength of the electromagnetic spectrum."

"Yes, sir." Drallondryn adjusted his signal strength downward, though it pained him to do so. The less powerful his scan was, the less information he would receive in return. "Judging by the state of the planet's technological development, I don't believe they are capable of detecting us."

"Maybe not." Aayshen began readying the small observation ship for entry into the atmosphere. "But I want no surprises when we land." He fed a final string of data into the navigation controls, then stared at the viewscreen in silence. On the planet's surface, flat patches of green and brown had given way to soaring mountains, their jagged peaks blanketed with what he assumed to be layers of glittering ice crystals. The brilliant blues of the planet's endless seas were now tinged in places with a cool, smoky green, a color he had never seen before in nature.

So strange. So beautiful. As different from his home world as night was from day. Savan, with its stark gray mountains and barren vistas of sterile sand, couldn't compare with this newly discovered world.

The Savanian settled himself into the padded command chair and fastened his seat restraints, glad that he would soon be free of the shuttle's cramped confines, even for just a little while. He was tired of breathing manufactured air, sick of the steel-walled sameness of life aboard a starship. It was the promise of a momentary escape from that life that had led him to take command of the probe ship himself, a routine duty that should have fallen to a lesser officer. Aayshen sighed, his pale gaze moving to a thin band of stars shimmering in the darkness. When was the last time he had felt a wind or the heat of a sun against his skin? Two years? Three?

"How long do you think we'll need to be on the planet's surface, Commander?" Drallondryn asked anxiously. The idea of landing on an alien world sent a shiver of apprehension up his spine. "I've never been part of a planetary survey before, and I'm not exactly sure what to expect." The inhabitants could be flesh-eating barbarians for all he knew.

Lost in thought, Aayshen stared absently at the milky veil of stars shimmering beyond the planet.

When Aayshen failed to answer, Drallondryn frowned and glanced sideways at his commanding officer, his cool, appraising gaze sweeping over the Savanian's pale face. Aayshen's features were sharp and lean, a study in angles framed by a thick mass of platinum blond hair, features which bore the unmistakable stamp of a Savanian genetics lab. But the eyes betrayed his designer as a renegade, an experimenter. They were the same crystalline blue as a Savanian star-rise, a color much at odds with the normal velvet-black of his race.

"Commander?" Deep lines of concern edged through the glossy black fur covering Drallondryn's brow. Aayshen was still staring into the darkness, his pale gaze focused on infinity. The Kri's frown deepened. For the past few days, ever since the shuttle had left its mother ship, the *Stellar Wind*, those ice-blue eyes had held a haunted, faraway look the Kri had never seen before, as though Aayshen Rahs were searching for something in the distance, something just beyond his reach. "Commander Rahs?"

Aayshen shook himself out of his reverie, his gaze angling to the furry dark shape sitting beside him. "Sorry. What did you say?"

"I just wanted to know how long we would need to be on the planet's surface."

"An hour or two, just long enough to collect routine air samples and biological specimens." The suggestion of a smile played across the telepath's angular features. He didn't need to read Drallondryn's thoughts to know what was bothering him.

15

"Are you worried about making landfall, Technician?"

The Kri's lips peeled back in a sheepish grin, revealing a needle-thin row of glistening fangs. "A bit, I guess." His bright yellow eyes darkened with a mixture of uneasiness and fear. What if his scans had been detected? "Do you really think the inhabitants might be aggressive?"

Aayshen shrugged, platinum-blond hair rippling across his shoulders. "If your assessment of the planet's communications technology is any indication, the inhabitants are barely beyond the primitive stage. Hopefully, we'll land, do the survey, and be gone before they ever know we were there."

Some of the tension faded from Drallondryn's eyes, but his apprehension remained firmly entrenched. It was his assessment of the planet's level of technology that had convinced the commander to risk a landing. He offered up a silent prayer to the gods and near-gods that he was right.

The smile touched the edges of Aayshen's mouth again as he studied the nervous Kri. "A touch of fear in a tactical situation is to your advantage, Technician. Don't suppress it. Fear keeps your senses honed to razor-sharpness." Through the years Aayshen had learned to control his fear, revel in it. It was the only thing that made him feel alive nowadays. The sensation was familiar, exciting. "Only a fool would not be frightened when faced with the unknown."

"Then I guess I am not a fool," the Kri said quietly. He felt a sudden need to know more about this mysterious blue planet. Knowledge was the only weapon against the unknown. He touched a pad on the console, and a pulsing, rhythmic sound suddenly filled the shuttle's control deck, punctuated at frequent intervals by a pounding beat that vibrated from the soles of their boots all the way to their fingertips. He touched the pad again to lower the volume. "Sorry, Commander."

Aayshen grimaced, his ears still ringing from the discordant noise he had been forced to listen to off and on for three days now. The horrid sounds were made by microwave leakage from the planet's atmosphere, the same signals that had been picked up in deep space by the *Stellar Wind* several weeks ago. It was the first indication that they'd had of intelligent life in this sector, and the reason the observation ship had been dispatched to investigate.

He frowned and shook his head in disbelief. Entertainment signals, Drallondryn had surmised, some form of music. But Aayshen wasn't so sure. How could anyone find such sounds entertaining? Listening did serve a purpose, though. Drallondryn was an expert in primitive languages, and with the help of the computer's translation programs, he had already assimilated a rudimentary knowledge of the most predominant language.

But knowing that didn't make listening to alien voices shrieking in those guttural, clipped tones a pleasant experience. Aayshen kneaded the center of his forehead, then fired the braking thrusters and rolled the small craft into position for entry into the atmosphere. "Contact with atmosphere in five seconds."

The nose of the shuttle began glowing orange-red as it skimmed across the outer fringes of the planet's upper atmosphere. Within seconds the orange glow vanished, and the shuttle plunged inside the atmosphere, careening downward into a blindingly blue sky.

"Crossing into night," Aayshen said a moment later, and the shuttle was suddenly immersed in darkness again as they crossed the boundary to the planet's nightside. He touched a rarely used control on the console, and the shuttle's curving wings swept forward, giving the small ship the appearance of an exotic bird gliding through the night-darkened sky.

As the shuttle began rocking back and forth, buffeted by the strong upper-level winds, Aayshen stared through the viewport. Nothing save the planet's dark and forbidding seas stretched beneath them, but toward the wide curve of the horizon the white haze of a million lights winked invitingly, like so many incandescent insects glittering in the darkness. "There," he said, pointing to the distant lights. "We'll bring the shuttle down on that land mass."

A shrill sound from the control console caused him to shift his attention. His somber gaze flickered over the bank of monitors until a blurry image on the proximity scanner caught his eye. "Sensor contact," he said as the electronic blip edged across the screen, moving swiftly, unmistakably in their direction. Aayshen muttered a Savanian curse under his breath. The tiny observation craft had no defensive armaments, no shielding to protect them from an attack. "It's on an intercept vector."

Drallondryn's claws dug deep ridges into the

chair's padded armrests. "So much for my technological assessment."

Aayshen clenched his jaw and stared bleakly at the speeding blip, then his eyes darted from the monitor to the darkness sweeping past the transparency. It was too late for second thoughts now. "We should have visual contact any moment now."

"Base, this is RM772." The Air Force pilot glanced at the electronic blip streaking across his radar screen. "I have the bogey on my scope. He's still hypersonic, moving along at better than Mach 2. I should have visual in about thirty seconds. What are your instructions?" Static crackled in his ears.

He switched on his night-vision gear and glanced through the canopy to the right of the F-15's cramped cockpit. "Eglin, what are your instructions?"

"RM772," a voice finally said. "You have clearance to fire. Repeat, you have clearance to fire. Splash the bogey."

"Uh, roger that, Eglin. Splash the bogey." Adrenaline surged through his bloodstream. The young officer checked his altitude and craned his neck to see through the canopy. Except for a dark patch of sky looming over him, he saw only stars. Clouds, the pilot thought. Then his eyes widened in horrified comprehension. The dark patch wasn't clouds. It was moving faster than he was and descending.

He screamed behind his face mask.

For a split second of time the stars disappeared, blocked completely by something big and dark

Jan Zimlich

streaking over the top of the jet with a scant hundred feet to spare.

Then as quickly as it had come, the object vanished into a curtain of clouds, leaving the Air Force pilot with a vague mental impression of clean, sleek lines and curving metal wings.

A high-pitched electronic tone sounded through the cockpit. The weapons system had a lock. His hand trembling, he thumbed a button and fired two air-to-air missiles.

Chapter Two

The shuttle brushed the top of a tree, then scraped across another, ripping limbs and a deluge of smaller branches from the slender trunks. Something large and dark collided with the left wing. Aayshen tensed, the muscles in his neck and back bunching involuntarily in anticipation of the impact.

The tail section of the shuttle came down first, slamming into the ground with surprising swiftness. Just as quickly they were airborne again, but the respite lasted only a brief moment. The shuttle touched down again, harder this time, wrenching Aayshen and Drallondryn sideways in their seats. Tortured metal screamed in protest as the small ship finally settled down on its belly, sliding wildly across the alien terrain, helpless against the force of its own momentum.

Jan Zimlich

A crackle of static shot through the electronics in the console; then the lights dimmed and sputtered out of existence, plunging the control deck into total darkness.

There was one final bone-jarring jolt; then suddenly, amazingly, it ended. A bulkhead gave one last protesting groan and fell silent.

Aayshen flexed his battered limbs experimentally and blinked in the near-blackness to focus his eyes. Hazy light from the planet's solitary moon was streaming through the viewport, casting silvery shadows on the shuttle's darkened interior and Drallondryn's still form.

"Technician?" The telepath trailed a finger across the Kri's temple and reached out with his thoughts, his mind brushing against Drallondryn's for one brief second. Aayshen sagged in relief. The Kri's thoughts were obscured by a thick bog of pain caused by a blow to his shoulder, but otherwise he was undamaged. Aayshen released the catch on his seat restraint and struggled to stand on uncertain legs.

"Drallondryn . . ." He grabbed the shoulder of his flightsuit and shook hard. "On your feet," he snapped in the tone which sent shivers up the spines of his junior officers. "We have to get out of here before whoever shot us down discovers where we crashed."

As if to prove his words, the shrill whine of an aircraft shrieked through the night-darkened skies above them. Aayshen glanced out the viewport, but saw nothing save for a tangle of green foliage. He shook the Kri's shoulder more forcefully. "Now, Drallondryn!"

The Kri cracked his eyes open and fumbled for

the release button on his harness. "I'm trying," he said hoarsely. His tongue felt thick, and his limbs felt like melted rubber. "I believe my shoulder is damaged. It hurts, but I don't think it's broken."

"Unfortunately, we don't have time to see to it now." Once Aayshen was certain that Drallondryn had regained his feet, he threaded his way through the darkness to the cabin hatch. "Activate the auto-destruct manually, and rig a time delay. I'll set it off myself when we're ready to leave the ship."

The fog of confusion lifted from Drallondryn's brain abruptly. "Yes, sir." He ripped open an access panel beneath the console and groped inside, thoughts of being captured spurring him to work faster.

"When you've finished here," Aayshen continued, "come to the cabin. Hurry." He punched the hatch switch, but the airlock to the passenger cabin refused to budge. Cursing silently, he flipped open a tiny panel in the frame and grasped a metal wheel, cranking the airlock open manually.

The hatch finally split open with a creaking wail. As his eyes gradually adjusted to the lack of light, he picked out the boxy shapes of the Kri's sensor equipment strewn about the cabin. Aayshen climbed over an acceleration seat that had been torn from its moorings, then cocked his head and listened to the shriek of chemical engines in the distance.

The sound galvanized him into action. Squinting in the dim light, he headed for the storage locker to the right of the hatch and stepped inside, reemerging a moment later carrying a pile of bulky equipment. He dumped his load on the tilted deck and made several more forays inside the locker, increasing the size of the pile with every trip.

Drallondryn stumbled over the remains of a sensor monitor as he felt his way into the cabin. "I've rigged the time delay, Commander."

"Good." Aayshen's last stack of equipment landed at Drallondryn's feet.

The Kri stared at the object curiously, wondering what he was supposed to do with it. The thing was large and dark, vaguely resembling the shape of a person.

"It's a reconnaissance suit," Aayshen said curtly. "Put it on." He picked up the top half of his own suit and shoved his arms inside, clamping the armored chest plate shut with a skilled ease born of years of practice. Next came the bottom half of the ponderous suit, then the protective boots and gloves, the entire process taking less than a minute.

Fully suited except for his helmet, he turned to the Kri, who was still staring at an armored chest plate with an expression hovering somewhere between curiosity and horror. "I would suggest you hurry," Aayshen grunted as he checked the energy levels on his suit's power pack. "Unless you care to be left behind."

Drallondryn slid his good arm inside a heavy sleeve. "I am a technician-scientist, Commander, not a warrior. I have never felt the need to familiarize myself with tools of war such as this."

Aayshen blew out his breath noisily and guided the Kri's injured arm into the other sleeve. "Then I suggest you 'familiarize' yourself quickly. Because you just became a soldier."

Cutting off any further protests, Aayshen stepped into the cramped locker again and surveyed the assortment of weapons stacked neatly inside. He slung two heavyweight pulse rifles over his shoulder and grabbed several hand weapons.

The Kri was fully suited when he exited the locker. "Ready?" Aayshen asked.

Drallondryn's helmet bobbed once in the dim light.

"Good." Aayshen tossed him a rifle and a hand weapon, then clipped his survival pack into a slot on the suit's back. After a final glance around the cabin, he snapped his helmet into place and activated the recon suit's com-set. "Blow the hatch, Technician."

A muffled whomp rattled the shuttle as the emergency hatch was blown. There was a hiss of escaping air and the heavy metal hatch burst outward, clanging to the ground amidst a jungle of torn limbs and broken branches.

Pale light from the planet's moon crept through the hole where the hatch had been. "Go!" Aayshen threw a portable transceiver pack to Drallondryn. "Take cover. I'm going to activate the destruct timer. We can't leave anything for the barbarians to find."

Drallondryn jumped through the hole in the shuttle's side. Unused to the bulky equipment, he landed hard atop a fallen tree trunk, crushing his tail between his backside and the heavy recon suit. He yowled in pain, then maneuvered himself behind an uprooted tree as Aayshen jumped clear of the shuttle and dove for cover beside him.

The first explosion fractured the ship's spine.

Wings snapped, and the passenger cabin collapsed into several huge pieces. The second explosion, more powerful than the first, sent a tower of fire soaring into the night sky. Flames licked greedily at the surrounding treetops.

Aayshen climbed slowly to his feet and stood in the shower of flaming embers and debris falling from the sky. He stared in silence at the shuttle's burning remains, acutely aware that all connections with his previous life had just been traumatically severed. They were stranded here for an unknown length of time. Aliens on an alien world.

Subdued and silent, Drallondryn appeared beside him, the glare of the flames reflecting off his darkened visor.

Aayshen studied him for a long moment. The scientist was depending on him, waiting for his next order. He sighed raggedly. The weight of command lay heavily on his shoulders this night.

Drallondryn watched the flames a few seconds longer, then angled his ponderous suit around to face Aayshen. "If fortune favors us, Commander, the planet's inhabitants will believe that we were incinerated in the explosion."

"Perhaps." Aayshen's eyes were drawn upward when he heard the muffled *whump, whump* of a different type of aircraft circling high overhead. He adjusted the shoulder strap on his rifle and hefted the transceiver pack. "But not if we stand around in the open much longer."

Drallondryn glanced at the dense vegetation stretching in every direction. "Which way?"

"There." Aayshen pointed to a small rise blanketed by a thick stand of trees. "Away from the sea." His boots sinking ankle-deep in the loamy soil, he trudged toward the north. Drallondryn followed.

"Jeezuz!" the helicopter pilot shouted, loud enough to be heard above the din of the rotor noise. Bright orange flames were climbing a hundred feet past treetop level, casting an oily pall of smoke into the Mississippi sky. "Whatever it was, Colonel, it sure doesn't exist anymore."

Lemanuel Chapman wasn't so sure. They'd already flown over the area twice and there weren't any flames then. The bogey hadn't exploded on impact. "Take us down for a closer look-see of the area, Lieutenant."

Light from the tower of flames danced across Chapman's vision, glinting off the Air Force helicopter's windscreen as they swept over the tops of tall pines in a wide loop. To the right, a dense stand of Southern pines gave way to coastal swampland stretching northward to a series of murky bayous and winding rivers. A little further north, 1-10 cut a wide swath across the flat terrain.

As the helicopter skimmed over the treetops for a final pass, Chapman fixed his gaze on a small marshy clearing. A glint of metal in the darkness brought him up short. His body stilled. Silhouetted by the orange glare of flames, two figures clad in black metallic suits and helmets were racing across the clearing, plunging headlong toward a stand of trees a few yards ahead. Then the black-suited figures dissolved into shadow, veiled by darkness and the surrounding woods.

Chapman's stern, dark features visibly tightened, and his hands began trembling with excitement. Two of them. They couldn't be allowed to slip away now. "Lieutenant! Get me a secure channel to Keesler Air Force Base! I want this area sealed off, and the EBE Search Team deployed on the double!"

The Air Force colonel began to laugh, whether from fear or joy he didn't know, and didn't care. He had been waiting and training for this moment for over ten years. EBEs—Extraterrestrial Biological Entities. Chapman laughed again, drawing an inquiring glance from the young pilot. The Air Force finally had an extraterrestrial ground-sighting by an impeccable source—the head of their own regional EBE Search Team.

Out of breath, Aayshen stopped and stared upward as the sound of engines receded in the distance. There were other noises now. Close at hand, he could hear the quiet drone of insects flitting through the dense foliage and the shrill chirps of night creatures calling from hidden perches high in the trees. The cacophony of odd sounds made him feel out of place on this strange world. But at the same time, that very strangeness was somehow exhilarating, as though he had just awakened into a different life on a new and intoxicating world.

A sharp jab in the back of his neck reminded him of who and what he was in no uncertain terms. The recon suit's electronics had monitored his change in mood and begun injecting him with the plethora of chemicals Command deemed useful on long planetside patrols. His face grew warm and flushed as stimulants to regulate his mood and keep his senses honed to a razor point were pumped into his bloodstream. He knew the injection would also contain the customary neural enhancers to boost his memory, giving him the ability to remember in exquisite detail everything he saw, everything he did and learned. Once the memory enhancers took hold, he would be able to assimilate the local language and customs with amazing rapidity, learning what he needed to survive in hours instead of the usual weeks or months. Motioning for the Kri to follow, he wended his way through the heavy vegetation, his boots sinking deeper into the mushy black soil.

Aayshen stopped and scooped up a gloveful of the soggy loam. His lips puckered in distaste. "What is this muck?"

Through his visor, Drallondryn eyed the contents of Aayshen's hand, his whiskers twitching curiously. "It seems to be a mixture of soil, water, decayed organic matter and vegetation."

"Uuckk." Grimacing, Aayshen dropped the oozing glob. "I hope the whole planet isn't made of this mess."

"On the contrary," Drallondryn replied, warming to the subject as his suit pumped pain-deadeners through his body. "My data indicated that the planet's topography and climate are amazingly diverse." He stopped to retrieve a delicately pointed leaf from the mud and stuffed it into his utility pouch for later study. "The climate extremes are particularly interesting," he droned on. "The area we are now in appears to be subtropical, that explains the—"

"Quiet!" Aayshen whispered as his suit bleeped an electronic warning. Something large and loud was moving beyond the slender trees. He swiveled his helmet back and forth to make the widest possible scan. Moving pulses of red light appeared across the inside of his visor, indicating the position and speed of the object.

Inside the confines of his helmet, Aayshen frowned in confusion. The target was moving at ground level in a fairly straight line, receding from the suit's scanning range rapidly. Another blip appeared, then several more, all tracking in the opposite direction at irregular intervals. His frown deepened. No matter what lay ahead, they had to keep moving. .

"Stay close and low," he said quietly, and took off at a fast jog, zigzagging through the maze of trees and wiry underbrush for cover. Then the landscape changed abruptly, and he was out in the open, exposed. He fell to the ground and inched his way up a small grassy embankment on his hands and knees until he reached a long metal barrier blocking his path. Aayshen studied the flimsy barrier, trying to discern its purpose. It was too low to be of any practical use.

A hazy beam of light suddenly stabbed through the darkness, and a small ground vehicle roared past, leaving behind the acrid stench of burning fossil-fuels. The corresponding blip on the inside of his visor edged slowly out of range.

Drallondryn lifted his head out of the tall grass and sniffed delicately. He could even smell the stink inside his suit. "Burning hydrocarbons," he whispered. "The barbarians must use them for energy." He turned the air scrubbers in his recon suit on high. The toxic fumes were beginning to make him feel light-headed. "Disgusting."

"Shhh!" Aayshen ducked into the thick grass as

another ground vehicle sputtered past, belching fumes and clouds of poisonous smoke. When the vehicle's lights had finally been swallowed by darkness, he rolled onto his back to face Drallondryn. He had no options. They had to cross the barrier and whatever lay beyond it. His helmet swiveled toward the Kri. "If you are forced to shoot, Technician, try to incapacitate only."

Drallondryn nodded nervously and unslung his rifle.

"Stay close," Aayshen said. "When I give the signal, we move." He climbed to his feet and surveyed the area beyond the barrier. For the moment, his visor was clear of sensor contacts.

"Now!" He scrambled up the embankment and vaulted the barrier effortlessly. Ahead of him two wide swaths of hard-packed rock sliced across the landscape, stretching out of his range of vision in either direction. His boots clattering on the smooth expanse of rock, he sprinted for the other side, Drallondryn close on his heels.

As they neared the dividing strip of vegetation, Drallondryn wheezed and staggered to a breathless stop. The pain in his shoulder was back, more intense than before, and growing stronger with each step.

Aayshen glanced over his shoulder and paused. The Kri had stopped out in the open. "Move, Drallondryn! Before we're both captured!"

"Please," he wailed, bending double to catch his breath. "I must rest for a moment. I'm not used to wearing one of these heavy suits."

A pulsing red light sidled into scanning range on Aayshen's visor. "Technician!" Mumbling a curse under his breath, Aayshen ran back for him.

31

Half dragging, half carrying the exhausted Kri, he started back for the opposite side and the safety of the trees.

Twin beams of light suddenly sliced through the darkness, capturing them in their hazy white glow. Aayshen groaned inwardly. Caught halfway across the last strip of paving, they didn't have time to run for cover. Deciding to hold his ground, he dropped to his knees and faced the huge object roaring toward them, the rifle aimed and primed.

The ear-splitting wail of a warning signal bellowed across the countryside. Aayshen clenched his jaw and tensed. There was another warning wail, then with a grinding roar, the vehicle swerved around them, skidding to a jerky stop in a choking cloud of burning rubber.

Aayshen sighed heavily, then spun on his heels and dropped to a defensive stance, leveling his rifle on the red lights blinking across the rear of the rectangular vehicle. They were supposed to be in hiding, not forcing an open confrontation with the natives. "Stay where you are, Technician," he ordered through his helmet mike. A door creaked open at the front of the vehicle. "Don't fire unless you're forced."

There was no need for the order to stay where he was. Drallondryn couldn't move. His boots seemed to have frozen to the paving. His hands shaking violently, he clicked the safety off his rifle.

The trucker leaped from the cab and peered into the inky shadows behind his trailer, his weathered face flushed with anger. The stupid idiots were still there, smack-dab in the middle of the road. "You morons!" he yelled. "You almost made me jackknife!" A little leery of the unmoving shapes, he patted the bulge in his back pocket, then marched resolutely down the shoulder of the road, emboldened by the comforting feel of the pistol pressed tight against his buttocks. He balled his hands into tight fists, growing more uneasy with each crunch of gravel beneath his boots. Normal people didn't stand in the middle of an interstate daring 18-wheelers to hit them. "What the hell's the matter with you buttheads?"

Aayshen's eyes darkened. The fat little barbarian's words were incomprehensible, but the challenge conveyed in his tone was understandable in any language. As Aayshen climbed to his feet with deliberate slowness, a sliver of moonlight stabbed through the blanket of storm clouds gathering in the west, illuminating the dark, polished surface of his recon suit.

The hairs along the back of the trucker's neck suddenly stiffened. The helmeted thing standing in the shadows was aiming the wrong end of an evil-looking gun directly at him.

A car horn blared and the frantic trucker flapped his arms for help as a pickup and a station wagon sped past without a second glance. His throat tightened. The robot-thing was barely 15 feet away.

Aayshen stood stock-still, his unwavering gaze locked on the nervous trucker. The barbarian had a weapon. He could feel it. "Don't move, Drallon-dryn. I'm going to disarm the barbarian and be done with this."

The trucker's hand began inching slowly for the back of his pants. "I got news for you buttheads," he shouted, his anger finally winning over fear. "Halloween's over . . . it's January, so cut the bull-

33

crap and put your costumes back in the closet. Save them and your bad jokes for next year." His gaze darted from one to the other, gauging their distance.

Aayshen's eyes narrowed behind his faceplate. *Botthaeds*. The barbarian had used that word and tone before. Undoubtedly it was an insult. "Can you translate what he said, Technician?" Aayshen whispered into the mike, puzzling over the garbled words.

A worried frown slanted across Drallondryn's forehead. "Most of it, but not all. He referred to us as body parts, mentioned something about slicing animal dung, then told us to save ourselves by getting into a storage locker for a long length of time."

Aayshen's left eyebrow slanted upwards. "You must have omitted something in the translation."

The Kri's fear deepened, adding ridges of worry to the sleek black fur covering his forehead. "I don't believe so, but I would need more data and practice for an exact translation." His fingers tightened around the rifle.

The trucker's hand trembled as it closed around the pistol. With a swiftness that belied his advancing years, he pulled the automatic from his pocket and squeezed off nine shots, emptying the clip in a few short seconds. His eyes widened in horror. The bullets had made sparks and a pinging noise as they ricocheted off the metal suits, but nothing more. Not one hole, not even a scorch mark was visible on either of them.

Drallondryn yelped and flinched reflexively at the sound of a projectile ricocheting off his recon suit. The pulse rifle jerked in his hands, and a six-foot section of metal on the rear of the trailer suddenly vanished in a blinding explosion of blue light. Jaw slack, he stared in disbelief at what he had done.

The pistol slipped from the trucker's nerveless fingers and clattered to the pavement. He took one look at the smoldering hole in his trailer, then screamed and ran, pounding down 1-10 as fast as his legs would carry him.

Feeling Aayshen's icy glare, Drallondryn shrugged helplessly. "I'm sorry, Commander. It was an accident."

Aayshen shook his head in disgust. He might as well have lit a signal flare. "Don't let it happen again." He took one last look at the burning trailer and a string of oncoming lights before sprinting for the woods again, altering their course slightly to the west to confuse any searchers.

Drallondryn fell into step behind him, watching Aayshen's tense back as they ran in silence.

After a long, uneventful hour, the thick foliage finally gave way to another vehicle path, one more narrow than the first and cracking with age.

Aayshen ground to a halt and studied a small green sign on the side of the pathway. Every populated planet had signs of one type or another, and they all meant something. "Can you translate that?" he asked, staring curiously at the sign's bold white lettering.

The Kri examined the lettering and searched his memory for any similar words.

ESCATAWPA

He shook his head in frustration. "Sorry, Commander. I have no idea."

Aayshen grunted, then moved past the mysterious sign, no longer bothering to conceal every movement. They had to find cover soon, a safe place to rest and recoup. Speed was the most important consideration now, and the vehicle pathways offered the quickest route of travel at the moment. Besides, he thought with a shrug, what more could possibly go wrong?

The first few drops of moisture spattered the top of his helmet, trickling down his faceplate like rivulets of sweat. Aayshen blinked in surprise at the liquid beading on his visor and stared upwards with wondering eyes. Drops of water were literally falling from the sky. He had heard and read of such a thing before, but had never witnessed it himself.

The tentative drops suddenly became a deluge, a streaming torrent of windblown water that pounded against his faceplate and obscured his vision.

Then his suit shorted out.

Chapter Three

"This . . . is . . . Jeopardy!" the announcer bellowed, loud enough to rattle pot lids a room away.

Laura Malek gave the pan of bubbling spaghetti sauce a vicious stir, splattering bright red tomato paste across the top of the stove. Being forced to listen to game shows day in and day out was bad enough, but did he have to turn the volume up so high?

"Turn it down, Grampa!" she shouted, struggling to make herself heard over the television's deafening roar.

A trickle of the splattered spaghetti sauce oozed down the front of the stove, staining the white enamel bright orange. "Dammitall," Laura muttered, and began wiping at the spill with furious swipes of a dishrag. "Grampa," she yelled again, more irritated by the second. "Please turn it down!" The roar from the television seemed to intensify.

Her eyes darkened to a deep, angry brown. If he wanted to sit on his butt all day long and stare at the TV, that was his business. But from now on, he was going to quit acting like a baby and wear his hearing aids. She already had one child to raise. She didn't need two.

Determined to have it out with the stubborn old man once and for all, Laura tossed the dirty dishrag atop the counter and stormed into the den, grinding to a furious stop beside his ancient recliner chair. She snatched the remote control from his withered fingers and hammered the mute button.

Garner Haines scowled at his granddaughter. "Turn the sound back on, Laura!" The perpetual frown etched across his wizened features grew more pronounced. "You're gonna make me miss the show." He made a grab for the treasured control, but the young woman skittered out of his reach.

Still guarding the remote, Laura perched herself on a sofa arm, digging her bare toes between the worn plaid cushions. "It won't kill you." He glared at her, and she glared back. "Why aren't you wearing your hearing aids, Grampa?"

"What?" Garner answered grumpily, eyeing the stolen control. "Speak up. You know I can't hear."

Laura rolled her eyes heavenward. "Give me patience," she mumbled to the ceiling, then yelled, "WHAT DID YOU DO WITH YOUR HEARING AIDS?"

Grumbling about impertinent young people, Garner shoved a bony, blue-veined hand inside a

38

pajama pocket and retrieved the hated things. He poked them into his ears and stared at his granddaughter sullenly. "Satisfied?"

"Yes."

"Good. Then give me back the control."

With Garner, life was a constant negotiation, an endless battle of wills and words. "Only if you promise to keep the volume down." Laura felt her irritation begin to drift away. It always did. She enjoyed their little battles, and had never been able to stay mad at him for very long.

"Agreed. Now give it to me and let an old man live his last days in peace."

Laura snorted. "You're not that old. Besides, you're too mean to die."

A wheezy laugh rumbled up from his chest, caught in his throat, and turned into a fit of coughing. "Not that old? Laura, I'm eighty-six."

The tight set to her delicate features melted away, replaced by a look that was both wistful and sad. Laura turned and stared listlessly through the half-open blinds behind the sofa, hiding her pained expression from his sharp blue eyes. Her pensive gaze swept over the squat row of dilapidated greenhouses, the acres and acres of withered brown saw grass and leafless pecan trees swaying in the chill winter wind. She placed her palms flat against a windowpane, feeling a hint of the numbing January cold through her fingertips. She didn't like to think about Garner's age, or the idea of him dying. When he was gone she and Bryan would be completely alone. No family, no ties. Nothing left but an aching hole in their lives too large to fill.

A bitter tear slid down her pale face, scalding

her cheek. The Malek family, her ex-inlaws, didn't count. When the divorce was final, they had vanished from her life entirely. They never even bothered to acknowledge Bryan's existence with an occasional phone call or birthday present, not even a simple card to let him know they cared. Some grandparents they were. The Maleks acted as if he had never been born.

Garner Haines's aged blue eyes wandered over his granddaughter's troubled features. He saw the pain etched across her heart-shaped face and knew its cause. Laura's life had always revolved around family, especially her parents. But they were long dead now, and he would be joining them in the not-too-distant future. Laura needed a new centering force in her life.

A calculating gleam suddenly sharpened his eyes, and he scrutinized her face intently, considering. At 31, her skin was still smooth and unlined, burnished gold by long days spent working outdoors tending the nursery and pecan orchard. The sun had also touched her blondish hair with fiery highlights, giving her wild permed curls a distinctive reddish cast. All in all, she didn't look much different than she had at 20. Still young and pretty enough to catch herself a new man.

His eyes misted over. Except for those infernal blue jeans she insisted on cramming her body into, Laura was the spitting image of her grandmother—God rest her ornery soul—and just as bullheaded, too. What Laura needed was a real man, not some sissy-boy like her ex-husband. She needed someone to take charge of her and that rambunctious son of hers, someone who'd make her dress like women were supposed to.

"Why don't you get married again?" he blurted out suddenly. "While you're still young enough to enjoy it."

Laura dropped her head into her hands. Not that again. "Grampa," she said wearily, "it's 1995, not the Dark Ages. I've already had one husband. I don't want or need another one."

"Hah! You sure were singing a different tune a few years back. Never seen a girl so fired up to get hitched. I think you just liked all his names."

Laura winced. The barb dredged up memories she would have preferred to leave buried. Braxton Edward Davis Malek IV. She had liked "all his names," she admitted to herself. Youngest son of an old, rich Biloxi family, Brax had wooed her, pursued and flattered her until she finally said yes and married him, never dreaming that he was after her money. She had discovered too late that his family had been broke for a generation, possessing only the ancestral home and a once-powerful name used as a calling card to gain entrance to country clubs and debutante balls up and down the Gulf Coast.

For the thousandth time she kicked herself mentally for being such a fool. She was no debutante, but her parents had left her their entire estate, including a tidy sum in insurance money—a fact which Brax or his family had somehow discovered. After they had married, he had whizzed through her inheritance in just four short years with a steady stream of new cars, club memberships, expensive suits and one harebrained investment scheme after another. And she'd let him do it because she'd loved him. What a moron she'd been.

41

Jan Zimlich

His last and most worthless scheme had been to buy the foliage nursery and 20 acres of pecan trees in the hind end of nowhere outside of Escatawpa, Mississippi. Then the money ran out and so did he, leaving her with a business to run which she knew nothing about, virtually penniless and eight months pregnant with a child he'd never paid a dime of child support for.

Laura willed her thoughts back to the present. Brax was out of her life now, married again, or so she had heard, to some other young fool down in New Orleans. And the past five years hadn't been so bad. Not great, but not bad either. The fancy car was long gone, traded in for a more practical Jeep Cherokee after Brax ran out on her. She had a decent, paid-for house, and a small business with which she could eke out a marginal living. But most importantly, she had Bryan, now a handsome, vibrant five-year-old who brought her immense joy and pleasure and made her solitary existence worth living. She was content with her life, happy to be on her own. The last thing she needed was a new husband. At least that's what she kept telling herself.

The old man wisely kept silent, choosing to spend the time watching the conflicting emotions flit across his granddaughter's face. In the end he realized that he had lost another round in their ongoing battle over Laura's future. With that disheartening realization came a fit of pique. "Well, now that you've quit mooning over your sissy-boy, you can finish fixing my supper."

The utter absurdity of his comment evoked a startled laugh from Laura. Brax may have been many things, but "sissy-boy" wasn't one of them.

42

Slimy toad described him better. She sighed, thoroughly exasperated. She'd gotten over Brax years ago, and Garner knew it. "I don't know why I put up with you and that mean mouth of yours, Grampa." The old coot was impossible to live with, but he did have her best interests at heart—most of the time.

"You put up with me because you're scared I'll cut you out of my will."

An amused smile ruffled the edges of her mouth. He didn't have a pot to pee in, and they both knew it. "Yeah, you're right. I'm after that Swiss bank account of yours." She climbed to her feet with a sigh and padded toward the kitchen to check the spaghetti sauce. "Supper'll be ready soon. Tell Bryan to wash up."

"You tell him. He's outside playing with that stupid cat of his again."

Laura hesitated in the doorway, her brows drawing downward in a frown. It would be dark before long. Too late for a five-year-old to be roaming around the fields alone.

"If I've told you once, I've told you a thousand times," Garner said in an all-knowing tone, "it's not good for that boy to live out here in the sticks with no other children to play with. He's beginning to think that cat actually talks to him."

"Don't you think I know that?" Her anxious gaze drilled into the back of Garner's head. Why did he always have to give voice to her worst fears?

The camouflaged army helmet slipped down low over his face as Bryan Malek crept over the levee and moved a little closer to the grove of ancient water oaks rimming the Pascagoula River.

43

His soft brown eyes, so like his mother's, grew watchful, alert. The enemy soldiers were hiding in the oaks today. They were using the stringy gray moss and thick leaves for cover.

He made a small gesture with his left hand, motioning for the sarge to move out. "Sneak up on them from behind," Bryan whispered. "You know what to do." He loved crawling through the tall saw grass with the sarge at his side, sneaking up on the evil forces of doom in their hidden camps.

Intent on gnawing a blade of half-dead grass, the black tomcat completely ignored him, as he did more often than not.

The five-year-old made a disgusted face. "You heard the order. Move out!"

The cat twitched his long black tail three times, a clear sign of impatience, and stared at the boy with inscrutable yellow eyes. He meowed angrily, as if to say, "Leave me alone or you'll regret it."

Bryan shoved the too-large helmet away from his grimy face and swiped at the blond-red bangs plastered to his forehead. "All right! Don't go with me. But you won't get the milk from my cereal tomorrow."

Indifferent to the threat, Sergeant Pepper pawed at a large beetle unlucky enough to meander into his line of vision.

"Be that way," Bryan said, and crawled to the edge of the oak grove. He would have to fight this mission alone. The dumb old cat would just get in his way anyhow.

A tree rustled to his right and Bryan froze, his eyes intent on the swaying leaves. Something was moving along a limb. Something big. Steadying the BB gun with his free hand, he drew a bead on the quivering leaves and waited.

The limb gave a protesting creak, as if it were supporting a heavy weight; then an arm and a leg appeared from under the thick canopy of leaves. A sliver of murky sunlight made its way through the dense foliage, glinting off dark metal. Then a large black helmet fell out of the tree, bounced several times and rolled to a stop.

Bryan stared at the helmet, eyes widening. A robot.

He adjusted his aim toward the tree and squeezed the trigger again and again with a trembling finger, firing a barrage of BBs at the invader.

The limb swayed and groaned. Leaves rattled. Wood snapped. Then a heavy branch crashed to the ground with a thud, followed closely by a big black robot.

Bryan leaped out of the weeds, too excited to stay still. "Yahoo!" he shouted, and streaked toward the tree with all the speed his short legs could muster.

Dazed, Drallondryn lay flat on his back and stared upward at the tree he'd been sitting in only a moment ago. He blinked to focus his bleary eyes, unable to remember how he had ended up in such an undignified position. His left ear hurt, and there was a stinging sensation on the top of his head, as though he had been hit by several small projectiles.

Bryan skidded to a clumsy stop less than five feet from the thing on the ground and gaped, dumbfounded. It wasn't a robot at all. The metal suit made it look like one, but its face was covered in black fur, and there were big pointed ears poking up from the sides of its head.

45

He edged a little closer, fearful but curious. If it wasn't a robot, what was it? Except for a twitch from a hand, the thing hadn't moved yet. It was just staring up at the tree like it was stupid or something.

Pointing the BB gun threateningly, he tiptoed up beside it and paused. It was as big as a human being, but it had a tiny little mouth and that fur and ears. "Don't move or I'll shoot." He poked at its leg with the barrel of the rifle, thinking it looked a lot like Sergeant Pepper.

At the sound of the alien voice, Drallondryn focused blearily on the small, pale face hovering above him, then on the metal tube the tiny barbarian was aiming at his chest. A weapon, obviously. He groaned inwardly. Commander Rahs would have his hide for this. Aayshen had left him behind to rest in the tree while he scouted the area, never imagining that he would be taken prisoner by a small barbarian.

So. He would just have to handle the situation on his own. "Please not to shoot me, small one, thank you very much."

Startled, Bryan took a step backward, his jaw sagging in disbelief. He gazed at the furry face warily. Cats didn't really talk, did they? He studied the fur and ears once more and came to the only logical conclusion.

"You're a mutant space warrior," he said suddenly, images from a dozen cartoon shows flashing through his mind.

Drallondryn lifted an eyetuft in a silent question. What in the universe was a mutant space warrior? "Please to explain term, thank you very much."

Bryan giggled. "You sure talk funny." His hold on the BB gun relaxed.

The Kri saw the small hand loosen its grip, and he relaxed a bit, too. Less concerned about his physical safety than he had been a moment before, he eased himself up to a sitting position. Laughter he understood. "You have a call-name, small one?" he asked, deciding to calm the alien's fears through conversation. Besides, the more the barbarian talked, the more of their language he could assimilate.

The child puzzled over the question for a few seconds. "My name's Bryan Christopher Malek. But everybody just calls me Bryan. What's your's?"

"Drallondryn Nrilfrrm e't Kri."

"Huh?"

He repeated it slowly, sounding out each combination of letters one by one.

Bryan stammered over the strange words, unable to form the sounds with his tongue. "Can I just call you Drallondryn for short?" A small, friendly smile slanted across his elfin face. "I can't say the rest."

"That is permissible." The Kri flashed him a quick, toothy grin in return, suddenly warming to the odd little barbarian. He sensed no pretense here, none of the emotional artifice common among other races, especially Savanians. Bryan Christopher Malek displayed his emotions for all to see, regardless of who the observer was. There was no detectable guile or deceit in the fragile creature's expressions or bearing.

He stared up at the small one eagerly. "I have many questions. Tell me of yourself . . . Bryan."

47

The child sank to the ground beside him and propped his chin on his knees. "Well, I'm five years old, and my mom says I have to go to kindergarten next September, but I don't want to. I wanna stay home." He pointed toward a long row of pecan trees, indicating the direction of his house with a stubby finger. "I live over there with my mom and great-grampa. He keeps his teeth in a glass and has gas all the time. Mom says it's because he's so old."

Drallondryn blinked, bewildered by the deluge of information pouring out of the child's mouth. The barbarians' thought patterns were obviously disordered and imprecise.

"Look at this," Bryan went on, holding his BB rifle out for inspection.

He examined it carefully. "A weapon, yes?"

Bryan nodded. "Grampa Garner gave it to me for my last birthday. Mom didn't want him to, but he did it anyway. She made me promise not to shoot anything alive." A guilty flush tinged his small face with pink. "Please don't tell my mom I shot you. She'll get real mad. I won't do it again. Honest. I only shot you because I thought you were a robot."

The Kri lifted a finger to his sore ear and touched it gingerly. The stinging sensation had almost stopped. The same could not be said for his bruised shoulder and tail, but those injuries had nothing to do with Bryan at all. He smiled gently. "I will not tell mom."

Sergeant Pepper chose that moment to leap out of the weeds and dash to the trunk of an oak tree. Digging his claws into the rough gray bark, he began using the tree as a scratching post, unmindful

48

of the alien sitting less than five feet away.

Drallondryn stared at the small black creature, too astonished to speak. Except for being a four-legged quadruped, its appearance was almost identical to that of a newborn Kri kit.

"Don't be scared," Bryan said, misjudging the look on his new friend's face. "That's just Sergeant Pepper. He's my cat."

Sergeant Pepper swiveled his head in Drallondryn's direction and blinked indifferently.

The Kri gaped at the creature's glossy black fur, then glanced down at the thick mat of fur covering his own gloveless hands. His mouth slack, he met the cat's unwavering yellow gaze, studied its ears, then touched his own face wonderingly. "Can he speak?" Drallondryn asked when he was finally able to find his voice.

"Of course not." Bryan rolled his eyes. "Cats don't know how to talk." Puzzled lines angled across his small forehead. "Except ones like you."

Tired of clawing at the tree, Sergeant Pepper plopped down on his haunches and began grooming the lower half of his body.

Drallondryn's mouth dropped further. Though they shared a disturbing number of physical characteristics, this cat-creature was definitely a lower life-form. A troubled frown creased across his brow as he scrutinized the red collar encircling the cat's thin neck. The purpose of the collar was uncomfortably clear. But even if it was an animal, no intelligent being had a right to hold a lower life-form in bondage.

He was about to question Bryan on the disturbing subject when an icy splat of water trickled down his face. Drallondryn glanced upwards at the swollen gray clouds. Not again. Last night had been miserable enough. He was tired of being cold and wet.

"I gotta go," Bryan said abruptly. "My mom will kill me if I get wet."

The Kri's yellow eyes widened in horrified comprehension. Kill him? These people really were barbarians. "Then go. I would not wish for such a thing to occur."

The raindrops were falling faster now, clinging in icy droplets to the child's blond eyelashes. Bryan pulled the army helmet down to protect his face and tugged his heavy jacket closed. He was going home, but what was Drallondryn going to do? Sit in a tree in the rain all night? "If you want, you can stay in my room tonight."

A bewildered frown rippled across his forehead. "Stay in your room?"

"You know, spend the night with me. My mom won't mind," he lied. Maybe she wouldn't.

His thin black lips slanted upwards in a warm smile. "Thank you very much, but I cannot remain here. Peoples are tracking me. If I stay, I might be captured." He gazed at the child steadily, his unblinking yellow eyes bright with urgency. "You must tell no one of me. No one, not even the being you call mom."

Bryan's eyes widened with fear. Really bad guys must be chasing after him. "I won't tell, even if they torture me . . . I promise."

Bryan flushed beet-red. "I'm not lying!" he yelled angrily. "He had pretty black hair on his face and hands like Sergeant Pepper's, squinty yellow eyes and big cat-ears on top of his head. And he could talk real good, too."

Lifting a bushy white brow, Garner Haines shifted his bulk and mouthed an "I told you so" to his granddaughter over the rim of his glass. It was one thing for the boy to think that his cat could talk, quite another for him to be having conversations with some goofy cartoon character.

Laura glared across the dining room table, then swung her gaze back to her son. "I didn't say that you were lying, Bryan. It's okay to have an imaginary friend."

"He's not imaginary!"

Exasperated, Laura squeezed her eyes shut for a moment, long enough to dredge up a little more patience. "Quit shouting and finish your supper, Bryan. We'll talk more about this tomorrow." It was useless to continue now. The argument had been raging ever since they sat down at the table. She glared at Garner again. He had been laughing at Bryan's tale and had accused him of making it up.

Bryan stabbed his fork into a mushy peach slice and pushed it around on his plate, shoving the spaghetti, turnip greens, and fruit into one runny pile. His nose wrinkled in disgust. "This is gross! I'm not going to eat it!"

Laura sighed, her patience strained to the breaking point. "Fine. Don't eat it. Go bathe and brush your teeth. You can watch TV in your room until you fall asleep."

To her surprise, he obeyed, padding down the narrow hallway toward the bathroom without the usual storm of threats from her and ridiculous excuses from him.

Shoving her half-eaten plate aside, Laura

propped her tired feet on an empty chair across the table and lit a cigarette, relishing the long slow drag of menthol. A curl of wispy smoke drifted toward the vaulted ceiling.

"That's a nasty habit, Laura," Garner commented between mouthfuls.

"Yeah, I know. You've told me often enough." She took another deep pull on the cigarette and watched the smoke absently, her mind ranging over all the things she needed to do the next day. Carrie, her foreman, would be at the greenhouses by seven, along with the motley collection of locals and down-on-their-luck drifters who comprised the nursery's small work force. She had to have their schedule ready by then. There were a thousand gloxinias in the east greenhouse that needed to be repotted. Fertilizing. Watering. A heater in house number two wasn't putting out as much heat as it should and someone had to fix it. And then there were the tables and tables of poinsettias that hadn't sold at Christmas. It seemed such a waste to just throw them out. She chewed on her lower lip worriedly. In this business, everything needed to be done yesterday. If she slacked off even a little bit, her inventory just up and croaked, or withered away in the bottom of a dumpster.

With a weary sigh, Laura stubbed the cigarette butt out in an ashtray. Trapped, that's what she was. The "For Sale" sign had been nailed up to the front gate five years ago, five long years without a single offer. She couldn't afford to move without selling the place, and absolutely no one was crazy enough to buy it. Catch 22.

Garner Haines finally laid down his fork and

belched softly. "Good dinner, Laura. Don't use so much garlic next time, though. You know it gives me gas." Gripping the edge of the table to support his stooped frame, he climbed to his feet and shuffled toward the den door. If he didn't make his escape quickly enough, Laura would ask him to help with the dishes. She always did when he wasn't fast enough. And then he'd have to make up an excuse of some kind.

But tonight she remained silent. Brooding, no doubt. Or worrying. Laura worried over every little thing. He forced his arthritic knees to move faster. The doorway was only a few feet away now. "You better check those greenhouse heaters," he said over his shoulder. "Weatherman says it's going down to twenty-eight tonight. My knees keep telling me the same thing."

The door swung shut behind him. Seconds later, the television began roaring in the den.

Laura cleared the big oval table, then made short work of loading the dishwasher. She didn't really mind all the housework, but as bone-tired as she was at the end of the day, she would appreciate an occasional offer of help. "Women's work," Grampa would always say. Or he would complain that his knees hurt, his shoulders, his hands or any number of other body parts. She slid the racks inside the dishwasher, smiling cynically to herself. What could she expect from a man who had been born over 80 years ago? A man waited on hand and foot by women for his entire life? Garner Haines was one old dog who was too ancient and stubborn to attempt new tricks.

As the dishwasher churned noisily in the background, she grabbed her down-filled parka off a hook in the utility room, pocketed a flashlight and left the warmth of the house behind.

Outside, the night air was chill and soggy, but the rain had finally slackened to a misty drizzle. Laura sucked in a cold, deep breath and lifted her face upward, heedless of the little puffs of steam her exhalations formed. To the west, the sky was beginning to clear as the cold front tracked eastward. Here and there stars shown through odd-shaped gaps in the heavy clouds, glistening like fragile jewels in an ebony crown.

Lighting another cigarette, she star-gazed for long minutes, enjoying the peace and simple beauty of the night sky. A sheet of plastic loosened by the wind slapped against a greenhouse roof, then fell silent, the sound replaced by the muffled whir of a far-off helicopter wending its way through the darkness. But that noise soon faded, too, swallowed by the wind and distance.

Reluctantly, she tossed the cigarette into a puddle and retrieved the flashlight. The heaters were waiting, and so was her bed.

The crunch of oyster shells under her heels was the only sound to break the stillness as she made her way down the narrow pathway, her eyes straying occasionally to the distant stars. At times like these she almost enjoyed living in the country. Almost.

Chapter Four

Aayshen bit a chunk off a soggy protein stick and grimaced. Even his food stick was wet. When he finally managed to choke down a tasteless mouthful, he stretched his long legs out on the dirt floor and glanced around their dismal surroundings. The ramshackle structure where they had taken refuge was rectangular in shape, covered in an opaque layer of synthetic material which did little to hold the cold at bay. Row after row of wooden tables lined the floor from one end of the structure to the other, all laden with dirt-encrusted containers of vegetation heavy with bright red blooms. He bit off another piece of the protein stick and sighed. At least they were out of the elements, the sky wasn't dripping on them anymore and there was a small heating device spewing out a little warmth.

He tugged the edges of his survival blanket tight around his shoulders. "I don't believe I've ever been this cold before."

Drallondryn licked the last morsel of his food stick from a claw and settled back comfortably against a wooden beam. "Although your body feels the cold more intensely here, the air temperature is comparable to a winter night in the polar regions on Savan. It is the combination of the high moisture content in the atmosphere and the wind speed which make you feel colder." He found a crumb he had missed and licked it from a claw.

"The cold doesn't seem to be bothering you." Aayshen stared at the Kri's dark fur enviously. "I'll probably be frozen solid by star-rise." His teeth began making that annoying click-click sound again, but not as loudly as before, and his limbs were no longer trembling. His body was gradually adjusting to the drastic change in temperature.

"Perhaps exercise would help keep you warm," Drallondryn offered.

Aayshen climbed to his feet and began to pace, stamping his boots every now and then to keep his feet warm. It would be four long days until the shuttle was declared overdue and a search ensued. And days after that before the *Stellar Wind* located them and they could hope for rescue. His fist began rapping an impatient beat on his thigh. They had to survive a week or more on a freezing, hostile world.

He paced to the end of the structure and pivoted. "Switch the transceiver back on, Technician, and continue the language lesson. If we are to survive the coming days, we must blend in quickly."

Drallondryn nodded and began fiddling with

the controls on the transceiver pack. The discordant noise that passed for music soon filled the air. He punched a button, adjusting the frequency downward until the throbbing music was replaced by a single voice delivering a speech in a grim monotone. "The local dialect is quite simple, really," the Kri began, "a combination of hard and soft sounds created with the tongue and throat muscles. The basic grammar and syntax are similar to Savanian, only modified in some instances. Unlike your language, in pronunciation much more emphasis is placed on vowels than consonants."

Aayshen's palm finally stopped its relentless rapping as he concentrated on the voice emanating from the transceiver. The chemical enhancers were hard at work. Already he could understand one word out of five, but speaking the language was a different matter altogether. "Goff," he said at last, attempting to imitate the voice on the transceiver.

"Golf," Drallondryn corrected. "Now try an entire sentence. 'I thank you very much,' which means you are grateful for help rendered."

"I thannk you verri—" Aayshen frowned and cocked his head toward the doorway, listening to a scuffling, scraping sound in the darkness beyond. "Quiet," he said in a whisper. "There's something outside."

Drallondryn clicked off the transceiver and shoved the equipment out of sight beneath a table full of plants.

The scuffling noise grew louder, closer. Aayshen lifted a hand and motioned for him to take cover, then dropped to a defensive crouch in the shadows near the door.

Laura shoved the flimsy greenhouse door open with the end of the flashlight and wrinkled her nose. The cloying stench of so many flowers packed into such a tight space always made her stomach churn. It smelled like a funeral home.

Telling herself to ignore the smell, she switched on the flashlight and played the light across the far end of the greenhouse where the ancient gas heater was attached to the wall. The narrow beam cut a white swath over a potting table and illuminated a long row of poinsettias heavy with blood-red blooms. Laura grimaced and aimed the flashlight to the left, hoping she'd be able to read the big wall thermometer from here and save herself a few steps.

The light touched another row of clay pots, revealing a profusion of ribbed green leaves and scarlet blooms, then grazed over something small and yellow glittering between two plants. She flinched in surprise and swung the flashlight back to the table. A second spot of fluorescent yellow appeared beside the first, glowing like a cat's eye caught in the beam of a headlight.

She blew out her breath in relief. Sergeant Pepper. "Here kitty, kitty. Come on, boy. You know you're not supposed to be in here."

A pot toppled over and rolled off the table, tumbling to the hard floor in a shower of dirt and broken clay. Her lips thinned. "Get off that table right now, Sergeant! I've got enough problems without having to clean up after you." She stalked toward the table, swinging the flashlight back and forth to scare the wayward cat out of his hiding place.

"If you don't come out now, I'm gonna nail your scrawny hide to a fence post."

A shadowy form suddenly bolted from behind the table and darted across the greenhouse, over-turning several more pots in its haste to flee. As the dark shape scrabbled to a far corner, it skit-tered through the wavering light to reveal an im-mense muddy shadow with glittering fluorescent eyes.

Too startled to scream, Laura took a stumbling step backwards, her grip on the flashlight tight-ening. For some reason, Bryan's description of the catlike cartoon character flashed through her mind, replaying over and over again like a scratched and worn-out record. A shudder of fear crawled up her spine. "I've got a gun," she warned in a small, frightened voice. "I'll use it if I have to." Even to her the threat sounded foolish. "Now get the hell off my property before I do something you'll regret."

The thing detached itself from the shadows and began creeping toward her. Something long and metallic glinted in the near darkness. A real gun? Her heart hammered against her ribs, so loud she could hear the blood pounding through her ears.

Brandishing the flashlight like a club, Laura backed quickly toward the door, only to be stopped cold when she slammed into something large and rock-hard. Oh, God, another one. She made a strangled noise low in her throat, then sucked in a deep breath and screamed as long and loud as she could, praying that for once Garner was wearing his hearing aids.

Aayshen muttered an oath and clamped a hand over her mouth to muffle her scream, cursing again when she sank her teeth into the heel of his palm.

His viselike grip loosened for one brief second, but that was all the time Laura needed. She twisted free and jammed an elbow into his chest, emitting a little screech as a bolt of pain shot upwards to her shoulder. Her elbow felt like it had smacked into a column of steel. Ignoring the pain, Laura scrambled through the door. Another scream clawed its way up her throat, but it died half-born when strong hands grabbed her from behind.

Aayshen jerked her back inside and slung her to the floor, pinning her beneath his body to still her flailing legs and arms. He glanced down at the terrified woman and winced. Her features were twisted with fear, and she was breathing in short, panicked gasps, her chest rising and falling in a ragged rhythm that matched his own accelerated heartbeat.

"Don't mess with me, bub!" she hissed between clenched teeth, more panicked by the second. "Let me go!"

She swung the heavy plastic flashlight toward the side of his head, but he deflected her blow with his arm. The flashlight popped out of her grasp and tumbled across the greenhouse floor, the hazy beam dancing crazily across the pale face suspended inches above her own. Her breath caught in her lungs and her mouth fell open in astonishment.

"My God," she whispered hoarsely. Burglars didn't look like this guy, did they? She'd never seen anyone with such perfect, chiseled features, so perfect they seemed unnatural somehow. In that brief glimpse she noticed there was something strange about his eyes, too, something missing. Icy blue and overly large, his eyes were so pale and clear they looked almost translucent.

Laura flinched in sudden horror when she realized what was missing. The cool eyes staring down at her were solid in color. Her arms and legs began flailing again. There were no whites in those pale blue eyes, none at all. She angled her head sideways and down in an attempt to bite his arm, but he simply shifted his weight to move her target out of reach.

"Taey makk d'nrae," Aayshen urged quietly, trying to reassure her that there was nothing to fear.

The sound of his husky whisper caused a startled frown to slant across her brow. What the hell kind of language was that? Danish? Norwegian? Her struggles intensified.

After an elbow slammed into his chin, Aayshen increased the pressure on her arms and legs to hold her squirming body in place. She couldn't be allowed to escape, not in her terrified state. If she did, the planet's authorities would undoubtedly be notified. Even now he could hear the distant sound of a search craft plying the darkness. He had to make her understand that he meant her no harm. *"Taey makk d'nrae,"* he repeated, his voice rising with impatience. "Nott fere . . . nott danger."

Laura continued squirming, but her frantic movements only served to press her body even closer to his, so close a long hank of his platinum-blond hair fell across her cheek. She twisted her head, snagged a few strands of hair with her teeth, and yanked them out by the roots.

He muttered a curse and jerked his head sideways to keep her from ripping out any more hair. "Technician!" Aayshen bellowed. "I could use your assistance."

Drallondryn crawled out of the corner where he'd taken refuge and lit an emergency torch, shining it on Aayshen and his prisoner as he approached. But when he caught sight of Aayshen sprawled in the dirt atop the struggling female, his fear dissolved and he quirked an eyetuft in amusement. "Now that you have her, what do you intend to do with her, Commander?"

Aayshen lifted his head and glared. "I find nothing amusing about this situation, Drallondryn."

Laura stopped thrashing and listened to their guttural voices in confusion, trying to determine what language they were speaking. It wasn't Norwegian. In fact, it wasn't any language she had ever heard. Her train of thought faltered as an even more terrifying realization dawned. They weren't just foreigners. They weren't people at all.

"As for what I intend to do with her," Aayshen continued, "I have no choice but to hold her as a captive. She's seen us." He glanced down into her dark brown eyes, sensing a glimmer of comprehension buried in their fear-glazed depths. "By now she has figured out who and what we are." His cool gaze locked with hers for long seconds. The glaze of fear had faded from her features, replaced by an air of suspicion and something else. Curiosity? The blue of his whiteless eyes deepened and his gaze narrowed speculatively. He was suspicious, too, and more than a little curious. "You did say that you were tired of being wet, didn't you, Technician?"

Relief flooded Drallondryn's sharp features. The female possessed a dwelling with artificial warmth, a comfortable, safe hiding place where they could wait out the days until rescue. "Most definitely."

Aayshen's piercing gaze settled on Drallondryn. "Until I have assimilated enough of their language to make myself understood, you will serve as interpreter."

The Kri nodded. "Of course."

"Good. You can start now. Convince her that we intend no harm. Explain the situation to her in the vaguest possible terms. The less she knows, the safer we'll be."

Drallondryn moved into the female's range of vision and hunkered down on the floor beside them.

All hint of color faded from Laura's face. The thing crouched beside her looked just as Bryan had described. Black fur on its face and hands, squinty yellow eyes, and cat-ears which angled up to narrow points on the top of its head. She blinked to refocus her eyes, but when she opened her lids again, it was still there.

The Kri waited for the alien's shock to subside before he spoke. At least he had her full attention now, and she was no longer trying to devour the Commander's hair. Finally he said, "It would be to the advantage of all if you were to promise not to attempt another escape. Perhaps then Commander Rahs would remove himself from your body."

Her lips parted in utter astonishment. This had to be a nightmare. A six-foot cat dressed in an armored suit had just spoken to her in clear, unaccented English. She bit down hard on her lower lip to wake herself up. But the cat was still there, and so was the guy with pale, determined eyes. Laura shook herself mentally. Think, stupid! Don't just lie here and be crushed to death. Do something. "Okay, you have it."

Drallondryn blinked. "Have what?"

"My promise." She glared up at the one called Rahs with angry, reproachful eyes. "Just get him off me before I suffocate."

Aayshen frowned in sudden confusion as a burning sensation began deep inside his mind, a hot flame of something indefinable pulsing through his thoughts, growing stronger, more intense. He sensed the swirl of emotion clotting her mind, felt the raw, hot anger directed at him as if it were his own. His frown grew more pronounced when he realized what had occurred. For one brief instant his thoughts had brushed against hers. But that was impossible. He had spent a goodly portion of his life learning to control his telepathic abilities, erecting impenetrable mental barriers to shield his mind from the errant thoughts of others. He shouldn't be able to sense the intimate thoughts and emotions of anyone without making a conscious effort to do so. He shouldn't be able to, yet he had.

His gaze burned into hers for an interminable second. She was bewildered now. He could feel it. Though she didn't understand it, on some level, she, too, had sensed the mental communion between them.

Shaken by the discovery that she had somehow penetrated his barriers, Aayshen released his grip on her arms and rolled sideways, hoping physical distance would put an end to the unwanted mental contact. His mind felt scorched and heated, scalded by the intensity of her thoughts.

As his weight lifted from her chest, Laura scrambled in the opposite direction and folded her body into an uncomfortable crouch, ready to flight or flee at the first opportunity. With her back against the leg of a potting table, she studied them carefully, her wide-eyed gaze sliding over each of them in turn. She swallowed the tight knot of fear clinging to the side of her throat and forced her face into belligerent lines. "Who the hell are you people? Or should I say, what are you?"

Drallondryn cleared his throat nervously. "I am a Kri," he said finally, as though that would explain everything. He inclined his head toward Aayshen. "He is not."

Laura's gaze traveled over his catlike features. He obviously thought she was blind, or stupid. "Gee, I hadn't noticed." She snorted scornfully. "Now tell me something else I don't know."

The Kri quirked an eyetuft, bewildered by her disdainful tone of voice and expression. "An unfortunate event has temporarily stranded us here. We were simply cold and wet, in need of shelter to escape the condensation in your atmosphere."

His use of the word "your" didn't slip past her unnoticed. Laura swallowed hard. The knot of fear was climbing up her throat again, threatening to strangle her. She had to get to a phone and call someone, but who? The county sheriff? State troopers? She discarded that idea as absurd. The troopers' office would probably log her as a crank caller, and Sheriff Rankin . . . he wouldn't know an alien if it bit him on the butt. "What do you

65

want with me?" she asked, trying to make her voice sound calm. Keep him talking, she told herself. As long as he's talking, you're okay.

Drallondryn hesitated, and his gaze met hers for a long moment. Couching his answers in vague terms was not only difficult, it bordered on the impossible. He could see it in her eyes, in her probing expression. She knew what they were, and she wanted specifics. He sucked in a breath and chose his words carefully. "Please comprehend. Our method of . . . transportation . . . has been destroyed, and we find ourselves in a most difficult situation. Rescue will not come for at least seven of your planetary rotations. We do not intend to bring injury to your body, but your discovery of us has left the commander with no other alternative. Until rescue arrives, we will take shelter in your home-place to insure your silence."

Laura bolted to her feet, anger and disbelief glittering in her dark eyes. This was insane. "You're going to hold me hostage? For a week?"

The Kri nodded curtly. "Possibly more."

She gathered herself for a lunge to the door and freedom, but the tall blond alien moved faster.

Aayshen planted his body in the doorway and clicked the safety off on his pulse rifle. *"Quiff e'h moh!"* he said roughly, telling her to stop, but she kept running toward him. He squeezed off a quick, carefully aimed warning shot, sizzling the dirt floor near her feet.

Laura froze, the hairs on the back of her neck standing on end. She stared in shock at the smoking hole not two feet from the toe of her shoe. A bolt of blue energy had streaked across the greenhouse, evaporating a chunk of dirt into nothingness.

Aayshen chastised himself for resorting to such unwarranted measures. Unwarranted, perhaps, but from the look on his captive's face, effective. "Drallondryn," he said in Savanian. "Tell her I am a dangerous being. Tell her I will not hesitate to shoot if she tries to run again."

"Please," Drallondryn said to the frightened woman, "if you value the health of your body, you will not attempt to escape." His eyes flickered to Aayshen. "You would not wish to antagonize the commander further. Do you understand?"

A short downward jerk of her head was the only acknowledgment Laura could muster. Her vocal chords seemed to have taken an unexpected vacation. There was no doubt in her mind that he would shoot again. And the next time might not be a warning.

A nod from Aayshen signaled Drallondryn to hurriedly gather their equipment and discarded recon helmets.

As the cat-thing moved about the greenhouse in a flurry of activity, Laura's gaze was drawn to the tall, slender alien standing near the door. He was watching her intently, a puzzled expression flitting over his shadowed features. She met his probing gaze for a long, tense moment, losing herself in the depths of his wintry eyes. Her thoughts stilled and grew calmer as she stared into those oddly compelling eyes. Without conscious thought or reason, she took several halting steps toward him, then blinked in surprise. A sudden frown rippled across her forehead. He'd made her do that somehow, drawn her toward him like a

67

moth lured by the glow of a flame. She knew it, could feel it in her bones. Her gaze narrowed with suspicion. He was telepathic or something, and if he could beam his thoughts at her and force her to walk across a room, what else could he do? She shuddered violently. God help me, she implored silently. Help me protect my child.

Aayshen shook himself mentally and shifted his gaze away from the woman. He'd felt it again, that brief sensation of mental communication, and this time they hadn't even been in physical contact. He kneaded the center of his forehead with the back of a thumb, wondering how it could be, and what it signified.

When Drallondryn finished collecting the equipment, Aayshen turned to the doorway, scanning the night-darkened landscape for signs of movement. His practiced gaze traveled over the gravel walkway and barren trees, up a slight incline to the rambling structure perched on top of the rise. Lights shone like beacons from several windows, but there was no trace of movement inside. He motioned for Drallondryn to move up the walkway with a wave of his hand. As he melted into shadow, Aayshen turned back to the woman. "Cumm," he said in slow, halting English. "Timme now."

Laura shook her head, planted her feet firmly in the dirt, and refused to budge. "No way. I'm not going anywhere." She wouldn't try to escape, but if he wanted her as a hostage, he was going to have to drag her up to the house kicking and screaming.

He lifted a pale eyebrow in response. Most of her words were incomprehensible, but the stubborn lines settling over her delicate features told him everything he needed to know. Before she had a chance to scream again, he grabbed her around the waist and slung her small body over his shoulder, stunning her into silence. Willingly or not, she would come. He stalked up the gravel path toward the beckoning lights, unmindful of the extra weight.

Dazed, Laura blinked to focus her wobbly gaze, but the view of her surroundings remained skewed, off-kilter, as if she were staring at the world upside down. Blood rushed to her head and she blinked again. She *was* upside down, hanging over his back like a sack of potatoes, her nose slamming into his metal armor with each step he took. No wonder she felt dazed. She opened her mouth to try and scream again, then clamped it shut as the gravel beneath his boots gave way to brick. They were too close to the back door for her to scream now. Too close to Bryan and Grampa. If she did, one of the aliens might do something stupid. Like blowing a hole in her son to teach her a lesson.

Aayshen stopped at the doorway and peered through a square pane of glass. All was quiet within, save for a steady hum of voices coming from another part of the structure. He listened for a moment, finally deciding the droning voices were artificial in nature, similar to the signals they had picked up on the transceiver. He settled the woman back on her feet and shoved her against the door, trapping her body between him and the door frame. "How manni peeples, this place?" he demanded, jerking his head toward the small door-window. He glared down at her fear-blanched face and waited.

Laura swallowed hard. He looked as if he were daring her not to answer, and she didn't want to find out what he would do if she refused. "Two," she told him finally. "Just my son and my grandfather." Fear, stark and vivid, glistened in her eyes. "Don't hurt them . . . please." A single hot tear spilled from the corner of her eye and slid down her cheek unheeded. "I'll do anything you want, just don't hurt them."

Drallondryn shifted his feet uncomfortably. What did she think they were? Barbarians? "We will not harm them," he said hastily, trying to allay her fears. "As long as you do as asked." He winced inwardly. That had to be added, too, for self-protection. A fearful captive was a well-behaved captive.

Aayshen couldn't tear his eyes away from the wet spot on her face. Unable to contain his curiosity any longer, he touched it wonderingly, then lifted his dampened finger into the light to examine the clinging moisture. He had encountered many different life-forms in his years, but none with leaking eyes.

Still curious about the phenomenon, he fumbled with the door latch until he mastered its operation, then twisted the knob slowly and stepped inside, reveling in the sensation of warm, dry air rushing over his face. The Savanian blinked in the bright, artificial light and walked through a small anteroom into a larger chamber, the echo of his boot heels striking the patterned stone floor sounding strange and overloud to his ears.

Equipment clattered against the walls and floor as Drallondryn crowded in after them, eager to leave the cold night air behind.

Releasing his grip on the woman abruptly, Aayshen walked slowly around the chamber, touching and feeling various objects to familiarize himself with their new surroundings.

Laura retreated to a far corner of the kitchen and pressed herself against a cabinet near the stove. Since this was her first opportunity to study them in normal light, she took full advantage. Her probing gaze settled on first one, then another, assessing, judging. Under the harsh glow of the fluorescent lights, they didn't look as menacing. Strange maybe, but not nearly as threatening. There were no sharp teeth protruding from unexpected places, or extra eyes where some other body part should be. Actually, they looked pretty human, except for the cat-thing's fur and ears, of course. He/she/it was busily piling the equipment atop her kitchen table, muttering to itself in a high singsong voice that sounded almost Chinese.

She shuddered and swung her gaze back to the one called Rahs. He was tall and rangy lean. Six feet three or four, at least. But his lanky frame and easy grace didn't fool her, not for a minute. Hidden beneath that thick metal armor was a powerful, muscular body. She had sensed that hidden power in the greenhouse, felt it pressing down upon her. She watched him roam about the kitchen with slow, sure movements, occasionally stopping to run a tapered finger over the formica countertop, the sink, a cannister, as though he were absorbing everything he saw in minute detail. He half-turned in her direction, eyes intent on the cabinets. Laura took a quick sharp breath and stared openly at the clear-cut lines of his pro-

71

file, mesmerized. He was even more handsome than she'd first thought. His pale, ascetic features were perfectly symmetrical, almost beautiful in an odd, exotic way. The word aristocratic came to mind unbidden.

She shoved the wayward thought out of her mind and tore her eyes away from his face. She couldn't allow herself to think of him in those terms—human terms. For all she knew, he might not even be male, but all of her senses warned her that he was.

The refrigerator compressor suddenly kicked on and began humming noisily. The catlike alien flinched and backed away, visibly startled by the abrupt noise. In the process he somehow managed to snag the electrical switch on the cabinet behind him with the butt of his weapon. As the garbage disposal came to life with a grinding roar, he leaped back toward the refrigerator, swinging the rifle around in confusion.

Stifling a startled laugh, Laura calmly walked to the sink and flipped the switch off before the wild-eyed alien began blowing holes in her kitchen. Her eyes sought the Kri's. "It's just a garbage disposal. You put stuff in and it grinds it up."

The dark tufts of fur above the Kri's eyes drew downward in bewilderment. "Excuse please, what is 'stuff'?"

Laura had to puzzle over that one herself. "You know . . . things."

"Things?"

She threw up her hands. "Never mind." The two aliens began talking among themselves, whispering back and forth in a language that sounded more European than anything. Norwegian again.

"Laura?" Garner called from the den. The drone of the television faded into silence.

Oh, God. Laura froze and clamped a hand to her mouth. Garner was still wearing his hearing aids. He'd heard them.

"Who are you talking to in there?" Garner shouted from the den. "We got company?"

She clutched at the Kri's metallic sleeve. "Please . . . he's just an old man. He won't hurt you."

"Laura? Is something wrong?"

Drallondryn glanced at Aayshen, who muttered instructions in Savanian, then turned his gaze back to the terrified female. "The commander has ordered that you answer. Tell him whatever you wish, but do not frighten him into doing a foolish . . . thing."

She nodded once and cleared her throat. "Nothing's wrong, Grampa," she yelled back, then paused a beat, choosing her next words carefully. "We do have some company, though."

"At this time of night?" Garner's voice sounded annoyed, and more than a little bewildered. "Who?"

Aayshen chose that moment to kick the den door open. Laura squeezed her eyes shut and prayed as wood splintered and the lower hinges broke off the frame.

The barrel of his pulse rifle swinging back and forth, Aayshen charged through the door, only to find the chamber empty of life save for a single aged barbarian, who was glaring at him with very angry eyes.

Garner climbed from the recliner chair, took a shuffling step forward, and gaped at the splintered

73

door. The center panel was warped and cracked where the heavy oak had been kicked, and the lower hinge had been ripped completely off the frame. He turned back to the crazy man holding a shotgun on him and glowered. "What the hell is going on here?" His blue eyes turned glacial. "I don't know who you think you are, young fellow, but you better get that gun out of my face right now!"

The old one's sharp tone of voice and fearless expression caused Aayshen to lift a pale eyebrow in surprise. He was either extremely foolish, or very brave. He wasn't sure which.

"Just look what you did to that door!" Garner raved, jabbing an accusing finger at him. "You're gonna pay to have that fixed, even if I have to take it out of your hide!"

Aayshen returned the penetrating glare in kind, then slowly shouldered the rifle, deciding the only thing dangerous about the barbarian was his acid tongue.

Laura jerked free of the Kri's grasp and rushed into the den. She grabbed Garner by the arm and propelled him backwards toward the fireplace, angling her body in front of him protectively as Rahs sprinted after her. Resentment smoldering in her eyes, she squared her narrow shoulders and turned to face them. "I've had enough of this!" Her angry gaze focused on Rahs. "I'm not scared of you people anymore. I'm damned mad! Now take your stupid rayguns and get the hell out of my house!" Chest heaving, she paused and waited for him to respond. When he didn't, she swung her glare to the Kri, who had hesitated in the doorway. "Tell him, cat." At least he was bright enough

74

Not Quite Paradise

to understand English. "Tell him I said to get out of here and leave us alone."

Garner squinted over her shoulder, trying to see who Laura was yelling at. But even with his glasses, all he could make out was a tall, dark shape standing in the shadowed doorway. "Who are these people, Laura?"

"Lunatics."

75

Chapter Five

Drallondryn's right ear twitched nervously as he edged into the room. From the rigid set to Aayshen's features, he knew the commander had grasped the content of the female's statement, if not the words themselves. He also knew that Aayshen was not pleased. The situation wouldn't deteriorate into violence, of that much he was certain. For the most part Aayshen Rahs was a tolerant being, but if the female barbarian engaged him in a clash of wills, the commander would win. Of that Drallondryn was certain, too.

He lifted his hands in what he hoped was a conciliatory gesture. "The commander understood enough of your words to comprehend their meaning. I regret to say that his decision will remain unaltered, no matter what your wishes." As he moved out of the shadowed doorway, the hazy glow cast by a table lamp spilled over his features. "We will remain in your home-place as long as necessary."

Garner's eyes widened. He didn't need his glasses to see that the thing walking across his den wasn't a person. "What the hell is *that*?" he asked in astonishment, making stabbing motions with a gnarled finger.

The Kri glanced over his shoulder and studied the strange assortment of furnishings lining the wall behind him, wondering if that could be what the old one was gesturing to.

"It says it's a Kri." Laura eyed the two aliens warily. "Whatever that is." She gave Garner's frail hand a reassuring squeeze, then jerked her head toward Rahs. "I don't know what the other one is, Grampa, but neither of them are from around here . . . I mean, well . . . I think they're from outer space or something."

Garner lifted a heavy white brow at that and gave his granddaughter a weary, reproachful scowl. Sometimes she treated him like a mental midget. "I'm old, Laura, not stupid. I may not know what it is, but I can guess where it's from." He squinted at the cat, his critical gaze sweeping upward from the shiny black boots to the ears which crested into tiny peaks on top of its head. "Can't say that it looks much like one of us, but at least it's not some bug-eyed lizard." His ancient blue eyes hardened behind the bifocals and angled over to the other one. Except for his queer eyes, he looked human enough. His eyes were like blue holes in his pale face, and his long hair was so blond it looked almost silver. Not bad to look at, though, if you could ignore the weird eyes.

"Outer space, huh?" Garner said. He wasn't overly surprised by the news. The Pascagoula area wasn't any stranger to visiting aliens and spaceships. There had been plenty of sightings through the years, including his own, and the one where two old boys claimed to have been floated off a riverbank by alien Frankensteins. "Doesn't really surprise me a bit. I saw a UFO once, you know, about forty years ago. Everybody laughed at me and told me I was nuts, but I knew better. I always thought the government was covering things up. This proves it, I guess."

Garner shook his head in wonder, stared at the two silent aliens for long seconds, then shuffled off to his recliner chair. Much as it pained him, first thing tomorrow he'd have to apologize to Bryan for laughing at him. "What's the world coming to?" he muttered, still shaking his head. "Dope dealers, crooked politicians, and terrorists weren't enough. Now we've got to worry about talking space cats barging into our house." He eased his bent frame into the faded green Naugahyde until he was almost comfortable. The television clicked back on. "Well, tell them if they're gonna stay around here, I want that door fixed." As the image on the screen flickered into focus, Garner turned up the volume.

Laura simply stared, speechless. Until this moment she hadn't been certain. Now she was. Garner had an advanced case of senility or something. There was no other explanation. Why else would he just accept the aliens' presence so matter-of-factly? As if this sort of thing happened every day?

She sank to the carpet in front of the brick fireplace, twining her fingers nervously through the matted beige pile. Judging by Garner's seeming indifference, he wouldn't be much of a help in the coming days. Whatever happened would be up to her, and how she handled herself might prove to be the determining factor in their survival.

Her chin tilted in a defiant angle as she glared at the tall Kri. "All right," she said in a clear, calm voice. "If you're going to insist on staying here, let's get a few things straight right now. First." She glanced at Rahs through narrowed eyes. "Tell him to put that raygun away." She jabbed a thumb toward Garner. "It's pretty obvious that he's not able to put up a fight, and my son is going to be scared enough when he wakes up. There's no need to make things any worse. You have my word that I won't do anything—as long as you leave us alone."

Relieved, Drallondryn expelled the tense breath he'd been holding. Even though he detected a rebellious edge to her voice, it appeared she had finally accepted the situation and would offer no more resistance.

"Second," Laura said in a flat, hard voice. "If either of you harm my son, if you as much as touch a hair on his head, I'll tear you apart limb from limb, rayguns or not. Got it?"

Drallondryn nodded curtly, then turned to Aayshen and translated her demands into rapid Savanian, adding that he thought her sudden acquiescence was more out of fear for her offspring than herself or the old one.

As he listened, Aayshen regarded her curiously for a long second. She was such a small, fragile creature, yet the fierce protectiveness burning like dark flame in the depths of her oval eyes told him that the Kri's insight held more than a trace of truth. If her chid were injured in some way, she would attempt to carry out the threat, regardless of the cost to her personally. And who would blame her if she did? Who were the alien barbarians here? She or they?

He lifted his hands palm up in the universal sign of peaceful intent. "We nott brinng harm to yourss." To show her that he meant what he said, Aayshen bent low, the seams of his suit creaking as he did, and slowly laid his rifle on the floor. The grip was still within easy reach, of course. He wasn't a complete fool. Without giving himself time to reconsider, he released the latch at his waist. The heavy black utility belt, along with the attached hand weapon, landed on the floor in an untidy heap. "Not harm," he repeated in a quiet voice, struggling over the strange words. "Not."

Laura drifted in and out of a restless sleep, fighting her way back to consciousness a slow degree at a time. At first she was only aware of the nerve-wracking sound of a jackhammer drilling through concrete, and a dull, throbbing pain in the right side of her neck. Gradually her thoughts cleared and focused. She was curled on the den floor, her head propped at an unnatural angle on the arm of Garner's recliner chair. That accounted for the pain in her neck. And Garner's incessant snoring explained the jackhammer.

The antique pendulum clock perched on the mantle began chiming in a melodic, muted voice. Still half-asleep, Laura counted the chimes. Six of them. She should have already been up and moving. The nursery crew would be arriving by seven.

Then she remembered.

She cracked her eyes open warily and flinched in surprise when she realized that Rahs was sitting on the brick hearth seat only a few feet away, his pale gaze intent on her face. She flexed the agonized muscles in her neck and returned his stare, her gaze sliding over his stern, chiseled features. Sometime during the night he had shed the bulky metal suit to reveal a simple black jumpsuit which molded itself to every line of his long, lean form. The startling contrast of his silvery hair and strange eyes against the dark, shiny material made him look even more exotic than before.

Of their own volition, her eyes flickered downward, resting briefly on his muscular thighs, then up to the telltale bulge visible through his tight black suit. Her throat suddenly went dry, and a rush of heat reddened her cheeks. Perverse curiosity, Laura supposed. She cleared the dryness from her throat, forced her gaze to a safe patch of wall beside the fireplace, and studied a crack in the Sheetrock. At least she knew he was definitely a male now.

For a fraction of a second, the suggestion of a smile hovered around the corners of Aayshen's mouth. He couldn't help but notice the downward course her eyes had taken, or their ultimate destination. Her curiosity was understandable, of course. So was his own. What he couldn't understand was why he felt such a strong sense of urgency when he looked at her, even as she slept, as though his curiosity was fast growing into an obsessive attachment. Each time his gaze lingered on her expressive features he discovered something unique and fascinating, some new facet of her character, her thoughts. There was

81

something quite appealing in the structure of her heart-shaped face, the set of her dark eyes, how the curls in her gold-red hair fell past narrow shoulders in such precise, silky ringlets. It was a uniqueness that was hers and hers alone. On Savan, conformity was the norm, physical and intellectual individualism considered impolite. But this was not Savan. On this world a strangely compelling mix of conformity and individualism seemed to rule.

Aayshen allowed his gaze to boldly slide over her slender body. More and more he wanted to explore the mysteries that lay beneath that eloquent face, those deep, changeable eyes.

His eyes were still boring into her. Laura felt it in the marrow of her bones. The sensation was disturbing, as if he knew things about her that he couldn't possibly know, intimate things about her that even her own mother hadn't known.

When the crack in the Sheetrock finally lost its appeal, she glanced around the den. The Kri-thing was sprawled on the sofa, an arm and leg dangling haphazardly over the side as he slept. She surveyed the den and the dark hallway leading to the bedrooms with one quick glance, making sure Bryan wasn't up and about.

For a second she panicked, thinking they might have hurt him. Then she remembered the promise Rahs had made, and relaxed a little. Strangely, she thought he would keep his word. As long as she cooperated, they would come to no harm.

Those pale, probing eyes burning into her began to make her increasingly uneasy. Her own gaze thinned and moved back to his face. "What are you staring at, Rais?" she blurted out in a chilly, defensive tone. "Or whatever your name is." The look was beginning to make her nervous.

"Aay-shen Rahs," he corrected, enunciating each syllable carefully. "Call-name is Aayshen." He folded his arms and leaned against the smooth blocks of stone behind him. "I stare in your face."

Laura blinked in surprise. Ten hours ago he only knew a few words of English. Now he had less of an accent than some of the locals she knew. "Well, quit looking at me like that. It gives me the creeps."

He searched his mind for a definition of the last word she used but couldn't find one. "What is 'creeps'?"

"You are."

His eyes darkened. The curious mixture of venom and apprehension in her voice told him he had just been insulted. But he wasn't sure how. "This stare in face disturb you?"

"Deeply."

Perplexed, he shifted his legs and leaned forward, elbows on his knees. "Explain, pleass."

Laura sighed wearily and scrubbed at her day-old eye shadow with the back of a hand. If she had to go into lengthy explanations every time she insulted him, it wasn't worth the effort. "Never mind. Forget I said it."

He stared at her for a long moment, trying to remember what the old one had called her. "Your call-name is Lawra?" The word felt strange on his tongue.

"That's close enough, I guess." Her expression turned sullen. "It's my turn to ask questions now. How did you learn to speak English so fast? A few hours ago you could hardly speak a word."

His brows bunched together as he struggled over an explanation within his ability to verbalize, and hers to grasp. He finally gave up and tapped an index finger against the side of his head. "Cheemicals, here."

"Oh, I see." Chemicals? Her stare grew more intense than his had been. Great. Alien dopeheads. "Well, that explains everything." She sighed and shook her head, then climbed to her feet, slow and easy so he wouldn't think she was making any sudden moves. One exaggerated footstep at a time, she edged toward the hallway leading to the back of the house. She hadn't been to the bathroom since the night before, a fact which her body was insisting that she remedy soon. "I've got to, a . . . got to go. Understand?" Besides that, the idea that one of them might have gone into Bryan's room was beginning to gnaw at her.

"Go?" Aayshen bolted to his feet.

His movement was so swift and silent Laura couldn't pinpoint the exact moment it occurred. Strong fingers latched around her shoulders in a viselike grip, pinning her between his body and the hall door. Their eyes locked, hers defiant, his calm and lethal. She tried to push away from him, but his grip only tightened. "Please. Let me go. I'm just going to the bathroom." He was so close his breath fanned her face. "If you don't, I'm going to wet my pants."

A platinum brow angled upwards in response, and his baffled gaze slid down the slender length of her body. Comprehension lighting his eyes, he released her abruptly.

Laura raced down the darkened hallway, palmed the light switch and kicked the door shut as she dashed inside the bathroom.

Aayshen slouched against the door frame and waited. He spent the time contemplating the vague pattern in the synthetic matting beneath his feet. Several minutes passed, and still he waited. Suddenly uneasy, he pressed an ear to the closed portal and listened for sounds within. There was a roaring, sucking noise, then only silence.

His uneasiness transformed itself into suspicion. There were glass windows in every room. She could have already escaped through one for all he knew. The hinge gave a protesting squeak as he pushed the door open with his knuckles.

Laura quit fighting with her tight jeans and glanced up, her face slack with disbelief. Her eyes glittered angrily. "What do you think you're doing?" Although her shirttail covered everything important, she jerked at the too-snug jeans frantically, desperate to pull them up and over her thighs before he got any strange ideas. "You can't just walk in here whenever you feel like it! Now get the hell out!" To her eternal relief, the jeans finally slid over her hipbones, even though her panties were still caught somewhere in the nether-reaches of her thighs. Laura fumbled with the zipper and offered up a prayer of thanks. "Don't they teach you any manners where you come from?"

Aayshen stared at her with a blank expression, wondering what she was so agitated about. Perhaps her race had some sort of cultural taboo about viewing a female's legs. He'd heard of stranger things before. He shrugged inwardly and turned his attention to the fascinating array of equipment lining the walls of the cramped chamber. A long blue counter marched down one side

Jan Zimlich

of the room, its focal point seemingly a deep, oval-shaped depression in the flat surface. At the top of the depression, two metal handles glinted invitingly. Curious, he turned one and took a startled step backwards when a spigot gushed a steady stream of clear liquid. For one brief second he was too stunned to react. Then he dipped a single finger into the chilly torrent and tasted. He closed his lids as the bead of moisture slid over his tongue. It was water, as clear and cool as the moisture which fell unbidden from the planet's clouds.

Laura watched his reaction with curious eyes. He was staring at the faucet like he had never seen one before. "It's just a sink, for God's sake. Don't they have water in outer space?"

His incredulous stare shifted to her. "No, nott so . . . much as your world." He turned the spigot off hurriedly, dismayed by the sight of so much water spiraling away to nothingness down what was obviously a drain. "Only little."

"Oh." An unpleasant thought suddenly occurred to her. What if they were here to steal water? She'd seen a movie about that once. "Well, you can't steal ours. My government will see to that," she informed him in a confident voice. "We'll fight you before we ever let that happen."

Indignant lines formed around his generous mouth. "Not stealers, my peoples." His expression darkened with an unreadable emotion. "Others are. Some day, maybe they will come." Aayshen fell silent, concerned that he had already told her too much. The less she knew about them, the better for all concerned. In theory, at least. Reality was a different matter altogether. Her people were ill-prepared to deal with the aftereffects of open contact with other worlds. They didn't even possess the technology to enable them to fend off a few determined water smugglers.

To Laura, his silence was more ominous than his cryptic words. She shook herself mentally. Lies, probably. Alien boogeyman stories to throw her off balance, keep her in line. For now, she'd play along since she didn't have much choice in the matter, not when her son was sleeping a room away.

Thinking of Bryan sent a new surge of uneasiness up her spine. She glanced sideways at Rahs. He had moved to her end of the bathroom and was examining the toilet, flipping the lid up and down to see how it worked. As he pushed on the handle and flushed, she slipped past him and rushed into the hall.

She eased Bryan's door open quietly and exhaled the tense breath she'd been holding. Cloudy light from the aquarium played across her son's still features. Laura stepped over a plastic superhero and tiptoed to the side of the bed, studying the small limp body and sleep-tousled hair. He was so still, so quiet. Just to reassure herself, she eased her fingertips across his brow, smoothing the golden strands back into some semblance of order. Then her fingers slid downward, across the slender chest, until she felt his ribs rise and fall in a slow, steady, rhythm beneath her palm.

Relieved, she gently tucked the heavy blue comforter around his shoulders before moving back toward the door, pausing for a moment to study the shadows in the room. An army of sightless robots and stuffed animals gazed back, mute sentinels who stood guard over their small charge

Jan Zimlich

from haphazard perches on a bookcase at the far end of the room.

After sidestepping a pile of dirty blue jeans and rumpled sweatshirts, she dodged the dead-eyed hero again, and backed slowly for the door.

A long, distorted shadow fell across the carpet and played over her son's sleeping features. Even before she turned, Laura knew it was Rahs. Her lips compressed into a tight, grim line. "This room is off-limits," she whispered coldly. "You hear me?"

Her mind told her to block the door, prevent him from entering the room, but for some reason her legs rebelled. She simply watched in mute, apprehensive silence as he threaded his way through the scattered maze of clothing and discarded toys, eyes intent on Bryan's sleeping form.

Aayshen paused near the bed and stared at the tiny form in fascination. The child was so young, so innocent. Just like this world. But it wouldn't be long before this planet lost that innocence. Once word of discovery spread, other ships would eventually come. The vast liquid and mineral riches were too great a lure to resist. And the result would be that this child would grow to manhood on an altered, different world, one where innocence no longer existed.

A look of profound sadness settled over his strong features as he watched the sleeping child. What were rare minerals, mere water when compared to this? Before him, close enough to touch, lay the greatest, most valued resource of all. A child. Continuance. A forbidden treasure he could never have.

He shifted his eyes from child to mother, the

sadness in his eyes replaced by calm acceptance. "Your peoples are fortunate," he told her in a quiet, gentle voice. "The Fates have blessed you with gifts one such as I can never receive." He turned on his heel abruptly and strode to the door.

Laura stared after him, perplexed by his odd choice of words and the strange blend of emotions she'd seen on his shadowed features. Curiosity first, then a deep, unexplained sadness. She paused by the door for a moment, her eyebrows pulling downward in confusion. Was she just trying to attribute human emotions to an alien? Or was the pain she had seen reflected in his eyes genuine?

"Mom . . ."

Laura blinked in surprise and rushed to the bed. "I thought you were asleep," she said in a whisper.

Bryan yawned and stretched. "I was, but I felt eyes looking at me and woke up."

"Go on back to sleep." She adjusted the covers and smoothed his rumpled bangs. "It's still early."

"I don't want to." He scratched at an itch on his thigh and fought his way out of the covers.

"Bryan, please, don't argue about it." Her breath escaped in a weary sigh. "Not right now."

"But I want to know why that man was in my room. Who is he?"

She dug at her eyes with the heels of her palms. He knew. So now what? "He's . . . staying here for a few days. One of his friends is, too." Laura sank onto the side of the bed and pulled his small body close to her chest. "I want you to listen to me carefully, Bryan, and do exactly what I tell you."

"Why?" The child sensed her fear and edged a little closer, clutching her arms tightly.

"Because you have to. Now I don't want you to get upset about what I'm going to tell you. It's very important that you don't." She hugged him closer. "Remember the story you told Grampa and me last night? About who you met down by the river yesterday?"

He nodded against her chest. "Uh-huh." This was going to be the talk she'd promised about pretend friends.

"Well, that . . . person you met is here in the house, and he brought along one of his friends . . . that man you saw."

Bryan bolted upright and grinned. "Drallondryn?"

"Something like that."

His grin turned smug. "I told you I wasn't making it up."

"I know you told me, and I'm sorry. Next time I'll believe you." Her fingertips brushed his cheek in a wordless gesture of apology. He was beginning to bounce on the bed in excitement. "Just settle down. We have to have a little talk."

"Not now! Drallondryn's here!" He scrambled to the end of the bed.

Laura made a grab for his leg and missed. Before she could stop him, he bounced from the bed and was gone, scurrying down the hallway in a blur of movement. "Bryan, wait!" Laura dashed after him.

As he angled around the hall door, Bryan spotted the Kri sprawled on the sofa. He did a little jig, then brushed past Rahs and landed in a frenzied heap atop the sleeping Kri.

For the second time in as many days Drallondryn opened bleary yellow eyes to find the small barbarian hovering over him.

"Yahoo! I knew you'd come back!" Bryan shouted, and began bouncing up and down on the startled alien's stomach. "I'm glad you didn't have to sleep in a tree."

Drallondryn winced as a tiny foot grazed his bruised shoulder. "I am glad to see you also, small one."

Laura froze in the doorway and stared in horror. Bryan was using the cat-thing for a trampoline, jabbing its stomach with his knees and feet. "Bryan! Stop that right now and get off of him!"

"Drallondryn doesn't mind." The jabbing slowed. "He's my friend."

"Bryan!" Her eyes shifted nervously to the left, to where Rahs was slouched against the fireplace, seemingly unconcerned, then back to the sofa. "Get off him . . . and stay off," she said in a warning voice. At the first opportunity they would have a long talk. Set some ground rules to avoid problems.

"Aw, Mom." He leaped to the floor.

"Go fix yourself a bowl of cereal." She glanced at the recliner chair. Garner was still snoring away, totally oblivious. "Fix Grampa Garner some, too."

"He doesn't like cereal."

"I don't care." Laura pushed on Garner's arm to wake him. "Today he eats cereal whether he likes it or not." Garner snorted and moaned but refused to wake up.

"Can we have sugar and bananas on it?"

"Go ahead," Laura told him. As Bryan darted to the kitchen, she decided the effort to wake Garner was pointless. He'd even snored through the last hurricane they'd had.

Drallondryn's ears had perked up at the word "eats." "Is this cereal some form of sustenance?" The thought of eating another soggy protein stick wasn't the least bit appealing.

She looked at the skinny alien and forced herself to meet his probing yellow eyes without flinching. "I guess you could call it that." His stomach growled, loud enough for Laura to hear the familiar sound a full ten feet away. "Go get some if you're hungry," she offered grudgingly. If left to their own devices, there was no telling what the aliens might decide to eat. Laura shivered. They might even decide that humans were tasty. "Bryan can show you what to do. Just keep your furry paws off my son."

He was on his feet in an instant. "Thank you very much." His thin black lips pulled back in a small, grateful smile.

As he ambled toward the damaged kitchen door, Laura got her first rear view of the creature since he'd shed the heavy metal suit. Her eyes widened. He actually had a tail. Long and thick, the catlike appendage spiraled downward out of a slit cut in the back of the jumpsuit, almost dragging the floor. At least she hoped it was a tail.

She stared at the door as it swung shut behind him, vacillating over whether she should stand guard over Bryan or not. The sound of her son's excited chatter and the rattle of spoons and cereal boxes was a little reassuring, but she was still uneasy. That tail . . .

"Drallondryn will not harrm him," Aayshen offered, sensing the reason for her renewed uneasiness.

Startled, Laura spun in the direction of the quiet voice. He had managed to sneak up on her again, and was staring at her with those deep knowing eyes. As if he knew things about her that he shouldn't. Even what she was thinking. She stared back at him suspiciously. "You can tell what I'm thinking, can't you?"

Aayshen shifted his feet, suddenly uncomfortable. It was an accusation, not a question, and one he chose not to answer. Instead, he feigned ignorance with a baffled look. "Not understannd."

The flash of guilt she saw in his fathomless eyes belied his words. He had understood exactly what she'd said and thought, and on some vague level she also knew that he was the only one of the two who was telepathic. Laura didn't know how she knew that, but she did. "Why don't I believe you?"

He didn't answer.

"Okay," Laura said. "Have it your way if you want, but you and I both know better." Strangely enough, the idea that he might be reading her mind didn't really bother her. She was more curious than anything. She would have to watch herself in the future, though, guard against any wayward or revealing thoughts.

Before he had a chance to frame a response, Drallondryn rushed back into the room and grabbed up his pulse rifle.

Aayshen tensed.

Eyes glittering with apprehension and fear, Drallondryn sucked in a deep breath and rattled off a torrent of rapid Savanian, gesturing wildly

93

at the back window with the barrel of his assault rifle.

Aayshen's face turned ghost-white. "How many?"

"At least three, maybe four," Drallondryn said in breathless Savanian. "Do we fight?"

Laura glanced from one to the other, unnerved by the cat's urgent, clipped tone.

Aayshen grabbed his discarded rifle from the floor and hammered the safety off. "If forced to, we'll fight." He gestured toward the bank of windows to his left. "Position yourself there."

Drallondryn dashed to the window as ordered and shoved the barrel of his rifle between the slats of the blinds, balancing the stock on the sofa's high back.

A thin stream of early sunlight filtered through the hole in the blinds, bathing a narrow slice of carpet with a dim white glow. Laura gasped, finally comprehending. It was almost seven. The nursery crew had arrived. Her panicked gaze darted to the mantle clock to confirm her fear, then swung back to Rahs. He was poised next to the window, a weapon in his hands, pale eyes surveying the area around her greenhouses through the blinds.

"No!" Laura shouted. "You don't understand!"

He turned toward her slowly. "Not interfere." His icy gaze flickered across her face before moving back to the window.

"They're supposed to be here! Those people work for me!" She clutched at his sleeve frantically, twisting the heavy black fabric between her fingers. "Listen to me . . . please." Fear welled in her throat as he finally turned. "If you stay in the house they won't even know you're here."

Aayshen stared down at the diminutive woman tugging on his sleeve, a skeptical frown clouding his rigid features. She was telling the truth. He could sense it in her thoughts, see the candor in her dark eyes. But it was only the truth as she knew it. No one could guarantee the behavior or actions of another. His frown deepened with uncertainty.

Laura sensed his hesitation and plunged on. "You asked me to believe in you last night when you promised not to hurt us. Now it's your turn. Trust me. Just leave those people alone. Let them do their jobs and go home. I'll give them time off. They won't be back until you're gone."

He rubbed the tip of a finger against his chin, considering. An open confrontation might bring about what he feared most—discovery and capture. Perhaps her way would be best. Safer. He dipped his head once in a wordless gesture of agreement, then signaled Drallondryn with a quick jerk of his eyes. The safety latches on their rifles clicked back into place.

Laura blew out the breath she'd been holding and wiped at her damp forehead with a shaky hand.

Someone rapped loudly on the back door.

"Mom!" Bryan yelled from the kitchen.

Laura froze as the back door creaked open. Oh, God, why now? Her heart hammered against her ribs.

"Carrie's here!" Bryan yelled again. "She wants to see you."

Heavy footsteps thumped across the tile floor,

moving slowly, inexorably through the utility room to the kitchen.

Her eyes glazing with sudden panic, Laura stood rooted to the floor, watching in horror as Rahs readied his weapon again with quick, sure movements. She didn't know what to do. Didn't know how to stop what was about to happen, or even if she could.

"Miz Malek?" The heavy workboots thumped closer. "You in there?"

The sound of Carrie's voice finally galvanized her into action. Unmindful of the consequences, Laura rounded on Rahs and batted the barrel of his weapon downward with the heel of her hand. "Put it down!" she ordered in a harsh, raw whisper. "Hide the Kri and your guns and let me handle this!"

Aayshen hesitated for a split second, glancing first at the doorway, then at Laura.

"You've got to trust me!" The panic in her eyes faded, and her voice turned soft, controlled. "You don't have a choice."

He gave her a brief, imperceptible nod. She was right. He didn't have a choice, not if they wanted to avoid capture. In one quick movement, he lowered his rifle to the floor and sent it sliding behind the sofa with the toe of his boot, then motioned for Drallondryn to follow suit.

Laura held her breath and moved toward the doorway as the Kri dove for cover in the shadows between the TV and sofa.

One weathered hand wrapped around a soft drink can, the other clutching a half-eaten doughnut, Carrie Cooner slouched into the den, blinking to focus her eyes in the dim light. The room was almost pitch black. "What's it so dark in here for?"

Laura squirmed, her mind racing to come up with a believable explanation. "Garner's asleep in his chair."

Carrie snorted inwardly. Nothing new about that. As she grew accustomed to the gloomy light, her piercing gaze zeroed in on Laura, who was just standing there wringing her hands, then took aim at the nervous stranger behind her. Her thin face scrunched up in surprise. Except for a few old friends, Laura hardly ever had company, male or female. Carrie's appraising eyes slid over the tall man with shoulder-length blond hair. To her knowledge, Laura had never had a good-looking hunk like this come to visit. Especially one dressed in a tight body suit, sorta like the kind those aerobics people jumped around in.

She forced her gaze back to Laura. "You sick or somethin', Miz Malek? We've been waiting on you down at the greenhouses for close to a half hour."

"No . . . I'm not sick."

Carrie gave her a suspicious look. Laura's face was the same pasty white as Ornell's backside, which had rarely seen the light of day since they'd married close to 20 years ago. And she kept twisting her hands around and around, like she was nervous or upset about something. "You sure?"

"I'm sure . . . I've just got company . . . from out of town."

It suddenly dawned on Carrie that it wasn't even seven yet. Too early for the hunk to come calling. He'd been there all night. She flashed Laura a sly, knowing smile. She'd been the nursery foreman here for nigh on six years now, since right before Laura's sniveling excuse for a husband ran out on

97

her. And in all that time Laura hadn't even had a date that Carrie knew of, much less a man to spend the night with. Her smile widened. It was about time.

Laura turned beet-red when she realized why Carrie was staring at her with that idiotic smile on her face.

Still grinning, Carrie brushed past her and barreled headlong across the room. "Hi." She stuck out her hand to the huge blond. "I'm Carrie Cooner. Miz Malek's foreman."

Aayshen tensed and stared down at her outstretched hand, uncertain of what he was supposed to do with it. Knowing some type of acknowledgment was expected, he tapped a closed fist to his chest in the Savanian gesture of greeting.

Carrie's forehead bunched in bewilderment and her hand fell back to her side. What the hell was that salute supposed to mean? Some kind of sign language? She cast Laura a questioning glance. "Is he deaf or something?"

"He doesn't speak much English," Laura offered lamely. "He's . . . Norwegian."

"Oh." Carrie's gaze narrowed with sudden suspicion and moved over his face again. There was something weird about him, especially his eyes. But every time she tried to get a real good look at his face, he moved off in another direction. Like he was hiding something. She turned back to Laura, her suspicion growing. "What you got a foreigner staying in your house for?"

Laura groaned inwardly. Why did Carrie always have to ask so many questions? Her mind churned over possibilities. "He's my cousin," she finally blurted out. That might work, at least with Carrie. Almost everybody in the county was related to Carrie in some fashion. "He's just here for a week or so . . . on vacation."

"Vacation, huh?" Carrie lifted a disbelieving brow. She had worked for Laura too long not to know when she was lying. And she was lying through her teeth right now. Besides, this guy didn't look anymore related to her than a rooster did to a cow. "Well, I guess I'll get back to work."

Laura grabbed her by the elbow and ushered her toward the kitchen. "Get everybody started to work on the number-two house. I want to clear out those poinsettias today."

"Okay." As she gave the foreigner one last suspicious glance, she caught a brief glimpse of Sergeant Pepper's tail whipping across the arm of the sofa. Confusion rippled across her forehead. She'd seen the cat down in the greenhouses not ten minutes ago. And he hadn't come in the back door with her. "What else you want us to do?"

"I'll be down after a while," Laura prattled on, propelling her through the kitchen. "I'll give you the rest of the work schedule then." Laura opened the back door and shoved her through. "See you in a little bit." She slammed the door shut and latched it, shaking with relief.

Carrie stared at the closed door for long seconds, her jaw drooping in astonishment. Laura had actually slammed it in her face. Her mouth snapped shut and her expression hardened. Something weird was going on here.

Determined to get to the bottom of whatever was going on, Carrie bent low and inched her way along the side of the house until she reached the den window. She scrunched down behind the overgrown camellias and waited, trying vainly to eavesdrop on the low conversation inside. A disgusted frown carved new lines across her face. Even with her ear pressed against the glass she couldn't make out what they were saying.

Fighting her way out of the briars tangled around her boot, Carrie rose from her hiding place quietly, her eyes roaming over the closed blinds for a hole she could peer through. Her frown vanished, replaced by a grin. Someone, most probably Bryan, had jammed something between the slats and bent them, leaving a nice eye-level peephole.

Palms pressed flat against the chilly glass, Carrie squinted intently and peered through the tiny opening. Something big and black scurried across her line of vision, but the blurred shadow moved out of sight before Carrie could force her myopic eyes to focus. She blinked and squinted harder, her gaze roving back and forth across the tunnel-like slice of the darkened room. Other shadows moved about, revealed in quick snatches by the flickering light from the television screen. The back of Laura's head, Garner's still hand resting atop the arm of his chair, a brief glimpse of the stranger's long blond hair.

Carrie shrugged inwardly and shivered in the biting wind. All was quiet inside. Except for the presence of Laura's so-called "cousin," everything seemed normal within the Malek household. But she couldn't shake the nagging feeling that something very weird was going on.

Sidestepping the withered brown stalks of a dormant hydrangea, Carrie slipped away from the house soundlessly, her thin mouth puckering in consternation. One of her husband's many pearls of wisdom came to mind as she walked downhill toward the greenhouses. "Don't ever trust nobody who won't look you in the eye," Ornell was fond of saying.

Carrie stopped in mid-stride and targeted the small brick house with one last distrustful glance. Ornell was almost always right about things like that.

Chapter Six

Steam curled and drifted around Laura's body as she doused her hair beneath the showerhead for the third time, the hot water cutting a dozen tiny channels between her shoulder blades. How long had it been since she'd had her last shower? Two days? Three? Her fingers caught and squeaked in a tangle of painfully clean curls. However long it had been, it seemed like forever.

She closed her lids and allowed the water to run down her face. It had taken a bit of cajoling, but she'd finally convinced the aliens that being allowed time in a bathroom alone was a cultural necessity, a place where humans went in search of needed solitude. The line of her jaw softened, and she huffed out an amused breath, water dribbling down her chin and mouth. Somehow the Kri had gotten the idea that her need for privacy was related to the practice of human religious beliefs, and she wasn't about to dissuade either of them of that bizarre assumption. Rahs could stand in the hallway and wait for her as long as he wanted, but she doubted if even he would dare barge in on her again. Hopefully, the bathrooms were now considered hallowed ground.

But as much as she'd like to, she couldn't hide from Rahs in the shower all day like a frightened little ninny. Her fingers caught in another tangle. Besides, she didn't think her hair could survive another shampooing.

Laura sighed and shook her head. She'd locked herself in the bathroom more than an hour ago. It was time to get out of the shower and check on Bryan again, make sure he still had all his fingers and toes. Time to deal with the real world. She laughed aloud, the sharp sound echoing once in the tiny shower stall. The real world, such as it was, didn't exist anymore. Not for her, at least.

While she hid in the shower, millions of normal people were busy drinking their morning coffee, reading the headlines in their newspapers and hurriedly dressing for work as they went about the monotonous rituals of everyday life.

But then, they weren't being held hostage in their homes by aliens from outer space.

She smiled cynically and gave her curls a last quick rinse. Lucky girl, that Laura Malek. She was privileged. Not many people had a giant black cat wandering around their house, or a tall alien warrior who watched their every move.

The thought of Rahs and how closely he watched her brought a frown to her water-streaked face. For the past two days he had shadowed her every move around the house, those pale, haunting eyes staring at her with an intensity she found completely unnerving. It wasn't the fact that he was watching her exactly, even though it annoyed her in the extreme. It was more the way he stared at her, as if he were peering straight through her skin into the depths of her soul.

She pressed herself flat against the shower wall, heedless of the chilly blue tiles against her naked back. Even more annoying was the knowledge that she'd found herself staring back at him on more than one occasion, meeting that strange, opaque gaze with a directness of her own that she couldn't explain. Granted, he was astonishingly handsome, possessing a well-muscled, rangy body, a thick mane of blond-white hair, and elegantly sculpted features that, together, lent his looks an air of exotic sensuality. But there was something else about him that caused her eyes to single him out for closer study. His every movement, every word exuded a cool veneer of self-command and quiet authority that clung to him like a second skin. Yet that was tinged somehow by a sense of restless isolation that seemed to emanate from a wellspring of unhappiness flowing from some hidden source. At times, she found herself wondering what that wellspring was, and what sort of life had caused its creation.

She pushed away from the shower wall abruptly, her frown now laced with self-doubt. Had she completely lost her mind? How could she possibly sense that he was restless or unhappy? For all she knew the very concepts might be as alien to him as he was to her.

Her chest tightened, and a pulse quickened at

the base of her throat. Not alien enough. Aayshen Rahs might not be human but he was male, all right. Ever since he'd arrived, her body had been telling her that in terms even a simpleton could understand. Each time he looked at her, each time she felt those eyes on her, a flush of answering heat crept through her veins.

"Stupid, stupid, stupid," she muttered to herself, and forced her mind to back away from any thoughts of him. She was just curious, that's all. Curious and scared out of her wits. Her mind was just reacting unconsciously to the stress, careening around in odd directions in search of a novel way to cope.

Angry with herself, she switched off the faucets abruptly, the torrent of water from the shower-head ebbing to a chilly dribble. Laura fanned the steam away from her eyes and pushed the glass door open, feeling around in the mist until her fingers closed around the bath towel she'd left hanging over the metal bar.

She dried her hair and body, then wound the thick towel about herself and stepped out of the shower. The fog of leftover steam seemed to thicken around her, so thick and heavy she could almost taste it in her mouth. She felt her way to the sink, and wiped at the hazy mirror with the back of a hand, rubbing back and forth until a wide, clear circle appeared in the center of the foggy surface.

After smoothing the tangle of wet curls from her face, Laura stared at the image of a scared young woman standing before her. She blinked once, her eyes widening in shock as they focused in on the reflection of the alien standing directly behind her.

Laura let out a startled screech and wheeled around, her dark eyes burning with fury as she glared up at his pale face. "Get out!" she screamed at him, hands clutching at the top of the towel frantically. She'd locked the door. She knew she had; so how did he get in? "I already told you that you can't just walk in here whenever you want! You agreed! You said you wouldn't do it anymore!"

Aayshen simply stared at her upturned face, unmoved by her anger, but growing more aware of her disheveled state with each passing second. "I made no such agreement." His cerulean gaze swept down the length of her small body, lingering for a moment on each curve visible beneath the thick swatch of nubby material wrapped tightly around her. Droplets of water clung to the silky expanse of thigh visible beneath the bottom of the blue cloth, the sun-burnished skin still slick and damp with moisture.

She clutched at the towel convulsively, her shock and rage swiftly turning into outright fear. Why did he have to keep looking at her like that? A surge of pink swept across her cheekbones. "I want you out of here, and I want you out of here now. Do you understand me?"

His curious gaze moved upward again, touching briefly on the soft mounds of flesh threatening to spill over the top of the material, then up the graceful column of her neck to the taut lines of her angry face. "I said I would grant to you a small number of time to be alone with yourself, if that was required of me," he told her impatiently. "You have takken far more than I wish to allow."

Her mouth fell open in surprise; then she snapped it shut again. Each time he spoke, his command of English had increased substantially. How was that possible? Whether from chemicals, as he'd said, or something else, the change was positively spooky. She shrugged off the thought and forced the anger back into her face and voice. Concentrate, she told herself, one problem at a time. "Look, let's get something straight right now. I've got a right to take a shower whenever I want, for as long as I want, without you or the cat barging in here and ogling me! Understand?"

The deep brown eyes glaring up at Aayshen were tinged with color, tiny flecks of gold that seemed to move and shift through the dark pools of her irises. Aayshen's platinum brows pulled downward in a curious frown. In the past few days he had studied every aspect of her expressive features, but each time he looked at her he still discovered something new and fascinating that he hadn't noticed before. What was it about this human that appealed to him so, made him want to delve more deeply into the mysteries hidden within the folds of her mind?

His angular face visibly tightened. Laura Malek was of no more consequence to him than a thousand other beings he had met through time. She, her race and her culture were simply curiosities, and his interest was the same as he would experience on any new world. "You understand. . . . " His voice was pitched deeper than normal, gruff and commanding. "You take so long in this place again, I no longer allow you time alone."

Laura glared at him, her forehead knotting with

107

indignation. Then she snatched her clean clothes from the counter and marched stiffly to the door, holding the back of the towel down as she walked. The door was closed, but the inside bolt had been moved to the unlocked position without any sign of tampering on his part. She stared at the bolt suspiciously, wondering just how he had managed that feat. Some sort of telepathy? She grabbed the knob and twisted, too mad and embarrassed to really care one way or the other, and fled down the hallway to the comparative safety of her bedroom.

If you really are a telepath, then read this, you jerk, she screamed at him mentally, and proceeded to throw every curse and oath at him that she'd ever heard.

Aayshen stared at the empty doorway, the endless string of invectives grating through his thoughts like metal against stone. Though he only grasped the full meaning of an occasional word, her intent was clear enough. The barest trace of a bemused smile ruffled the corners of his mouth. The human mind was far more agile than he'd thought. Instinctively, Laura Malek had already made the connection that his telepathy could be a double-edged sword.

Still cursing him mentally, Laura slammed her bedroom door, tossed the pile of clothes atop the flowered bedspread and hurriedly slipped into her panties. He might walk in any second. Closed doors meant nothing to him, neither did locks, obviously, so she'd just have to dress and undress as quickly possible. No more long showers either.

After giving the closed door a wary look, she hooked her lacy bra, tugged it into place with shaking fingers, and threw on a long black sweater and leggings. Only then did she allow herself a little sigh of relief.

She cast another glance at the door. Somehow she wasn't surprised to find the door open again and him standing there, his blond head almost touching the top of the frame. Embarrassment stained her face red. How long had he been there? "Would you please quit following me?" she grated through clenched teeth. "It's driving me nuts!"

Aayshen leaned against the door frame and stared. He didn't bother trying to explain, or comment on her outburst. She understood full well why he felt compelled to guard her. Whether she liked it or not, she was his captive, one who'd done little to inspire his trust. The fact that he found immense pleasure in such an ordinary task was a secret he would never share, not with her or anyone. He folded his arms, settled his shoulder more comfortably against the wooden frame, and continued staring at her.

Laura threw up her hands in resignation. What was the point? It was obvious that he would continue to watch her, no matter what she did or said, so why fight it anymore? She would just have to ignore him in the future, go on about her life as if he weren't there.

Steadying herself with a ragged breath, she walked to the dresser, picked up a comb, and proceeded to rake it through her blondish curls, wincing every now and then as the teeth snagged on a wet tangle. If he insisted on watching her, he could just go right ahead and do it. He could follow her around all he wanted, watch as she cooked and cleaned, watered in the greenhouses,

109

and did the mountain of dirty laundry piled in the hamper. If he wanted, he could even watch while she scrubbed the toilet. She'd bore him to tears with the everyday details of her life, and make him wish he'd never laid eyes on a planet called Earth. And through it all she'd just bide her time, waiting patiently until an opportunity presented itself to get help.

"Will it hurt?" Bryan's small face was pinched with worry. He considered jerking his hand away and making a run for his room, but he'd already agreed to let Drallondryn do it, and a promise was a promise.

"There will be no pain." Drallondryn sensed the boy was on the verge of fleeing, and tightened his grip on the child's thin wrist. "I doubt very much if you will even feel it." The Kri flicked a tiny button on the sampling tube and pressed the device tight against Bryan's palm. A pinpoint burst of air drilled through layers of skin and tissue and formed a small circle of suction; then the air pressure reversed and the blood sample was siphoned back into the tube.

"See?" Drallondryn snapped a seal over the collection tube and placed it inside his specimen case, along with the sliver of fingernail he'd clipped from the child's thumb. "No pain."

Bryan stared at his palm in surprise. He couldn't even see a red mark where the thing had bitten him. "Neat."

"I'm just going to cut a small portion of your body hair now." He lifted the heavy sewing scissors he'd found in a drawer and snipped several pieces of hair from the base of the child's neck.

The scissors moved toward his bangs.

Laura walked through the hall door and froze. The Kri-thing was kneeling behind her son, a pair of scissors poised in midair. "Just what in the hell do you think you're doing?" she yelled at the startled alien.

Drallondryn dropped the scissors abruptly and lifted his hands, his yellow eyes round with fear. "I meant no harm," he tried to explain.

Enraged, Laura dumped the basket of dirty towels to the floor and rushed across the den. She snatched up the scissors and advanced on the Kri. "I warned you what I would do if you so much as touched a hair on my son's head!"

He extended a hand palm up, the short locks of Bryan's blond-red hair a vivid contrast against his sleek black fur. "It . . . it was only a very small amount of hair. Truly, I meant no harm to him."

Laura blinked and stared down at the contents of his palm. A hank of Bryan's hair? What was going on here?

Cold fingers suddenly latched around her hand, and she felt the scissors slide from her grasp. She glared at Rahs from the corner of her eye. Her shadow had managed to sneak up on her again.

"Drallondryn," Aayshen snapped, the line of his jaw hardening with disapproval. Their situation was precarious enough as it was. "What have you done to the child?"

"I was simply gathering biological samples, Commander." Drallondryn held his breath, uncertain which of them looked angrier. "I apologize if I've offended anyone."

Bryan scrambled to his feet and tugged on his mother's sleeve. He glanced up at her worriedly.

111

Her face had gone white, and her mouth was set in a hard, thin line. "Don't get mad at Drallondryn, Mom. I told him he could do it," he said in a rush. "I've been helping him collect samples of stuff to take back to outer space with him. Leaves and bugs and all kinds of other weird things. My hair and a piece of my fingernail are going, too." He didn't tell her about the blood. From the look on her face he knew that would just make things worse. "Drallondryn's going to study them so he can find out more about us and Earth. Pretty cool, huh?"

Distrust clouded her face and narrowed her eyes. She gave the Kri a glare that was cold enough to freeze solid rock. "And just what do you plan to do with my son's hair and fingernail up there?" All sorts of thoughts ran through her mind, nightmarish scenes from a hundred different movies she'd seen through the years.

The Kri's ears twitched, and his tail whipped back and forth nervously. "Scientific research, nothing more. The hair and nail contain human genetic information that will prove invaluable in our studies of your race."

Her suspicion lingered.

Drallondryn cleared his throat. "I had hoped you would be willing to provide me with samples also."

"Come on, Mom." Bryan tugged on the sleeve of her sweater again. "We already got samples from Grampa Garner."

Laura's brows rose at that. She glanced sideways at the cantankerous old man. As usual, he was snoring peacefully in his recliner chair. "He let you?"

"Well, not exactly," Bryan said. "He called Drallondryn a bunch of names and threatened to hit him with his cane. So we just waited until he fell asleep."

Laura stared down at her son's earnest face, then glanced at the nervous alien. "You cut his hair while he was asleep?"

Drallondryn winced and edged backwards a bit.

"It was just a little bitty piece," Bryan explained, "and the end of his thumbnail. He probably won't even know they're gone."

She coughed and bit back a startled laugh. Garner would have a hissy fit if he knew what they had done. And she wasn't going to be the one to tell him, at least for a while. She doubted if her grandfather would take too kindly to the notion that a hank of his hair and his thumbnail were about to boldly go into outer space. She frowned suddenly. That was assuming Rahs actually kept his promise to leave.

She sighed deeply and pointed a finger at the Kri. "All right, you're forgiven this time, but I'm warning you, don't do anything like that again without my permission first."

The Kri bared his fangs in a relieved smile. "I swear it."

"Okay, then." She shot the Kri another wary look, then retrieved the basket of towels. "Bryan, I've got to go down to the greenhouses and water in a few minutes." Garner was still asleep, and she really didn't want to leave her son alone with the scissor-happy Kri. "Why don't you come with me?"

"Can me and Drallondryn both go?" Bryan pleaded. "We can look for more specimens out-

113

side. I saw a lizard on the patio the other day."

Laura considered the idea for a moment, weighing the pros and cons. In the end, her son's excited face was the deciding factor. That and the fact that it had been several days since he'd had any fresh air. "All right, just for a little while. Stay close to the house, though."

The Kri's eyes cut to Aayshen, who gave him permission with a downward jerk of his head.

"Come on, Drallondryn!" Bryan raced toward the kitchen, the catlike alien not far behind. The back door slammed shut.

Laura closed her eyes wearily and kneaded the center of her forehead with the back of a hand. She'd just given her five-year-old permission to go out and play with an alien. "I must be losing my mind," she muttered to herself. She shook her head, then trudged toward the utility room with the basket of laundry.

Aayshen followed her through the kitchen, wondering just how many times she was going to throw clothing into the boxy, white machine. She had made countless trips since morning, tossing clothes into one machine or the other, then rushing here and there about the house in a frenzy of bone-numbing activity. She had scrupulously cleaned every crevice and scrubbed every item she passed along the way. He suppressed a heavy sigh. The novelty of watching her every movement had begun to wear a bit thin.

She brushed past him, rummaged through the refrigerator, and dropped the last of the carrots and celery into the stock pot simmering on the stove. The soup wouldn't be ready until tomorrow, but fooling with it, as well as the housework, was keeping her mind off the fact that Rahs was still shadowing her every move. She stirred the green liquid and allowed herself a tiny, satisfied smile. No doubt about it, he was definitely beginning to look quite bored by it all.

Her smile faded as she turned to face him. "Well, if you're going to insist on following me, you better come on." Sooner or later he'd get sick of tagging along behind her. "I have a lot more work to do in the greenhouses." She hurried back to the utility room. Yes, indeed, he'd soon be sick enough to leave her alone.

Aayshen lifted a brow and followed after her, out the door and down the sloping pathway that led to the cluster of buildings where she'd found them that first night.

As she disappeared inside one of the buildings, he paused for a moment and stared around him in mute wonder. It felt good to be outside, to feel the wind moving through his hair. The sky above him was a clear, shocking blue, a copse of trees near the river a green so deep and rich it almost took his breath away.

He lifted his face skyward and closed his lids, savoring the moment, the sensation of sunlight warming his face. How many times in his life had he seen such vibrant colors, felt the warmth of a sun beating down on his bare skin? Heard the soft thud of his own footsteps as they fell upon solid ground? A shadow of regret moved through his pale eyes. The dark vistas of empty space and the cold metal decks of a starship were the only realities he knew.

His everyday world was measured in inches, not the distance between horizons. For the most part he lived his life within the confines of a starship, surrounded by steel and sharp angles, artificial light and sterile, windless air. On the rare occasion when he did make planetfall, his time had been spent overseeing the gathering of information about newly discovered worlds, endless surveys and maps of new star systems or, more often than he liked, waging outright war. Keeping the peace, Command called it, damping the fires of rebellion that sometimes flared to life among the scattering of worlds that were a part of the Planetary League. And at the end of each battle, at the end of every dreary day, he had begun to find that he'd lost another tiny piece of his soul.

Gravel crunched beneath his boot heels as he trailed after Laura Malek, the sights and sounds of Earth still permeating his thoughts. He couldn't help but feel a trace of envy for the humans who called this planet home. To live on such a beautiful world, to see and experience such wondrous things each day was a gift of incalculable value. Did they know what they had? Did they realize that the very gifts nature had bestowed on them could soon be lost? Their culture was still young, their technology still struggling to keep pace with the transformations wrought by change itself. The faceless bureaucrats, scientists and bioengineers had yet to wreak their havoc upon this youthful world. But their time would eventually come, just as it had so long ago on Savan and countless other worlds. Change gave birth to more change, until the process spiraled out of control. In a millennium or two Earth's resources would be depleted, its vast seas sucked dry, the trees dead and gone, all sacrificed in the name of progress. Eventually,

116

it would happen. It always did. And then humans would know what it was like to lose their souls.

But that was the distant future. The Earth of the present still possessed an untamed beauty that enlivened his senses, a harvest of exotic pleasures and new experiences that he would gladly feast upon. His footsteps quickened. Watching Laura Malek, no matter what she did, was one of those exotic, earthly pleasures.

He walked through the open doorway and paused. The air in the greenhouse was thick and muggy, and a thin haze of sunlight was seeping through the plastic roof, casting murky shadows across the tables of plants. His eyes followed her while she worked, her slender form bent low as she dragged a heavy length of hose. Just being near her made him feel alive in a way he'd never felt before.

Chapter Seven

The morning had dawned bright and clear, with
a faint hint of tropical warmth drifting inland on
the stiff Gulf winds. Eyes squinted against the
winter glare of the Mississippi sun, Colonel Lemanuel Chapman stretched the slats of the mini-
blinds another inch apart to improve his view of
Keesler Air Force Base's squat buildings and carefully tended lawns.

The constant hum of base activity was familiar
to the Air Force officer. After 19 years in the service and countless bases around the world, the military and its regimentation were his home. Duty,
honor, country were more than words to him.
They were his life, the only home he knew.

His dark face tightened. His whole way of life,
his entire world, were threatened now. Extraterrestrials with unknown and unimagined technol-

ogy were loose in the Mississippi countryside, roaming at will around the country he had pledged to protect and defend.

The consequences were terrifying.

Burkett, Chapman's aide, slipped into the borrowed office quietly and hesitated near the heavy oak desk. "Phone call, Colonel."

The blinds snapped back into place as Chapman turned slowly from the window. "Who is it?"

"It's Washington, sir, General Moss of the National Security Agency. He insists on speaking with you. He says he has to give an update to the Threat Assessment Committee of the Joint Chiefs of Staff at ten, and wants to talk to you before then."

Chapman picked up a gnawed pen from the desk and began rapping it against his knuckles in an impatient, staccato beat. Rufus Moss. Of all the gung-ho brown-nosers that Washington could have sicced on him, Moss was by far the worst. One corner of Chapman's mouth twisted into a pained grimace. Careful, he reminded himself. General Moss was a *smart* brown-noser, one with a John Wayne fixation and a rep for making rash decisions.

Chapman sank into the high-backed chair. "I'll take it here."

Burkett nodded crisply and turned on his heel. The door snicked shut behind him.

After allowing Burkett a few seconds to transfer the call to a secure line, Chapman stabbed at a glowing button on the desk phone with the end of the pen. "Colonel Chapman here."

"Lem?" A thousand miles away, in the faded architectural splendor of his Washington office, the

Marine general leaned back in his expensive leather chair and gazed out a window at the D.C. skyline. His domain. "That you, boy?"

A cold stony expression settled over Chapman's ebony features. He was beginning to think that the general's constant use of the word "boy" was intentional. "It's me, General," he said in his most amiable voice. Beneath the khaki uniform and rows of campaign ribbons, Moss was an arrogant jerk, and always would be. "What can I do for you, sir?" He took a deep breath to steady his temper. Moss enjoyed making him mad.

"Well, for starters," Moss began in a soft, Virginia drawl, "you can tell me what's going on down there. Your people have had over three days now to put a lid on the . . . ah, situation. But from what I've been told, it sounds like you're no closer to containment than you were the other night." He slouched back in the plush leather chair. "Some members of the Threat Assessment Committee are beginning to get real nervous. And our friends over at CIA in Langley are getting a bit twitchy about the delay. They want the extraterrestrials, Lem. They want them in custody real bad."

Chapman's dark eyes turned flint hard. "Sir, my team has been working on this around the clock, but we're chasing shadows down here. Rumors."

"The committee wants results, not excuses, Colonel."

"Do you think I don't?" Chapman's temper was fast reaching the boiling point. He'd had only four hours of sleep since that first night. Some of his men even less. "The search grid has been narrowed to a hundred square miles of nowhere bordering the Alabama-Mississippi state line. A rat can't leave Jackson County without me knowing it, much less two extraterrestrials wandering around the woods in atmospheric suits." He massaged his temple with the end of his thumb. "My trackers think they're running scared and have probably gone to ground somewhere. We're going to start a house-to-house search—quietly of course, so we don't stir up the locals."

Moss paused for a moment, considering. "Then do it, Colonel. Just remember, we don't need any reporters or some yahoo Mississippi sheriff nosing around."

"General, sir." Chapman sighed heavily, no longer caring if Moss noticed his impatience or not. "My people know the drill backwards and forwards. Their covers are already in place and they're ready to go. The locals will never suspect a thing."

"They better not, or the committee might decide to send their own man in to take charge of this mess."

The ballpoint pen snapped in two. Their own man. His name was Rufus Moss, no doubt. "You just tell the committee to let us get on with our job," Chapman said in a brittle voice.

"Your job, Colonel, is to give me results."

"Yes, sir." Chapman bit down on his temper. Rufus Moss was searching for an excuse to step in and take operational command. "You'll get the EBEs, but I need more time. If my people just start banging on doors all over the countryside, the natives are bound to get restless. We've already chased off one nosy tabloid reporter who was sniffing around down here after the trucker's story hit the wire. There'll be more if I move too fast."

Moss laughed shortly, a harsh, hollow sound. "What about that loudmouthed trucker?"

"He's been dealt with, too. He's on his way home to Pineville, Louisiana, right now. He won't be chatting with any more reporters."

The news elicited another harsh laugh from Moss, this one edged with approval. "All right, I'll hold off the committee for another couple of days. You just be sure that whatever your team does, they do it fast. And while you're at it, tell those scientists analyzing the ship remains to get their butts in gear, too. Their preliminary reports weren't exactly illuminating."

"Anything else?" Chapman glared at the phone.

"I want updates every six hours until you've captured the EBEs."

It took a moment for Chapman to realize that he was listening to a dial tone. He dumped the receiver back into the cradle and rubbed at his weary eyes. In a few days it would all be over. A week at the most. He could sleep then.

The awkward silence thickened, broken occasionally by the clink of a glass or the familiar sound of a fork scraping against china. The lack of dinner conversation was familiar to Laura, too, evoking painful memories of her marriage and silent meals with Brax. But in an odd way this present silence was somehow comforting, as if the strange group of people clustered around the mahogany dining room table had formed a tentative alliance with each other in the last few days. As if they had all come to grips with the reality of their

situation and decided to deal with it by not dealing with it at all.

Laura frowned at her own thoughts and
crunched down on a piece of lettuce, realizing she,
too, had been handling the situation in unrealistic
ways. The past few days had been imbued with a
dreamlike quality of normalcy, a sense of the com-
monplace that she had purposefully interjected
into their household routine. Breakfast at seven,
lunch at twelve, and dinner at six. And in between,
all of the mundane tasks she usually performed to
keep her house, business, and family functioning.
Never mind that there were aliens wandering
around her house, eating those clockwork meals
with them and watching her every move. She had
stuck her head in the sand, pretended they weren't
there and blissfully continued on with her life like
nothing had really changed.

The lines of concentration deepened along her
brow as she looked around the table. Bryan was
seated directly across from her, fiddling with the
food heaped on his plate, as usual, while Garner
slurped and chewed his way through dinner with
the same array of sound effects she'd heard for
years.

"Eat, Bryan." After the long silence, her own
voice sounded overloud to her ears. "Don't just
play with it."

Bryan folded his arms defiantly and stared at his
dinner in disgust. Split-pea soup and salad. It was
worse than gross. "Can't I have pizza instead of
this stuff?"

"Don't start. It's all we have." Her freezer was
almost empty, and she had cleaned out the vege-
table bin to make the soup. Laura shot the Kri a

venomous glare across the width of the table, watching as he devoured his third bowl of soup with uncontrolled zeal. "Thanks to him. He's eaten everything in the house that doesn't bite back." She stared as Drallondryn aimed a spoonful of soup at his mouth and missed. Diced potatoes and green liquid landed on the varnished mahogany with an audible splat. Undaunted, he tried again, this time extending several claws to prevent the potatoes from slipping off his spoon. The soup soon vanished down what Laura had come to believe was a dark, bottomless pit.

Drallondryn pinched a slice of cucumber between two claws and held it suspended above his plate, examining its perfectly rounded shape. "Is there some special significance to the shape of this consumable?"

She shrugged. "Not that I know of, Dra—" Laura stopped herself in surprise. She'd almost referred to the cat-thing by name, as if he were a flesh-and-blood dinner guest. What was she doing?

Bryan pretended to eat a few bites of salad, then swung his legs to the side of his chair. "May I be excused? *Gilligan's Island* is on."

"Go ahead." Laura sighed. She couldn't force-feed him.

A flash of anticipation glimmered in the Kri's yellow eyes. Gilligan and the Skipper were fast becoming the high points of his days. He scraped the last spoonful of soup from his bowl and swallowed it hurriedly. "I wish to be excused also," he said, careful to follow Bryan's lead in dealing with the required cultural amenities.

Laura shook her head in disbelief as her child

and the Kri clambered out of their chairs and rushed through the door. The sound of muffled voices and canned laughter soon filtered into the room from the den.

She stared blankly at the empty doorway for an interminable second, picturing the two of them as she'd seen them the night before—stretched out on the den carpet in front of the TV side by side. Laughing, talking, just two friends watching an old rerun together.

She forced her mind back to the present and took a bite of a biscuit, chewing as she thought. The sense of normalcy was insane, a Pollyanna ruse she'd used to trick herself into believing that everything would be back to normal soon. But how could it be? Even if the intruders magically disappeared tomorrow, her family would be forever altered. There were two aliens sleeping in their house, sitting at the dinner table with them, beings who had insinuated themselves into their home and lives with alarming ease and rapidity.

Perversely, Laura no longer felt fear in their presence, only a vague sense of uneasiness which had more to do with the aliens' similarities to humans than their physical differences. Aside from Rahs's strange eyes and the Kri's fur, they weren't that much different from her or Garner or Bryan. They were people, too, she supposed, with all the emotional and mental baggage the definition entailed.

From beneath her lashes, she stole a quick glance down the oval table to the chair at the end where Brax used to sit, a place now filled by the enigmatic Rahs. Surreptitiously, she studied his pale, compelling eyes, the clear-cut lines of his features and the confident set to his shoulders. Ever since he'd barged in on her when she was getting out of the shower, she had found herself watching him more and more, unconsciously searching for something she couldn't define.

"Pass the butter, Laura."

Rahs lifted his gaze to meet hers, and Laura lost herself in his magnetic eyes, mesmerized by their cool blue depths. There was an air of calmness and isolation about him that spoke of strength and serenity, a hidden layer of his personality that she both feared and envied.

"Laura," Garner repeated in an impatient tone.

She blinked to clear her thoughts and transferred her attention to the opposite end of the table. "What?"

"I said pass the butter." Garner gave his granddaughter a probing glance. She'd been acting queer for the last couple of days. Subdued and preoccupied. "Or do I have to walk down there and get it myself?"

"Oh." Laura hastily shoved the plastic dish in his direction. "Sorry." She felt Garner's sharp eyes boring into her, and squirmed in the straight-backed chair, refusing to look at him head-on. Her cheeks grew warm and flushed when his gaze remained fixed on her face.

Garner's knife sliced into the stick of butter. "You've been awful quiet the last couple of days." The tip of his knife swung in an arc that encompassed the alien, then he stared suspiciously at Rahs as an unexpected thought suddenly gelled in his mind. The two of them were together almost all the time, so Rahs could keep an eye on her.

Supposedly. "Is something . . . or someone both-ering you, Laura?"

The red stain on her cheeks crept over her entire face. His mind was as dirty as Carrie's. "Of course not." Her voice carried just the right amount of indignation. "Nothing's bothering me."

"Don't get your back up. I've seen the way Silent Sam there looks at you sometimes and was just wondering."

The scarlet flush spread down to her fingertips. "Grampa!" she whispered urgently. "He under-stands more than you give him credit for. Don't give him any ideas!"

Garner deposited the butter on his biscuit and lowered the knife to the edge of his plate. He stared at Rahs speculatively. The icy blue eyes were still riveted on Laura, watching her every move. "Oh, I don't think I've given Silent Sam any ideas," the old man said. Obviously, he already had them, and that thought made Garner finally give voice to the question that had plagued him for days. "You think outer space people do it like we do?" he mused aloud.

"Drop it," Laura warned in a threatening voice.

"Hey." Garner rapped the edge of the knife against his glass to get the alien's attention. "Just out of curiosity, how do you people make babies?"

"Grampa!"

Aayshen quirked a platinum brow in surprise and gave them both a swift, bewildered look. "Ba-bies?" he repeated.

Garner rolled his eyes. "That's right, how do you reproduce? Make little alien children?"

The Savanian frowned, finally comprehending.

"I am not allowed that privilege. Few warriors are."

Garner coughed into the folds of his napkin to hide his astonishment. "You're not allowed?"

"Shut up, Grampa." Laura's voice now carried a steely edge.

His curiosity piqued, Garner propped his elbows on the table and leaned forward intently. "You mean your government decides who can and can't have children?"

Aayshen shifted in his chair, disquieted by the direction the conversation had taken. "Only ones such as I are forbidden the life-gift."

"What makes you so different?" Garner pressed.

"Because I am a conditioned soldier, and we are not allowed to make decisions for ourselves."

The old man gawked at him. "Why not?"

"Grampa, stop it."

A muscle in the Savanian's right cheek visibly tightened. "Our ways are not yours, humann. You would not understand."

Garner waved a gnarled hand in resignation. "Okay, I'll drop it." He stared long and hard at Rahs, and dabbed at the corners of his own mouth with a napkin. "I was just trying to be friendly."

Friendly? Laura raged to herself. As usual, Garner was sticking his long nose where it didn't belong. And judging by the hostile look on Rahs's face, he might get his nose bobbed if he brought the subject up again. "Go check on Bryan, Grampa," she suggested, trying to diffuse the situation.

He pushed away from the table and rose to his feet. "If you insist." He shuffled off to the den, taking the hint.

The door swung shut behind him, leaving Laura acutely aware that she was now alone in the dining room with Rahs. She fidgeted nervously in her chair, then shoveled a forkful of salad into her mouth and forced herself to swallow.

The uneasy silence grew more oppressive than it had been before. Unsure of what to say or do, Aayshen poked at the greenish liquid in his bowl with the tip of his utensil. Several bits of meat Laura had called ham floated to the surface. His throat tightened. Animal flesh.

Laura rummaged in her shirt pocket and produced a bent cigarette, lighting it as she watched Rahs stare uncertainly at his half-eaten food. The look on his face spoke volumes. "Sorry I didn't have more vegetables, but I'm out of almost everything. Your Kri friend eats his weight in food every day." She paused a moment and pulled on the cigarette, then blew a cloud of smoke toward his end of the table. "Unless you want to starve, you're going to have to let me make a trip to the grocery store."

His nose wrinkled in disgust as the chemical fog began stinging his eyes. He coughed and turned a little paler.

"Sorry." Smiling innocently, Laura exhaled another swirl of haze in his direction. Blowing smoke in their faces had become one of her fondest pleasures in life. Their revulsion never failed to amuse her. "Does that bother you?"

He nodded once in reply, his cold eyes thinning with a hint of suspicion. She had asked that question many times now, and his reply was always the same, yet every few hours she would produce another of the thin white sticks and repeat the process. The noxious chemicals made him feel light-headed.

"About that trip to the grocery store . . ."

Aayshen glanced down at the bits of pink animal flesh floating in green liquid. "Is there edible vegetation at this store-place?"

She suppressed a relieved sigh. Getting his permission to leave the house was going to be easier than she had thought. "Lots of it." Her mind churned over possible ways to get help. A quick note to a cashier, or a telephone call to the sheriff's office might do the trick.

Aayshen laced his fingers under his chin and studied her bland expression carefully. He still didn't trust her, and probably never could. "Then we shall make a trip tomorrow."

We. Her hopes plummeted with the single word.

A kaleidoscope of images flowed through Aayshen's mind, quick snatches of sound and shapes and colors. The child's smiling face . . . whispered words that had no meaning . . . a sudden veil of mist settling over a cityscape crowded with unknown people and odd-angled buildings . . . Bryan's face and body vanishing in the thickening mist.

A black haze of terror suddenly enveloped the telepath.

Where's my son? Laura cried out silently. What have you done with him?

Aayshen awoke with a startled gasp, his heartbeat pounding in his ears. As the dream images began to fade into memory, he sucked in a ragged breath and glanced around the night-shadowed

130

bedroom. All was quiet. The room was dark and still, the only sounds his and Laura's breathing.

Just a dream. Her dream. His heartbeat slowed, and he settled his head against the door he'd been sleeping against the last few nights. He'd been caught inside her nightmare, an unwitting passenger on her flight of imagination.

He massaged his temples wearily. What was happening to him? Laura Malek had even begun to invade his sleep, as though some sort of telepathic link were forming between them, binding his thoughts to hers in a way that he found disquieting in the extreme.

His worried gaze moved to the woman sleeping in the center of the large wooden bed, her slight form huddled beneath several layers of blankets. She was moaning softly, still caught in the throes of the nightmare that had startled him from a deep sleep.

Careful not to make any noise, Aayshen climbed to his feet, and slowly made his way to the side of the bed. A shiver of awareness slid through his veins as he stared down at her sleeping face, a halo of silken curls fanning across the top of the downy pillow. Her lips were parted slightly, her dark lashes fluttering gently as she dreamed. As he watched, a tiny frown passed across her heart-shaped face, then faded into nothingness, her features smooth with sleep once again.

She was so beautiful, so utterly different from anyone he had ever seen or known. Her nearness was like a drug to him, his attraction to her a reality he could no longer shrug off as mere curiosity. He sighed deeply, trying to understand, considering the possibility that it was the very fact that she was different that held such appeal to him.

Through the centuries Savanians had become cynical and hardened, indifferent to anyone or anything save themselves. The concept of family, of the unselfish, protective bond that so obviously flourished with Laura, her child, and her grandfather, was beyond their realm of experience. His people were nothing more than emotionless automatons who went through the motions of life without conscious decision, mindless members of a moribund society that no longer possessed the capacity to feel.

Until recently, he had never thought to question his way of life, never wondered what it would have been like to have had a mother soothe his fears, or care so deeply she dreamed of him in her sleep. He had been born to a life devoid of nurture or family, trained to be what he was and nothing more, while elsewhere in the universe people were allowed to have hopes and dreams.

She stirred beneath the covers, her body shifting restlessly as she slept. Aayshen reopened his eyes, saddened by the turn his thoughts had taken. What would it be like to live as she did? To have children, a family? To know what it was like to be loved? He bent down abruptly and touched her hair, allowing the silky strands to drift through his fingers. Unfortunately for him, he would never know.

Laura lay stock-still, her sleep dulled senses coming alive with an abruptness that caused her heart to hammer against her ribs. Even though her lids remained tightly closed, she knew with an unnerving certainty that he was standing beside her bed. She also knew that he had touched her. Gently, carefully, his fingers had brushed through her hair, a whisper of movement that could almost be termed a caress. She continued to feign sleep, worried that he might touch her again, and wondering why he had.

Laura sensed rather than saw when he moved away from the bed, stole through the shadows, and resumed his vigil by the door. She listened to the small sounds he made as he settled on the floor. Seconds passed, and a ghostly silence settled over the room.

Only then did she release the tense breath she'd been holding and allow her lids to open just enough to survey the darkened bedroom. A haze of silvery light had crept through the curtains, throwing odd-shaped shadows across the walls and floor. She glanced sideways at the clock perched on the nightstand, the numbers glowing bright red in the pre-dawn darkness: 4:35. Too soon to get up, too late to fall back asleep.

She stared at the ceiling, her heart rate accelerating as she thought of the long-awaited opportunity the new day would bring. Within hours she would be on her way to the grocery store, her first and perhaps her only chance to slip a plea for help to someone in the outside world.

There are aliens in my house. Come and get them.

A frown rippled across her forehead. For some reason, the idea of delivering that message had begun to hold less and less appeal.

Laura emerged from the closet in her bedroom clutching a pile of rumpled clothing. "Here, try

133

these on." She hesitated for a moment, then tossed a pair of faded blue jeans and an ancient ski sweater on the top of the bed, along with a pair of mirrored sunglasses she'd found in a drawer. "I don't know why I saved them. They belonged to my ex."

Aayshen gave the strange clothing a dubious look. The heavy blue tunic might suffice, but the trousers appeared to be far too short for his legs. "X?" He tried on the sunglasses and glanced in a mirror, satisfied they would shield his eyes from human view.

"Former husband." She frowned and brushed an errant curl from her forehead. "Bryan's father."

The sunglasses joined the clothing atop the bed. "This husband . . . he is your mate?" Confusion clouded his light blue eyes.

To hide her discomfort, Laura moved to the dresser and began fiddling with the cluster of perfume bottles perched atop a white lace doily. "Not anymore. He left me before Bryan was born." She scrubbed at a layer of dust coating the top of a bottle. Why was she telling him this anyway? He was an alien. What did he know about anything?

Aayshen studied her rigid stance intently, watching her body language for clues to why she was so agitated. Even with the aid of chemical enhancers, four days of cultural assimilation hadn't improved his understanding of Laura Malek or her culture. Nothing made sense on this strange world. Why would this man choose a mate, then leave her? "Why did this husband reject you?"

She winced at his choice of words and shrugged one shoulder. He wouldn't understand, even if she did tell him, so it really didn't matter if he knew the gory details or not. "The usual reasons . . . other women, money."

His eyes darkened, and his brows knitted together in a bewildered line. "Humann males must place much value on the mating ritual and wealth."

Laura's hand slipped, and a bottle of cheap drugstore perfume toppled over, taking several other bottles with it. He understood far more than either she or Garner had realized. Her eyes were drawn to his reflection in the tall mirror hanging behind the dresser. "Some do, I guess." Laura swallowed nervously, averted her gaze from the mirror, and made a halfhearted attempt to rearrange the fallen bottles. "If you insist on going to the store with me, you're going to have to wear the jeans and sweater," she said hastily, trying to steer him to a less painful topic. "You can't walk into the Piggly Wiggly dressed in that black getup."

Aayshen sensed her growing unease and wondered at its cause. He shrugged inwardly and tugged off his boots, then touched a fingertip to the small magnetic seal hidden beneath the collar of his flightsuit. Soundlessly, the dark material unsealed itself and whispered open in vertical lines down his chest and legs, rippling to the carpet in a mound of soft black folds.

She righted the last of the bottles and turned. Her jaw slid open in shock and her breath caught in her lungs. He was just standing there with his back to her, buck naked, staring at the sweater and jeans as if he were uncertain of what to do with them. Laura knew she should run for the door, flee before she saw more than she wanted to see, but curiosity and shock held her in place.

Her wide-eyed gaze traveled an involuntary path down the length of his spine, grazing over taut, corded muscles and pale, pale skin.

"Good grief!" She squeezed her lids shut and covered her eyes with the back of a hand. "I didn't mean for you to strip! Put something on, will you?"

Aayshen turned slowly, baffled by her outburst. "Why are you . . ." He searched his mind for the appropriate word. "Anxious."

"You can't just walk around naked whenever you feel like it!"

"Why not?"

Her lids fluttered open, as if they had a mind of their own. He was facing her now, and her gaze stilled on his long, lean form, the hint of muscles rippling beneath the smooth expanse of his chest. As her gaze drifted lower, past the tapered lines of his waist and hips, a shiver of awareness throbbed through her bloodstream.

"Oh, God." Somewhere deep inside her, a hot, raw ache flared into sudden life. "Just put your clothes back on . . . please." Laura forced her eyes to close again and covered her face with her hands. Any questions she might have had about Savanian anatomy, or his masculinity, had been laid to an abrupt and permanent rest.

Aayshen shook his head, completely baffled now. Humans obviously had cultural strictures against the baring of flesh in the presence of others. But that didn't explain the profusion of half-clothed images he'd seen on Laura Malek's television, or in the glossy pages of the books Drallondryn was so fond of leafing through. "If that is your wish." He shook his head again and shrugged back into his flightsuit. Earth society was a study in contradictions.

Half in anticipation, half in dread, Laura finally mustered enough courage to peek through her fingers. She let out a long audible breath. Thankfully, he was clad in the black outfit again. "Just put the sweater and jeans on over that."

He fumbled his way into the itchy tunic, then coerced his legs into the uncomfortable trousers, pulling and tugging until he forced them up to his waist. He glanced down. The bottoms of the heavy pants narrowed into tight bands beneath his knees, and the front flap hung loose below his waist. "Like so?"

Her gaze drifted downward and rested briefly on the patch of black material visible beneath the open zipper. "Not quite. You have to fasten the front."

He fought with the stubborn closure for long seconds, managing to snag his flightsuit with the mechanism in the process. "This metal thing will not function." He sighed in exasperation.

Wariness shadowed her expression as she closed the gap between them. She stopped in front of him and steeled herself to purposefully touch him, another of the many firsts she'd endured in the past days. "Move your hands. I'll try." Fingers trembling, Laura jerked the dark material free of the zipper and forced the tab upwards. Her hands were shaking so bad it took her several seconds to fasten the top button. "Okay, put your boots on." She blew out a relieved breath and took a half-step backwards, but her hasty flight was stayed when his hand closed firmly over her upper arm.

He stared down at her upturned face with a puzzled expression, grateful that she'd deigned to help him, and curious as to why she did. She was so changeable, unpredictable. "Why did you assist me, Laura Malek?" he asked in a husky voice, uncomfortably aware of how close her body was to his.

The muscles in her arm quivered beneath his burning touch. "I don't know," she said quietly. His strange, hypnotic eyes searched her face and she found herself drifting deeper and deeper into their wintry depths. Her body shuddered from her fingertips to her toes as he reached into her thoughts, drawing her mind into his just as he'd done on that first night.

For a few seconds, she pressed her lids shut and allowed the odd feeling to wash over her, enjoying the sensation of closeness, oneness, the cool orderly texture of his mind. Her body felt numb, her limbs paralyzed by the intensity of his thoughts. Somewhere in the distance she heard the sharp heave of ragged breathing, the primitive sound of a low, anguished moan, and wondered what sort of creature could have made such agonized sounds.

Stunned by the intensity of the contact, Aayshen jerked his hand free of her arm and staggered backwards in surprise. A single touch was all it had been, a simple gesture of gratitude, yet it had led to other things, deeper things that should not have occurred. Forbidden things which were best left buried in the darkest recesses of a Savanian commander's mind.

Laura's eyelids fluttered open, and she stared at him with dreamy, absent eyes. Something strange had happened, but she wasn't sure what. Her thoughts cleared and focused. The agonized moans she had heard had come from *her,* sounds of passion that had slipped unconsciously from her own lips.

Scarlet heat stole across her face, leaving two angry red marks high on her cheekbones. Oh, God, what did he do to me? Her dark eyes glittered with a mixture of humiliation and fear.

"I did not intend to intrude on your mind," he said softly. Masking his own turbulent thoughts with a deceptive calm, Aayshen clenched his hands into fists behind his back, and struggled to regain control of his body and mind. "Humanns must be sensitives, able to share thoughts from peoples gifted with the mind-send." The simple explanation was for her benefit, but it did little to unravel the mysterious reasons for her physical and mental reaction, or his own.

His nails dug into the center of his palms, burrowing deeply into the yielding flesh until his thoughts focused on nothing but the stabbing pain. He was a Command officer, bred and conditioned since infanthood to serve and obey. Duty was the all by which he lived, the creed which guided his every breath. There was no place or purpose in his life for an intimate joining with this woman.

He stilled his thoughts by sheer force of will and shoved a foot into a high black boot. "Do not grow anxious without need." The boot slipped all the way up to his knee, shielding the too-short hem of the trousers from prying eyes. "I shall forbid myself to touch your body again."

Still shaken, Laura averted her eyes from his

steady gaze and grabbed her purse off the dresser, busying herself by fumbling around its crowded interior for her car keys.

"See that you don't," was all she said.

Chapter Eight

The low, plaintive chords of an Elvis song pulsed from a jukebox as Chapman paused inside the entrance of the deserted Pizza Hut, his eyes sweeping over the sea of empty tables crowding the restaurant's interior. Hardly the setting for a close encounter. But every lead had to be checked and double-checked.

"We don't open for lunch till eleven," a woman trilled in an impatient, clipped tone.

Chapman made a slow half turn, angling his lanky body toward the checkout counter and the woman's voice. Her hand hesitated over the cash register buttons and her gaze thinned, as if the sight of a stranger was cause for suspicion and fear.

"I said we're closed, mister."

He forced his lips to part in a tight smile. "Doris Arnette?"

Still suspicious, the middle-aged woman took a step away from the counter, her fingers clutching nervously at her rumpled uniform shirt. Doris wished now that she had remembered to relock the door. "Who wants to know?"

Chapman flipped open a small leather wallet and flashed a false ID and badge. "Special Agent Grissom, Federal Bureau of Investigation."

Her wary expression turned incredulous. "What's the FBI want with me?"

"Just the answers to a few questions, that's all." He pulled a pad and pen from an inside coat pocket to make the questioning look official. "On Monday at 1:07 A.M., you placed a call to the Jackson County Sheriff's office and reported a disturbance in the restaurant's parking lot. I need the details of the disturbance and a physical description of the suspects."

Doris rolled her eyes and sighed. "For goodness sake, I gave all that information to the deputies the night it happened, then again to some young fellow who came in here the next day." She pursed her lips in disgust. "Look, I've been working double shifts all week, and I'm worn slap-out. Do I have to go through it all again with you?"

"Yes." There was a subtle shift in his tone, a sharp edge of annoyance which revealed more than the single word.

Her bravado wilted under his determined glare. "It was no big deal, really. I locked up the restaurant about a quarter to one and was walking around back to my car when I heard something behind the dumpster, like somebody was fooling around back there. Believe you me, I was some kind of scared, a woman alone at that time of night in this day and age. All sorts of things ran through my mind, so I jumped in my car and locked the doors real quick."

Elvis's voice finally faded, and a blanket of silence settled over the empty restaurant. "So?" Chapman pitched his voice lower since he didn't have to compete with the jukebox anymore. "What happened then?"

Doris folded her arms as if to stave off a sudden chill. "I'm not real sure, it happened so fast. When I started the car and wheeled around to get the hell out of the parking lot, my bumper clipped one side of the trash dumpster. I looked out the rearview mirror before I gunned it and saw two guys wearing motorcycle helmets jump up from behind my car and take off running down the side of the building. That's about it. It was raining cats and dogs at the time, so I didn't see much else." She rubbed her forearms with her hands to warm them, thankful to have escaped the close call. "I was scared they were going to break into the restaurant, so I drove on down to a pay phone at a convenience store and called the sheriff from there."

He scribbled some more. "Which direction did they go?"

The heavyset woman jabbed a finger toward the woods bordering the opposite side of the highway. "They were headed north, on foot."

Chapman closed the notepad slowly, still uncertain if the sighting warranted any more investigation or not. The intruders could have been bikers or some kids on a lark, or any number of

143

other explainable things. But this was Escatawpa, only miles from the crash sight, too close to just shrug it off. "Thank you for your help, Ms. Arnette. I'm sending a forensic team in this afternoon to check your parking lot and the dumpster, and an artist to draw a sketch of their helmets based on your description." He walked toward the door.

"Hey," Doris called after him. All this for two punks sneaking around a parking lot? "What'd they do, anyway?"

Chapman turned and gave her another thin smile. "We suspect they might be illegal aliens." His smile vanished as he strode through the door and sprinted across the empty parking lot to his waiting car.

Burkett switched on the ignition as he slammed the car door. "Anything, Colonel?" his aide asked.

"I don't know. Maybe." The timing was right, just hours after the crash. But the very idea of EBEs sneaking around a Pizza Hut parking lot was ludicrous. Chapman warmed his hands in front of a heater vent and unbuttoned his overcoat. "I want the team to go over the area again just to be sure. Full sweep." He stared at the entrance of the restaurant for long seconds. Doris Arnette was staring back at him through the glass door, her anxious face pressed tight against the diamond shaped panes. "And tell them to keep using the FBI cover. It seems to work best with the locals."

"Yes, sir."

A tight, burning sensation began building beneath Chapman's rib cage, crawling slowly up his esophagus as Burkett eased the government Ford into light traffic on Escatawpa's main drag. His dark features twisted into a pained grimace. Too many cups of coffee, and too little sleep. "Find a drugstore before you make that call, Burkett. I need some antacid."

"Right away, sir." Burkett's gaze moved over the cluster of faded gas stations and ramshackle car lots lining the two-lane highway, finally settling on the small strip shopping center they had just left. The car turned abruptly and bumped its way back across the sprawling parking lot, then angled into a handicapped parking space. "This okay, Colonel? I didn't see any drugstores."

Chapman eyed the neon lettering and smiling pig's face on a sign above the store. "Fine. Keep the heat on. I'll just be a minute." Tugging his coat closed against the damp Southern wind, the Air Force intelligence officer dodged a mud-filled pothole and hurried into the nearly deserted grocery store.

A couple of bored-looking cashiers were stationed around the registers, yawning and killing time by gossiping with each other until the few customers in the store were ready to check out. He glanced at his watch. It was only 10:15, too early for most shoppers, he supposed.

After bypassing the produce department, Chapman wandered down the narrow maze of aisles in search of the drug section, nodding occasionally to acknowledge the probing looks cast his way by several housewives. The acrid scent of laundry detergent touched his nostrils as he rounded a corner of another aisle, veering right to avoid colliding with a basket parked in his path. The basket's owner, a small, 30ish woman dressed in jeans and a heavy parka, gave him a swift, startled glance before shoving the overloaded cart against a shelf stacked high with pet supplies.

"Sorry," the woman said, and produced a wan, apologetic smile.

Her dark brown eyes drilled into his face for a tense second; then her gaze slid nervously to the opposite end of the aisle, lighting on a pale, long-haired giant clad in sunglasses, too-tight jeans, and an out-of-date ski sweater. The giant was staring intently at the selection of canned fruits. Chapman's mouth twitched with amusement. This guy gave new meaning to the word white. He looked like he hadn't seen the sun in at least five years, maybe longer. It took all kinds, Chapman told himself. Even men who bleached their hair platinum white and wore riding boots to the grocery store. His glance lingered on the rangy blond for a split second before darting back to the woman.

Chapman gave her an automatic half-smile, nodded, and continued on his way, frowning in surprise when she moved to block his path again. His frown turned impatient.

Laura sucked in a quick breath to calm herself, and released her grip on the scrap of paper clutched in her hand. This was the only time Rahs's watchful eyes had left her since they had entered the store. Her first, and possibly last opportunity to pass the hastily scribbled note. The loose-leaf sheet fluttered to the red tile floor, landing wrong side up.

Irritation flashed in Chapman's eyes. The silly woman was just staring at the fallen paper with a blank expression, as if she expected him to play out the tired old roll of gallant Southern gentle-

man. He muttered to himself and stooped to retrieve it, saw a few words peripherally like
potatoes and bread, and offered the paper back to
her without reading the other side. "You dropped
your list, lady."

Laura stood stock-still, her panicked gaze
swinging wildly to the end of the aisle. "I . . ." Rahs
was moving toward them, suspicion written in
cold lines across his stark features. Her hand
shook as she reached for the paper. "Thank you,"
she mumbled in a strained voice, and hastily buried the note inside a pocket of her jeans.

Bewildered, the Air Force officer watched as a
nervous red flush raced across the woman's
cheeks, and her eyes clouded with apprehension.
He swiveled his head to follow the direction of her
gaze and tensed. Trouble was heading toward
them. Chapman could feel it in his bones, sense it
in each of the blond behemoth's pantherlike
strides and the stiff, watchful set to his sharp features. Even though his eyes were hidden behind a
pair of mirrored aviator glasses, Chapman knew
they were hostile. Jealous husband? Irate boy-
friend? He wasn't going to wait around to find out
which.

After dipping his head slightly, he gave the
woman a pitying look, and hurried off to find the
antacids. As he turned down another aisle, a small
uncertain frown carved a path across his forehead. Something about the guy hovered around
the edges of his mind, some connection just out
of reach.

Aayshen glided to a silent stop and stared into
Laura's fear-blanched features with wary, suspi-

147

cious eyes. "Why did you talk with that human?" His tone was terse, demanding.

Panic gnawed at her vocal chords. Laura made a low, raspy sound as she cleared her throat, the only sound she could make for several seconds. "I dropped my grocery list, and he picked it up for me. That's all." She backed away from him slowly, crowding against a shelf of dog food to place her body out of reach. If he touched her now, even accidentally, or tried to read her thoughts, the telepath might discover the truth. Silently, she began reciting the words to a nursery rhyme in her head, trying to blank any thoughts of the note from her mind.

Aayshen's skepticism lingered. He watched the play of emotions across her delicate features and recognized the lie for what it was. Didn't she realize that he could force the truth from her if he wanted, invade her thoughts with no more effort than was required to see or breathe? But this was neither the time nor the place to risk a mind-touch with her. If nothing else, the last few days had taught him that exploring Laura Malek's mind could produce an unpredictable reaction from him as well.

The pale planes of his face shifted into taut, somber lines. The truth would have to wait. "You have chosen enough food-things," he said roughly, and propelled the grocery cart toward the front of the store.

Laura followed, staring silently at his back. She didn't know if he had accepted the lie, and that made her edgy.

When they reached the checkout lanes, Laura commandeered the cart and pushed it up to a bored cashier who was busily filing her nails. Laura began tossing a mountain of groceries atop the conveyer belt, hoping she had enough money in her purse to cover what would surely be an astronomical bill.

As the cashier weighed and rang up one plastic bag of vegetables after another, Laura's eyes found Rahs again. He was waiting near the exit doors with a tight-lipped, impatient expression, looking much like any other American male waiting on a dawdling wife.

"That be all today?" the cashier said finally.

Laura blinked and directed her attention to the woman's chubby face. "Oh . . . that's all." As the register began tallying a final total, her gaze angled over the cashier's shoulder to a customer three lanes away. Her eyes skimmed across the familiar features of the man waiting for his purchase to be rung up and bagged, the same man who'd retrieved her fallen note.

All trace of color drained from Laura's face. He was staring at Rahs with a fixed, stony look, probing the alien's face and body with sharp, distrustful eyes. She scrutinized the well-dressed man intently, from his neatly trimmed military haircut to the costly gray suit and overcoat. No one dressed like that in Escatawpa. The word "government" was stamped all over him, and the realization sent a cold shudder of dread spiraling down her spine. The man knew, or suspected, what Rahs really was.

"A hundred and eighty-two dollars and seventy cents."

The cashier began the painfully slow process of bagging her groceries as Laura scrabbled through

149

the dark recesses of her purse, digging around until she unearthed her well-worn wallet. The man's gaze had never wavered, and Rahs still seemed oblivious to his relentless stare.

She hesitated for an uncertain second as she weighed her decision. The note was still hidden in her pocket. All she had to do was slip it onto the counter along with the money. So simple. Her hand wavered. If Rahs were captured now, away from the house and Drallondryn, Bryan and Garner might pay for her mistake with their lives. She plopped two hundred-dollar bills down atop the counter, then hurried the cashier along by stuffing food into the grocery bags herself. The note stayed hidden in her pocket. There was no telling how the Kri would react—or retaliate, if Rahs were captured. For her family's sake she had to get Rahs away from the man and the store in one piece. At least that was what she kept telling herself, repeating it like a litany until she almost believed it.

Laura crammed the last bag inside the basket, grabbed her purse and shoved the cart out of the narrow lane, tipping it on two wheels as she swerved toward Rahs.

"Miss . . . you forgot your change!"

"Keep it," Laura shot back. The man was walking toward Rahs now, his strides slow and determined.

Aayshen finally glanced up, his brows pulling downward in a puzzled frown when he saw Laura and the cart rushing to the doors at a reckless speed.

"Come on, sweetheart," she gushed in a loud, artificial voice. The smile she plastered on her face was just as phony. "I need help pushing the basket."

The Savanian's frown deepened, but he did as instructed. Though her expression reflected an entirely different emotion, he could sense Laura's fear, smell it building in the air.

As he fell into step beside her, Laura's fingers dug into his elbow. "That man," she whispered urgently, "he's watching you. I think he knows what you are."

Chapman closed the gap between himself and the pale-skinned man wearing sunglasses. It wasn't just the guy's oddball looks that had piqued his curiosity. Something almost tangible seemed to hover around the tall blond, nothing he could put his finger on, but it existed nevertheless. It was a disquieting alienness that permeated the air around him, and made the hairs on Chapman's neck refuse to lay down. There was something too practiced, too controlled about the man, a lethalness that Chapman was all too familiar with. The man had the look of a trained and blooded soldier. The Air Force officer's heart hammered in his chest, and his pace increased.

Laura cast a nervous glance backward as the cart rattled across the sensor mat and the door flew open automatically. Rahs had stopped and turned, cold eyes moving warily over the stranger walking toward them. The stranger was barely ten feet away now, closing on them fast. She clutched at the back of the ski sweater and jerked Rahs backward.

"Come on!" she hissed at him. As she rammed the basket through the narrow exit, a rear wheel snagged on the door frame and caught.

151

"Hold it right there, miss," Chapman ordered quietly. His gaze never wavered from the blond's sharp features. As the woman turned back to face him, he flashed the fake FBI badge. "I'd like a word with you people."

The smell of fear was stronger now. Laura's, the human's. Aayshen tensed, mind and muscles reacting automatically as he assessed the situation. The human had the ready stance and cold trained eyes of a warrior, one who would not allow his quarry to slip away unbloodied. The Savanian didn't need to see the weapon to know it was there, tucked within the folds of the human's clothing. His senses sharpened, eyes grew hooded, watchful, as a lifetime of mental conditioning centered his mind, focusing his thoughts only on the human male and the threat he represented.

"Step away from the door, please." Chapman's right hand drifted toward his coat and the gun concealed inside. Neither one of them moved. The woman was rooted to the floor, her face blanched white with fear. The man, if that's what he was, was staring at Chapman with a vacant, impassive expression, as though he were concentrating on something unseen. "I don't want to use force, but I will if I have to," Chapman warned them.

As if it were guided by invisible hands, the grocery basket suddenly freed itself and lurched over the threshold, spilling a roll of paper towels as it careened across the sidewalk and clattered over a curb. Chapman's attention was pulled to the unexpected noise, his gaze flickering over the runaway basket for a split second too long.

Behind the dark sunglasses, Aayshen's eyes were dull and heavy-lidded, as though he were half-asleep or caught in the throes of a waking dream.

Chapman felt his ears pop, as if the air pressure had suddenly changed; then something closed around his upper body with a viselike grip. He gasped and stumbled backwards, pain stabbing through his shoulders from what had felt like a powerful physical blow. He blinked twice, confused. The blond man hadn't moved, was still staring at him from behind the mirrored glasses. Chapman forced himself to ignore the searing pain and reached for his gun. He staggered again, arms and hands flailing vainly for the pistol as he reeled like a drunken marionette dangling from invisible strings. The air wheezed out of his lungs in one huge, raspy sigh as something hard and invisible collided with his chest.

Laura choked down a frightened, startled cry and watched in horrified fascination as the man, his badge, and a bottle of medicine suddenly flew in three different directions, hurled up and backwards by a nonexistent blow. "Oh, God," she breathed.

Chapman came down for a landing atop a checkout counter sprawled on his back, a full 20 feet from where he'd been just a second before. Dazed, he stared fixedly at the high white ceiling, his glazed eyes swimming in and out of focus. Don't lose consciousness, he ordered himself, but his brain refused to cooperate. A thick veil of darkness settled around him.

The sound of a cashier's high-pitched screech filtered through Laura's mind, galvanizing her into action. A female customer added her voice to the bedlam, creating a cacophony of frightened screams. "Let's go!" she whispered to Rahs, and offered up a silent prayer that the government man was still alive.

As though he were waking from a deep sleep, Aayshen turned and walked through the door, each movement slow and exaggerated.

She jerked on his sweater to hurry him up. "We've got to get out of here!" With Aayshen close on her heels, Laura retrieved the grocery cart and shoved it across the asphalt at a dead run. A man in a dark green car glanced up from a newspaper as they ratcheted past, but no one else in the parking lot seemed to notice or care.

God help me. Laura fumbled in her coat pocket for the keys, then rammed the metal basket into the driver's side of her battered Cherokee, carving new scratches into the navy blue paint. Her fingers trembling from cold and fear, she swung a back door open and began slinging the grocery bags inside. A paper sack split down one side, disgorging its load of vegetables across the seat. Laura swore under her breath. She should just forget about the bags and leave, but they had to eat, and she wasn't about to leave 200 dollars worth of groceries behind, not after what she'd been through to get them. "Help me, dammit!" she snapped at Rahs, who seemed more concerned with the man in the green car than anything else. "Quit worrying about him! He's nobody!"

Aayshen wasn't so certain. His thoughts touched the suspicious young human for a fraction of a second, long enough to know for sure. Their eyes locked. The sheet of newspaper the human had been reading drifted downward and his head lolled backwards against the seat of the vehicle.

A package of hamburger meat splatted against the pavement. "Are you going to give me a hand or not!"

Aayshen swiveled his gaze around. He stared first at his own hand, then hers, wondering how he could accomplish such a thing.

"Oh, for God's sake! Never mind!" She tossed the last two bags inside and slammed the door. "Get in!"

Chapman eased himself off the conveyer belt and shifted his battered body into a sitting position. He touched his chest gingerly. Possibly one broken rib, maybe more. He tried to remember how it had happened and why, but his mind still refused to cooperate.

"Stay still, mister. We called an ambulance for you. They should be here pretty soon now."

The cashier's concerned features swam into sudden focus. "I'm fine," he said. A vague, uncertain memory stirred within his mind, lingered for a second, then came into sharp focus. The woman . . . The odd, vacant look on the blond man's face. Chapman had been reaching for his gun when something grabbed him and slung him across the grocery store, something strong and powerful that wasn't physically there. His heart thudded wildly against his aching ribs. Some form of telekinesis? A physical manifestation of mental energy? "Just help me off of here, will you?" He winced as the woman helped him to stand on unsteady feet. "How long was I out?"

"Five minutes or so."

His dark gaze moved beyond the press of faces clustered around him, tracking over the front of the store in search of the woman and the man.

"If you're hunting for that blond-haired fellow you was talking to by the door," the cashier offered, "him and the woman lit out of here a few minutes ago, right after you throwed yourself on the checkout counter. They're long gone by now."

The realization of what she had said hit Chapman full force. She had seen it happen. He clutched at the woman's wrist, fingers pressing into her flesh anxiously. "Tell me exactly what you saw. How did I get on the counter? Was I hit? Did he touch me physically?" His convulsive grip tightened. "Where the hell did they go after I blacked out?"

"Nobody touched you, mister." The cashier tugged her wrist free of his insistent fingers and took a wary step backwards. "It was just like I said, you throwed yourself up there. So don't you go trying to sue nobody, because I'll testify that you did it yourself." She fingered the ID wallet she'd found on the floor, giving the gold FBI shield a final, leery look. "I'll testify even if you really are some kind of FBI man." She handed the ID back to him.

Chapman ground a closed fist against his forehead, furious with the woman, and furious with himself for approaching a possible EBE without backup. Damn. He'd screwed up royally. "Forget about that, woman, and just tell me where they went!"

"How should I know?" She glared for a moment, considering. Maybe he really was FBI. "They took off in one of those Jeep-like cars. A black one, I think."

Chapman glared into her pudgy face. "You think? Was it black or not?" His eyes grew sharp and hard. "You checked her out—who was she? A regular customer?"

The woman shook her head from side to side. "Can't rightly say. I'm new here, so I don't know the regulars by sight yet. And that Jeep could have been another color, I suppose. Blue maybe."

Annoyance flickered in his eyes. The cashier was being purposely obtuse, but from what he'd seen, that was standard behavior in this part of the country. "Think, woman, how'd she pay? By check?"

Her head wobbled back and forth again. "Cash money."

Chapman shot a commanding look at another cashier, a scrawny woman with a thin face and a surprisingly large chest, then glared at the small crowd of whispering customers gathered around her. "I want a name," he demanded in a curt, chilly tone. "Escatawpa's just a flyspeck on the map. One of you people *had* to recognize her!"

A sudden, stony silence fell over the women. Several of the Piggly Wiggly's customers drifted away, grumbling and whispering among themselves as they collected their baskets.

"Flyspeck? You sure got your nerve, mister." The scrawny cashier who'd bagged his purchase folded her arms across the front of her uniform and glared back. "I've never seen that woman before in my life. The man either." Her eyes narrowed, as though she were daring him to challenge her word. "So why don't you just take

157

your Yankee self and move on out of here."

She was lying through her teeth and Chapman knew it. "I want her name, lady, and I want it now."

The remaining locals closed ranks around the cashier like an overly protective family. "We've got nothing more to say to you, Mister Government Man," the cashier grated. She waved a bony hand in dismissal. "Find her yourself." The Mississippian's voice was edged with a steely note of finality.

Chapman ground his teeth together in frustration. He wasn't getting anywhere. "All right, you people can have it your way . . . for the time being." His lips tilted upwards, more a grimace than a smile. "But I'll be back." He glanced at the white name badge pinned to the cashier's uniform shirt. Bobbie-Jean Cooner. Wouldn't be hard to remember that name. "Count on it, Ms. Cooner."

He scooped up his bottle of antacid and marched toward the door, mustering as much dignity as his ribs allowed. His fingers trailed over the small, tender area in the middle of his chest. Any trace of doubt he might have had about the blond man's identity faded from his mind, replaced by a certainty born of painful experience. Chapman quickened his pace across the parking lot, rushing toward his car at a near run. No one but an EBE with paranormal abilities could have sent him flying across the store like that, an EBE who had delivered an invisible mental blow aimed and timed so precisely that it barely injured him at all. The intention had obviously been to incapacitate, not kill. Otherwise, Chapman would be on his way to the morgue.

Chapman slid into the Ford's passenger seat and slammed the door, grunting in pain as he pulled it shut. He scanned the parking lot hopefully, but there was no one in sight.

His aide glanced at him sleepily, the eyes behind his thick glasses glazed and confused.

"Burkett, did you see a big blond man and a woman run by here a few minutes ago?"

"No . . ." Burkett took off his glasses and rubbed his eyes. "Wait, yes, I did. They passed right in front of the car. Weird-looking guy, and a woman pushing a grocery cart. I was wondering why they were in such a big hurry when . . ." His brows came down in a frown. "Funny, I don't seem to remember anything after that."

A chill rippled down Chapman's spine. "Get on the phone and request a secure satellite patch to Team Base. Tell them to contact the Mississippi and Alabama state police."

Burkett started punching buttons on the cellular phone.

"I want a complete rundown on everyone within a hundred square miles who owns a dark-colored utility vehicle, no particular make or model," Chapman ordered in an urgent voice. "Names, addresses, descriptions—everything on record. Level-one priority. I want the information as soon as possible."

Two minutes later Burkett snapped the phone back into its base. "They said it'll take a while, sir. No one knows exactly how long."

Chapman grunted in acknowledgment. "In the meantime, drive."

Burkett threw the gear shift into reverse. "Where to, Colonel?"

"Keesler, the base hospital. I think I have a couple of broken ribs." He popped the safety seal on the bottle of antacid and took a chalky swig. "And like it or not, we're both going to be spending the next few hours undergoing decontamination."

The announcement drew a blank expression. "Sir?"

"We might be contaminated. You because you've been in close contact with me, and me because I think I've been in close contact with an EBE."

Burkett's blank look transformed itself into disbelief. "An extraterrestrial? Where?"

Chapman released a weary sigh, leaned his head back against the seat and kneaded the center of his forehead. He found it hard to believe himself. "In the Piggly Wiggly."

Chapter Nine

The Cherokee kicked up a hazy cloud of orange dust as Laura sped down the narrow dirt road, slewing around potholes and mini-ravines gouged in the clay by the last heavy rains. She rounded a sharp curve and bumped onto a secondary, more desolate road, one which would eventually lead to pavement and home.

Aayshen stared at the landscape sweeping by in silence. The tangle of trees embracing the pathway grew thicker, a dense, vibrant jumble of scent and color. A small winged creature arced across his line of vision, flushed from its hiding place by the ground vehicle's mechanical roar. Eyes on the gangly trees, he tugged off the uncomfortable sunglasses and massaged the bridge of his nose. His expression turned pensive. Savan, with its stark gray mountains and sterile landscape, couldn't compare with this planet. Earth was so alive, so beautiful.

The Jeep hit a dip in the road and bottomed out, its undercarriage scraping across hard-packed clay. Laura winced as the alien's head slammed against the ceiling with an audible thunk. Glancing sideways, she gave him a feeble half-smile. "Sorry about that," she said nervously, more to break the awkward silence between them than to apologize. Neither of them had said a word since leaving the parking lot. "I didn't do it on purpose."

His head swung in her direction. "Please slow your velocity before our bodies are harmed." Her piloting skills left much to be desired.

After a quick look through the rearview mirror to make sure they weren't being followed, Laura eased off on the gas pedal and slowed until the speedometer dropped below 30. No one was behind them, not now at least. She swallowed hard and mustered enough courage to ask the question that had been gnawing at her for the last ten minutes. "That man in the grocery store . . . I know you did that to him. He isn't dead, is he?"

Aayshen shifted in his seat, his eyes on the terrain flashing by the window. "The human still lives."

Her shoulders sagged against the back of the seat. Thank you, God. He hadn't said how he'd done it, though. "Did you do some sort of mind-thing to him?"

"Mind-thing, yes. I have been conditioned to act in such ways when danger to myself or my people is near."

Laura shivered despite the stuffy warmth blowing from the heater vents. "You can't just . . . think someone dead, can you?"

He lifted a platinum brow. The mental abilities that had been genetically bred into him were extensive, but not so powerful that he could kill with a single thought. Not intentionally. "With my mind, no. But I cannot allow us to be captured. My training forbids this."

Laura fought to keep her hands steady on the wheel. If cornered, he would kill if he had to. No doubt about it. So she would just have to make sure he was never cornered again.

The orange-red dust grew thicker, settling over the hood and windshield as their speed dropped to a leisurely 15 miles per hour. She checked the mirror more carefully this time, then relaxed her convulsive grip on the wheel and sucked in a deep, ragged breath. "I haven't seen another car for the last couple of miles." The shock of what had happened at the Piggly Wiggly began to fade with distance. "I think it's safe to head home now."

Aayshen watched her curiously as he felt her fear begin to ebb, his opaque eyes grazing over the soft planes of her face. Refracted light cast a shadow across her right cheek, a dark sliver which moved slowly downward, touching her changeable features with a cool shade of gray-green. Fascinated by the play of light against her cheek, he lifted one hand to brush a fingertip across the sliver of shadow, but stopped just shy of his destination. His hand pulled back abruptly and fell to his side. Aayshen frowned and stared at his clenched hand curiously, as if it were some strange, horrid thing with a will of its own.

Laura gave him a sideways, quizzical glance. His pale features had taken on a remote, almost

Jan Zimlich

brooding look, as though he were pondering an escape from the dark flames of his own personal hell. She cleared her throat. Maybe he was. Perhaps his hell was her, and a planet named Earth. "That guy you knocked across the store was FBI, part of our government. He won't give up. The FBI will keep searching until they find you, no matter how long it takes. It would be a whole lot easier on you and me both if you just gave yourself up."

A muscle in his jaw clenched, and his eyes turned a glacial blue. "Then I will fight these FBI persons." There was determination in his voice, as well as a lethal undertone. "We will not be captured by them or any other humans."

She cast another questioning glance his way. The somber, brooding look had dug new lines across his brow. "So what's the big deal about you and the cat being captured? The government wouldn't go to this much trouble to find you if they had any intention of hurting you."

The tense, uneasy lines deepened along his forehead. She and her people were innocents, primitives who knew nothing of the universe save for their own little world. "Humans are not yet ready for open contact with other worlds. It would be dangerous."

Laura laughed, a short, brittle sound tinged with amusement and disbelief. "Dangerous? For who? You or us?" Her own government had obviously shot his ship down, and was now trying to capture him. She shook her head. Typical knee-jerk reaction. "Except for the military, I think most of us humans are more than ready to make contact with the big unknown. Just about everyone I know already believes in the possibility anyway. Even Garner. No one will be too surprised."

"Dangerous for you," he said softly.

His quiet tone caused her gaze to shift from the road to him. The blood drained from her face abruptly. His features were frozen in a stiff, anxious expression, as though he were contemplating the end of the world. "Dangerous in what way?"

"All ways." His lips flattened in a tight, grim line. "Your culture will be changed forever. Your government will want our science, and if they capture us, especially the Kri, they will surely steal that knowledge by force. With this information, advances in technology that now take your people decades to achieve will occur in days. Everything you know will be altered." He fell silent for a long moment. "I have seen this happen on other worlds. With such drastic change, much unrest will come. Your people will fight among themselves. They will not be able to accept or adjust."

Thoughts of a new Cold War, of governments fighting each other over possession of alien technology, made the blood chill in her veins. Wars fought with alien weapons of unimaginable and unspeakable power. She stepped on the brake and brought the Jeep to a sudden, bone-jarring stop. The idea of contact with other worlds had suddenly taken on a different, more ominous meaning than it had before.

She closed her eyes. It was too much to absorb. She rubbed the center of her forehead with the back of a hand. Let him be captured by the government and risk—what? If she believed him, maybe the end of the world. But if he continued hiding in her house, the lives of her own family were at risk.

"Okay, I guess we'll just have to make sure the FBI doesn't find you again," Laura said finally. No more notes to strangers. She didn't really believe him, but she wasn't willing to stake her family's lives on the possibility that he was lying.

She stared out the windshield in silence, her dark brown eyes burning with a combination of frustration and helplessness. What the hell was she doing in the middle of all this anyway? She was just an ordinary person, a nobody from Jackson County, Mississippi. Why her? Why ruin her life?

The dark intensity of her thoughts pressed in on Aayshen's mind with startling force. Uncertainty, indecision, distrust, and a hot flame of anger. He could feel them all, but mostly her anger at him. His own thoughts stilled, and his expression grew wary. "If you hate me so very much, why did you aid me in the food-place?" he asked, growing suspicious of her motives now as before. There was only one way to discover the truth. He steeled himself mentally and reached into her thoughts, a light, cautious exploration that only probed the surface layers of her mind.

All the fear, anger and frustration Laura had so carefully held in check simmered to a sudden, violent boil. He was trying to get inside her mind, a place where no one had a right to be, least of all him. There was no way to protect herself from such an assault, and for that she hated him. If he wanted he could effortlessly sift through every stray thought, every errant feeling hidden within the protective folds of her mind. Even the unwanted feelings she had about him, her own uncertainty about her reasons for helping him. Worse still, on some deep, raw level, she realized that she wanted him there, wanted to feel that violent surge of awareness coursing between them once again. And for that, she hated herself.

"Get out of my head." Her eyes burned with hostility. "I don't have to tell you squat."

When she refused to answer, Aayshen's features clouded with escalating doubts. She had talked with the FBI person just minutes before the confrontation. Something had transpired between them. "Tell me, Laura," he demanded. Then his voice turned cold and deathly quiet. "How did that human know we were in the food-place?"

Her chin tilted to a defiant angle. "How the hell should I know? He was just there."

Aayshen's hand snaked across the gap between them and latched around her elbow, trapping her flesh beneath steely fingers.

She tried to twist away. "Let go of me, dammit! You said you wouldn't touch me again!"

His fingers dug into her pliant flesh. She was hiding something. He could feel its fleeting presence in her thoughts. "Speak now, or I will force the truth from your mind."

Laura let out an angry screech and tried to twist her legs around to kick him, but he just trapped her thighs with his body and pulled her down on the seat. Her head bumped the steering wheel, then the armrest. Eyes smoldering with rage, she lashed out with her free arm. The sound of her palm connecting with his jaw cracked through the chilly air like a rifle shot.

"Let go of me or I'll turn you in myself!" The

imprint of her palm stood out starkly against his pale skin.

Aayshen pinned her arms beneath him, then clamped a hand to the side of her face, a fingertip digging into the skin around her temple. He sucked in a deep, ragged breath, then forced his way into her thoughts, a quick mental thrust that jabbed through the outer layers and levels of her mind, deep enough to know that she had only told him part of the truth. Images of a sheet of paper and the man in the food-place flashed rapid-fire through his mind. "You gave the human a message. . . . " Had her help only been an elaborate ruse, one designed to shield the fact that she had already informed her government? "Why did you aid me? Is this only a false escape?"

"No!" She could feel him inside her, digging, probing. "He didn't even read the note, I swear!"

Aayshen pushed deeper, ripping through the thin wall of defiance she had created to veil her most intimate thoughts. Her emotions and memories flowed into his mind like a rising tide, and with that river of knowledge came the truth. His thoughts stilled in surprise. The subterfuge and betrayal he had expected to find were only phantoms, figments dredged from his own distrust. His anger evaporated, replaced by confusion and a tangle of discordant feelings. He had violated her, forced his way into the core of her mind unnecessarily, and with that realization came an overwhelming sense of shame. Her thoughts were still coupled with his, so he apologized the only way he knew how. The mind-touch that had been crude and violent only a moment ago became a gentle thing, a subtle exploration and conveyance of regret.

An unexpected torrent of strange images and feelings suddenly filled Laura's mind, tenuous, vague, a delicate haze of conflicting emotions that enveloped her within a soft cocoon of fragile warmth.

And with the drifting sensation came a rising wave of awareness. She could feel the hard, coiled strength of his body pressed close against her, and felt a surge of familiar heat in response. Their eyes met across a wide sea of disparity. Hers dark with shock, his pale and hesitant. Time seemed frozen in that one heated moment.

Laura couldn't move, couldn't speak. Those strange, enigmatic eyes were inches above her, so deep and wintry blue that she felt as though she could glimpse infinity in their crystalline depths.

His hands slipped up her arms, pulling her body tight against him. Aayshen shuddered as the blood thrummed through his veins like liquid flame, a forbidden heat he had been conditioned to never feel, never desire. His fingers sought and found an errant lock of gold-red hair, and he marveled at its soft, rich texture. A fingertip gently traced over the creamy skin of her cheeks and full, parted lips, then down to her delicate chin and curving, graceful neck, touching a woman as he had never done before.

Her body began to move against him of its own volition, her arms and legs desperate to draw him closer. Her trembling hands burrowed beneath his sweater to the dark coverall beneath, palms sliding back and forth across the wide expanse of his back, gingerly exploring the corded length of muscles hidden underneath the black, silky material. A sweet, hot ache bloomed in her thighs and groin, and she longed to feel his pale, sinewy flesh pressed against her own.

The wave of erotic images she projected into Aayshen's thoughts sent a dizzying rush of unfamiliar warmth through his mind and heated loins. She wanted him in the male-female way, wanted him to join with her body as well as her mind. Aayshen groaned low in his throat. She did not know the consequences of such a joining, could not know that what she wanted would bind them together as one, minds and souls forever intertwined. She wanted the one thing he was forbidden to give.

His eyes, hot and bright with newly awakened desire, burned into hers like cool blue diamonds. He wanted her, too, wanted to take her here and now, possess this fragile human in every way, but to do so would only bring pain and grief to both of them.

I am not human, Laura, he whispered in her thoughts. *I am a Savanian soldier, a warrior destined to serve my world and nothing more. The Fates have already woven the threads of my life long ago. You have your own destiny to fulfill . . . as do I.* He withdrew from her mind gently, slowly, until their thoughts were barely touching. She didn't understand, couldn't understand, what it meant to join with a telepath. *For both our sakes, do not ask more of me than I am allowed to give.*

The warm, drifting sensation gradually lifted from her mind, and the hot currents of uncontrolled desire began to slowly ebb. Echoes of his whispered words danced like a fitful rainfall on the edges of her memory. The Fates . . . destiny . . . for both our sakes . . . She gazed up dreamily into his alien eyes, uncertain of what had happened, or if he had spoken aloud.

Then reality returned, and with it shameful memories of how her body had responded to his. Her cheeks reddened with an embarrassed flush. He had brought her dormant senses to life, awakened a rush of sensuality she had thought long dead.

As his body eased away from her, Laura retreated to the far side of the seat, horrified by the feelings he'd aroused in her. Even more horrifying was the realization that she still wanted him. Her hands shuddered as they closed around the steering wheel. He was an alien. She stared in silence at a thick green patch of kudzu bordering the dirt road. What in God's name was wrong with her?

Chapter Ten

Carrie Cooner propped her elbows atop the Cimarron Club's sticky tablecloth and studied the gaunt, nervous woman seated across from her.

"Well?" Bobbie-Jean Cooner prodded, tired of waiting for Carrie to tell her what she thought. "Say something."

Carrie lifted a skeptical brow which threatened to vanish beneath uneven bangs. What was she supposed to say? She'd known Bobbie-Jean her entire life. They had graduated the same year from East Central High, gone on to marry first cousins. Their children played together, their husbands drank and fished together. Carrie bit off the end of a french fry and chewed on it slowly, then washed the greasy lump down with a swig of draft beer as she mulled over what Bobbie-Jean had told her. She knew Bobbie-Jean, and never once had Carrie doubted her word about anything. But this . . . "You sure it's an FBI man following you, Bobbie-Jean?"

"Of course I'm sure!" Bobbie-Jean almost yelled, her voice shrill with paranoia. "Who the hell else would be following me?" Curious stares from a group of men clustered around the Cimarron's dingy bar caused her to lower her voice. "Those government men were in the store all yesterday afternoon, for heaven's sake, snooping around and trying to get the names of everybody that was there that morning."

At first, the Piggly Wiggly cashier had been thrilled to discover that the FBI was following her. It hadn't taken her long to realize that a big black car was mirroring every turn she made as she headed home from the store, twisting down the narrow dirt road that zigzagged back and forth across the Alabama-Mississippi line. Hard to hide something like that when the car kicked up a dust cloud visible a quarter mile away. It was the most exciting thing to happen to Bobbie-Jean, or to Escatawpa, in years. But in the hours since her discovery, the excitement had begun to fade, replaced by trepidation, and a heavy dose of paranoia.

She lowered her voice even further and gave her cousin-in-law a meaningful look. "Mostly what the FBI wanted to know was the name of the woman driving the dark-colored Jeep, and if anybody had seen that blond fellow before."

The sun lines on Carrie's forehead gathered in a tight frown. "Think anybody in the store squealed?"

Bobbie-Jean shrugged. "Can't say for sure. I

173

don't think any of them really knew who Miz Malek was. She's not a regular down at the Pig."

"Yeah," Carrie said. "That's understandable. She's from Biloxi originally. And for the most part she does her shopping in Pascagoula."

"I wouldn't have even known who she was if it weren't for you," Bobbie-Jean added. "Remember? I came by the nursery last year and you introduced me. That's the only time I've ever laid eyes on her." By rights, the FBI should be following Carrie, not her. Carrie was the one who worked for the woman. "But even if somebody in the store did recognize her, that Yankee FBI man made everyone so mad they weren't in the mood to do any talking." She shifted nervously in the hard-backed chair. "I'm telling you, Carrie, your Miz Malek's gotten herself into something I don't want no part of."

A sudden whoop of male laughter caused Carrie to flinch. Her gaze grew leery and swung around the bar, lighting every now and then on the customers she didn't know. Everything seemed fairly normal. The laughter had come from an alcove at the far end of the drafty bar, where their husbands, Ornell and Ricky, were busy cheating each other in a heated game of eight ball. Disgusted with herself, Carrie shook her head. She was beginning to catch Bobbie's paranoia. She was also beginning to have serious doubts about Laura Malek's "houseguest."

"Who's this blond guy, anyway?" Bobbie-Jean asked. "The way those FBI people were acting, you would have thought he was a spy or something."

Carrie's attention moved to a cheap white napkin stamped with the bar's steer-head logo. She began shredding the top layer with nervous fingers. "I told you I only saw him over there that one time last Monday morning. Miz Malek said he was her cousin, and that he was here on vacation from Norway."

"Yeah, right." Bobbie-Jean snorted. "So she just closes up the nursery and gives everybody two weeks off so she can show her cousin the big 'sights' of Escatawpa." She shook her head in disbelief. "You didn't really buy that vacation crap she fed you, did you, Carrie?"

"Of course I didn't. I'm not that stupid." A defensive edge crept into her voice. She had believed it, sort of. "But why that guy's staying in her house is none of my business. Miz Malek's been good to me, and I'm not about to do anything that'll get her in trouble with the law."

"Trouble?" Bobbie-Jean hissed. "I'm the one who's got trouble. What am I supposed to do? Just let the FBI follow me around for the rest of my life?"

"They're not going to follow you around forever, Bobbie." A long strand of brown hair fell in Carrie's eyes. She shoved it behind an ear impatiently. "You just go on about your business and pretend like they're not even there. What's the harm in that? In a few days they'll be sick of dogging you all over the county and head back to wherever they came from."

"Easy for you to say." Bobbie-Jean threw a nervous look over her shoulder as the front door swung open and two strangers sauntered into the Cimarron. She turned back to Carrie, her face turning a sickly shade of white. "That's them!" she said in a high-pitched whisper. "Those are the guys who've been following me!"

Carrie angled her head toward the door.

"Don't do that!" Bobbie-Jean pinched her arm. "Don't let them see you looking."

Carrie looked anyway.

"Stop it! If they see you looking they'll know we know what they're up to!"

"Shut up, Bobbie." Carrie sighed and rolled her eyes. "You sound like a total fool. Just sit there and try to act normal, okay?"

Bobbie-Jean blinked back a haze of tears. "What do we do?"

"Nothing." Carrie's gaze cut back to the strangers, who were busy ordering beers at the bar. She looked them over carefully. Both men were fairly well-built, in their late 20s or early 30s, with short military-style haircuts and the same stiff-jawed expression carved into their faces. Twins, sort of. They were even dressed more or less alike. Both were wearing unfaded blue jeans, plaid flannel shirts buttoned just a tad too close to their necks and brand-new boots that had probably never seen a layer of dust.

Carrie lifted a brow. If they were trying to blend in with the locals, they were doing a really bad job of it. Even worse, the two young government men had cowboy hats perched on the tops of their heads. "Wrong state, guys," she muttered to herself.

"What?" Bobbie-Jean scrunched down in her chair, trying to look inconspicuous.

"Those guys look like they're on the way to a country line dance, Bobbie. You sure it's them?"

"Yes, I'm sure. I got a real good look at them a while ago when I stopped for a hamburger." She folded her arms across her chest and leaned forward. "What am I going to do, Carrie? I don't like this. I don't like this one bit." She clutched her arms tighter. "I'm getting scared."

Carrie reached across the table and squeezed her hand. "Like I said, they'll get sick of tailing you in a few days, and this will all be over with. Just keep quiet until then. Don't even tell Ricky."

Bobbie-Jean's head wobbled back and forth vehemently, and her face settled into rigid lines. "I'll give it another day or so, but that's all, Carrie. If those government people haven't quit pestering me by then, I'm gonna tell them or Sheriff Rankin what they want to know. The only reason I didn't tell yesterday was because that other FBI man started talking to me like I was a pile of dirt."

"Okay, okay." A worried frown slanted across Carrie's forehead. What had Laura gotten herself into? "Give me a few days, Bobbie-Jean, that's all I ask. Just don't go running your mouth until I talk to Miz Malek and find out what's going on. You understand?"

Bobbie-Jean made a show of sighing a couple of times to prove she was agreeing reluctantly. "All right. A few days and that's it."

"Thanks." Carrie's frown deepened. As soon as she got up the nerve, she would pay Laura Malek a little visit.

"Well, are you in or not?" Garner reared back in his chair and gave Laura and the cat his best poker smile. "Make up your minds." He glanced at his cards again just to be sure. Nothing. Not even a pair of deuces. His smile widened, dentures gleaming a bright, artificial white in the glare of

Jan Zimlich

the light fixture suspended above the kitchen table. "Come on, we haven't got all night."

Laura studied his shark-smile through narrowed eyes. This time she wouldn't give the old coot the satisfaction of beating her. Let him beat the Kri if he wanted. Besides, she was sick of listening to the two of them argue, and tired of passing endless hours playing cards or staring at the walls. Except for the brief trip to the grocery store the morning before, she hadn't done anything or been anywhere for almost a week. All she did was sit and wait—for what she didn't know.

She gave her battered watch a squinty, impatient look. It was getting late. Bryan had been in bed for hours now, and she wanted to find Aayshen before she turned in herself and settle things between them once and for all. She wanted to tell him that she wasn't going to be held prisoner in her own home any longer, that they should just get the hell out and leave her alone. What harm was there in trying? A sudden spurt of determination flickered in her dark eyes. She had been a scared little wuss long enough. "Anybody seen Aayshen lately?"

Garner glanced at her out of the corner of his eye. First names now. Something more than a trip to the grocery store had happened yesterday morning. Laura had been edgy ever since, pacing around the house and making a general nuisance of herself, while Rahs had just made himself scarce. He wasn't even watching Laura anymore. "Not since supper." The way they were acting was making everyone edgy. "Why?"

Her shrug of indifference was feigned. "Just curious, that's all."

Drallondryn gulped down a mouthful of choc-olate-chip cookie, licked away the crumbs stuck to the rim of his mouth, and focused his attention on Laura. "The commander has been acting a bit preoccupied since yesterday. Perhaps he has gone outside to meditate."

"Enough about Rahs," Garner said testily. "Are you two in or not?"

Laura's fingers began tapping a restless beat atop the circular oak table. "Count me out, Grampa." The restless, spasmodic tapping spread to her leg and foot. "I've had enough."

As she laid her cards facedown on the table, Garner's smile grew obscenely large. One down, one to go. "All right, cat, it's time to fish or cut bait."

"Excuse?"

"Put up or shut up, moron."

The Kri's hand hesitated over the dwindling pile of coins stacked neatly in front of him. His fore-head rippled with suspicion as he fingered several dull brown coins and targeted the old human with a long, searching look. He had seen that expres-sion on Garner's face once before. Bold. Confi-dent. It was the same expression Grampa had worn the first time they played this game, right before he declared himself the winner.

He waffled over his options a few seconds longer, then tossed the required coins in the mid-dle of the table and added two more. "I lift your Abraham Lincolns with an additional two."

Garner rolled his eyes toward the ceiling. "How many times have I got to tell you people? You're supposed to say, 'I raise you,' not lift!"

"All right. I raise you two Abraham Lincolns."

Drallondryn's thin lips puffed out petulantly. "Silly language," he muttered under his breath. "No one ever says what they mean or means what they say. Completely illogical."

"What?" Garner thumped his hearing aide with the end of his thumb. "Speak up."

The Kri eyed the heavy cane propped against the ancient one's chair. Grampa had already used it on him a few days before when he made the mistake of calling him an old gas expulsion. "Your hearing device must have malfunctioned again." He extended the claws on his left hand and scratched at a nagging itch on his neck. "I said nothing."

Garner gave his left hearing aid another sharp rap. Stupid things. They never worked right. He was sure he'd seen the cat's lips move. "Bull. You're always muttering or writing about something."

"That is a complete exaggeration." His claws dug deeper, raking through his fur at a furious pace.

Sighing, Laura glanced at each one in turn, sagged in her chair and waited for the never-ending argument to explode again. It wouldn't be long now. The tension hung in the air around them like a gathering storm.

"Is not," Garner fired back. "I've been listening to you whine and jabber about this and that for almost a week." He poked a finger toward the spiral notebook and ballpoint pen that was always sitting near the Kri's elbow. "And there's no telling what kind of insults about humans you've been scribbling in that book of yours." Page after page of the notebook was filled with neatly written gibberish, indecipherable squiggles and lines that looked more like hieroglyphs than writing.

The Kri's eyetufts pulled downward in an incredulous frown. "I? Your complaints and insults are more hideous than the Skipper's. If I were the Little Buddy, I believe I would be tempted to just vaporize you and be—"

"Oh shut up!" Garner made a disgusted face and shook a fist. He would forever rue the day when this particular alien had discovered TV, especially reruns. "If I hear one more word out of your mouth about Gilligan, or any more of your infernal questions, I think I'll puke!"

"Puke?" The Kri stopped scratching and reached for the notebook and scriber. The last few pages of his notes were reserved for the compendium of obscure human colloquialisms he was compiling for the Kri linguistic archives. "I have not seen or heard that word before." He scribbled hastily. "What does it mean?"

Garner glowered, his heavy white brows descending until they almost covered his sagging eyelids. "It's French for ass!"

"I do not wish to be called a body part in any language." Drallondryn's eyes thinned to sullen yellow slits. Grampa was even more insufferable than usual. "Especially by an ignorant barbarian such as you."

The spidery network of veins crisscrossing Garner's forehead pulsed bright blue. "Ignorant barbarian, am I?" A gnarled hand closed around the head of his cane. "Say it again, cat. I dare you. No moth-eaten bag of fur is going to call me that and get away with it!"

"My fur has not been eaten by native insects,"

Drallondryn said, outraged. He straightened in his chair and fingered the stiff, smelly thing hidden beneath the collar of his flightsuit. His almond eyes clouded with anger and embarrassment. "It is merely . . . infested."

Garner blinked, glanced at Laura, then Drallondryn, then back at Laura again. Comprehension slowly dawned. "No, don't tell me. Fleas?"

Laura nodded reluctantly. She had hoped Garner wouldn't find out. Knowing would just give him more grist to grind out of his insult mill. "A gift from Sergeant Pepper, I guess," she said. From the corner of her eye she shot the alien a quick, sympathetic look. He didn't seem too happy about wearing the dog collar she'd bought him at the grocery store, but she hadn't had much choice. It was the largest one the store carried. "How's the flea collar working out?" she asked quietly, feeling a twinge of empathy for the hapless alien. Strangely enough, of the two, he seemed the most human emotionally. Whenever Garner insulted him, the Kri seemed genuinely hurt.

Drallondryn sighed morosely. "It smells unhealthy."

"A flea collar!" His fit of pique forgotten, Garner made a strangled noise that turned into a brittle, gleeful laugh.

Drallondryn tilted his chin to a dignified angle and stared at the ceiling above Garner's head, refusing to meet the human's irritating gaze.

"Did you buy it a litter box, too?" He threw back his head and cackled again, oblivious to the Kri's embarrassment. "Can't have it leaving messes in the corner."

Sudden anger lit Laura's eyes. He'd been lobbing insults at the alien for days now, and she was sick of it. "Leave him alone, Grampa. Drallondryn is not an 'it,' and you damn well know it." She pinned him to his chair with a glacial look. "There's no call for you to treat him like that." The anger spilled from her eyes to her face and voice. "He's an intelligent being. They both are . . . unlike someone else I know."

Garner stared at his granddaughter in astonishment. Laura was boiling mad, madder than she'd been since he gave Bryan the BB gun for his birthday, and for what? A couple of aliens who'd broken into their home and were holding them hostage? "What's gotten into you, Laura? If I didn't know better I'd think you were actually defending it—him."

Laura surged from her chair, sending it crashing to the tile floor in her haste to rise. She balled her hands into tight fists to still their violent trembling. "I am not defending him!"

Drallondryn's jaw went slack, and his gaze ricocheted from one human to the other. Something more than a simple argument was occurring here, an undercurrent of tension that he didn't quite comprehend.

"Could have fooled me." Garner couldn't deny the evidence any longer. It wasn't just the cat Laura had gotten on her high horse about. Silent Sam was at the bottom of this. "Then tell me, just who *are* you defending? That Rahs fellow?"

The question and its implications caused Drallondryn's gaze to swing back to Laura. He nodded inwardly, finally understanding. He'd had his own suspicions, too.

Laura stared mutely at Garner for long seconds, anger and confusion warring for control of her features. Who was she defending? And why? Confusion finally won the battle. Hands still clenched at her sides, she walked stiffly to the utility room and grabbed her parka from a hook.

"Where are you going?" Garner called, suddenly uneasy.

She shoved an arm through a sleeve and paused, her hand wrapped around the doorknob. "Outside. I need some air." The door slammed shut.

Drallondryn gave the old human a troubled, knowing glance. The commander was outside.

"Air, my ass," Garner grumbled.

The night was cool and damp, thick with the lingering promise of mild days and a false spring to come. Another in the endless series of winter storm fronts had pushed eastward, allowing the gradual return of muggy Gulf air. Laura knew the respite would only be temporary, a few days at most, but the change was welcome and long overdue.

She hesitated at the end of the curving walkway where brick and gravel met, uncertain of where she was going or why. Downhill, the small cluster of greenhouses stood dark and neglected. A sheet of plastic crackled in the light breeze, as if to remind her of responsibility and work to be done. Tomorrow, Laura promised herself. Tonight she was too restless and angry to work. She needed time to brood and think.

She pulled in a deep, calming breath and stared into the darkness, listening to the quiet rustling of wind through night trees. What in the hell was the matter with her anyway? Garner was always insulting someone, or accusing her of one thing or another. Nothing unusual about that. He'd simply implied that her interest in Rahs went beyond the realm of curiosity. So why had she gotten so mad?

Because it was true. The admission froze in her mind with fearful clarity. There was nothing normal about the wild surge of sensations she experienced whenever he touched her, the strangely sensual way her body had responded to his. Whenever he was near, a flush of excitement thrummed through her blood, as if the thread of awareness that flowed between them had suddenly been electrified. Every fiber of her senses had come alive when he touched her the morning before, and again in the car when he'd invaded her thoughts.

He'd felt it, too. She knew he had. What had happened between them had scared him enough that he'd finally quit hounding her every footstep, a turn of events that she'd hoped and prayed for only a few days before. But now that he had ended his constant vigilance, she felt an odd emptiness, as if her world had turned a little bleaker without him around. She missed the tension, the heart-pounding excitement and fear she felt when he was near, the sense that at any moment, any given second, he might touch her again, and maybe, just maybe, she would lose control and surrender to him.

A dull, aching warmth rushed through her bloodstream, and her pulse quickened to a faint, thready beat. Even the thought of him made her body want to feel those sensations again.

The ache grew to a hot, gnawing pain, dredged from that part of her she had thought long dead. He's not even human, Laura reminded herself. An alien. To think of him in such intimate terms was insanity. Her heartbeat throbbed in her ears. It was a madness she was powerless to resist.

Without conscious decision, she turned to the southwest and walked instinctively toward the grove of dormant pecan trees. Dried leaves crunched beneath her shoes as she hurried through the orchard. He was out there somewhere. She could feel him.

As she searched among the long rows of winter-bare trees, a ribbon of moonlight sliced through the clouds, its silvery glow revealing the pale silhouette of a familiar form. Startled, Laura ground to a sudden stop and pressed herself flat against the trunk of a tree. Eyes on the distant heavens, he was kneeling motionless amidst an undulating patch of saw grass, arms folded across his bare chest so that his fingertips touched the tops of his shoulders. She peered around the trunk of the tree and watched. A piece of equipment, small and rectangular, was sitting on the ground a few feet from him, half hidden by tall grass and the branches of a fallen limb. Pinpoint lights pulsed on the top of its flat surface, alternating in rhythm and color from a hazy green to a painful shade of orange.

Her curiosity soon changed to fascination as the minutes passed and Rahs still hadn't moved. There was something compelling about his statuelike stance, in the way the moonlight brushed across his sculpted profile and platinum hair, something almost mystical that struck an answering chord deep within her.

A vague twinge of uneasiness mottled her forehead with an uncertain frown. Whatever he was doing, it might not be meant for prying eyes. She moved deeper into the tree's shadow and took a hasty step backwards, intent on fleeing her hiding place before he spotted her. A twig snapped beneath her shoe, the sharp crack of brittle wood sounding loud in the wintry stillness. Laura sucked in a terrified breath and froze.

Aayshen's head swung in the direction of the telltale sound. His eyes burned into the shadows around the tree, searching for the woman he knew was there. Even from a distance he could sense her presence, her thoughts, smell the clean, salty scent of her human skin. "There is no need to conceal yourself," he called to her softly. "I felt your presence long ago."

He looked toward the communications-pack for a fleeting second, switching it off with a single thought. All but one of the pulsing lights faded to dark. The beacon light continued to shine bright orange as the tachyonic transmitter resumed broadcasting an emergency signal across space and time.

A guilty red flush crept over Laura's cheekbones as she edged out of the shadows. "I didn't mean to intrude on whatever it was you were doing." She moved closer, eyes straying across his bare chest again. His discarded sweater was lying on the ground in a limp pile near his equipment, but she wasn't about to ask him why he'd taken it off. "I'm sorry."

"You did not intrude." In truth, she hadn't. He had realized hours before that trying to boost the comm-pack's signal with his mind was an exercise

187

in futility. Just as his halfhearted attempt to meditate had been.

His arctic eyes darkened with an unreadable emotion as Laura came to a stop directly in front of him, so close he could feel the heat from her body. Somehow he'd known she would come to him this night. Either consciously or unconsciously she had found her way to him, answered the same inexplicable call that echoed through his own blood of late. Two restless minds and bodies searching for solace. Souls aching to touch and be touched.

"Did you have need of me?" He rose from his knees in one fluid movement.

"No, not really . . ." The flush on her face turned scarlet. "I was just . . . getting some air." Even to her the excuse sounded lame. "I guess I'll go back to the house now." She turned to leave.

"Wait." His voice was gentle, more a plea than a command. "Do not go yet. Stay with me for a while."

Laura turned back slowly. Uncertain of what to say or do, she simply stared at him in mute confusion. She stamped her feet to ward off the damp night chill and shifted her weight from one leg to the other.

A thick, awkward silence hung between them. Laura tilted her face upward to stare at the distant heavens, wondering which of the far points of light he called home. "Can you see your star from here?" she said finally, the silence making her nervous.

His gaze was drawn upward to the thin veil of stars visible through scudding clouds. He searched the sliver of sky for a glimpse of familiar stars, but found no sign of Savan's aging binary suns. "No. If there were fewer clouds, perhaps."

"Is it so different there . . . where you come from?" she asked hesitantly.

His pensive gaze swept over the verdant, alien landscape, the limbs of trees shifting in the cool breeze. She lived on a world that was still young, evolving, ablaze with the vibrancy of life. "Very different," he said slowly, choosing his words with care. "On Earth, life and water are everywhere . . . strange bright colors . . . the smell of growing things in the air." Hazy light from Earth's solitary moon threw halos around the tops of trees. So beautiful, so wild and free. "There are not so many colors on my world. The mountains, sky and sand are much the same. Dry and gray. The trees are small and few, nothing like here, and the seas are long dead, emptied many centuries ago." He stared at the quiet river and ebony sky. "Two suns burn in Savan's sky, one bright, the other dim, and complete darkness falls only once in a very great while."

Laura wondered what it would be like to live in such a place, to rarely see a night-darkened sky. "What about the people?" she asked quietly, determined to keep the flow of words going, to learn more. "Are they all like you?"

"No. Only a very few." He was quiet for a moment, thinking of his life, the aching emptiness of the decades he'd spent between the stars. "A few of us are gifted by scientists with the thought-abilities before we are born, given strong bodies and minds, then conditioned to think and act in certain ways, all to make us better warriors." He stopped for a moment, startled at himself for telling her so much. But strangely, telling her felt right. Comfortable. "We are born for one purpose only, to live out our lives in service to our world. Duty requires that we choose nothing for ourselves."

Laura stared in shock as the meaning of his words slowly penetrated. "You mean they created you just to be a soldier?"

"Yes."

"My God." She shook her head in disbelief. His genes had been shuffled in some Savanian laboratory, assembled like a box of Legos by unfeeling scientists so he would be better, stronger, more intelligent, only to be condemned by his creators to a life of service that sounded uncomfortably close to slavery. She stared at the trees in silence. She couldn't think of anything to say.

A sound akin to a sigh escaped his lips, mingled with the wind and faded. "On your world all humans are allowed to choose their own path in life. Each being is free to make his future as he wishes." To those on Earth, even giving birth was a simple matter of preference. A trace of bitterness crept into his eyes and voice. "Among my people the Fates rule all, and we have no choice."

Laura frowned in confusion. "I don't understand. What do you mean when you say 'the Fates'?"

His shoulders tensed, and he closed his eyes. How could he explain the unexplainable? "Humans believe in a force . . . a great power who watches over the universe, do they not?"

"Yes," she said slowly. This was a new, spiritual side to him that she'd never seen before. "We call it God."

"We have such a belief. We believe that our lives are destined by the Fates before we are born." He opened his eyes and stared down at her upturned face. "The Giver of life chooses the thread . . . the Weaver spins it into the cloth that is us . . . the Taker is that which rises from the dark to cut the threads at the end of our lives."

She lifted a brow. If she'd understood him correctly, the Fates were their version of predestiny. "Some humans have beliefs that are similar to your Fates. Here, we call it predestiny, the idea that every aspect of our lives has already been determined before we're born."

He gave her a long, searching look. "You understand," he said in a voice tinged with surprise.

"I understand, but that doesn't mean I believe it. There's such a thing as free will, you know, the ability to choose for yourself. We wouldn't have been given that ability if we weren't meant to use it."

Aayshen sighed. The concept sounded so simple when it came from her lips. Free will. Every human had the ability and the right to determine his or her own fate. How could he make her understand that his beliefs, though completely the opposite of hers, were an integral part of his life, the very fabric that bound his culture together? In the end, he didn't try. "Your people are indeed fortunate. They have so much more than they know."

A sudden breath of cold wind rushed through the trees, twining long strands of red-gold hair around Laura's shadowed features. She lifted her gaze upward, forcing herself to meet his ice-blue eyes. "When you talk about us, our planet, you make Earth sound like some sort of paradise. It's not, you know."

"Paradise?" The word sounded strange on his tongue.

She smiled slightly, wryly. "Heaven, nirvana, paradise . . . An old Earth legend of a beautiful, peaceful place where there are no problems. Everyone lives happily ever after when they go there."

A sad, comprehending expression stole across his face as drifting clouds obscured Earth's moon, turning the treetop halos from cool silver to a darkening gray. Night creatures called from hidden branches, lonely, plaintive sounds. Paradise. There was no such word in any language he knew. "If this paradise place truly exists, it is here, on your world."

Laura's gaze moved over the familiar landscape, the thick stands of fragrant pine, the grassy levee and ancient water oaks looming in the distance, all the sights of home she had taken for granted time and time again. These things looked different now, as though she were seeing Earth's wild beauty through someone else's eyes. His eyes.

He was so very different from her. They came from different cultures, had memories and beliefs they could never really share because they lived such utterly disparate lives. But did any of that truly matter? Did the fact that he was different somehow lessen the feelings she had for him?

She turned to him then, beginning to understand and appreciate his quiet, inner strength, the ingrained sense of duty and purpose that had made Aayshen Rahs what he was. And with that first, faint glimmer of understanding came an irresistible urge to discover more.

A thick, warm tide of desire rose within her. She wanted to touch him, know him, feel the strange heady sensation of his thoughts once again, be the one who drove away the air of aching loneliness that seemed to hover around him like a melancholy cloud. She wanted him, Laura admitted to herself—on any terms. Even if what they had together lasted only an hour, a day, or a single minute.

With a trembling hand she sought and found the sharp planes of his face, fingers brushing against, then retreating from cool, alien skin. Her dark brown eyes met opaque, startled blue ones across an infinite sea of space and diversity. Who or what he was no longer mattered to her. "I want you, Aayshen," she said in a husky whisper. "For whatever time we have, I want you." The words were out now, hanging between them, and couldn't be taken back. "Do you understand?"

He lifted a hand to her still face; then with a gentleness born of uncertainty, he brushed a silky tendril of hair away from her cheek and traced the outline of her jaw with a fingertip. "I understand." His finger grazed her mouth, her chin, his touch growing more urgent. He wanted this. And if this brief instant in time could stave off the numbing emptiness of his life, he would forever be content.

Laura stood stock-still, unable to move or breathe. Her skin felt scorched, heated by the intensity of his touch. As the flood of sensations began to grow and build, her gaze strayed downward from his face to his bare chest and arms, skimming over the smooth expanse of alabaster skin. She groaned softly and reached out with a tentative hand.

Aayshen took a shuddering breath, reveling in the unfamiliar sensation of her fingertips gliding across his skin. "A joining between us will not be as you . . . imagine, Laura, not as you have known. Once done, it cannot be undone."

She dipped her head and stared at him expectantly, waiting for what she knew would come, wanted to come. It was inevitable, had been since that very first night. "I don't care." She drew closer to him, her hands exploring the hollows of his back. "I want you. I want you to make love to me."

Her eyes caught and held his as she fumbled with the fastenings on her parka. The heavy jacket slid to the ground, followed swiftly by her clothing. She stood before him, trembling, the gentle swell of her breasts barely brushing against the taut muscles of his chest.

A shudder of anticipation coursed through his body as he explored her face and throat with his lips, her salty-sweet flesh warm and silky against the coolness of his mouth. Blood thrummed through his veins, so loud he could hear it pounding in his ears.

Laura groaned low in her throat as the forgotten warmth of a male hand enveloped her breast. With trembling fingers, she unfastened his jeans and slid them downward over his tapered hips, eager to see and feel his body pressed against hers.

She stared at him and sucked in a sharp, awed breath. His body was lean and sinewy, gloriously chiseled and formed. Her hands moved over his pale skin, exploring the lines of his slim hips and muscular thighs. He was beautiful, perfect in every way.

At her touch, Aayshen's senses spiraled out of control. Roughly, almost violently, he pushed her downward, lowering himself along with her until they were both kneeling, face to face, bodies barely touching. He brushed a hand across the side of her face and probed the hollow of her temple with the tip of a finger, searching for the neural pathways needed for a joining.

"Are you certain?" he asked in a raw, strained whisper. His fingertip dug into her skin, and his shadowed features grew still and serene.

She dipped her head, her body quivering in anticipation. A tremulous smile lifted the edges of her mouth. God, how she wanted him. "I'm certain."

A startled gasp slipped from her throat as something warm and feathery caressed her mind, and with it came an unexpected wave of dizziness and vertigo. Reality faltered, and she felt her body begin to drift, as though time and gravity had suddenly lost their sway. She squeezed her lids shut against the vertigo, wondering fleetingly if they were floating in air. She could no longer feel the cold ground beneath her legs, and the sharp blades of saw grass had stopped prickling her knees.

There is nothing to fear, a soft voice whispered in her thoughts. Strong arms folded around her, crushing flesh to pliant flesh.

From a distant reality Laura realized the warm, comforting voice had come from within. Her lids fluttered open, and she gazed up at him dreamily, aware in a vague sort of way that they seemed to be surrounded by a dim, incandescent aura. His fathomless eyes were inches above her own, his angular features lit by that eerie half-light.

Laura stroked his cool cheek, and wound her fingers through his silky hair, pulling his shuddering body closer. As her thighs parted to receive him, a pulsing, burning sensation began to build behind her eyes, blooming outward through her mind and body like a white-hot tide rushing through her veins.

He took her then, his hardness driving into her again and again. She cried out and arched her hips in tandem with his burning thrusts, her limbs twining about him to draw his heated body even closer.

He was inside her, around her, part of her, his mind and body one with hers. Instinctively, she lifted a trembling hand to his forehead to complete the mental circuit raging between them, fingers pushing deeply into his pale skin, searching for release, searching for more.

The tide of heat became a raging torrent, and her senses came alive in ways she had never imagined. She could see herself through his enigmatic eyes, feel the aching intensity of his wonder, joy, and fevered passion as though it were hers alone. His movements turned urgent, hungry, and Laura fed that hunger by answering his thrusts with a rhythm that matched his own. And through it all those strange, pale eyes continued to hold hers, twin blue suns burning hot and bright with the flames of new-born desire.

The world around her suddenly dissolved, and a wash of light and vibrant color filled her mind. "Oh, God," she moaned softly. They were soaring, hurtling upwards through the wash of light to a sea of glittering stars.

Aayshen closed his lids, her slender form pulled tight against him. *This is what it means to join with a telepath,* he whispered in her mind.

A sharp cry of ecstasy slipped through her lips as the aura seemed to explode around them in a cascade of sensations and golden light. She felt his body shudder, and the stars flared, streaming outward in a wave of heat and rapture she thought would never end.

Chapter Eleven

It was a perfect day, the bright, chilly sky a clear, sharp-edged blue peculiar to Southern winters. Afternoon sunlight clawed through the tops of the water oaks and dappled the ground in cool shades of gold and shadow. The thick awning of leaves, still deep green despite the season, moved restlessly in a fitful breeze, the raspy sighs like the slow in-outs of quiet breathing.

Laura rested her back against the trunk of a weathered oak and allowed her gaze to roam over the wide expanse of the Pascagoula River as it slid quietly past. A flock of cranes rose from the dense scrub and twisted cypress trees lining the far bank, white wings beating against the deep blue sky in a graceful choreography of strength and speed. She smiled to herself as the cranes arced around a bend in the river and vanished. The day was glorious, and she was content, a serenity of body and spirit stronger than any she could ever remember.

"Did you see the cranes, Bryan?" Laura said, gesturing toward the thicket where she'd last seen them.

"Yeah," he answered in a dull, disinterested voice. He was sprawled across the tattered old quilt near Laura's feet, chin propped in his small hands. Sergeant Pepper was curled beside him, dozing in a patch of sun. "Big deal. They're just a bunch of birds."

Frowning, Laura wrapped her arms around her knees and stared at her young son worriedly. A picnic along the river had been her idea, a mother-son thing they had done on a regular basis in the past, even in the dead of winter. Today, it had gotten them out of the stuffy warmth of the house for a few hours and into the outside world, regenerating a strained semblance of that Pollyanna normalcy into their lives. At least Laura thought it had. She studied his small rigid features for long seconds. Now she wasn't so sure. The cranes had never been "just a bunch of birds" before. It seemed like she was the only one enjoying the outing. "Something wrong, Bryan?"

His lower lip quivered, and he turned hurt, accusing eyes on his mother. "Why did *he* have to come?" He jerked his head toward the placid river.

Unconsciously, her dark eyes shifted to the tall, stoic figure standing sentinel on a crust of land along the riverbank, his brooding gaze focused on nothing and everything. Laura sighed. She should have seen this coming. Most of her time had been spent with Aayshen in the last few days. Too much time to suit a five-year-old who'd had his mother's undivided attention his entire young life.

"Aayshen had to come, Bryan. He wouldn't have let us leave the house without him."

"Why?" Distrust, raging jealousy, and curiosity skittered across his gamin features.

"Well, I guess because he's worried we might tell somebody about him and Drallondryn, or that somebody other than us will find out that they're here." Laura folded him into her arms and held him close. "He is a soldier, after all. It's his job to make sure something bad doesn't happen."

Bryan glared at Aayshen's back. His mother had invited him to come along. Not Drallondryn, not Grampa, just him. And Bryan was beginning to suspect the reason why. He'd caught his mother making moony-eyes at him more than once. The child's face bunched into a frown. It would have been more fun if Drallondryn had come. They could have played catch or collected leaves for Drallondryn's specimen case. Commander Aayshen hardly ever said a word. He just stood around all the time staring at his mother or the trees.

"How come you spend so much time with him?" Bryan demanded. "He hardly ever says anything."

Her mouth curved into a soft, unconscious smile. Memories of the last two nights slipped through her mind unbidden. It wasn't words that bound them together. "That's just the way he is, Bryan. I'm not sure he even knows how to be anything other than a soldier," she added quietly, more to herself than to him. She shook herself mentally and ruffled the child's red-blond hair.

"Besides, have you ever really tried to talk to him, Bryan?"

The child hung his head.

"I thought so." She tipped his chin up with a finger. "As for me spending time with him, he'll be gone soon. Then it will be just you and me again."

Bryan heard the trace of wistfulness in his mother's voice and looked into her face, noticing a glint of something strange and sad in her eyes that he'd never seen before. His suspicion turned to certainty. His mother had even worn a dress today, the one with the big purple flowers she saved for special occasions. He'd heard Grampa Garner mumble that her wearing it was a bad sign, but he hadn't understood what he meant. "You really like him, don't you, Mom?" he said, suddenly comprehending.

"Yes," she said truthfully. "I do." She did like him, but underneath the surface, the relationship she had with him couldn't be measured in such simple terms as like or dislike. With each passing day her feelings for him had deepened, evolving into a new emotion she found hard to define.

The wistfulness returned in the form of a smile, but her eyes were dark and troubled. He was her lover, as well as her captor.

The idea of his mother being involved with any man was new and strange to Bryan. She hadn't even been out on a real date as far back as he could remember, although Grampa had told him that she had once or twice not long after the divorce. "Does he like you back?" The picnic was sort of like a date. That's why she was wearing the dress.

Laura's smile faded abruptly. "I think so." She sighed and turned slightly, watching as Aayshen paced a few steps down the riverbank, the wind and sun rippling through his blond-white hair. "Yes, I think he does." Something had changed about Aayshen in the last two days, ever since they had given in to lust and loneliness and spent the night wrapped in each other's arms. He still wanted her, she knew, still felt that strange thread of oneness flowing between them, and he had acted on those feelings more than once since that first night. But there was a remoteness about him even deeper than before, a tense, somber watchfulness that she couldn't drive away, and couldn't fathom. As though he were holding himself apart from her by sheer force of will.

She watched him for long seconds, a curious frown rippling across her forehead. There was so much about him she didn't know. Even in those few blissful moments when their minds touched and mingled, she had learned very little, as if he had erected a mental wall behind which no one was allowed. What was he really like inside his skin? What lay beneath that calm, solemn exterior? Was he even capable of anything more than what he had already given?

Her frown deepened. She'd probably never know. Sighing, she fished in a paper sack and handed Bryan the remains of their sandwiches, as well as a bag of stale bread. "Here, Bryan. Go feed this to the turtles. Aayshen will probably want to go back to the house soon."

"Okay." He scooped up the bread and hurried downhill to a low section of the riverbank that had caved in, creating a small pool of stagnant water along the edge of the muddy embankment. Cattails and marsh reeds and scrub jutted from the thick, syrupy water, as well as a tree stump that had washed downstream in a flood the summer before. Ignoring the alien standing quietly beside him, he threw a crust of bread atop the blackish-brown water, then another, and waited impatiently for the turtles to make their appearance.

Aayshen stared down at the boy and the water curiously. The child seemed to be waiting for something. "Why are you throwing food into the water?" he finally asked, noting for perhaps the hundredth time that the child's dark eyes were exact replicas of his mother's.

"It's for the turtles." He threw another piece of crust. "My mom and I do it all the time."

"Turtles?"

Several dark brown heads appeared at the edge of the reeds, plowing swiftly toward the bread. Others followed from beneath the tree stump, their oval heads and hard, mottled backs bobbing up and down in the dark water. The bits of crust soon became the spoils of war as dozens of small turtles fought and snapped at the bread. A few brave minnows darted and weaved beneath the murky surface, dashing through the midst of the battle just long enough to grab a pinch of bread and flee.

Aayshen stared in fascination as Bryan tossed more bread into the fray to fuel the primitive battle of survival. He knelt down on the bank for a closer look. Some of the creatures were dark green, with smooth rounded backs, while others had more elongated bodies, and a hard ridge of brownish-gold rising from their shells. "Are there many other water-creatures on your planet?" he asked the boy.

Jan Zimlich

"Zillions of them. Fish and whales and dolphins and all kinds of other stuff, more than anybody can count. There're sharks, too, but you have to watch out for them because they'll eat you. Some are so big they can swallow you whole."

More than anybody could count. Aayshen stared at the water. Oddly, he hadn't given much thought to the idea that Earth's vast seas might be teaming with biological life. So much he would never know. "What do these sharks look like?"

"Kind of like those minnows down there, but a whole lot bigger, and meaner." Bryan gave the alien a surprised look. "Haven't you ever seen a fish or a turtle before?" he asked, warming to his newfound role as instructor.

Aayshen continued to stare at the turtle-creatures, thoroughly fascinated. The diversity and abundance of life on this world was staggering. It would take at least a dozen lifetimes to completely explore Earth's land and seas, maybe more. "No, nothing like these creatures."

"You have any fish at all where you come from?"

His thoughts drifted back to Savan, the arid, distant world of his birth, the home he'd last seen over three decades before. "Most of the water on my world is underground, and the creatures that live in it are too small to be seen with the eyes." Savan was just a memory now, of no more importance than a dozen other worlds. His home was between the stars. He smiled gently at the boy. "There is a creature on one planet I have seen which looks a small bit like your turtles, but it is far larger, perhaps as large as your house, and eats soil to live."

Bryan gave him a sidewise, startled glance, cu-

204

riosity glinting in his dark brown eyes. "It eats dirt?" He shook his head in wonder and sank to the ground beside him, eager to hear more. "Wow. I bet you've seen a lot of other weird stuff out in space, too. Must be great flying around out there and visiting all those planets, huh?"

"Sometimes." His pale eyes took on a distant, faraway look. "Most times it is just dark . . . and empty."

The child cast him another sidewise glance. He seemed sad almost, as if he didn't really like being in outer space. "My mom says you're a soldier. That's what I want to be someday. I bet you've fought in a bunch of wars out there, haven't you?"

He turned then and stared at the child, his opaque eyes darkening with an unreadable emotion. "Yes, many battles . . . too many." He could feel the boy's longing and youthful envy, his childish exuberance for the heat of battle. "War is not a thing you should seek, Bryan. To be a warrior is to eventually lose your soul." His voice faded into silence, and his expression turned bleak.

The strange look on his face warned Bryan not to pursue the subject any further. The child felt the need to comfort him somehow, so he moved a bit closer to the tall alien and stared at the turtles with him, enjoying the silent comradery, and the quiet blossoming of understanding between them.

They watched as a turtle sated itself on the last of the bread, then dragged its bulbous body onto the bank directly beneath them. The small turtle lay there in the sun, its long claws digging furrows in the mud. Still curious, Aayshen leaned over to pick it up.

205

Jan Zimlich

"I wouldn't do that if I were you," Bryan said, his voice rising in alarm.

"Why not?" His hand closed around the brown and gold shell, and the turtle's mouth latched onto his thumb. Aayshen winced and shook his hand to free his finger, but the tenacious turtle refused to release its painful grip.

"That's why." Bryan clapped a hand to his mouth to smother a snicker. "I warned you not to do it. Those are snapping turtles."

Aayshen pulled his hand up, turtle and all, and stared at the wet brown creature attached to his hand. "When will it release me?" He was amazed by the amount of force it was exerting.

"When it's good and ready." The child laughed aloud, amused by the sight of the huge alien with a turtle hanging off his hand. He knew he shouldn't laugh, but he couldn't help himself. "Carrie told me that once a snapping turtle's got you, it won't let go until it thunders. She said one bit her husband on the lip and was stuck there for a whole month, but I think she was lying about that."

Aayshen studied the creature and his thumb intently. A sharp, gnawing ache was spreading from his finger to his hand. He climbed heavily to his feet and glanced around in dismay. "When will it thunder?" He knew he could pry the jaws apart if it were truly necessary, but he didn't want to kill the turtle in the process.

"I don't know." Bryan turned toward the trees, where his mother was propped against an oak staring at the sky. "Mom! Aayshen has a turtle stuck on his finger and can't get it off!"

Laura used a tree root for leverage and pulled

206

herself upright. She shielded her eyes with a hand and stared down the grassy slope. Aayshen and Bryan were standing side by side along the river-bank, just as they'd been for the last five minutes or so. "What?" she yelled back, and started walking, the soft folds of the dress billowing around her as she moved. "I didn't hear you." He'd said something about Aayshen but she wasn't sure what.

"Aayshen has a turtle stuck on his finger!"

"He's got a what?" Laura ground to an abrupt halt near the riverbank and stared, blinking in the afternoon glare.

Embarrassment flooded across Aayshen's angular face, and he displayed his hand for her to see.

Laura burst out laughing.

"I told him not to pick it up," Bryan said, "but he did it anyway."

He shook his hand again, but the turtle refused to budge. The bone in his thumb was beginning to feel as if it were being crushed in a vise.

Laura lifted a hand to her mouth to stifle her giggles, but the effort proved futile. He was just standing there, the turtle dangling from his hand, that cool air of composure she'd grown so used to replaced by a grim look of almost childlike pique. Her peal of laughter was low, throaty, and joyous. The implacable warrior had been felled by a lowly turtle. "I'm sorry," she said, gasping for breath. "I know it hurts. It's just . . . it's just so . . . ridiculous."

An impotent glower spread over his features. "Please remove this creature." He sat back down and laid his hand and the turtle on the ground. "I have no wish to cause it injury."

Laura scrounged around the riverbank until she found a stout oak branch. "Let's try this." She tried to shove the end of the stick between the turtle's powerful jaws. The turtle didn't even flinch. "Don't worry. I'll get it off." She jabbed the stick again to no avail, then looked up at Aayshen, trying her level best to hide her amusement. "At least it's a small one, no more than a pound or two."

"Yeah," Bryan added. "A big one might have snapped your finger clean off."

Aayshen grimaced. Their comments weren't exactly comforting.

The turtle's head moved away from the stick, then it released his finger abruptly. Aayshen snatched his hand out of harm's way, and heaved a relieved sigh as the creature turned slowly and lumbered toward the river.

Bryan danced in circles around the retreating turtle until he lost interest, then barreled past them and up the slope. "I'm going to tell Drallondryn what happened!" he yelled over his shoulder, and started running toward the house.

Laura turned back to Aayshen and shook her head in disbelief. She was glad it was winter, and the snakes were hibernating. He could have reached down and picked up a water moccasin just as easily. "Let me see your finger."

He held up his hand for inspection, and Laura bent close. Except for a tiny gouge or two, the skin wasn't broken, but there was an angry red and blue line running around his thumb. He'd have a hell of a bruise before long. "No permanent damage. Some ice will help, though." She led him up the slope to the spot beneath the tree, and fished a cube from the small cooler she'd brought along. "Here. Hold this against your finger. It'll keep the swelling down."

Aayshen flexed his finger experimentally. "Do not trouble yourself." His chin lifted a notch, and the mask of self-composure slid over his sculpted features once again. "I feel no pain."

"Right." Laura almost laughed aloud. Were men alike everywhere? She pressed the wet cube into the palm of his hand. "Drop the invincible-warrior routine and do it anyway."

Aayshen tried to stare her down, but in the end he sat down on the blanket and did as instructed.

"I do have one suggestion for you," Laura said in a mock-serious voice. The look of wounded pride on his face was just so . . . male.

He glanced up expectantly.

"You don't know a lot about this planet yet. In the future, when someone tells you not to pick something up, listen." A glint of mischief stole through her eyes. "There are worse things on this planet than snapping turtles. Much, much worse. You might have accidently picked up a snipe . . . or even a land-shark, so don't do it again."

Aayshen lifted a platinum brow. Bryan had said nothing about sharks being amphibious, or anything about a creature called a snipe. His forehead knotted in a suspicious frown. Her eyes were bright with silent laughter, and her lips trembled with barely suppressed mirth. There was no need to read her thoughts to know she was teasing him, and deservedly so. He grinned in return, a devastating smile that transformed his features; then his smile turned into a deep chuckle, something that would have never happened before he came to Earth. "I will be more careful in the future. I'm sure these . . . snipes and land-sharks are very dangerous beasts."

Laura suffered another fit of the giggles when a mental image of Aayshen and the turtle flitted through her mind. She allowed the attack to run its course unhindered. It felt good to laugh again, to release the pent-up tension and near-hysteria that had been building inside her for so long. She sat back against the oak tree and wiped the tears from her eyes with the sleeve of her dress. "I'm sorry, Aayshen. I just couldn't help myself."

He lifted a hand to her cheek in silent wonder, then stared at the wetness glistening on the tip of his finger. Water had leaked from her eyes and coursed down her face, just as it had on that first night. He touched his fingertip to his lips and tasted. Salty, vaguely sweet, just like her scent. "Your eyes . . . why does water fall from them?"

Her amusement faded, and she gazed at him steadily. He was so changeable, so unpredictable. "Different reasons. Strong emotions cause it." His aquiline face was alight with an almost childlike curiosity, a gentle innocence that belied the fine lines etched around his mouth and the haunted, ageless look that shadowed his eyes. Except for the fine webbing of lines at the corners of his mouth and deep-set eyes, his skin was youthful and baby-smooth, completely devoid of the vagaries of aging. Yet there was something timeworn about him that was inconsistent with that childish innocence, as if he knew nothing of life except duty and the heat of battle.

"Aayshen," she said softly, "tell me about yourself."

He sprawled sideways on the quilt, facing her, and propped his chin in a hand. How much should he tell her? He stared at her for a long moment, considering. How much would she understand? "There is not much to tell," he said finally. "The first ten years of my life were spent in a special place on Savan where telepaths are sent for conditioning. We were trained to be soldiers, taught how to control our mind-abilities, then assigned to the Corps."

Her brows pulled downward in disbelief. Surely she hadn't heard him right. He was sent somewhere as an infant to be trained as a soldier? "What about your family? Where were they during those years?"

"I have no family." A sudden frown moved across his stark features, and he shifted uncomfortably, avoiding her eyes. "Telepaths are not allowed to form . . . attachments with anyone, not even among themselves."

Her disbelief turned to utter horror. His own people had stripped him of home and family, sent him off to some alien boot camp when he was born, then forbidden him to have an emotional relationship with anyone? A surge of anger tightened her throat. "Why would they do such a thing to anyone?" An even deeper realization suddenly sharpened in her mind. Was the intimacy that they'd shared forbidden, too?

He gave her a long, probing look, her final, silent question echoing through his thoughts. But he didn't allow her to hear his answer. She was better off not knowing, not ever realizing the ter-

211

rible price he would pay for joining with her. Once he was gone, she would continue on with her life, immune to the repercussions because of her humanity.

"A Savanian soldier cannot share what is not theirs to give, Laura. Nothing exists for us beyond our duty. We go where we are ordered, fight when we are commanded to fight. If telepaths were to bond themselves to others, our loyalties could be divided, and the oath we have sworn to the Corps would then be meaningless. No soldier can serve two masters." He frowned then, guilt and uncertainty shadowing his face and eyes. He had already bonded with another, violated every precept of his conditioning by allowing emotion to cloud reason for a single night, and in doing so, he had condemned himself to a lifetime of sorrow and regret.

He sighed raggedly. Tomorrow, or perhaps the day after, he would leave here. But he would never have a single master again.

"Sounds to me like you lead a pretty grim life," Laura said tightly. The more he told her, the less she liked what she heard.

He smiled sadly and trailed a fingertip along the side of her face. She cared about him, and with that knowledge came a current of warmth that overshadowed thoughts of a future without her. "It is not all so very grim, Laura. I have seen and experienced things that you can never imagine." He gazed at her steadily, his eyes clouding with memories of the dark silence between stars, the pastel beauty of a distant nebula, a sea of galaxies glittering like flinty jewels in the endless night. "I have seen many wonders in the years I have spent out here . . . along the frontier."

"The frontier?" she said absently, still brooding over the cruel reality of his life. "What do you mean?"

He pointed toward the sky, toward the vast emptiness that lay beyond the thin blanket of Earth's atmosphere. "This is the frontier, Laura. Earth's star is far past the edges of civilization. Even though our ships travel at speeds your technology is not yet capable of, it takes many years to cross the void between stars."

"I guess that means you don't get to see your home very often." She leaned closer to him, closer to the tapered finger moving across her cheek in slow, gentle spirals.

He shook his head slowly. "Because of the time required, serving on the frontier is a lifetime duty." He stared at the blindingly blue sky, her gold-flecked eyes, the veil of silky curls moving around her face in the fragrant wind, committing the sights and smells to memory. The haunting beauty of the universe could never compare to the wonders he had seen and experienced on Earth. "Someday I will die out there, as I was meant to."

She pulled away from him abruptly. "Do you mean you won't ever see your home again?" Laura asked in disbelief.

He shrugged one shoulder in resignation. "No." There was no bitterness in his voice, only acceptance. "The Giver chose the thread of my life long ago."

Incredulous, Laura simply stared at him. Then an angry frown skittered across her features and she found her voice again. "Let me get this straight. You're just going to fly around on that spaceship of yours for the rest of your life, doing whatever someone billions of miles away orders you to do. Never see your home again, or have a home for that matter, risking your so-called life doing their bidding, all because some little scientific toad messed around with a few genes in the lab one day and created you. Is that right?"

He heard the anger in her voice, but didn't fully understand the reason for it. "I was created for this life."

"But you never chose it. Someone did that for you before you were ever born."

A gentle smile lifted the corners of his mouth. How naive she was, oblivious to the vagaries of the Fates and an unfeeling universe. "Laura, you forget what I am. Our ways are different from those of your people."

Laura closed her eyes for a moment and sighed. He was right, of course. She'd been applying her own values and beliefs to his life, judging him and his culture by human standards. Her anger flagged, replaced by the same resignation she'd heard in his voice. "I haven't forgotten, Aayshen." She smiled sadly and stroked the side of his face with her palm. His skin felt cool and soft against her own, almost cold to the touch. He couldn't change what he was, any more than she could herself. "I just don't want to remember," she finally said.

On impulse she bent close and touched her lips to his in a feathery kiss, accepting him and all that he was with the simple gesture.

When she drew away from him, Aayshen gave her a puzzled frown and touched his parted lips, then trailed his fingers over the soft curve of her mouth. "What does this mean . . . this touching of lips?"

"It's called a kiss." She kissed him again, deeper this time, her mouth joined to his in a gentle exploration. "Do you like it?" she breathed against his cheek.

A shiver of awareness rippled through his body. Their eyes locked for a long moment; then he touched his mouth to her warm lips, marveling at the rush of desire such a simple act could arouse. "Very definitely."

Chapter Twelve

Lem Chapman jumped from the helicopter's open door and sprinted across the landing strip, bending low to protect his face from the rush of cold air stirred by the rotor blades. The awkward, half-stooping position sent a jab of pain through his fractured ribs as he hurried over the concrete to where Burkett was standing at the edge of the tarmac, patiently waiting his arrival. His young aide was leaning into the mini-hurricane created by the rotor wash, one hand tucked securely around a leather portfolio, the other clutching desperately at his uniform cap to hold it in place.

As soon as he was clear of the sweeping blades, Chapman straightened both his body and his wind-whipped uniform and stalked toward the collection of massive aircraft hangars squatting along Keesler Air Force Base's endless runways.

Burkett huffed along in his wake. "Did the lead in Meridian pan out, Colonel?"

"A waste of time," Chapman said over his shoulder. "There was no actual sighting. Just your average looney claiming to have been kidnapped by a spaceship—three years ago. The guy was crazy as a bedbug."

Chapman slackened his killing pace only long enough to return the crisp salutes offered by a phalanx of security guards stationed around the perimeter of a cavernous hangar. "What about the car? Any news on that yet?"

"Jeep, sir." Burkett sifted through the sheaf of papers in his briefcase as he hurried to catch up.

"Jeep, car, what's the difference? I just want it found." The Air Force colonel ground to an abrupt stop at the final security checkpoint and presented his identity cards for inspection.

Burkett finally found the papers he was hunting for. "Of the five hundred and twenty-seven names of dark-colored Jeep owners compiled by the Department of Motor Vehicles, we've narrowed the list down to two hundred and four possibles. Field personnel have been assigned to investigate each of the remaining names, but except for the description you gave of the female driver, we don't have much else to go on yet. The state hasn't provided the necessary photo IDs for us to cross-reference against the list."

Chapman frowned and shook his head: 527 names and 204 possibles. Did everyone in southern Mississippi own a four-wheel-drive? "What's the holdup on the photo IDs?"

"Apparently, most of the sorting is being done by hand. The State of Mississippi is still in the process of computerizing some of their records."

"Oh, great, that could take forever." Chapman massaged the center of his forehead with a fist. The search had gone from bad to worse in the last couple of days. At least two extraterrestrials were playing the gawking tourist in local hotspots like the Piggly Wiggly and Pizza Hut. Harmless, maybe, but God only knows where else they had been, or what they were up to. "Get on the phone to Washington. Ask them to put more pressure on the state people. I want those photos by tonight."

"Yes, sir."

Burkett hurried off as Chapman walked through a small, unobtrusive entrance to the right of the massive hangar doors and paused, surveying the work in progress with a critical eye. A charred lump of metallic debris, by far the largest recovered from the crash site, hung suspended from the arm of a crane, turning slowly in the fluorescent glare of a maze of overhead worklights as it was carefully lowered into a crate on the cement floor. A bevy of white-coated technicians and scientists swarmed around the hangar, faces grim and set as they carefully sorted, catalogued, and photographed bits and pieces of the alien spacecraft's blackened remains. Chapman stared, shaking his head. Over a thousand fragments had been recovered from the woods, some close in size to the twisted lump being lowered by the crane, others, most in fact, smaller than the end of a thumbnail. Slivers which did nothing to reveal the nature of the alien craft, or its missing passengers.

"Lem, boy," a smooth, unctuous voice said behind him. "Good to see you again."

Chapman had to force himself not to stiffen as

he turned, an equally unctuous smile sliding masklike across his tense features. "General Moss. Good to see you, too." The hangar doors had cracked opened, and a long line of somber, suit-clad men were filing into the hangar, all armed to the teeth. Whether they were military, National Security, or a rapid-response team from some other federal agency, Chapman didn't know. It didn't really matter either. They were Moss's men, body and soul. He wasn't really surprised. He'd half-expected this moment since their phone conversation four days ago. So maybe the best thing to do was to dispense with all the social amenities and cut to the chase. "What are you doing here?"

There was a hint of triumph in Moss's eyes. "You know why I'm here, Lem. You and your bug-hunters screwed up big time. This was supposed to be a quick operation, in and out of the area with a minimum of fuss and bother." Moss's eyes turned flint-hard. "Since 'Air Force Intelligence' seems to be a contradiction in terms around here, the Threat Assessment Committee has given me operational command—with the Joint Chiefs' blessings. My orders are to get results, no matter what it takes. So don't get in my way, Colonel, or question my methods in any way. You're number-two on the totem pole now."

Chapman had a sick feeling in the pit of his stomach. John Wayne had just ridden in, guns blazing. There was no telling what would happen now.

Darkness fell with surprising swiftness. One moment the sky was gray, hesitating between night and day; then the sun dipped beneath the horizon, painting the trees in lengthening shadows. As the stars began their slow arc across the sky, Laura spread the ragged quilt atop the levee, carefully arranging the patchwork folds into a downy rectangle.

When she was finished, she smiled to herself and stared at the results of her handiwork. The blanket was ready, and two glasses were perched atop the tiny cooler where a bottle of white wine had been left to chill since early afternoon. Her heartbeat drummed in her ears. The grassy levee and old quilt were going to be used for much more than stargazing tonight.

She paused in surprise. What was wrong with her? She was as giddy as a love-starved schoolgirl getting ready for her first date. Her hands were even trembling, and her heart was hammering so loudly she could feel it pounding against her ribs. She shook her head in silent wonder and laughed aloud. The Laura Malek who'd led such a quiet, ordinary life was gone, replaced by a new woman who was alive and vibrant, her body thrumming with excitement and sensuality that had been long suppressed.

Something else had changed, too, she realized. The ghost of Brax was finally gone, buried deep within a coffinlike part of her memory, a wooden stake driven through its callous heart. The new Laura was ready and willing to meet life head-on, free to steal a piece of happiness from life wherever she found it, even if that happiness lay in the arms of a lover from a distant world.

A breath of chilly wind moved through her hair, blowing her curls into wild disarray. Laura shivered slightly, despite her heavy parka, and brushed a windblown curl away from her face. With the coming of darkness, the temperature had begun a slow downward slide, bringing another fleeting taste of winter to the Mississippi Coast. Warm sheets, a mattress, and the privacy of her bedroom would have been far more comfortable for what she planned, but she had Garner and Bryan to consider, as well as Drallondryn. They didn't know, and couldn't possibly understand. So to hell with the cold and wind. She'd make love to him in the top of a tree if she had to. Just being with him was all that really mattered.

She turned toward the muddy river, searching the darkness with her eyes. Aayshen was walking through the oaks, his tall figure weaving in and out of the stand of trees as he made his way back to the levee. A gauzy veil of moonlight pushed through the trees, washing his hair and face in a haze of silvery light. Her pulses quickened, and a slow flood of desire crested through her blood. His arrival had filled her world with magic, and changed her life forever more.

A sudden realization beat against the edges of her mind like the quick fluttering of a bird's wings, then crystalized into conscious thought so abruptly it left her breathless with surprise.

I love him. She stared at him in astonishment as he climbed the slope of the levee, the soft, dewy grass rustling with his every step. God, help me, I do.

"Laura?" Aayshen frowned and paused a few feet shy of where she stood. Even from there he could feel the intensity of her emotions, a strange web of warmth that seemed to flow around her in pulsating waves. "Is something wrong?"

She blinked, glanced at him for a moment then quickly looked away. "No." You're a fool, Laura Malek, she chided herself. "Nothing's wrong." She collapsed onto the carefully arranged blanket and patted the soft material. "Come . . . sit next to me, Aayshen."

He settled down beside her, throwing a suspicious glance at her every now and again from the corner of his eye. Some sort of change had come over her in the few minutes he'd spent walking along the riverbank. Tension, an odd rush of happiness, anticipation. Her emotions were tangled together into something unfamiliar that he couldn't quite define. Curious, he reached out to touch her thoughts, but pulled back abruptly when that tide of emotions began flowing through him in hot, scorching waves. He sucked in a startled breath, his mind scalded by the intensity of the telepathic contact.

For a fraction of a second Laura had felt the familiar sensation of oneness and warmth that came when he peered into her mind. Her hands trembled violently as she opened the cooler and fished the wine bottle out of a thick pool of melting ice. If he touched her thoughts again, she'd lose complete control, and all her plans for a slow seduction would be for nothing.

Wine trickled into the grass as she over-filled their glasses with wobbly hands. She sipped at both rims for a moment to stop the spills. "Here, drink this," she told him finally, and handed him a wineglass.

Aayshen stared at the contents of the glass warily. "What is it?"

"Wine. Go ahead, try it."

222

He took a cautious sip, gave her a surprised look, then tossed down the rest of the glass. The dry, sweet liquid tingled as it slid down his throat. "It's good." He held the glass out for a refill.

Laura lifted a dark brow. Her plans didn't include him getting stinking drunk. "Okay, but don't drink this one so fast." The bottle and crystal clinked together as she poured him another glass.

"Why not?" Taking the warning to heart, he sipped more slowly this time, memories of what had happened with the turtle still fresh in his mind.

"It might make you feel strange if you drink too much too fast."

Aayshen blinked to focus his eyes. He already felt strange. As if his body had been transformed from a solid state into a warm, heady fluid. The warmth spiraled through his blood, kindling a storm of desire that left his senses reeling in shock.

"Aayshen?" Laura said worriedly. His face was flushed, and he was staring into the darkness with a vacant, zombielike expression, the wineglass poised in midair. It had never occurred to her that he might not react the same to alcohol. Her anxious voice rose half an octave. "Are you all right?"

He angled his head around and gave her a devastating smile. "I'm very fine."

"Good. You had me scared there for a minute. I thought I might have poisoned you."

"I'm very fine," he said again. The storm in his blood had begun to subside, but not the aching desire. He gave her a long, smoldering look.

Her brow climbed a notch higher. "Obviously." She tugged the glass free of his hand and dumped

223

the rest of his wine into the grass. "I don't think you need any more of that."

He leaned toward her suddenly and brushed a hand along the tantalizing band of flesh visible around her ankle, his fingers stealing upwards beneath the dark material of her pants.

"No, Aayshen." She drew a shuddering breath, then gently pushed his hand away. "I don't want you to touch me, and I don't want you to poke around in my head either. At least for a few minutes."

Confusion darkened his opaque eyes. Ever since that first night she had welcomed the touch of his mind and hands. "Laura. . . ."

She rose on her knees and faced him, a slow, sensuous smile playing over her shadowed features. "Tonight is different . . . special." Her eyes, dark with expectation, caught and held his. "Don't move, don't talk, don't even think," she whispered. "All I want you to do is feel."

He was completely bewildered now. "I don't—"

"Shh." She lifted a finger to his lips to belay any questions. "You're about to learn what the word seduction means, Aayshen Rahs." She eased the heavy knit sweater over his head, each movement slow and painfully exaggerated; then her hands trailed across his muscular shoulders and down the corded length of his arms, his bare skin smooth and cool beneath her eager fingers. A tremor ran through him as she nuzzled his ear and caressed the hollow at the base of his throat with her lips and tongue.

His breath caught in his lungs as a current of pleasure surged through his wine-heated blood. Her lips moved from his throat to his chest, lingering attentively for a moment at the crest of each nipple. The heat turned into exquisite pain as her mouth drifted lower, searing a fluttery trail across his abdomen. A low, ragged sound slipped from his throat.

Her caresses grew bolder, more demanding, when she heard his agonized moan, proof of his passion that emboldened her even more. His body trembled, and a rush of desire swept through her, an ache so deep and powerful that her heart felt hollow inside.

She pulled away from him, fingers shuddering with sudden urgency as she hastily shed her own clothing, then slipped his boots and pants off one by one. It was a hollowness only he could fill.

Gooseflesh danced along her arms as a chilly wind gusted across her bare skin. Laura ignored it. Her universe had narrowed to this single moment in time, the pale eyes that were following her every move, the need to feel his silky-smooth flesh pressed against hers once again.

She knelt before him, her hands twining through his satiny hair before they finally stilled on his sharp-angled face. Her eyes clung to his, and her universe narrowed even more. She moved against him, slowly at first, the tempo building as the seconds passed.

Aayshen groaned, a deep, tortured sound that mingled with the wind and faded into the night. He clenched his hands against his thighs to keep from crushing her to him, but it was so very, very hard. Every nerve-ending in his body was ablaze, a fire so hot and torrid he would soon lose any semblance of control.

She lifted his hands to the sides of her face,

clasping and cradling his lean fingers against the flesh at her temples. "Connect with me, Aayshen," she whispered, and opened herself to him in every way. "I want to see the universe through your eyes again."

A small cry broke from her lips as they hurtled and soared into an endless sea of stars, the light streaming around them in a timeless wave of unremitting pleasure.

In the afterglow of their lovemaking, Laura clung to him, her trembling body spent and breathless, yet filled with a deep sense of contentment she'd never felt before. "I love you Aayshen Rahs," she breathed against him.

He held her tightly, the meaning of her words threading around him in a delicate web of warmth and fierce emotion. The web tightened, tangling him inside, and Aayshen drew a shaky breath. He finally knew, finally understood what it meant to love and be loved, and that knowledge shook him to the depths of his soul.

"Stay with me," she pleaded, and her arms slid up and around his neck, drawing him closer. "I can't bear the thought of losing you."

He kissed her cheek, his fingers moving gently through her silky hair, and buried the truth in his heart, armoring himself against a lonely, loveless future, and the aching sense of loss he would soon feel. The threads of their lives had intersected, merging together for just this one brief moment in time, but that joyous twining would soon come unraveled, and their futures unfold along disparate lines. "When the time comes, I have to go back, Laura."

A tear slid down her cheek, dampening her face

with salty moisture. "How much longer do we have?"

"A few days. Less, perhaps."

She held him tighter, determined to wedge a lifetime of living into that short span of time. A few days. And then she'd lose him forever.

Drallondryn pressed his face against the window, eyes scanning the night-darkened landscape for any sign of Aayshen and Laura. He had watched them hours before as they walked toward the levee, the sun slowly fading in the western sky; he had been a silent witness when they paused and faced each other, bodies twined together before they vanished into the waning light.

A pained expression stole across the Kri's face. Something indefinable had passed between Commander Rahs and Laura Malek in the last few days, something the Kri had only sensed intuitively, but which troubled him nonetheless. Ever since the first night on Earth, he had felt the stirrings of an odd intimacy between them, as though they were privy to some secret no one else was allowed to share. He had seen it in the quiet, questioning glances they exchanged, the way their eyes met and lingered for long, probing moments, the sudden shiftings of anxious limbs, still faces. Words no longer seemed necessary between them, as if they were communicating in the spiritual, sensuous language of bodies and minds.

Impossible, Drallondryn told himself. Aayshen Rahs was a genetically conditioned officer, rendering him incapable of forming an emotional commitment to anyone or anything save his ship, his government, and the crew who so willingly served him. But the growing intimacy between Aayshen and Laura signified some sort of drastic alteration in the Savanian's psyche, a baffling deviation from the norm.

The Kri folded his arms across his chest to stave off a sudden chill. Was Aayshen so changed that he was no longer the instinctive warrior he was born to be? Was he still capable of making the sometimes brutal decisions necessary in a tactical situation?

"They've gone off together again," a quiet voice said behind him, "haven't they?"

Drallondryn continued to stare out the window, searching in vain for another glimpse of the pair. "Yes." He turned slowly. "But perhaps we concern ourselves without need."

Garner snorted. "In a pig's eye. I might be half-deaf, but I'm not stupid, or blind either." He glanced toward the television to see if Bryan was listening. Surrounded by a platoon of plastic soldiers, the child and Sergeant Pepper were sprawled on the carpet in front of the TV, seemingly absorbed with each other and some boring sitcom.

The old man looked at the Kri again and lowered his voice to a terse whisper. "I think we both know what they've been up to the last couple of days." He sighed and shifted in the recliner chair. Naugahyde groaned in protest. "What are you so worried about anyway? She's my granddaughter, I'm the one who should be doing all the worrying around here. She might get herself into trouble."

"Trouble?"

"The worst kind. You know, make a little Savanian."

The Kri smiled thinly and paced across the room, hands clasped beneath his chin. "Hardly. Such an occurrence would be genetically improbable. Their bodies are too different." He paced back to the sofa and resumed his vigil by the window.

"Not that different," Garner muttered, and blew out a noisy breath. "They wouldn't be out there in the woods if they were." When the Kri failed to comment, Garner glanced at his sharp profile, noting how the fur on his forehead now seemed permanently ruffled with anxious lines. He'd looked that way ever since Laura had gone outside for "air" the other night. "You seem more bothered about the idea of them together than me. What's got you so upset?"

Drallondryn perched himself on an arm of the sofa and stared at the old human intently. He needed to voice his concerns to someone, and the ancient one seemed willing to listen. A common foe, even fear, sometimes forged an unlikely alliance. "It is not the idea of a physical relationship between them that concerns me." He picked at a claw nervously. What he was trying to put into words seemed disloyal somehow. "That the relationship even exists should not be possible at all." He picked up a book from a low table and ran his fingers across the smooth surface, enjoying the slick touch of Earth-leather against his fur. Animal hides, he reminded himself, and set the book back down. The fact that they were still hiding in the humans' dwelling didn't bode well for all concerned. "That we have remained so long in your home should also not be possible. The commander should have ordered us to leave here im-

229

mediately after his confrontation with the searcher." He shook his head in disbelief. "The decision to remain was tactically unsound and has increased considerably the risk of being captured."

Garner lowered his eyebrows in a thoughtful frown. Too bad they hadn't left. It would have solved a lot of problems. "Are you trying to tell me that you think he won't leave because of Laura?"

The Kri shrugged noncommittally. "It is a possibility." Sergeant Pepper leaped from the floor to the sofa and looked at the Kri expectantly. Drallondryn obliged by stroking the top of the cat's head, a curious sensation, but one he was growing to enjoy.

The old man watched as the alien petted a smaller version of himself with slow, gentle strokes. It was peculiar how such a sight seemed almost normal now. Even stranger was the knowledge that in the past week he had grown so accustomed to having the aliens around that the thought of them leaving or being captured made him realize he would probably miss them a little. "So what are you going to do about it?"

"Nothing." He lifted his hands and tail in a gesture of impotence. "I am not military. Such a decision lies within the realm of a trained warrior."

"Well, maybe you should discuss it with him, especially if you think it's dangerous to stay."

"Perhaps." It took a few moments for Drallondryn to digest the idea. A confrontation with the commander was not a thing to be taken lightly.

"Do it then." Garner knew he was pushing hard, maybe too hard, but it was time someone tried. "It's not just your lives we're talking about. You're putting ours at risk, too." He jerked his head toward Bryan. "Think of the boy. You want to see him get hurt?"

The Kri hesitated for a moment, then climbed to his feet and padded across the den, careful not to step on any of Bryan's toy humans. Sergeant Pepper scurried after him as he made his way through the kitchen to the back door, eeling back and forth between his legs. He would wait outside for Aayshen to return, convince him that staying any longer would be dangerous for them all.

Bryan watched his cat and friend vanish into the utility room before turning accusing eyes on his great-grandfather. "Drallondryn's my friend, Pawpaw, and Mommy likes Aayshen a whole lot. She told me. Why are you trying to make them leave?"

So, he'd been listening after all. Garner sighed and rubbed at the narrow space of skin separating his lip and nose. "Come here." He held out his arms and Bryan burrowed into his lap. "They gotta go sometime, boy, you know that."

"I know."

Garner gave his arm an awkward pat. "But if they stay here much longer, they're bound to be caught, and I know you don't want that. The sooner they leave, the better, for all of us."

A persistent sound, much like the high-pitched whine of an angry insect, began buzzing in Garner's ear. "Damnitall." Scowling, Garner shook his head and reached for the offending hearing aid. "I'm gonna flush these things down the toilet!"

Bryan looked around the room curiously. "That bug-noise isn't coming from you, Pawpaw."

The whine increased in pitch, and a corresponding burst of static shot through Garner's right hearing aid. "What the hell is it then?"

Carrie was standing in a dark spot near the side of the house, vacillating over whether she should knock or spy, when the back door slammed open and a shadow stalked across the patio. She jumped in surprise and dove for cover behind an overgrown azalea, not anxious to confront the Norwegian, or explain to Laura why she was creeping around her backyard. Hell, she wasn't even sure why she was doing it herself.

She swore silently. Instead of diving into the bush like an ignorant fool, she should have just said hi and made her presence known. Now it was too late. If she climbed out of the bushes, Laura would just think she'd been spying, even when she hadn't. Not yet anyway.

From the shelter of the azalea's thick branches, Carrie crouched and watched as the shadow walked to the far end of the patio and plopped into a wrought-iron chair. Light from the utility room spilled through the panes in the top half of the door, bathing the figure seated in the chair in a hazy white glow. She blinked and squinched her eyes closed, but when she dared another look the fuzzy black thing was still sitting there.

A costume, Carrie told herself. Has to be.

Her legs started shaking, and a chill rushed down her spine. Somehow she knew there weren't any buttons or zippers on this costume. Whatever it was, it was real. She eased deeper into the azalea, and started praying harder than she ever had, adding an apology for missing so many Sundays in church.

Drallondryn heard a furtive, scuttling sound from the tall bushes near the end of the house. He cocked an ear and turned, half-rising from the chair. "Commander, is that you?"

Something cold and wet touched Carrie's hand. She yelped and bolted out of the azalea, scrambling toward the patio on her hands and knees to get away from whatever had touched her. Behind her, Sergeant Pepper hissed once then ran off into the darkness.

Carrie's face went white when she realized the black thing was less than ten feet away, flicking a thick black tail back and forth and peering at her with glowing yellow eyes. Terrible, unearthly eyes. For one brief second neither of them moved, then the thing started walking toward her. Carrie clambered to her feet, let loose with a frightened scream and ran, farther and faster than she ever had.

Too stunned to react, Drallondryn stared after her, his tail whipping around in agitation. The human had seen him, that much was certain. The question was, what would she do?

Downhill, footsteps thudded across the damp grass, then hurried over the gravel walkway. Hands clasped together, Aayshen and Laura rushed out of the long shadows cast by darkness and plowed through the low bushes rimming the patio.

Laura's fearful gaze swept over the empty patio before settling on the anxious Kri. "What happened? We heard someone scream."

Drallondryn tried to shake off his rising fear, but found that he couldn't. "The woman . . . the one who came here the first day . . . she was hid-

233

ing in the bushes." He turned to Aayshen, his expression bleak. Capture was imminent, only a matter of hours, perhaps minutes away. "She saw me, Commander."

"Carrie?" Laura's face went ghost-white. "Carrie was here? She saw you?"

The Kri bobbed his head. "Yes." He pointed a hand toward the overgrown azaleas. "She was hiding under the branches when I came out to await your return."

"Oh, God." Laura's hand tightened around Aayshen's. Too soon. What they had together was magical, almost mystical. She wasn't ready for it to end. Not yet. "Oh, God."

Aayshen drew a shuddering breath and searched her face with troubled eyes. "What will she do?"

"She'll tell." Her hands started shaking, and she felt a hot rush of tears sting her eyes. "I know Carrie. She'll tell somebody."

He touched the side of her face gently, unmindful of the watching Kri. The thought of leaving, of never seeing or touching her again was like an aching wound deep within his flesh, one that would never heal. But the decision to leave had been delayed long enough. His selfish needs had overshadowed his training, and placed them all at terrible risk. "Then we must leave here. At once."

"No," Laura said, startling herself with the vehemence contained within that single word. Deep in her heart, she had known from the beginning that he would eventually leave, but not so soon. It wasn't fair. She shouldn't have to give up her last few days with him because of Carrie, not when she'd just discovered her love for him. Every second they spent together was precious to her, time she would treasure and be thankful for until the end of her days. It wasn't fair that someone could rob them of that time, not Carrie, not the government, not anyone. And she sure wasn't going to just stand by and let him be captured—or worse.

Her face settled into stiff, determined lines. "I'll stop her. I'll talk her into not telling anyone." She'd beat her into silence if she had to. "I know I can do it."

"Laura . . ." As much as he wanted to believe her, he knew that he couldn't.

"Don't try to stop me." She tried to jerk free of his hand, but he refused to release her. Carrie hung out most nights at the Cimarron Club. That would be her first stop. "Let me go, Aayshen."

She met his determined glare with one of her own. "You've got no other place to go," she said. "Don't you see? Where are you going to run to?" The far-off sound of a helicopter echoed across the winter sky, as if to give substance to her desperate plea. She gestured toward the encompassing darkness. "Those government people are out there right now, searching the area for you. You'll never be able to get far enough away to escape, not without my help. What we need is time—time enough for me to smuggle you away from here somehow, get you to a place where you'll be safe until your own people come for you."

He stared down into her imploring eyes. Instinct and training told him to leave, flee this place before the emotions raging within him seized complete control. But there was a certain logic in her reasoning. They didn't know the countryside, and if they were captured, the trail would undoubtedly lead back to Laura, a chilling eventuality that could place her and her family in mortal danger whether they left or not. A shudder of fear crawled down his spine. He could not leave her to face that possibility alone.

His hands slipped up her arms, drawing her into the protection of his embrace. In the end there was no decision to make. "We will stay," he murmured into her hair. "But you will not seek out this woman alone. I will be with you."

She sagged against him in relief, wound her arms about him for a brief second, then pushed away with the palms of her hands. "Let's go then." She rushed toward the back door to get her keys and purse.

"Drallondryn." Aayshen glanced at the dubious Kri. *"Quehf kln e'h mas,"* he said in quiet Savanian, ordering him to fetch a hand weapon from its hiding place in the greenhouse. If the searchers had set a trap, he would be ready.

A worried frown slanting across his features, Drallondryn dipped his head in acknowledgment, then hurried to the greenhouse. Within a minute he was back, the barrel of the plasma gun glinting dully in his hand.

Aayshen checked the charge, then shoved it into the waistband of his pants, tugging his sweater down to cover its bulk.

"Be careful, Commander," Drallondryn said, his frown deepening.

A bleak smile lifted the edges of his mouth. "I will."

Laura ran back out the door, the car keys jangling in her hand. "Let's go."

*　　*　　*

Drallondryn stared after them long after Laura's vehicle had roared to life and vanished into the night, watching and worrying over what unexpected perversity the Fates had in store. A strange, almost peaceful calm stole through him. Whatever would be, would be. It had all been decided long ago.

He turned slowly and walked into the house, aware on a half-conscious level that a fundamental change had occurred within Aayshen Rahs. Whether he realized it or not, the duty-bound Savanian had fallen prey to the siren-song of Earth and its peculiar people, had found something here that was lacking in his life, something that would make his return to his previous existence a painful experience. But return he would, for there was no other possibility. Aayshen Rahs belonged among the stars. There was no place for him here. This was not his planet or his race, and never would be.

Drallondryn shook his head and sighed as he walked through the utility room, pitying Aayshen for the wrenching sense of loss he would soon confront.

Garner's house shoes slapped against the kitchen tiles as he shuffled toward the Kri. The old man glowered. "Would you turn that stupid thing off?"

"Pardon?" Drallondryn shook himself out of his reverie, his browtufts setting in a puzzled line.

"That noise . . . turn it off." He cupped his hands over his ears and swung his head toward the breakfast table. "It's about to drive me crazy."

As the whining sound slowly registered, Drallondryn followed the direction of Garner's gaze, searching for the source of the electronic noise. The air rushed from the Kri's lungs in a startled gasp. Amid the jumble of equipment piled on the table, a single light was pulsing atop the comm-pack, shifting back and forth in hue from bright green to a deep, reddish-blue. He stared at the flashing light with a fixed, almost reverent expression.

"What is it?" Garner looked curiously at the Kri. "What does it mean?"

Drallondryn bared his canines in a joyous grin. "The signal light means that our ship is within range to lock onto the emergency beacon. We will be leaving soon." His smile suddenly faded, and his eyes shifted to the darkness beyond the kitchen window. It also meant that Aayshen's troubles were about to begin.

Chapter Thirteen

Chapman yawned and stretched back in his chair as another grainy image began to form on the computer screen, assembling itself into an electronic photo a few thousand pixels at a time. The blurry face that eventually peered back at him was a man's with thick jowls and a massive head shaped like a flattened .45-caliber slug. A physical description, along with the man's driver's license and the make and model of his car, was printed beneath the electronic photo in neat, bureaucratic lettering.

He made a face at the image. According to the information, the slug-head owned a Japanese pickup, not a Jeep. It figured. The paper-shufflers in Jackson had taken days to provide him with the information he'd requested, and at least half of what they had finally sent was either incomplete or just plain wrong.

Muttering under his breath, Chapman scrolled through the next few screens with barely a pause between them. He was in the M's now, the digitized names and faces erecting themselves like a child's building blocks across the computer screen. Mahoney, Alex J. Malbis, George, no middle initial. Malek, Laura H. Mallory, Gladys B.

His finger hesitated above the return key as his eyes and brain struggled to overcome weariness and connect what they'd seen. Something in one of those half-formed faces had triggered a recent memory. He paged back to a previous screen and waited impatiently for the building blocks to reform.

The lower half of a woman's face slowly took shape, the horizontal lines racing across the flat screen to add depth and detail to the electronic photograph. A well-shaped nose appeared, followed by deep-set eyes and a forehead framed by a halo of digitized curls.

Chapman's mouth curved in an unconscious smile as he leaned closer to the screen and stared, memorizing every nuance of the familiar face. "Well, hello there," he whispered to the driver's license photo.

His gaze angled downward to the information listed at the bottom of the screen. Now he had a name and address to connect with the face. "Nice to see you again . . . Laura H. Malek."

The crunch of oyster shells beneath the tires sounded like small explosions as Laura angled the Jeep across the Cimarron Club's sprawling parking lot. She wove her way through a maze of spindly pine trees that sprang from the white shells without rhyme or reason, their slender trunks scarred and twisted from close encounters with the bumpers of countless cars.

A line of blue neon above the door proclaimed the club's name, an M sputtering in and out of existence every second or so. In the ghostly blue light thrown by the sign, Laura saw Carrie's battered gray pickup parked by the door.

After backing into a shadowy spot to the side of the cement block building, she switched off the car and listened as the twangy strains of a honky-tonk song filtered through the still night air.

She turned to Aayshen, who was surveying the parking lot and low-slung building with the cool detachment of a soldier on the verge of battle. "Just stay in the car like we agreed," Laura said slowly. The look of concentration on his face was disquieting. It reminded her again of just who and what he was. "I'll go in and talk to Carrie by myself. It won't take long. You just sit tight and keep out of sight."

Behind the mirrored sunglasses, his wary gaze swept over the strange surroundings. Some inner sense was screaming a silent warning, telling him to not let her leave his side. He felt danger gathering around them, the hot prickle of a coming battle riding the air. "No." He fumbled for the door handle, the plasma gun hard and comforting against his rib cage.

She clutched at his arm to stay his sudden movement. "Aayshen . . . please. You can't go in. I think I can stop her, but if you're with me, it'll just make things worse. I know these people. You've got to trust me on this."

Against his better judgment, Aayshen capitulated. He sighed and brushed a hand across the side of her face. Perhaps his uneasiness stemmed more from his fear for her safety than reality. How had this fragile creature gained such a hold on his mind and soul? he wondered to himself. She had imprinted herself so indelibly into the essence of his being that he knew he would spend the rest of his days reliving this one brief moment in time. "All right. I will wait," he told her.

He drew her closer, and his lips moved hesitantly over her silken cheek until he found her mouth and claimed it with a savage intensity. Blood sang in his veins, and he felt the now-familiar ache spreading through his loins once again. His thoughts touched hers, and he basked in the heated rush of emotion she returned. He knew then that he could deny her nothing, and he would gladly give his life in exchange for hers.

Breathless, Laura pulled away from him, startled by the urgency and intensity of his kiss. She tamped down the embers of desire flaming within her. This wasn't the time or the place. She traced the outline of his jaw and soft, full lips with her fingers and smiled. "You're a quick learner, Aayshen Rahs." It was only yesterday that she'd taught him how to kiss beneath the oak tree. She moved across the seat and shoved the car door open before passion overcame reason. "I'll be back in a few minutes."

The sound of her footsteps receded, and a thick, uncertain silence settled around him. Too still. Too quiet. His gaze swept over the darkened parking lot, the vehicles sitting here and there, the gnarled tree trunks springing from the white shell. Aayshen's senses suddenly came alive. A trio of shadows had moved and shifted among the trees, creeping stealthily in his direction.

Cursing himself for several kinds of fool, Aayshen eased the hand weapon out of his waistband and checked its charge again, then slipped out the car door quietly.

"Come on, Carrie," Ornell begged. "Tell 'em just like you told me."

"Go to hell." Carrie's response drew a burst of laughter from the small clump of listeners gathered near the middle of the Cimarron Club's battered pine bar. Her stony glare chiseled a hole in her smirking husband. Ornell was going to pay for this. She'd tracked him down at the Cimarron to tell him what had happened and ask his advice. Instead, he'd announced to God and everybody that his wife had gone on a bender. "I'm not telling them diddly."

Ornell swung his beer gut and the barstool toward his wife and lifted a palm to his heart. "Honest to God, hon, I won't poke fun at you no more. Just tell them how that giant raccoon chased after you down at the Malek place."

The description evoked another storm of laughter, drowning out a maudlin Randy Travis song. Ricky Cooner, Bobbie-Jean's husband and Ornell's cousin, leaned on his pool cue and swigged down a glass of beer. "Tell us, Carrie." He hitched a cowboy boot onto the base of a stool and leered. "That must have been some raccoon."

Carrie's gaunt face flushed beet-red. Even

Bobbie-Jean was laughing at her, the same Bobbie-Jean who had prompted her little trip down to Laura's in the first place with her wild tales about strangers and the FBI. "It wasn't a damn raccoon, Ricky." Anger took a backseat to common sense. They might as well have called her a liar. "I said its face and ears were all pointy, kinda coonlike, but it was big, about six feet I think." She tilted her chin and gave the group a sour, challenging look. "All black it was, with shiny fur and yellow glow-in-the-dark eyes," she told them, her voice gathering momentum as she talked. "It was just sitting on Miz Malek's patio, big as you please, until it saw me. Then it jumped up and started coming after me, so I ran like hell."

Ricky and Ornell hooted as Mary Beth Shelton, the Cimarron's night-shift barmaid, dumped an overfilled ashtray into a napkin, then drew Carrie another mug of draft. She set the beer in front of her on the bar. "Don't get so worked up, Carrie. It was probably just somebody dressed up in a costume." Her dime-store eyelashes fluttered up and down, tiny crow's wings beating against plump cheeks, as Bobbie-Jean puffed smoke in her direction. "Mardi Gras is just a month or so away, maybe Miz Malek was trying her outfit on."

"It wasn't some kind of suit." The maze of sun lines around Carrie's mouth grew rigid as she grabbed her mug and tossed down its contents in three gulps. "Look, I don't care if you morons believe me or not, because I know what I saw. It was just as real as Bobbie-Jean sitting over there on that barstool." She motioned to Mary Beth for a refill with a jerk of her head. Her hands had been shaking ever since she'd run away from the Malek place. So far the beer hadn't helped. "The more I think about it, that other fellow didn't look right when I saw him either. He's different from the black thing, but there was something real spooky about him."

Ricky snickered, but the others were more subdued, uncertain, as if they were beginning to half-believe her, even though they weren't quite certain that they should.

"You must have really tied one on this afternoon, Carrie," Ricky said, the only one eager to pursue the subject further. His eyes slid to Ornell in search of encouragement. "What did this other fellow look like, a giant pink possum?"

Her flinty stare was cold enough to chip stone. "Shut your ugly face, Ricky." Her right hand knotted into a hard fist. "Or I'm going to hurt you real bad."

Ornell Cooner angled his bulk from the barstool and moved to stand between his wife and his cousin, arms spread placatingly. "Now, Carrie. There's no call to carry on like that. Ricky was just foolin' with you. We all were."

Carrie sniffed and tilted her chin. "For your information, Ricky, I wasn't drunk. Ask your wife, she'll tell you. She's seen the blond guy, too." Carrie jabbed a thumb toward Bobbie-Jean, who winced and turned away, pretending not to be a party to the conversation. "She saw him down at the Pig the other day with Miz Malek. Go ahead, tell them, Bobbie-Jean. There's no reason not to anymore."

Ricky turned and gave his wife a puzzled stare. So did Ornell. "That true, Bobbie-Jean?" Ricky said. "He the same guy that caused such a ruckus down at the store?"

The Piggly Wiggly cashier made a pouty face and propped her chin in her hands. As far as she could tell, the FBI had quit following her, so the whole thing really didn't concern her anymore. It had been kind of fun while it lasted. Bobbie-Jean sighed. "Yeah, one and the same. Big, good-looking guy, kind of weird, though. Spooky. That FBI man was sure hot to get his hands on him."

Carrie nodded vigorously. "Miz Malek said he was acting weird because he's a foreigner, but I think she was lying."

"So?" Ornell interjected. "Miz Malek's entitled to have a man in her house if she wants."

"That other thing's no man," Carrie shot back. "Hell, it's not even close." Her voice trailed off into silence. What was that thing on the patio? Worried lines bunched across her brow. Lots of strange things had been happening around Escatawpa for the last week or so. Strangers were everywhere she looked, doing a bad job of looking inconspicuous, or driving big cars and dressed in fancy suits. Helicopters were flying all over the place day and night. What if she'd been wrong not to tell Bobbie-Jean to call the law? Her frightened gaze settled on her husband. "I gotta do something, Ornell. Miz Malek's out there all alone with a little boy and that crazy old man."

"Call the sheriff then," Ornell said. "Tell him where that fellow is that the FBI is looking for." He wagged an admonishing finger in her face. "Just don't tell him what you saw tonight. He'd just think you're one of those fools hollering about alien monsters and UFOs."

"Aliens? You mean like from outer space?" Ricky snickered again. "Maybe they're pod people." He leaned over Carrie's shoulder and whispered in her ear. "That's what happened to you, Carrie—you've been podded."

Carrie stomped on his instep and drove an elbow into the hollow spot beneath his rib cage.

"Oow!"

"I told you to shut up, Ricky." She spun around to her husband. "Give me a quarter, Ornell. I'm going to call Sheriff Rankin."

He fished in a jeans pocket and produced a quarter. "Just remember what I told you. Don't go blabbing to the sheriff about what you saw out there."

"I won't." A breath of chilly wind touched Carrie's face as the door to the Cimarron Club swung open. The sudden breeze curled through the room, sending a stray napkin left on the bar fluttering toward the concrete floor.

Bobbie-Jean glanced up and froze. "You better use that quarter real quick, Carrie."

Carrie's face turned bone-white. Laura Malek was standing in the doorway. "Oh, Lord."

Laura paused in the doorway to give her eyes time to adjust to the tavern's dim lighting. There wasn't much to see, really, just rough pine walls and a few scarred tables and mismatched chairs scattered around a cold cement floor. The Cimarron had a generic, small-town feel about it, the same assembly-line look found in a thousand other bars littering the South. And with their jeans and plaid flannel, the customers looked like they had been pounded from the same cookie-cutter mold.

She sucked in a ragged breath when she spotted Carrie. She and Ornell, as well as several other locals, were standing in a knot around the bar, their watchful eyes drilling into her with a mixture of suspicion and fear. Her knees trembled as she made her way to a rickety table in the back of the bar and sat down. How much had Carrie told them?

Carrie watched her for a few seconds, trying to decide what to do, then picked up her mug and walked to Laura's table. She set the mug of draft on the table and gingerly lowered herself into a chair directly across from her.

Their eyes met, and Laura struggled to keep her composure. What in heaven could she say that would convince Carrie to keep quiet?

"No sense beating around the bush." Carrie's gaze turned flint-hard. "I saw that black thing down at your place. You gonna tell me what it is or not?"

"What black thing?" Laura swallowed.

Carrie leaned toward her and stared. "Don't bull-crap me, Laura. I've always been able to tell when you're lying. Tell me the truth right now, or I'll just get right out of this chair and head to the phone. I know you were down at the Piggly Wiggly the other day, and I know what happened."

Laura squeezed her lids shut and propped her forehead in her hands. Carrie wasn't going to make this any easier. "It's best you don't know, Carrie. What you don't know can't get you into trouble."

"I know who you are, Laura. That bit of information alone has already caused more trouble than you can shake a stick at." A tight frown settled over Carrie's face. "There's FBI men crawling all over the county hunting for you. They've even been trying to find out who you were by following Bobbie-Jean around, just because they suspect that she knows you, too. What do you think they're going to do when they find out we've been protecting you?"

"I'm sorry," Laura said. "I didn't know."

Carrie gave her a piercing look. "That black thing's some kind of alien, isn't it? That's why they're so hot to find you."

Laura stiffened, then buried her face in her palms, rubbed at her eyes, and heaved a resigned sigh. Carrie had already figured things out for herself. "Yeah," she admitted miserably.

Carrie's fingers began drumming the table top. "That blond fellow who's been staying with you . . . him, too?"

Heat rose in Laura's cheeks in response to the question. She nodded woodenly, unable to form intelligible words. "Him, too," she said finally.

"What did you tell me he was your cousin for?"

She shrugged and folded her arms. "I didn't have much choice, Carrie. When Aayshen came, he wasn't exactly an invited guest." An absent smile tugged at the corners of her mouth. "The last few days have changed all that."

Carrie slugged down the rest of the beer. Laura's face had softened when she mentioned him, a sudden rush of warmth that had filled her eyes. Was something going on between her and the blond man? Her fingers drummed louder. "You and your boy in any danger?"

"Not from them." She reached across the table and stilled Carrie's fingers, covering them with her

Jan Zimlich

own. "Please . . . I'm begging you, Carrie." Her hand tightened around Carrie's. "Don't call anybody, not yet. I'm scared. I couldn't stand it if anything happened to him. If they catch him there's no telling what they might do to him."

Carrie sat back in her chair and stared at Laura intently. There were tears in Laura's eyes now, threatening to spill down her cheeks at any second. She didn't seem frightened, just worried and more upset than Carrie had ever seen her. It was the kind of worry reserved for a child, a husband, or a lover. Her brows vanished beneath her bangs. "You love him, don't you, Laura?" she said in a wondering voice.

Another nod, swifter this time, and the tears slid downward. Laura wiped at her face with the back of a sleeve. "I know it's crazy and stupid, but I love him so much it hurts. Nobody's ever made me feel like he does. Nobody." She choked back a sob. "In a few days he'll be gone, and I'll never see him again. I know that, Carrie. But I can't stand the thought of losing him, not yet."

Carrie expelled a long, weary sigh, wondering how she would feel if the tables were turned and Laura called the law down on Ornell. She sighed again. The quarter was still burning a hole in her jeans, and the pay phone was only 20 feet away. But 20 feet or a thousand miles, what did it matter? Laura Malek had been good to her through the years, better than her own mother had ever been. She couldn't turn the blond man in to the law, any more than she could turn in Laura herself.

"Okay." Carrie shook her head from side to side, chastising herself for being such a pea-brained

250

fool. What kind of mess was she getting herself into? "I've been working for you for a goodly number of years now, and you've always treated me right. I won't go against you on this, Laura, not unless I have to. Besides, you deserve to have a little happiness after all this time . . . even if this fellow is an alien."

More tears welled in Laura's eyes, but this time they were tears of gratitude. "Thank you." A small relieved grin animated her face and chased away the last vestiges of fear. "I owe you, Carrie. Big time."

Carrie grinned back and patted Laura's hand. "And you'll pay me back, too. I'll make sure of it."

The door to the Cimarron Club swung open with a protesting groan. Behind them, Bobbie-Jean let out a little squeak of surprise as the doorway filled with dark, shifting shapes. Blue light from the club's neon sign spilled across the entrance, and the shapes solidified into a trio of dark-clothed men.

Carrie gave the newcomers a suspicious once-over as they paused in the doorway, blinking in the neon gloom. Clad in fancy wool overcoats and shiny city shoes, the three men were too well-dressed, too Yankeefied to be from anywhere near Jackson County.

One of the strangers, a big, cocky looking fellow, eyeballed her in return; then his cold gaze moved to Laura and stilled. Carrie felt a clammy shudder pass down her spine as the man glanced at what looked like a photo clutched in his hand. She searched out Laura's hand and squeezed it as the three men formed a loose wedge and began moving toward the table.

For a fleeting second Carrie's gaze locked with Laura's. Still clutching her hand, Laura half-rose from the table, then sat down again, resignation etched across her features. She knew who the men were, too.

"Hell's bells," Ricky Cooner slurred, oblivious to the scene unfolding around him. He pointed his beer mug at the strangers. "What is this place tonight? Grand Central Station?"

Carrie shot the fool a murderous look over her shoulder, but the beer had killed off too many brain cells for him to notice much of anything.

Ricky drained his mug, dribbling part of it down the front of his flannel shirt, then staggered toward the closest of the newcomers, grinning stupidly. "Any of you boys shoot pool?"

In response, the man shoved the oiled and shiny muzzle of a 9mm automatic pistol in Ricky's face.

Bobbie-Jean screamed, a high-pitched, echoing shriek that ended on a breathless, exaggerated sob. Several of the Cimarron's customers dove out a back window in the pool room.

For a fraction of a second, Ricky just stared at the gun; then the alcohol fog lifted from his brain and he threw up his hands. "Hey, buddy. No need to pull a gun. I'm not going to mess with you." He backed slowly toward the bar.

The man holding the gun snatched a badge from his pocket with his free hand and lifted it for them to see. "We're with the FBI, folks. No cause for alarm. Just stay where you are and don't interfere. We'll be out of here in just a minute."

The other two quickly moved into positions on either side of Laura, gun arms extended.

"Laura H. Malek?"

She nodded, too frightened to speak.

"Are you the owner of the dark blue Jeep Cherokee sitting on the side of the building?"

She nodded again. Oh God, Aayshen was in the car. Had they caught him already?

"Place the palms of your hands on top of the table and don't make any sudden movements, Mrs. Malek." The cocky-looking guy flashed Carrie a glance. "You, too."

They did as instructed. Laura's terrified gaze darted back and forth from one government agent to the other, finally settling on the bigger of the two. He was the one who had spoken, and was obviously in charge. "What do you want with me?" she managed to croak.

"You'll have to come with us, ma'am. I'm not authorized to say any more at this time."

Carrie's pale face began turning an angry scarlet. Who did these guys think they were? Coming in here, ordering people around and pulling guns on law-abiding citizens. She didn't care if they were government men or not. It wasn't right. "Hey, fellow, aren't you supposed to read her her rights or something before you haul her off?"

He shot her an impatient look. "Stay out of this, lady. This has nothing to do with you."

"Like hell it don't." She met his glare with one of her own. "If you won't tell me, then you just get the county sheriff on the phone, 'cause you're not taking her anywhere until we know what's going on!"

The sudden glance of fear and confusion that passed between the men gave Carrie pause.

"Nobody's calling anyone," one of them finally

said. "Just get up from the table, Mrs. Malek. Real slow and easy."

Something akin to dread set up permanent residence in Carrie's gut. She kicked Laura under the table and warned her not to move with her eyes. Why would they be scared about calling the sheriff unless this whole thing wasn't on the up and up? "I think you boys are lying." She was beginning to wonder if they were government people at all. "You aren't really FBI, are you?"

The bigger agent locked a hand around Laura's elbow and jerked her from the chair. He pointed his gun at the back of her head. "Just walk toward the door, Mrs. Malek, and no one will get hurt. We have authorization to use whatever force is deemed necessary to take you into custody. So don't make things difficult."

Before she had time to think about the repercussions, Carrie drove her left knee into the bottom of the rickety table, upending her side. An ashtray and her mug slid toward Laura as the table defied gravity and teetered uncertainly on a single wooden leg.

Laura toppled backwards along with her chair and the table, jerked her arm free, then scrabbled sideways on the floor, trying to regain her feet to make a run for the door. A small explosion to her right chipped a little hole in the cement. Laura froze and stared at the hole in sudden horror. Someone was actually shooting at her. Then she heard five more explosions in rapid succession. Wood splintered and flew from a chair beside her and something tugged at her sleeve. Laura stared dumbly at her forearm. There was a small tear in her dark green coat surrounded by a circle of bright red. Christmas colors, she thought to herself. The circle was wet and sticky, and growing by the second.

Screams of shock, both male and female, echoed through the Cimarron. Out of the corner of her eye Laura saw Carrie hurtle over the top of the bar and vanish from sight. Other customers were huddled behind barstools, frozen like startled deer caught in the glare of headlights.

Glass shattered somewhere behind her, adding to the nightmarish sounds, then a dark figure dove through the splintered window and rolled across the slab floor.

"Laura!" Aayshen screamed in a ragged voice. He pointed the plasma gun and a thick stream of blue-green light stabbed across the room, searing a rounded hole through a wooden beam above the door. A wisp of gray smoke curled upwards and the smooth edges of the hole glowed bright orange.

The agents dropped behind tables for cover and stared at the smoking beam in shock, the afterglow of the laser light still burning behind their eyes.

"Here!" Laura scuttled beneath a table and flattened herself against the cement floor. "Aayshen, help me!" She pressed her cheek to the concrete and choked back a frightened sob.

Aayshen crawled toward her on his elbows until their faces were only inches apart. His features tightened with rage when he saw the bloodstain on her arm. "Stay where you are," he whispered. Much as he would like to kill the humans, he knew it would only make their position more tenuous. He had to get Laura out and tend to her wound.

255

Anger burned hot and bright in his eyes as he adjusted the gun's beam and targeted a section of wall just over the attackers' heads. Several bullets thunked into the concrete beside him. Aayshen's lips thinned as he fired again. A foot-long width of wall glowed bright orange, and vanished from existence, exposing a maze of rusted plumbing and smoldering electrical wire. Sparks danced and flew from the wall and the overhead light fixtures. The lights flickered twice; then a thick bog of darkness enveloped the Cimarron.

Hazy light from a vapor lamp in the parking lot threw scattered beams through the shattered window. An unnatural silence settled over the room, a quiet so still and complete that it rang in Laura's ears.

As her eyes gradually adjusted to the dimness, Laura heard a sound to her left and turned. A small figure suddenly loomed up from behind the bar. Her eyes widened in surprise and horror. Carrie had risen from behind the bar clutching what looked like a shotgun.

"Laura!" Carrie yelled into the darkness, "I don't know what's going on here and I don't care!" She clicked off the shotgun's safety and smiled grimly, grateful for once that most clubs kept a loaded gun stashed behind the bar in case of trouble. "You just take your fellow and run! If those guys try to come after you, I'm gonna pump their butts full of scattershot!"

A series of little sounds came from the back of the bar where the strangers were hiding. Shoes scraping across the floor, urgent whispers. Carrie pumped the shotgun, then closed her eyes and squeezed the trigger. The gun went off with a heart-pounding roar, the recoil throwing her into a shelf behind the bar. Scattershot ripped through the darkness, making tiny sparks as it ricochetted off concrete and wood. "Get out of here, Laura!" Carrie screamed.

Aayshen pulled her from beneath the table and half-dragged, half-carried her toward the open door, the barrel of the plasma gun weaving back and forth as he ran. He paused in the doorway for a split second and focused his mind on the three attackers.

Carrie emptied the other barrel into the ceiling as Laura and the blond man vanished through the door. A few seconds later an engine roared to life, and she heard the sound of a car plowing through the oyster shells at high speed.

Silence reined for several minutes; then one of the strangers staggered toward the front of the bar, lurching into chairs and tables like a drunken man. The agent rubbed his forehead, trying to clear the cobwebs from his brain. Something strange had happened but he didn't know what. For just a moment he'd been in a stupor, unable to move or think. As the confusion lifted, he shouted an order, and the three agents stumbled out the Cimarron's door in pursuit.

Across the bar, Ornell climbed from beneath a barstool and stared at his wife in horror. "God Almighty, Carrie. You shot at a government man."

Bobbie-Jean crawled from her hiding place and started crying. "Heaven help us! They'll send us all up to Parchman Prison for sure!" Her wails turned into hiccupy sobs.

"Oh, shut up, Bobbie-Jean." Carrie brushed off the seat of her pants and laid the shotgun atop the bar. If nothing else, she'd given Laura a few minutes' head start. Her mouth was set in a hard little line. "I don't trust those guys. Somebody go call Sheriff Rankin and tell him to get down here right now."

Chapter Fourteen

Laura squeezed her lids closed as the Cherokee raced down Kali Oka Road, tires screaming on the narrow black asphalt each time the car rounded a curve. She pressed a hand against her arm to staunch the flow of blood and offered up a silent prayer. They were doing well over 90, and Aayshen was at the wheel. Heart pounding, she risked a quick glance sideways. His angular features were cool and composed, his eyes fixed on the darkened road with a quiet confidence. She seemed to be the only one worried by the fact that he had never driven before.

He felt her thoughts on him and flashed her a concerned look. "How is your arm?"

"It stings, more than anything." She lifted one shoulder in a half-shrug. "The bullet must not have gone very deep. If it had, I think I would be in a lot more pain than this. Of course, I've never been shot before either."

The white rail fence bordering Laura's property flashed by the window a series of horizontal lines. Aayshen stepped hard on the brake. The tires squealed, and the Jeep's rear end fishtailed wildly as they bumped down the long driveway, skidding to a jerky stop on a strip of blacktop beside the house. He jumped from the car and pulled her door open, lifting her out as gently as he could. Her body cradled against his, he hurried toward the back door at a dead run.

At the kitchen table, Drallondryn flinched in surprise as the door flew open and banged against the wall. The Kri wheeled around, just as Aayshen burst out of the utility room.

"Commander! The ship has locked onto the emergency beacon. We should have voice contact within the hour!"

Aayshen began shouting orders in a terse, clipped stream of rapid Savanian.

The Kri's mouth dropped open when he saw that Aayshen was carrying Laura. He stared mutely, not quite grasping what Aayshen had tried to tell him. There was a large splotch of crimson blood on Laura's sleeve. "Commander?"

A wave of apprehension swept over Aayshen's features. The signal lock had come too late. "Find me some type of medical equipment," he repeated in English, "then pack our gear while I see to her injury. An hour is far too long to wait for pickup. We've already been discovered." He rushed across the kitchen to the den.

Garner glanced up from the magazine he'd been reading when Aayshen rushed into the room carrying his granddaughter. The old man struggled out of his recliner chair. "Laura!" Her face was ghost-white and her arm was covered in blood.

"I'm okay, Grampa," she said as Aayshen laid her gently on the sofa. He began tugging off the torn coat to examine the wound.

His eyes dark with fright, Bryan ran up to the sofa and peered at the blood on his mother's arm. His lower lip trembled.

"There's nothing to get upset about, Bryan," she said soothingly. "I promise."

Garner gave the alien an accusing look; then his eyes cut back to his granddaughter. "What happened, Laura?"

She blew out a ragged breath and shook her head, still incredulous. "I think I got shot."

"Shot?" Garner shuffled closer to see as Aayshen jerked on the sleeve of Laura's sweater and ripped it open at the seam. "By who?"

"A federal agent of some kind, at least I think that's what he was." She winced as Aayshen probed the jagged flesh around the edges of the wound.

"Gross." Bryan's fear was gone, replaced by a five-year-old's morbid fascination with blood and gore. "There's stuff coming out of a little hole in your arm, Mom."

Garner peered over Aayshen's shoulder and studied the wound. His breath heaved out in a relieved sigh. "Doesn't look too bad, Laura. Looks like the bullet must have just grazed you."

Drallondryn appeared carrying an assortment of bath towels and an emergency kit from his suit pack. Aayshen swabbed some of the blood away with a towel, then opened the kit and touched a small cylindrical tool to her arm, cleansing and deadening the wound with the tiny device.

The stinging stopped abruptly, and Laura blinked in surprise. Her arm still throbbed a little bit, but other than that she felt as good as new. She moved her arm back and forth in disbelief. The flow of blood had ended, and the only visible mark on her forearm was a thin brown line. She gave Aayshen a wan, grateful smile, but the smile never reached her anguished eyes. "Good as new." A hard knot of despair had wedged in her throat. He was leaving, and she would never see him again. "I guess it pays to have an alien around the house sometimes."

"Humph," Garner muttered, and shook his head. "It wouldn't have ever happened if it hadn't been for him."

The truth of his words hit Aayshen with sickening force. He had remained here long after it was prudent in order to be with Laura for his own selfish reasons, to protect her from things real and imagined. Instead, he had nearly caused her death. A deep, terrible pain such as he had never known gnawed at his chest. He gazed at her in despair, the opaque blue of his eyes flat and lifeless. "I caused this. If we had left as we should have, you would not be injured."

She lifted an arm and touched his satiny hair, then cradled his cheek in her palm. "There's nothing to be sorry about, Aayshen. I wouldn't trade the past few days for anything." Tears welled in her dark eyes. "Not for anything."

He squeezed his lids and heart shut against the pain, the hot ache of impending loss. His expression grew hard, brittle, and when he opened his eyes again they were cold and emotionless.

Laura watched as the dull veneer of Savanian composure slid masklike over the sharp planes of his face once again, leaving no trace of the gentle lover she had come to know and love. She glanced away, unable to watch the transformation any longer. He had closed his heart to her, shielded himself from the pain of loss by shutting down his emotions.

He turned away from her. "Drallon-dryn,"Aayshen snapped in a cold, sharp voice. The Kri was wandering about the room in a state of confusion, equipment thrown here and there in haphazard piles. "Hurry with your preparations." He rushed toward the kitchen to retrieve the transceiver pack. "We leave immediately."

"I'm trying, Commander." The harried Kri finished sealing several organic samples inside protective tubes and dropped them inside his pack. Then he directed his attention to the collection of books and knickknacks piled around him, trying vainly to decide what to take, and what to cast aside. Everything Laura had given him would prove invaluable in some fashion to League sociologists and scientists, but what he could take was limited to the number of items he could carry in his suit pack.

His gaze paused and came to rest on the cat curled on the floor beside the fireplace. He stared longingly as Sergeant Pepper yawned and stretched, then wound himself into a half-circle and resumed his nap. Although he had blood and fur samples from the cat, as well as several dead specimens of the tiny insect that had plagued him so in the past few days, the idea of appropriating the creature itself was quite appealing.

But one look at Bryan's profile and he knew that he couldn't. The child trusted him. He shook off the impulse and rifled through a few of the much-worn pages of the dictionary, then jammed the heavy book inside his overfilled pack. The dictionary would go, as well as a thick text on human medicine and anatomy, even if he was forced to leave everything else behind. A picture book on Earth tropical vegetation followed, plus an old newspaper and a large book about some place called Egypt.

With the addition of the books, his pack was so full the vacuum seal refused to engage. He sighed and glanced in dismay at the mounds of small household objects strewn around the carpet. He really didn't want to leave any of it behind, especially the little carving of a creature Laura called a horse, and the tape Grampa had made him of yesterday's episode of *Gilligan's Island*. He'd have to build a device in order to play the tape, but that wouldn't be difficult. The human-made machine was so crude, a Kri kit could make one.

Garner shuffled in from the kitchen, his slippers making slapping sounds as he walked. "Here." He tossed a box of trash bags on the floor. "From the looks of that pile of junk you're planning to cart out of here, I thought you might need these."

Drallondryn stared at the rectangular box, wondering what he was supposed to do with it.

"They're trash bags," Garner explained. His knees creaked as he bent over and ripped one free of the box. "You can use them to haul all that stuff in when you leave." He fumbled with the slick green plastic until he finally found the opening.

As Laura watched the preparations, her dark eyes glinted with an indefinable emotion. Only a week ago their leaving would have been an answer to a prayer, but now . . . now the only thing she felt was a gaping emptiness.

She slipped off the sofa and followed Aayshen into the kitchen. He was hunched over the breakfast table, elbows folded in front of him as he spoke into the boxy piece of equipment in low, muffled tones. Laura strained to hear, but his words were incomprehensible. Since those first frantic days he'd said little in his native tongue. There was a soothing, almost melodic quality to his language, a compelling mix of slurred vowels and sharp consonants as one word seemed to slide unnoticed into the next.

Even though she couldn't comprehend the meaning of his words, Laura knew he was trying desperately to make contact with the incoming ship. But from his grim expression she surmised that so far his effort had failed.

Standing quietly in the doorway, she folded her arms across her chest and listened to his calm, resonant voice. There had been times in the last week when he hadn't sounded so cool and self-assured, moments when that familiar voice had been edged with emotion and uncertainty. But that was gone now, hidden behind the wall of indifference he was attempting to erect between them.

For a single impulsive second, she wanted to tear down that invisible wall and rip away the cold mantle of authority that had settled around him, get right in his face and scream, "Look at me, I'm the same person I was yesterday, the same one you made love to only hours ago!"

But she didn't. She couldn't. Laura rubbed tiredly at her aching shoulder with the side of her hand. What would be the purpose anyway? What they'd had together was strictly temporary, nothing more than a pleasurable diversion from the cold reality of disparate lives. They were aliens to each other, and always would be. Maybe his way of dealing with the pain was better. Easier.

Her expression was as cold and brittle as his when she pulled her thoughts back to the present and found his haunted, azure eyes riveted on her face.

Startled, Laura flinched in surprise and looked away. She hadn't noticed when he'd quit talking or that he had begun watching her with a bold, unsettling intensity. Her gaze wandered the length of the kitchen, then cut back to him and rested on his still features. She cleared her throat. "How soon will you leave?" Her voice came out small and ragged, almost a whisper.

Aayshen punched a small colored grid at the base of the comm-pack to switch the transmission frequency from voice-relay back to automatic send. "Very soon." A light flashed from blue to amber as the transceiver resumed transmitting emergency coordinates in a series of tight-pulse tachyonic bursts. "The ship is still beyond voice range, but I am sure they have dispatched a rescue craft by now."

She nodded once, a slow, sullen acquiescence, and hugged her arms closer to her chest. "I guess you'll be glad to get back to your own people."

"Yes." His ice-blue eyes held her in place. "Glad." He couldn't summon the emotion to match the word. A lifetime of obedience forced his mind to flinch away from that train of thought. "I belong there."

He rose and walked to the bank of windows flanking the table, slipped his fingers between the blinds and forced an opening in the flexible metal. Beyond the window, the night was quiet, damp and still. The slender crescent of Earth's ascending moon hung high in the sky, painting the treetops with bold glints of silver-white. The trees turned silver, then gray, then were swallowed by black as a heavy mantle of thick clouds obscured the moon from sight.

"Will you ever come back?" Laura asked quietly. She held her breath and waited. The question seemed to resonate between them.

He turned slowly and held her gaze, but there was no trace of emotion in his eyes. Inwardly, he was dying by slow degrees. "No, I will never return here."

Her chin lifted by a fraction of an inch. She'd needed to hear him say it, to confirm what she had always known. Wordlessly, she turned on her heel and walked to her bedroom to change out of the ripped sweater. If he wanted to build a wall between them, she'd be more than glad to hammer a few nails herself.

She sat on the edge of her bed for a few moments, staring at nothing, then pulled a heavy red sweater from a drawer and tugged it over her head, wincing a little when she raised her injured arm. Her thoughts gradually cleared, and her black mood lifted a bit. Maybe with him gone her life would return to some semblance of normality. Bryan didn't need this kind of turmoil and strangeness in his life, and at his age, Garner didn't either. She sank back down on the bed again. Tomorrow she would concentrate on earning a living again, and everything would be as it was. But deep in that secret place she kept hidden from casual view, she knew a terrible truth: Nothing in her mediocre life would be the same again.

"Excuse me . . ."

She glanced up to find Drallondryn standing in the doorway, watching her with an odd expression. He was wearing the metallic suit she'd first seen him in.

"I wanted to say thank you and good-bye . . . and to wish you well." He had already said his farewells to Bryan and Grampa. Laura was last. "I wish. . . . " Something akin to sympathy glittered in the alien's yellow eyes. "I wish for both your sakes that we had never come here."

A small, wistful smile touched the corners of her mouth. So Drallondryn knew. She supposed that Garner did, too. Sighing deeply, Laura stood and crossed the room. She gave his metal-clad arm a gentle squeeze. "I don't have any regrets. I just wish that things had turned out . . . differently."

The Kri stared at her intently. "He will return to his own reality," he said in a quiet voice, "where he was meant to be. There never was any other outcome."

"I know." Laura's voice was raw, ragged with suppressed emotion. Her hand slipped down his arm, and she clasped his fingers warmly. "Good-bye, Drallondryn." He was kind and gentle and considerate. She would truly miss him. "I'm glad I got the chance to know you."

He gave her a small, embarrassed smile, then

turned and hurried down the hallway. Laura followed him slowly to the den. Aayshen was there, suited in his warrior's armor once again. He was pacing back and forth near the front door, as though he were anxious to put time and distance between them.

She stared at him, but didn't say anything as Drallondryn hefted several trash sacks onto his back.

"I'm ready, Commander," the Kri said.

Aayshen checked the front windows again before opening the door. He gazed into the enveloping darkness with uneasy, watchful eyes as a sliver of moonlight stabbed through low clouds. His senses were warning him that something was wrong.

The wind stirred languidly outside the window, and he saw a furtive movement among the winter-bare trees. His body went cold and still as a dark, hunched shape flitted once across his line of vision, then melted to black.

Too late. His hands bunched into fists at his sides.

"Teams of two," Chapman whispered into his headset. "Teams of two at all times."

Dark, muted shapes, more shadows than men, merged with the wind-ruffled saw grass and dissolved into night. Chapman's nose filled with the rich, loamy smell of Mississippi dirt as he hunkered down lower on the slope of a small drainage ditch, elbows digging for a comfortable purchase in the moist earth and sharp yellow grass. From his vantage point along the narrow asphalt road, he had a clear, wide-angle view of Laura Malek's home and yard, including the navy-blue Jeep Cherokee parked on a strip of blacktop to the right of the house.

The house itself seemed innocent enough, an undistinguished mixture of bland old brick and simple lines that would have been more comfortable in the 1950s than now. The porch lamp was on, and a glimmer of inviting light shone behind several front windows. Smoke drifted from the chimney in lazy gray spirals, giving the setting an air of pastoral tranquility that was uniquely American. But Chapman knew that that outward normality sheltered something far different inside.

The face of his watch glowed milky-white as he checked the time. "Three minutes, mark," he said quietly.

Four black-clad shadows flitted soundlessly past a corner of the house and vanished again, their pale hands and faces darkened with sooty stripes of camouflage paint.

"Everyone knows the drill," he said into the headset, watching anxiously for more telltale movement as the 12 two-man teams settled into their assigned positions around the house. "The extraterrestrials' armaments and mental abilities are unknowns, so no unnecessary risks. Sharpshooters are to remain with your team partners at all times, but remember, there are at least three civilian hostages in there." He fell silent for a moment. "I don't want any mistakes. We're here to do a job and do it well. The primary mission of this team is to capture and contain the EBEs, not exterminate them."

One by one his men signaled that they had moved into position. He checked his watch again and began counting down the seconds. "Two minutes."

Chapman snugged heavy night-vision goggles down on his face and switched to infrared, turning the nighttime landscape a queer color of grayish green. The thermal signatures of a dozen men appeared, hunched blotches of red and yellow hidden from the view of ordinary eyes by scrubby bushes and the limbs of trees.

"Sixty seconds." Chapman tensed and shifted, as did several of the colored splotches visible through the goggles.

A crackle of static shot through his headset and the sound of Burkett's voice filled his ear. "Seeker, this is Dodger One, come in!" His aide's tone was half-muffled, half-shrill with panic. "Come in, Seeker!"

Instinctively, Chapman swung the goggles to his left and glanced toward a sharp bend in the deserted asphalt road. A quarter mile beyond the curve, Burkett and a backup team had been stationed at a makeshift roadblock, diverting any northbound traffic for the duration of the capture and containment. He thumbed his mike switch. "Dodger, this is Seeker. What the hell's going on down there?"

"We've got problems, Seeker!" Burkett shouted. "The county sheriff and some heavily armed locals have run the barricade! I'm sorry, sir, there were just too many of them."

Chapman cursed under his breath and glanced at his watch: 30 seconds. "Hold your positions!" he shouted to the containment teams through the headset. "I repeat, hold your positions." Through the goggles he could see the first yellow shimmers of light and heat rounding the curve. "We have civilian intruders inside the outer perimeter." He was going to skin Burkett alive.

Two patrol cars emblazoned with the crest of the Jackson County Sheriff's Department sped side by side around the curve, emergency lights spinning in quick flashes of urgent blue against a background of darkness. A steady convoy of vehicles followed, their headlights crisscrossing the wooded landscape in a sharp angled maze of white.

First one sheriff's car, then another roared past Chapman into the crescent-shaped driveway, squealing to jerky stops directly in front of Laura Malek's house. A motley collection of pickups and cars rolled into view, and the front portion of the convoy began braking along the shoulder of the road. Several dozen people spilled from the vehicles' interiors. Flashlights bobbed and weaved in the darkness, combining with the glare of headlights to illuminate the excited knot of people beginning to mill along the side of the road. The barrel of a shotgun glinted metallically in the shifting light.

Chapman muttered another oath. There was a steady procession of cars still streaming around the curve, at least 30 or so, judging by the headlamps. Any chance they'd had of taking the EBEs by surprise had long since vanished. "Stay undercover and hold your positions until further orders," he told his men.

He climbed from his hiding place inside the ditch, pushed the heavy goggles up on his forehead and stared mutely at the scene unfolding around him. For the moment, the crowd of locals seemed content to stand and watch from behind a white rail fence running down the property line, but their numbers were growing by the second. Chapman spotted several children among the sea of humanity, chasing each other around a pickup truck and shrieking in delight.

The sheriff and four of his deputies had climbed from their cars and were standing in the driveway with their backs to him, clumped in a hesitant little knot less than 50 feet from the front door of the house. In the blue glow of the rotating lights, they presented a tempting target. Chapman fingered the holster strapped to his waist. He was tempted himself.

He crouched and zigzagged toward the driveway, coming to a silent stop a few feet behind them. "Just what in the hell do you people think you're doing?" Chapman hissed through clenched teeth.

Startled, the sheriff and his deputies wheeled around, eyeing the speaker with suspicion and a trace of fear. Bob Rankin gestured to his men to quit fumbling at their gunbelts, and met the black-clad man's cold stare with one of his own. He saw that the stranger was dressed in some type of black military garb from head to toe, with night-vision goggles perched on his forehead.

"Took the words right out of my mouth, mister," Sheriff Rankin said. There'd been rumors flying around for over a week about government people sneaking all over the county. Those rumors didn't seem so silly anymore. "Now suppose you just tell *me* what the hell is going on down here." He waved a hand toward the crowd shuffling around the road. "I've got a bunch of hysterical people on my hands shouting about aliens from Mars and FBI men having a shootout in a local bar."

"You are interfering with an official government operation, Sheriff." Chapman's mind raced over the possibilities. All of his men were accounted for, so who had gone into a bar identifying themselves as FBI? His mouth thinned. General Moss must have turned his goon squad loose as soon as he was given the information on Laura Malek, and they had somehow found her first and created this mess.

"Sheriff," Chapman said slowly, "you, your deputies, and that mob over there have exactly sixty seconds to get out of here." He glanced toward the house. It was too quiet. Even with all the commotion, there'd been no sign of activity inside. "One minute, Sheriff."

Rankin bristled. "Or what? You gonna call Washington and gripe about some hick sheriff interfering with your 'official government operation'?" He flashed his teeth in his best country-boy smile. "I got news for you, Mr. Whoever You Are. Like I told that skinny little jerk down at your roadblock, I already called Washington, and the FBI said they don't know doodley-squat about you or your so-called operation. In case you didn't know, impersonating a government official is a federal crime."

Chapman suppressed a groan. Murphy's Law in action. The Washington Bureau was supposed to have transferred any requests for information directly to National Security. "Your minute is up, Sheriff. Get going."

Rankin's smile turned deadly, and he stabbed a finger toward a bank of azaleas that were concealing several more black-clad men. "I'm not going anywhere until I get some answers. So why don't you just tell this old hick what you and all those fellas hiding over there in the bushes are up to? For all I know you might be some kind of Middle Eastern terrorist outfit."

"Don't be ridiculous!" Chapman felt a rush of heat in his face.

"Am I?" The smile faded, and Rankin's mouth set in a hard, calculating line. "I've got half-a-dozen charges I could run you in on right now. So start talking. Tell me why you people have been pretending to be FBI, and what all this crazy talk of aliens and rayguns is all about. I've got a bunch of witnesses from the Cimarron Club who claim your boys were shooting at the lady who lives here and some big guy with a raygun, and that there's a giant raccoon or something holed up in this house."

He poked an accusing finger in Chapman's dark face. "When I got to the Cimarron, the shooters had already taken off, but there was some blood on the floor, and the inside of the place had been shot to hell and back. Now, I don't take very kindly to strangers taking potshots at the good people of this county. So you start explaining and I'll listen."

Chapman rubbed the bridge of his nose and watched the house as he thought. What now? The Sheriff's Southern good-ol'-boy routine didn't fool him. Rankin was sharp and determined, too sharp for his own good. And if the aliens really were inside, he couldn't very well take them down with the sheriff and a crowd of spectators watching. He reached inside a zippered pocket and handed his military ID to Rankin.

Jan Zimlich

Rankin shined a flashlight on the identification. "That's the spirit . . . Colonel Chapman, if that's who you really are." What was an Air Force Intelligence officer doing here? "A little cooperation between professionals never hurt anybody."

Chapman heaved a resigned sigh. "Look, Sheriff. We're dealing with a possible hostage situation here, one that might have severe ramifications on this country's national security." He gestured toward the crowd lining the road. Where had they all come from? Their numbers had swelled to at least a hundred now, and more headlights were visible in both directions. He watched as several laughing men hoisted lawn chairs from the bed of a pickup and set up ringside seats along the shoulder of the road. "I don't know why you brought all of these people along with you, but you've got to get them out of the area. I can't guarantee their safety."

Rankin removed his hat and smoothed his ruffled pompadour as he studied the shifting mass of humanity. Although he still saw a few rifles and shotguns held by itchy-looking men, as more and more people arrived, the crowd's somber watchfulness had given way to a festive air. Kali Oka Road had become an event. "I can tell you've never lived in a small town before, Colonel. I didn't bring those people with me. They got wind of something going on down here and just naturally piled in their cars and followed. It's a national pastime down in these parts. I couldn't blast them out of here with a howitzer now."

Chapman buried his face in his palms. Any minute now he would wake up and realize it was all just some hideous dream.

"Besides," Rankin continued, "other than a few old boys liquored up on beer and carrying shotguns, there doesn't seem to be anything around here that even remotely looks dangerous. Looks to me like the Maleks aren't even home. And I sure haven't seen any little green men sneaking around hereabouts . . . just a bunch of big ones dressed in black." He fiddled with the brim of his hat, then scrunched it back onto his head. "All this crazy alien talk will die down in a little while and everybody will head on home, so why don't you and your boys just sit tight for a bit and wait them out?"

The anger and frustration Chapman had carefully held in check boiled across his face. "You don't seem to understand what's going on here, Sheriff. I don't know who or what is in that house, but it's my job to go in there and find out. I've got orders, and cooling my heels while a bunch of sightseers stand around and gawk isn't part of them. So you either get those morons out of here, or I'll do it at the point of a gun!"

"Hey, Sheriff!" someone in the crowd yelled. "When we going to see us some of Carrie Cooner's aliens? Tell 'um to come out and have a few beers!" A spurt of laughter followed the anonymous taunt; then several other voices took up the demand.

"That's it." There was a distinct hardening of Rankin's eyes as he dropped all pretense of Southern affability. "I've had more than enough of this crap for one night." He turned his back on Chapman and quick-stepped toward the door.

Chapman stared after him in disbelief. "What in God's name do you think you're doing?"

Jan Zimlich

"What you should have done an hour ago," Rankin tossed over his shoulder. "I'm going to put an end to this nonsense once and for all." As Chapman shouted frantically into his headset, Sheriff Rankin scrunched his hat down tighter, then climbed a single step to the concrete landing and pushed the doorbell.

A few seconds later the door squeaked open and Laura Malek peered out a tiny crack. "Yes?" She didn't open the screen.

Rankin took a startled step backwards. He hadn't really expected anybody to answer the door. "Um . . . Miz Malek?"

Laura's eyes were wide and luminous in the glare of the porchlight. She wet her lips nervously. "What do you want, Sheriff?"

He shifted his weight from foot to foot, suddenly uneasy. The blue lights were still flashing on his patrol car, and the crowd was growing noisier by the second. The woman wasn't deaf or blind, so why hadn't she come outside to see what was going on in her front yard? "Sorry to bother you at this hour, but we've got a little situation out here that I think you can settle for me."

"Oh? What kind of situation?" Laura's lips betrayed her rising fear with an apprehensive quiver.

"Well." Rankin's cool gaze passed over her mouth and face, noting the nervous tremor. "It seems there's some sort of wild rumor going around that you were in the Cimarron Club a while ago and there was some, ah . . . trouble of some kind, and that a stranger staying here at your house might be involved. I'm sure this is all just a big misunderstanding, so if you'll just let me and a couple of my boys check around the inside of your house for a minute, we can clear·all this right up and get out of your hair."

Laura stared at him for long seconds, then sent a quick, furtive glance over her shoulder. "I'm sorry," she said, and shook her head slowly. "I can't let you do that."

"Can I ask why not?" Rankin felt a clammy tingle along the nape of his neck. His sixth sense, which had saved his bacon more than once, was screaming that there was someone hiding behind the door.

"Let's just say it would be better if you didn't."

"Better for who?" Rankin backed carefully to the edge of the landing. His eyes never wavered from the doorway.

"For everybody." Over Rankin's shoulder, Laura caught a glimpse of someone familiar crouched behind the trunk of a sheriff's car. The man from the Piggly Wiggly was here, too.

"You know I'm not going to be able to do that, Miz Malek," Rankin said. His hand closed around the butt of his pistol. "All those military boys out in your yard won't be able to either."

Terror mounted in her eyes and voice. "Just leave us alone for a little while longer, Sheriff. I promise you nothing will happen to me or my family as long as you stay out of it."

The tingle on his neck sped down his spine. "Who's in there with you, Miz Malek?" He slipped the pistol from its holster. "Are you being held hostage?"

"Please don't push this, Sheriff." Her voice was frantic now, pleading. "All they want to do is leave. Just let them go and nobody will get hurt."

The crack in the door suddenly widened and a tall, long-haired blond appeared behind Laura Malek, towering over the top of her head by a full foot or so. Rankin glanced up and found himself staring through the screen door into a ghostly face inhabited by the most piercing, intense eyes he'd ever seen. His feet froze to the concrete as the man made several jerking motions with the wide metal barrel of a massive gun.

"Okay," Rankin said quietly. "I get the message." He holstered his gun and lifted his hands to waist level. "Loud and clear." He gave Laura Malek one last look. "If they don't really want anyone hurt, tell them they have to come out of there quick with their hands above their heads. It's the only way."

After an abrupt about-face, Rankin fled to safety behind his patrol car and crouched low on the blacktop drive. Chapman and his deputies were waiting for him.

"That was a stupid stunt," Chapman grated, glaring in the darkness. "You going to get those people out of here now?"

Rankin gestured to his deputies, who split into pairs and sprinted toward the road. "Well, at least you know for sure there really is someone inside the house," he said. "Weird-looking fellow with a big-ass gun . . . as big as one of those shoulder-held grenade launchers, but different, more streamlined." He took off his hat and scratched at his graying hair. "I've seen a lot of guns in my time, but I've never seen anything like that before."

Chapman snorted. "I'm not surprised." Rankin

still didn't get it. "You see anyone besides the blond man?"

"Nope, just him and the Malek woman. How many do you think are in there?"

"Two probably, plus the Malek family. That makes five."

Behind them, the crowd of locals grew noisier and more belligerent as the deputies moved through the sea of people, waving flashlights and ordering them to disperse. A scattered few broke away from the main group and headed for their cars, but the vast majority greeted the news with angry shouts and refused to budge.

Kali Oka Road's first ever traffic jam ensued when a small line of cars pulled onto the narrow strip of asphalt, only to become entangled in head-on gridlock as they met other cars that were still arriving. Horns blared, and a bemused Rankin watched as the entire cheerleading squad from East Central High poured out of a late-arriving car and gathered in a tight, practiced line along the side of the road.

"Oh, great," Rankin muttered. Word of strange doings out on Kali Oka Road had spread a lot faster than he'd imagined. "The basketball game must be over. Every pimple-faced teenager in the county'll be out here before long."

Pom-poms shook in a flurry of maroon and gold as the cheerleaders began their impromptu performance, leading the crowd in a series of frenzied chants.

Through the blare of car horns and shouts of "Go, Go, UFO!" Rankin heard several angry cat-calls directed at him and his deputies, berating them for trying to break up the biggest party that Escatawpa had ever had.

"I think we got us a problem," he said to Chapman.

Chapman slid down to a sitting position on the hard blacktop and watched the bedlam with a stunned expression. Cheerleaders. "I don't believe this." People in the forefront of the crowd had begun passing around buckets of fried chicken and tossing beer cans to waiting hands from an endless stream of ice chests. "This can't be happening."

Chapter Fifteen

"What are you going to do?" It was the second time Laura had asked Aayshen that same question, and the second time she'd received no reply. "They're not going to let you just walk out of here." She leaned forward on the brick hearth-seat and swung her head to watch him as he paced across the carpet, his heavy boots leaving deep indentations in the thick beige pile. Panic tried to claw its way up her chest and throat. His pale eyes were flat and cold, and his fingers were continuously clenching and unclenching around the stock of his weapon.

Her worried gaze angled toward the floor. Bryan was curled on the carpet near her feet, pushing restlessly at the afghan she'd tossed over him as he slept. Instinct drew her hand downward to smooth her son's tousled bangs. Across the room, Garner was sitting in his chair as though this were just an ordinary night. But tonight he had the television muted, and there was a stiff watchfulness about his aged face and body that she'd never seen before. He was scared, too.

"Half the county is outside that door, Aayshen," Laura said as he moved past her again. "If you try to shoot your way out people are going to die."

Aayshen paused near the door and adjusted the chest plate on his recon suit. The suit itself was no longer functioning, but the hardened metal would serve as protection from projectile fire. Unfortunately, Laura and her family had no such protection. He clicked the safety off on his pulse rifle. "I have no wish to make war, Laura." The flat timbre of his voice carried a sharp edge of resolve that belied his words. "But if your people attack, we will fight back. It is their choice to die."

"Oh, I see." There was anger in her tone, as well as frustration. "So what will you do? Shoot them all?"

"If I must." He started pacing again, moving past the back windows where Drallondryn was stationed, then back toward the door. "I will not allow them to harm you again . . . or make us prisoners."

Her dark eyes burned holes in him. "The price of your protection is too high, Aayshen. I won't pay it, not if it means those people out there will die."

Drallondryn half-turned from the window, his attention divided between their bitter words and the shadowy darkness outside. "The ship will be here within two hours, Commander," he said evenly. "If we can hold the house until then per-haps—"

"Perhaps what?" Aayshen said darkly. "As Laura said, they will not allow us to just leave this place." His pale brows drew together in a frustrated frown. There would be a confrontation, one he would easily win; the only question was how many lives would be lost in the process. "When the shut-tle arrives, they will attempt to take the ship, as well as us."

As the noise outside built to a frenzied, shouting crescendo, dread etched new lines around Aaysh-en's mouth and eyes. If Laura and her family were caught in the crossfire of a firefight, he would re-taliate, and the ground would run red with human blood.

Chapman's mouth thinned to a hard line as he peered at the house over the trunk of Rankin's car. Nothing had changed. An inviting haze of yellow light still shone dimly behind drawn curtains and shades, but there was no sign of movement or ac-tivity inside, nothing that seemed even remotely amiss. His brows drew together in a worried line. What was going on in there? What were they plan-ning?

He pulled his head down and sank to the ground beside the tire well, then turned his attention to the noisy mob gathered along the road. Contrary to Rankin's assertion that the crowd would just drift away, their numbers seemed to have actually swelled in size, at least three or four hundred, he guessed. Although there was still an occasional chant of "Go, Go, UFO!" for the most part, the gawkers had settled down to party. Both country

285

and rock music were blaring from a dozen competing car radios, and combined with the laughter, shouts and drone of excited conversation, the profusion of sound was almost deafening. Several teenagers were dancing to an unknown beat atop the roof of a car, while others clapped and cheered them on. No one even seemed interested in the house anymore. They were too busy having a good time.

To Chapman, Kali Oka Road looked and sounded like some out-of-control block party. Even with the dozen or so reinforcements the sheriff had called in to handle crowd control, things were beginning to get out of hand. Time was running out, and short of calling in an airstrike, there didn't seem to be any way to end the spontaneous celebration.

Chapman activated the mike on his headset. They couldn't wait any longer. His team was here to do a job that was vital to United States interests, and they were going to do it, even if they had to take the house and the EBEs while an audience watched. "Sharpshooter teams six and twelve," he whispered into the mike, "advance to within twenty yards of the rear of the house and hold. All other teams prepare to move in on my command."

Sheriff Rankin ran across the yard in a half-crouch and slipped to the ground beside Chapman, just in time to hear the Air Force officer whispering orders into his headset. He stared at Chapman in disbelief. They were getting ready to storm the house. Anger cut deep lines across Rankin's forehead. There were hundreds of civilians lining the road, and hostages in the house. "You crazy son of a bitch . . . you're gonna try and take the house, aren't you?"

Chapman glared at him in the darkness. "Back off, Sheriff. This doesn't concern you."

"Like hell it don't! This is my jurisdiction! Besides the woman, there's an old man and a little boy inside that house! What if one of them gets hit?"

Dark shapes flitted down the sides of the house, and static shot through Chapman's ear as his men began keying their mikes to signal they were in position. Ignoring the sheriff, Chapman held his breath and counted off the final seconds in his head. "Go! Go! Go!"

Rankin grabbed the top of Chapman's flak vest and squeezed. "I swear to you, mister, if anybody gets hurt, I'm going to take it out of your hide!"

There was a sudden, muffled whump from the back window, followed by the crystalline tinkle of exploding glass. Laura's heart thudded wildly against her rib cage. Too stunned to react, she stared wordlessly at Aayshen as a second window exploded in a hailstorm of glass. Several small dark objects flew across the room and began spewing thick clouds of gray smoke as they rolled to a stop.

Aayshen moved with blinding speed, firing at the tear-gas grenades with pinpoint accuracy. Three daggers of blue-green light stabbed into the carpet and the cylinders shimmered out of existence.

"God Almighty!" Garner stared in shock at the haze of smoke drifting over the scorched carpet. His jaw sagged open. The alien had moved and fired so fast his motions were just a blur, faster than was humanly possible.

Small chips of brick and mortar suddenly erupted from the fireplace and leaped past Laura's face, then something long and dartlike dug into the carpet inches from Bryan's head.

"Bryan!" Laura screamed, and threw herself atop him.

Aayshen dove toward the fireplace, slung Laura face-first to the floor and rolled atop her and the stirring child, covering their bodies with his own. Several more projectiles impacted on his back, pinging harmlessly off the shell of hardened armor.

"Dae Nkke!" Aayshen yelled to the shocked Kri, ordering him to protect Garner and defend the house any way he could. *"Tovrammas!"* The crying child squirmed beneath him, struggling to break free. Aayshen pinned him with an arm.

Drallondryn dragged the old man from the recliner chair and fell on top of him as gently as he could. The sound of breaking glass could be heard from every room. One of the knifelike things buried itself in the arm of Garner's chair. "Commander! What should I do?"

"Stay down!" Cursing in low Savanian, Aayshen rose up on his elbows and fired blindly through the back windows. A thin shaft of blue heat stabbed through the shattered glass and burned across the darkness in a horizontal line. There was a scream outside, low and hoarse with pain. Footsteps thudded away from the house.

Aayshen's jaw went rigid. It was time the foolish humans learned what sort of destruction his weapons were capable of wreaking. He upended

288

a heavy wing chair and shoved Laura and Bryan between the chair and the fireplace, then scrambled on his hands and knees to the front door and fired through the wood.

A solid stream of light lanced outward from the bottom of the front door, sizzled and smoked across the roof of Rankin's patrol car and angled upwards into the night sky. The top of a huge pine tree cracked and groaned, then crashed to the ground behind them, guttering flames and smoke rising from the scorched tree trunk. Panicked screams from the crowd and a scattering of applause accompanied the light show.

"God Almighty!" Rankin blinked away the afterglow behind his eyelids and stared at the roof of his car in amazement. A six-inch section of beige metal had been turned into a channel of smoldering gray slag.

Chapman tackled the stunned sheriff, then dove to the blacktop face-first and belly-crawled for cover behind the rear bumper. "Keep your fool head down, Sheriff! You want to get your face burned off?" He lifted his gaze upwards, his mind tracing over the beam's awkward trajectory. It was obviously a warning shot, otherwise they would both be very dead. Rankin's car had just happened to be sitting in the beam's angle of ascent.

Bob Rankin rolled onto his back and wiped grit from a brush burn on his cheek. "What in the hell was that?"

"That, Sheriff, is why I wanted those civilians out of here."

"I've never seen anything like it before! It looked like a laser or something!"

"Or something." Chapman smiled grimly in the

darkness. "And I *know* you've never seen anything like it before."

Despite the chill, Rankin's forehead broke out in a clammy sweat. "Oh, my God." His arms and hands started trembling.

"I see you're finally beginning to get the picture, Sheriff."

Chapman's headset crackled to life, and a frantic voice filled his ear. His teams positioned around the rear of the house were in disarray. For some reason neither the tear gas nor the tranquilizer darts had worked, and every time his men got close to the rear windows, someone inside opened fire with a laser. Only one casualty, thankfully. One man had had several of his fingers burned off and was being attended by a medic.

"Pull back," he ordered reluctantly. "Pull back." A frontal assault obviously wasn't the answer. He needed time to think and regroup.

Numb with shock, Laura stared in disbelief at the carnage that had once been her den. Aayshen had upended most of the furniture, shoving it against doors and shattered windows to block the den off from the rest of the house. A light pall of smoke still hung in the air, but the smoke itself had been rendered harmless by the chill night air creeping through the broken windows. Glass littered the floor, and dozens of needlelike darts were sticking willy-nilly out of the carpet and upholstery. Tranquilizer darts, she surmised. At least she hoped that was what they were.

Beside her, Garner pulled a dart from the carpet and studied the sharp tip. The thin cylinder was filled with amber fluid.

"Careful, Grampa. There's no telling what's in it."

Garner snorted and propped his back against his overturned recliner. "Probably something strong enough to drop an elephant in its tracks." He tossed the dart into the fireplace. "At least they weren't trying to kill us."

"That's comforting." Laura rocked back and forth, a still-whimpering Bryan cradled against her chest. Oddly, the idea that the soldiers had only been shooting darts did bring her a small measure of comfort. A sudden shiver of fear chilled the back of her neck. The darts could have been bullets just as easily. Next time they probably would be.

Garner stared at Aayshen in mute wonder, stunned by the changes wrought in him by the attack. The tall, quiet alien was prowling the confines of the den with the fluid grace of a caged panther, his body and senses attuned to the slightest sound or movement. His reality seemed to have narrowed to this single moment in time, as though nothing else mattered except the soldiers outside and the coming battle. This was the darker side of Aayshen that Drallondryn had tried to warn him about, the instinctive warrior immune to the vagaries of emotion. The perfect soldier.

Garner glanced at Laura, who was watching Aayshen's movements with pain-filled eyes. "Did you see him earlier?" Garner said quietly. "He moved so fast it didn't look real . . . like a movie in fast forward."

"I saw," Laura answered in a dead voice. She watched as Drallondryn began moving around the room, collecting the darts and throwing them into the fireplace.

Bryan curled himself tighter against her chest. "I'm scared, Mommy." A stream of tears rolled down his face.

"Shhh." She pulled him closer. "It's going to be all right, Bryan. I promise."

Some way, somehow, she had to put a stop to this, end it before anyone else was hurt. She'd heard a scream outside the first time Aayshen fired through the windows, an anguished, anonymous sound that was still echoing through her mind. She had to end it before everyone outside was killed.

A quiet, yet desperate look of resolve settled over her features like a mask of stone. "Hold Bryan, Grampa." She handed the child into Garner's waiting arms and climbed to her feet.

"Where are you going?" Garner said, alarmed by the single-minded look on his granddaughter's face.

She scooped up one of the bath towels Aayshen had used on her arm and walked toward the front door, her steps firm and determined. "I'm going outside to talk to them."

Aayshen beat her there and blocked the door with his body. Their eyes met for an interminable second, hers dark and filled with purpose, his opaque and unreadable. In her eyes he saw the bitter truth. They were aliens to each other once again, strangers with no common ground. "I cannot allow you to leave here," he told her softly. The pulse gun lay hard and heavy in his hands.

She tried to duck under his arm to no avail. "Move out of the way, Aayshen. You've shed enough blood for one night. I'm going out there to talk to them, and you're not going to stop me."

He sucked in a breath to steady himself, then reached out with his mind to rekindle the broken threads of what they had shared. The link between them was still intact, but he found no solace there, only a dark, empty sadness for what they had lost, and burning contempt for what he was. He drew back from the emotional onslaught, both mentally and physically. "Don't judge me by human standards, Laura," he said raggedly. "I cannot change what I am."

Anger flared hot and sharp in her eyes. "Yes, you could, if you wanted to. You're not a machine programmed to kill."

A sad, melancholy smile lifted the corners of his mouth. In many ways he was a machine, one designed and bred by his own race to deal with the harsh unpleasantries of life. He and the others like him were the brutal alter egos of his people, the dark, ugly side condemned to do their bidding, while the rest of the populace were free to live out their days on a safe, tranquil world created by the lifeblood of others.

"End it, Aayshen," she told him desperately. "End it now before anyone else is hurt. All I ask is that you try."

Uncertainty such as he'd never known boiled through Aayshen's mind. Because of the genetic material contained within his cells, he had been condemned to follow a rigid set of rules that dictated his every action in a given situation, to serve and obey without question. But why was that? His uncertainty turned to resentment. Why should he be compelled to do the bidding of faceless Savan-

293

ians light years away, driven by instinct to inflict injury or death on the hapless humans sent to protect their little planet from alien invaders?

He was wavering. Laura could see it in his eyes, in the turmoil etched across his rigid face. She clutched desperately at his armor-clad arm. "You don't have to fight them, Aayshen," she whispered. "You can be anything you want to be, do anything you want to do. Let me walk out that door and try to find a way out of this for all of us." Her fingers tightened on his arm. "Please. If you can't do it for yourself, then do it for me."

His gaze met hers for a timeless moment, and he realized then that he would try simply because she asked it of him. The pulse gun trembled in his hands. Then his grip loosened abruptly and he lowered the weapon to the floor. Was it treason to desire freedom from the conditioning and training that governed every aspect of his life? Unnatural to follow his heart instead of a rule? He stepped away from the door. "Go. If they wish to talk, I will listen."

Laura let out a short sigh of relief, then reached up and touched his cheek. Wordlessly, she opened the scarred door a few inches and stuck a hand through the crevice. "Don't shoot!" she yelled. "I'm coming out to talk!" She flapped the white cotton towel back and forth inside the narrow gap between the door and screen, a flag of truce or surrender. She wasn't sure which.

A thin, excited cheer echoed toward her from Kali Oka Road, rising and falling across the darkened landscape in response to her shouts. Laura stared in amazement. There were hundreds of people lining the road in front of her house.

She pulled in a nervous breath to steel herself, then shook the bloodstained towel again. "I'm coming outside now!" The crowd fell into an expectant silence.

The porch light threw murky shadows across her face as she pushed the screen door open and stepped outside. She paused uncertainly on the steps, the towel hanging in front of her like a threadbare, rectangular shield. Less than 50 feet away, a cluster of people were hunched behind a sheriff's car, but she couldn't make out individual faces. "Sheriff Rankin?" Laura yelled. "Are you out there? We need to talk!"

Chapman grabbed Rankin by the shoulder to keep him from rising. "This is my ball game," he whispered furiously. "You hear me, Sheriff? If anybody talks to her it's going to be me."

"What for?" Rankin shook off the restraining arm and glared. "So you can get close enough to blow them all to kingdom come?" He grabbed his car's rearview mirror to help lift himself from the pavement, but went stock-still when he saw Chapman reach for his side arm.

Chapman toyed with the trigger and gave Rankin a nasty smile. "We're not going to have a turf war over this, Sheriff. Is that clear?"

For a split-second, Rankin considered calling his bluff. His fingers crept toward his holster. Then he saw the truth in Chapman's eyes, and carefully relaxed the muscles in his hand. This was a man who never bluffed. "Okay, have it your way. Just answer me one question, Colonel. Why should that woman trust you about anything? After you endangered her boy's life with that stunt you pulled a few minutes ago, you'll be lucky if she doesn't shoot you herself."

"Trust has nothing to do with it." Chapman eased his side arm back into the holster and climbed to his feet in one fluid movement. "She'll talk to me because she doesn't have any other choice." He walked slowly around the front of the car to the brick pathway, cast a wary glance at the house as the front door snicked shut, then ground to a halt midway to the porch. "Mrs. Malek?"

Laura nodded, and stopped a few feet shy of where he was standing. Her gaze roved over him suspiciously. The last time she'd seen him close-up he'd been sprawled across a checkout counter in the Piggly Wiggly. This time he wasn't dressed in a fancy suit. He was wearing some sort of black combat outfit, and there was a gunbelt strapped to his waist. She could detect no remorse or sympathy for her situation in his cold features, only a deadly determination that sent a chill spiraling down her spine. "I asked to speak to Sheriff Rankin, not you," she said in a hoarse voice. "Where is he?"

He shook his head slowly. "Sorry, ma'am. I can't do that. My authority supersedes his. You talk to me here, right now, or you can just turn around and walk back in the house . . . and face the consequences. What happened a while ago was a cakewalk compared to what will happen next."

A flash of anger burned in her eyes. Ever since she'd encountered this man in the grocery store the situation had gone from bad to worse. Now he was threatening her, and she had no doubt that he was dead-serious. She angled her gaze to the right and picked out the vague shapes of several armed men hiding in the shrubs near the front of the house. "Who *are* you people?"

His body stiffened slightly. "Special Operations Team, Air Force Intelligence."

"And you?"

"Colonel Lem Chapman." He gave her a curt, self-confident smile. "So if you've got something to say, you better say it to me. I'm the only one authorized to negotiate with the extraterrestrials."

"Extraterrestrials?" She manufactured a look of childlike innocence. "What are you talking about?"

His smile faded, and his eyes turned hard and brittle. "Cut the crap, lady. I've been tracking them for over a week now, ever since an Air Force pilot fired on their craft over the Gulf. I've seen the blond one before, remember? And I know what he's capable of doing. I also know what they are, and I know they're inside your house." He took a step closer, his gaze boring into her face. "Let me talk to them through you . . . before this situation gets completely out of hand."

Their eyes locked for a fraction of a second; then Laura's left shoulder rose and fell in a resigned half-shrug. This was what she wanted, wasn't it? "Well, then, Colonel, I guess you better come inside."

Chapman looked startled. "Inside?"

Under different circumstances, Laura might have laughed. His stunned expression was almost comical. "Of course you have to come inside. I'm not 'authorized' to negotiate on their behalf, Colonel. You want to talk to them, you do it face-to-face." She turned toward the house, then glanced back over her shoulder. He still hadn't moved. "Are you coming?"

His feet seemed to have frozen to the brick. He'd trained for this moment for over a decade, fantasized about what it would be like to be face-to-face with a true extraterrestrial, actually have a conversation with an EBE. But now, now that the opportunity had finally presented itself, he felt strangely removed from reality, as if this were all happening to someone else.

He waved a hand to belay her. "Just a moment, Mrs. Malek. I'll need a couple of minutes to inform my men and suit up."

A suspicious frown slanted across her features. "What do you mean, 'suit up'?"

"Get suited in protective gear. The EBEs—extraterrestrials—may be contaminated in some way. They may represent a serious biological hazard to humans."

Laura did laugh this time, although to her the laugh sounded like the hysterical cackle of an insane woman. What he suggested was ludicrous. "A biological hazard? They've been in my house for over a week and none of us have come down with any alien plague." She held up her hands and turned them palm up for examination. "See? No purple spots here, Colonel."

To her surprise, he took a wary step forward and began a cautious examination of her hands, although he was careful not to touch her. Laura snatched her hands away angrily. He was acting like she had suddenly thrust two cobras into his face. "Come on, Colonel. You've been watching too many movies. Don't you think I'd know by now if there was anything wrong with them?"

"Not necessarily." He spoke briefly into his headset, ordering his men to stay alert when he went inside. A few seconds later two men rushed out of the darkness carrying a large black case which contained the protective gear, then proceeded to help Chapman clothe himself in the bulky white anticontamination suit. "It's team protocol to wear protective gear," he explained to her, "when dealing with an unknown bio-hazard."

Laura shook her head in disbelief at his elaborate precautions. "Trust me," she said quietly, "if there was anything wrong with him, I would be the one to know."

As his men pulled the visored hood over his head, Chapman heard her muttered comment and frowned. What did that mean? The soldiers grabbed the empty case and ran back into the darkness. Chapman switched on his air supply and activated the suit's outside mike. "I'm ready."

"It's about time," Laura mumbled, then walked toward the porch. Chapman shambled after her in the ponderous suit.

Laura pushed what was left of her front door open and paused, almost blinded by the sudden light. "Aayshen?" She didn't need to see him to know that he was near. She could feel his presence. "It's all right. One of them is coming in to talk."

As he stepped across the threshold, Chapman forced himself to breathe at a more normal rate. If he started hyperventilating while he was wearing the suit, he'd fog up the visor and wouldn't be able to see. He followed Laura Malek into the room, his nervous gaze darting back and forth behind the transparent face shield. The den was in disarray, with broken glass and overturned furniture scattered everywhere. The old man, Garner

Haines, was sitting on the floor near the fireplace. Beside him, a solemn-eyed boy of about five or six was staring at Chapman apprehensively, as though the colonel himself were an alien who had just dropped out of the sky. The boy was frightened by the anticontamination suit, he surmised.

The front door slammed shut behind him. Chapman flinched and wheeled around, his lungs heaving in and out at an accelerated rhythm again. The tall blond alien had been standing behind the door all along, and was now staring down at him with a curious, almost amused expression.

Chapman swallowed hard, a sound that was amplified several times through the suit's microphone. The long-awaited moment had finally come, and now that it was here he couldn't remember what he had been trained to say. "I . . ." Those strange blue eyes . . . there were no whites in them! No sclera at all! What did it mean? Did his eyes refract light differently than a human's? Could he see in different spectrums? Infrared? Ultraviolet? Chapman stared at the alien in mute wonder. There was so much he wanted to know. So many questions he wanted answered.

A slight sound behind him caused Chapman to swing his head in the direction of the noise. "Oh, my God," he whispered to himself as a dark head appeared from behind the upended sofa, followed by a long, thin body clad in metallic armor. Its eyes were a brilliant yellow and its hands and face were covered with a sleek coat of heavy black fur. Although the creature was vaguely human in size and shape, it had upright, feline ears, as well as an animal-like alertness about its pointed features. Chapman stared incredulously. It did sort of resemble a big black raccoon, or a garish cat, or both.

A small, satisfied smile tipped the corners of Laura's lips. She was enjoying Chapman's astonished expression. Immensely. The cold self-confidence he'd displayed outside had been replaced by a slack-jawed, incredulous stare. "I think you can close your mouth now, Colonel."

Chapman's mouth snapped shut, but his rapt gaze remained fastened on the catlike alien. The more he stared, the less human it looked. What sort of world could have produced such a creature?

"Why don't you sit down, Colonel," Laura offered. When he failed to respond, she grabbed the Air Force officer by the elbow and guided him toward a chair.

"Huh?" Chapman forced himself to concentrate. "Right, maybe I better." He sank into the wing chair gingerly. His knees and ankles didn't seem to want to support him.

Aayshen pushed away from the door frame and followed, giving the human suspicious glances as he perched himself atop the overturned sofa. He suppressed an amused smile as his gaze slid over the human's ridiculous white attire. The poorly designed suit would do little to protect its wearer.

Chapman's throat constricted, and his forehead broke out in a cold sweat. His eyes were drawn back to the tall, furred alien. A thousand questions he wanted to ask churned through his thoughts, but his tongue froze and refused to phrase a single one. About the only thing he could muster from his torpid brain was a vacant, wondering stare. They were extraterrestrials, living, thinking beings from a distant, unknown world that he could only give shape to in fanciful imaginings or half-formed dreams.

"I . . . am . . . Colonel Lemanuel Chapman," he said in an overloud voice, "of the United . . . States . . . Air Force." He turned to Laura suddenly. "Can either of them understand what I'm saying?"

Laura rolled her eyes. "They can understand just about anything said to them." He was treating Aayshen and Drallondryn like they were some sort of alien half-wits. "Just talk normally, Colonel. They have a better grasp of English than most people I know."

"Okay." Chapman took a deep breath and gestured toward the tall blond. "Is that one in charge?"

"Yes."

"Does he have a name?"

"Of course he does," Laura snapped. "He's not a chair leg. His name is Aayshen Rahs. That's two words in case you couldn't figure that out."

"All right!" Chapman frowned, and clicked on a small recorder attached to the front of his suit. The alien was just sitting there, staring at him with those pale, unearthly eyes, eyes which seemed to drill right through him. "Mr. Rahs, sir . . ." He began parroting the short spiel he'd been trained to say. "As the highest-ranking representative of my nation present at this time, I am authorized by my government to gather preliminary information from you which will be used by my superiors to ascertain whether or not you and your companion should be regarded as threats to the internal security of the United States of America, and the overall security of the entire planet."

The probing eyes continued to watch him, as if the alien had taken his measure and found him wanting in some way. Chapman forced himself to break contact with that unearthly gaze. This wasn't going at all like he had imagined. "If you cooperate with this process and answer all questions accurately and truthfully, we can avoid an armed confrontation and begin negotiating the terms of your surrender to my government."

Laura stared at Chapman in disbelief. Was that all the government was willing to negotiate—the terms of Aayshen's surrender? She'd been naive to think the military would allow any other outcome.

"What is the name of your home world?" Chapman began.

Aayshen glanced at Laura, who just stared at him in return. Then he looked back at the suited human. "My planet is called Savan . . . Colonel Chapman."

The Air Force officer flinched in surprise. The alien had spoken in clear, concise English that contained hardly a trace of an accent, and the accent that was there sounded almost Southern. Was that how he had learned the language so quickly? By mimicking Laura Malek? He cleared his throat. "Are you and the, a . . . your companion . . . from the same planet?"

"No. Technician Drallondryn is Kri."

"Technician?"

Aayshen motioned for Drallondryn to step forward.

Drallondryn came around the end of the sofa and paused uncertainly a few feet shy of Aayshen. "I am what you call a scientist, Colonel," the Kri explained. "I specialize in alien cultures and languages."

Chapman gaped at the animal-like alien for long seconds. His command of English was even greater than the blond's. "What is the purpose of your visit to our planet?" Chapman asked.

The Kri's browtufts drew downward in a bewildered frown. "To gather information about your planet and race, of course."

"The purpose of your visit isn't military in nature?" Chapman stared hard at Aayshen Rahs, studying the alien's lithe body and tense, watchful expression. There was no doubt he was a soldier of some kind.

"No," Aayshen said flatly. "It is not. We came here to make maps and collect specimens, nothing more."

"I see." Chapman had no idea whether he was being told the truth or not. But it didn't really matter. Government interrogation specialists would discover the truth later, one way or another. "Where are your home planets located?"

"Very far from this world," Aayshen said. His eyes cut to Drallondryn, signaling the Kri to remain silent. He would not give the human information that could be used against them.

"I need a more definite answer than that. I need to know exactly how long your space flight lasted." Chapman felt a sudden surge of excitement. This being was from another star system, proving that light-speed travel was truly possible. "Your ship must have reached speeds in excess of the velocity of light. What is your source of power?"

"It takes many years for light to travel here from our stars," Aayshen said, pretending that he hadn't quite understood the question.

Chapman stared at him intently. Was the alien being purposefully obtuse? "How many years?"

"Very, very many."

Laura hid a smile behind her hand. In his own way Aayshen was toying with Chapman. He had no intention of revealing anything of importance.

"You're not being very cooperative, sir." Chapman frowned. "These are important questions you are obligated to answer."

"Why?"

"Because my government requires it."

"For what purpose?"

Behind the visor, Chapman's face contorted with a mix of astonishment and frustration. How could he even ask such a question? "You came here to gather information about us, now we want to learn about you. An equal trade—knowledge for knowledge. We want to learn about your people, your planet, the rest of the universe. With that knowledge we might be able to better our own world . . . change it forever."

Chapman's eyes glazed at the prospect of such a future, a brave new world in which the United States alone wielded immense technological and economic power. "The technological advances alone would propel this country into a new golden age."

Laura stared at Chapman in growing horror. She saw the future he described, saw it in the naked hunger glittering in the soldier's unfocused eyes. The race was about to begin again. One nation pitted against another, a new, more dangerous Cold War between countries armed with alien technology and weapons of unspeakable power.

Aayshen had warned her that this would happen if he were captured.

The Savanian rose suddenly, folded his arms across his chest and paced toward the fireplace. Then he retraced his steps to the sofa, stopped, and turned to Chapman, the lines of his face hard and bleak. He had to convince the human that the knowledge he sought would not be beneficial to his world. "What you suggest is not an equal trade, Colonel. Your race is not yet ready for contact with other worlds. Your culture is still young, still struggling to cope with the changes wrought by advances in your own technology." He shook his head firmly. "I will not give your people the information you seek. Your country, your world would not survive the transformation you desire."

Chapman eyed him carefully. "What do you mean we wouldn't survive?"

"There have been other worlds such as yours, though none so beautiful as this, planets whose peoples stole or received the knowledge that you seek. The changes occurred too quickly. The people could not cope. They warred against each other, against us." His voice turned flat, emotionless, as bloody memories of the senseless carnage on Mintak IV flitted through his thoughts. "Those worlds no longer exist."

As Chapman stared into those wintry eyes, he felt a sudden, irrational chill, a deep sense of foreboding that shook him to the depths of his soul. Dark images of a world gone mad slithered through his thoughts like some snakelike collage, memories of blood and death that the alien was implanting telepathically. And in that freeze-frame of time, Chapman knew with an awful, overwhelming certainty that the alien had spoken the truth, that he had been on that world and witnessed the carnage firsthand.

"Such knowledge is power," Aayshen said softly, "and power corrupts. Do not corrupt your world."

Laura moved to stand at Aayshen's side. Unconsciously, her fingers twined themselves around his. "You've got to listen to him, Colonel. If he allows himself or Drallondryn to be taken prisoner, sooner or later someone will figure out a way to make them talk. They'll use that knowledge to build bigger and better weapons. It will all be top secret, of course, but eventually there'll be a leak somewhere, and a hundred other countries will follow suit." Her fingers tightened around Aayshen's. "Please, Colonel. Just let them go. A rescue ship is already on its way to pick them up. Just let them walk out the door and leave. For our sake, as well as theirs."

Chapman stared at them mutely. She was dead-on about what would happen. General Moss, or someone like him, would make good use of the information. The United States would have the upper hand for a year or two, a decade at most; then the technical knowhow would spread like a cancer across the world because military secrets were the most fleeting of all. The dangers were great, but the benefits would be incalculable. Earth would be transformed virtually overnight. Surely the benefits outweighed the risks. Didn't they?

Chapter Sixteen

An antique pendulum clock perched on the mantle ticked off the seconds one by one. Chapman stared at the clock face as he debated with himself, watching time pass with each back-and-forth swing of the brass arm. Time was the enemy now. The situation wouldn't remain static for long. At some point events would spiral beyond his control. It wouldn't be long before General Moss charged in at the head of his calvary. But even if Moss didn't show up, someone was bound to make a mistake, maybe even him, a mistake that might be paid for in blood and lives.

A decision had to be made by someone. But could he in good conscious allow the extraterrestrials, and the opportunities they represented, to just walk out the door? Should he?

He looked at the aliens, whose wary glances

matched his own. Being in this room, sitting here with them was the high point of his career, the culmination of his dreams for the last ten years. But now that he had finally chased down that dream, he could feel it slipping through his fingers with every swing of the pendulum. No matter what he decided, he would never have the chance to personally know or understand these aliens, to see the Earth through non-human eyes. He would never learn the answers to the philosophical questions about life and the universe that had long plagued mankind. He would have to content himself with the sure knowledge that the human race was not alone in the cosmos. There were indeed other intelligent species wandering the galaxy in search of their own answers, diverse species which might someday become mankind's friends and allies—or deadly foes.

The motion of the pendulum blurred as he watched its rhythmic movement. Was present-day humanity capable of determining whether these particular aliens could be considered friend or foe? Deep down he knew the answer to that question was no. But it was a question he had no right, or authority, to answer. That job belonged to others.

Chapman's anxious features, lined with indecision just a second before, softened and untensed. For better or worse, he had made the decision. He unfastened the hood of his anticontamination suit and lifted it off his head. Alien bugs be damned. It was hot in there.

"I'm sorry." His gaze shifted from one EBE to the other. "I can't allow you to leave." In truth, he doubted that he could stop them from leaving if they brought the full force of their weapons to bear. But he had to try.

Aayshen's pale eyes caught and held the human's for long seconds. He nodded slightly, a silent gesture of acknowledgment from one warrior to another. "I understand."

"It's not my decision to make," Chapman said, mesmerized by the alien's compelling blue eyes. The sense of impending loss was strangely acute, as if he were being cheated out of something so valuable he couldn't hope to calculate its worth. "My superiors should be arriving shortly. With time I'm sure you can come to some sort of agreement that will avoid an armed confrontation."

"No," Aayshen said quietly. "There is no more time, Colonel."

"Then I guess we have nothing further to say." Chapman slipped the hood under his arm and stood. "I can't allow you to leave. I have to try and stop you."

Aayshen climbed to his feet and moved to stand directly in front of Chapman, glaring down at the human from his greater height. "And I cannot allow you to succeed." A small, cold smile lifted the edges of his mouth. "I could force you, Colonel. It would not be difficult." His hand snaked out and his fingers made contact with Chapman's temple.

The air rushed out of Chapman's lungs as a mind as bright and cold as a searchlight swung through his thoughts, illuminating the darkest recesses of his inner self in a brutal display of telepathic ability.

"Aayshen!" Laura yelled. Chapman's face bore the same look of surprise and shock she'd seen in the grocery store. "Stop it!" She tried to pull his arm away, but her fingers slid off slick metal. "Leave him alone!"

The telepathic searchlight retreated as swiftly as it had come. Chapman gasped and staggered backwards, staring at the alien in shock. In a single instant the telepath had searched through the contents of his mind, rummaging through his memories like someone searching the nooks and crannies of an attic for a forgotten box of keepsakes. Rahs now knew everything there was to know about him. He knew and understood Chapman's fears and secret longings, the inner conflict that was raging within him between honor and duty. But most of all he knew the United States military backwards and forwards. Tactics, deployment, the Capture and Containment Team's standing orders. Everything.

Chapman sank back down into the wing chair and dropped his face into his hands, trembling uncontrollably. Child's play. What the alien had done to him had been child's play.

Laura grabbed Aayshen's arm again and forced him to meet her gaze. "What did you do, Aayshen? What did you do to him?"

He gazed down at her for long seconds, uncertain how to answer. Guilt and defiance shadowed his cerulean eyes. "I did not harm him, Laura. Colonel Chapman understands what I did . . . and why."

Laura turned. "Colonel?"

Chapman bunched his hands into fists to stop the trembling. What a fool he was. In a split second's time the alien had ably demonstrated just how puny and pointless his efforts had been. What fools they all were. Him, General Moss, Air Force

311

Intelligence, the officials at National Security, all the strutting warhorses in Washington who'd convinced themselves that the United States had the innate right and the ability to capture an alien from a more advanced civilization in order to extract strategic knowledge. Had it ever occurred to any of them that the reverse might be true? That by the merest touch an alien might be able to render the government militarily helpless in the face of a hostile enemy? Thank God he was only a colonel. Rahs might have easily done the same to General Moss, a member of the Joint Chiefs, or even the President himself. It wasn't beyond the realm of possibility. Nothing was anymore.

Chapman rubbed his eyes with his fists and glanced up at the alien standing before him. A saying he'd heard over and over since he was a child kept ringing through his head. Be careful what you wish for . . . You might get it.

"The information . . ." Chapman said quietly, both terrified and fascinated by how easily the alien had probed his mind. "Will you use it against us?"

Aayshen felt a pang of remorse for what he had done. The human looked so disconsolate, as though he had betrayed his country. "Only if I am forced."

The Air Force officer nodded slowly, still in shock. God help him. God help them all. "Go," Chapman said hoarsely. "I won't try to stop you." In truth, he didn't want to anymore.

"There will come a day," Aayshen told him softly, "when your race and mine will meet openly as friends. In time that day will come, but it is not now. Until then your world will be watched . . . and protected if need be, but we will not protect you from yourselves, or interfere unless we are forced. That is our way, Colonel."

Chapman gave him a slow nod of acceptance. Their way was better. Safer. He understood now, understood on a primal, instinctual level what the alien had been trying to tell him. Humans weren't ready for contact with this race or any others. Only time would prepare the way, enough time so they could meet on an even footing, equals in every way.

A relieved sigh rattled up from Drallondryn's chest. "Thank you, Colonel, thank you very much." The Kri grinned broadly, his fangs glittering whitely in the lamplight.

Chapman sighed. He felt strangely subdued, like a small child chastised for trying to sneak a forbidden treat. "How soon do you leave?"

"The shuttle should arrive any time now," Drallondryn told him.

Chapman sighed again and stood, resigned to the perverse irony of his situation. To protect his country he had to betray it. But if he was going to help the aliens make their getaway, then he would have to do so with all the skill he possessed, an act some would view as collaboration. "Then get your gear together and be ready."

Aayshen watched the human carefully. "What of your men, Colonel?"

"There won't be any trouble. My men are soldiers. They'll follow orders. I don't think there'll be any problem with Sheriff Rankin or his people either. As for the others . . ." He shrugged. By now they were probably too drunk to care one way or another.

Garner made a snorting sound, but remained silent. There'd already been trouble—plenty of it, and probably more to come.

"Take everything with you," Chapman instructed them, "or destroy it. When this is all over and done with, the science boys are going to tear this house apart. Don't leave anything behind for them to find."

Laura dumped a book into one of Drallondryn's trash sacks and gave Chapman a startled look over her shoulder. "What do you mean, they'll tear my house apart?"

Chapman shook his head in disbelief. The woman really was naive. "Mrs. Malek, you've been harboring *aliens* in this house. You've been breathing the same air, eating the same food. The specialists are going to go over you, me, your son, Mr. Haines, and every inch of this house with a microscopic comb, and probably run every medical test on us known to man."

Her face turned parchment white. Losing Aayshen was bad enough. Now she had to cope with the idea of strangers poking and prodding at them in the name of science. The possibility made her skin crawl. "They can't do that!" Breathing the same air, eating the same food? She had been far more intimate with an alien than that. What if they discovered that she and Aayshen were lovers? What would they do to her then? "The last I heard this was still a free country!"

"It is, but the government is responsible for the health and safety of all its citizens, not just us. So far my team hasn't picked up anything but normal background radiation around your property, but until complete tests are run we can't be certain that you and your family aren't contaminated with some sort of radiation, or an extrasolar bug which could spread to the general population. I doubt if they'll find anything, but they have to be sure." He gazed at her intently. "So do you."

She hugged her arms to her chest as if to ward off a sudden chill. A kaleidoscope of fleeting images tumbled through her mind, quick glimpses of antiseptic laboratories and sterile examination rooms, the cold, clinical stares of nameless doctors bending over her. But what they had in store for her and her family was nothing compared to what would happen to Aayshen and Drallondryn if they were captured. "I understand why, Colonel, but I don't have to like it."

Chapman touched her shoulder with a white-gloved hand, but she flinched away. Why was she so upset? A few days or weeks, then it would all be over. "Let's worry about one thing at a time," he said. "We still have to get them to their ship. It's not going to be easy, and I'm going to need your help to do it."

"I'll do whatever you want." She sighed. "I just want them out of here safely, Colonel. They deserve that much from us."

"I'll do everything I can to insure their safety, as well as your family's. But there are no guarantees."

"I understand." She was taking a huge risk by placing her trust in Chapman, but then life itself was a risk, wasn't it? An endless series of high-stakes gambles that could either make or break the human spirit in the space of a single second.

Laura forced herself to calm down. Her course in life had been set days ago, the moment Aayshen

Rahs had laid claim to her body and heart. Her chin lifted to a defiant angle. So what if the world found out that she'd been intimate with him? She wasn't ashamed of anything she'd done. In fact she was proud of herself for finding the courage to reach out and grab what life had so unexpectedly offered her. Making love to Aayshen had been the most wondrous thing she'd ever experienced, a glorious, intimate joining of bodies and minds that went far beyond the physical into the realm of the spiritual. They had shared something so deep and personal that no one could ever take those feelings away from her, or diminish them in any way. No matter what happened, Aayshen was a part of her now, and always would be. Time and distance were irrelevant. The bond between them was too strong, too intimate. They were two parts of a whole now, two minds and souls twined together for . . .

Her thoughts stilled, and her startled gaze flew to Aayshen. There was a high-pitched sound in her ears, and the room and everyone around her seemed to recede into a formless cloud of misty gray. Only Aayshen remained, his pale, stricken eyes burning into her with a dizzying intensity. She understood now, understood with perfect clarity the true meaning of what he'd said to her beneath the trees that night.

A joining between us will not be as you imagine . . . not as you have known. Once done, it cannot be undone.

What was done could never be undone. He'd meant those words literally, but she hadn't understood then. The strange bond that had been forged between them would never die, or grow muted with the passage of years. Time no longer mattered. Aayshen was an integral part of her now and forever.

She choked back a sudden, anguished sob. After tonight, she would never see or touch him again, and with that realization came a surge of grief such as she'd never known. Without him, she would never be whole again.

Aayshen stood before her, his pale eyes shadowed with misery and despair as her emotions washed through him in hot, aching waves. The resonance between them was stronger and deeper than he had ever imagined, crumbling the barriers he'd erected in his mind to hide his emotions. "Forgive me, Laura," he whispered in a strained voice. "I did not wish to bring you pain." As a telepath, he had joined with her in the only manner he could: an irrevocable bonding that stretched beyond the shells of their bodies into their minds and souls. But because she wasn't telepathic, he had foolishly thought the differences between them would spare her from the anguish a physical parting would bring. He had believed the psychic pain would be solely his, and that once he left, her life would be much as it was. But that was not to be.

Laura stared into his face, the torment she felt reflected in the depths of his azure eyes. There was a tightening sensation inside her mind, as if immovable bands of steel had stretched taut between them, amplifying every thought and painful emotion to an unbearable intensity. "What I'm feeling . . . it's not all from me, is it?"

"No." He sighed raggedly and tried to bring his emotions under some semblance of control, but

Jan Zimlich

found that he could not. Even though she was not a true telepath, the bond granted her the ability to sense his every thought and feeling as though it were her own.

The invisible wall he'd erected against her suddenly shattered, and the truth flowed between them like a river of light. Tears glittered brightly in Laura's eyes, but they were tears of joy, not sorrow. The dark veil of grief lifted from her mind. His love for her was like a living thing singing through her veins, a sweet explosion of emotion and desire that threatened to consume them both. A deep sensation of peace swept through her. It wasn't lust that had bound them together. He had loved her from the very beginning, and always would.

"Let's go," Chapman urged. "You people have to get out of here fast. If one of my superiors arrives I won't be able to help you."

He eased the front door open, then glanced back over his shoulder and frowned. Laura Malek and the alien soldier hadn't moved. They seemed frozen in place, their bodies only inches apart, their glazed eyes locked on each other with a heated intensity Chapman found disquieting. The Air Force officer felt awkward and out of place, as if he were a voyeur who had stumbled upon a pair of lovers engaged in an act of intimacy. Nothing existed in the world beyond themselves.

He sucked in a startled breath. It all made sense now. Laura Malek's certainty that his environmental suit wasn't necessary, her continued attempts to insure the aliens' safety, and her obvious reluctance to submit to a medical examination.

Sometime in the past week the telepathic alien had become her lover.

Laura buried her face against the cold metal armor covering Aayshen's chest. The abiding certainty of his love imbued her with a deep sense of peace and fulfillment. *I don't want to lose you, Aayshen.* Her fingers wound themselves around his tapered waist. *Not now.* The words hadn't been spoken aloud, yet she knew he had heard her, and understood. *Stay with me.*

Strong arms folded her within the gentle circle of his arms. Her intoxicating scent drifted around him, and his heartbeat quickened at her nearness. *I cannot stay here, Laura. You know this.*

Then take us with you! We can go wherever you decide, wherever you want!

No. His grief was a raw, aching knot inside his throat. She could not be a part of his life because he had no life of his own. *That is not possible.*

A small, sorrowful smile trembled over her lips. *I know, but I had to try.* As long as she knew that his love for her was real and alive, she would persevere, even though the future that stretched before her was a bleak, lonely void.

What the Fates gave us, they have taken away, but I will never forget you, Laura, or cease loving you. You will always be with me in my thoughts.

She locked herself within the warmth of his embrace and tilted her face toward his. *Does it have to end this way?*

There can be no other ending. He twined his fingers through her silky hair and held her close; then his lips slowly descended to claim her as his own.

She returned his demanding kiss with reckless

abandon, utterly oblivious to the presence of any-one else in the room.

Chapman cleared his throat and glanced away. Clearly, what they had together was more than a brief encounter. Much, much more. The heat they were generating was almost palpable, as if the air around them had been electrified in some way. Telepathically, perhaps? He looked to the Kri in hopes of an explanation, but Drallondryn was pre-tending to stare at the floor, obviously uncom-fortable with the scene they were witnessing. Garner Haines's reaction was much the same. Only the boy was watching, his expression a blend of curiosity and stunned surprise.

Their lips parted and reality returned by slow degrees. Laura pulled away, trembling and breathless. She caressed his cheek one last time. "You'd better go now," she told him softly.

He touched her hair, her eyes and her face with gentle fingers, then traced the inviting outline of her full lips. A shudder of desire coursed through his body. "Good-bye, Laura." His hand fell limply to his side, and he turned away.

"I'll go first," Chapman told him. "Give me a couple of minutes to tell them I've granted you safe passage, then follow me out the door. I'll sig-nal you when I think it's safe."

Aayshen nodded, and picked up his pulse rifle as Drallondryn hefted several green trash sacks onto his back.

Chapman slipped out the door and activated his headset, quickly giving his men a new set of orders as he hurried down the front steps, stripping off the bulky suit as he went. The thought that his men might not obey the orders never crossed his mind. They were a team, trained and molded to function and fight as a single entity. And he was their commanding officer, had been since the team's inception.

Their movements swift and silent, members of Chapman's elite unit began shifting into new positions, fanning out by twos to form a semi-circle between the road and the house.

The dark shape of Sheriff Rankin's head popped up from behind the patrol car. "You all right, Colonel?" Rankin called in a worried voice. "I was beginning to think those people might have done something to you in there."

"I'm fine." Chapman paused halfway between the car and house, his practiced eyes scanning the grounds for any sign of danger.

Bands of people were still gathered up and down the road, though not as many as before. The laughter and beer were still in abundant supply, but the music wasn't as loud, and the block-party atmosphere seemed to have faded a bit. Just a few hundred rowdy diehards determined to stay until something happened. Chapman smiled grimly to himself. They were about to get their wish.

"You gonna tell me what's going on?" Rankin cast a nervous glance over his shoulder. A line of heavily armed soldiers had silently materialized between him and the road, moving into positions a few feet behind him. "Come on, Colonel, what are your boys getting ready to do?"

Chapman's attention finally swung back to Rankin. He sucked in a breath and lifted his chin. "Well, Sheriff, there's been a little change in plan. I've decided to grant them safe passage out of the house."

"You what?"

"You heard me. When they walk out that door in a few seconds, I don't want you or your deputies to interfere in any way. No trouble of any kind. My men have orders to make sure those people on the road don't get out of line either."

Rankin blinked twice, amazed. He'd never dreamed that the spit-and-polish Air Force officer would agree to let the aliens go. "I hope you know what you're doing."

"So do I, Sheriff." Chapman's voice was soft and low, laced with uncertainty and a twinge of fear. He turned toward the house and signaled with a wave of his arm. No matter what happened, he would be held accountable. And what he was doing would be construed as treason by some.

The screen door swung open, throwing a rectangle of yellow light across the grass at Chapman's feet. Laura Malek stepped onto the porch, her son clutched tight against her hip.

"There's people on the porch!" a voice shouted from the road, an announcement followed by the high-pitched screech of a rebel yell. The crowd on Kali Oka Road suddenly came alive, surging past Rankin's pitiful line of deputies in a mad scramble to reach the white rail fence and claim a ringside seat. The cheerleaders started chanting again.

Carrie Cooner squirmed through a gap between two men and elbowed her way to the fence. Laura Malek was on the porch, one arm draped protectively around her son. She clutched at her husband's shoulder as Ornell, Bobbie-Jean, and Ricky fought their way up behind her. "Look, Ornell! What'd I tell you? The thing I saw. It's behind

Laura, standing in the door. You see it?"

"I see somethin'." Ornell squinted until it came into sharp focus.

"Jeez, Louise!" Ricky blurted. "It looks like some kind of big raccoon wearing a metal suit."

"See, I told you, Ricky!" Carrie smiled smugly. "Didn't I?"

"Yeah, you tole me all right." Ricky tossed down the rest of his beer. "But you didn't say nothing about a metal suit."

"It wasn't wearing one when I saw it last!"

A shiver ran up Ornell's spine and the hairs on his arms stiffened into brittle curls. Next time Carrie told him some wild tale he'd listen a little closer. "What the hell is that thing?"

"It's an alien," Carrie said matter-of-factly. "What else?"

Ricky snorted and popped the tab on another can of beer. "Hell, I think it's just some guy in a raccoon suit."

"Oh, sure." Carrie rolled her eyes. "If that's all it was, all those soldiers wouldn't be here, now would they?"

Ricky swayed into her and gave her a bleary-eyed grin. "A bunch of hoopty-do about nothing, if you ask me." His beer-belch sounded like a small explosion.

Several teenagers standing next to them tittered.

Carrie grimaced, and took a hasty step away from the hot blast of beer-breath. "Bobbie-Jean needs to have her head examined for marrying you."

Another explosion rumbled up from his chest. "She loves me, don't you, sweetheart?" Ricky glanced around, but didn't see his wife among the sea of faces pressed around them. He bent over the top of the fence and scanned the crowd in both directions. "Where'd she go?"

"She's probably asleep in the car," Ornell offered, which was where he'd like to be. It was late, he'd had too many beers, and his shift at the shipyard started at six in the morning. He considered asking Carrie to go home, but knew that she wouldn't, not until she knew the Maleks were safe.

A strange, muffled sound suddenly filled Carrie's ears, reverberating across the eastern sky. A chill swept over her. "What's that?" she asked quietly.

Ornell cocked his head and listened. "I don't know," he whispered back. Instinctively, he pulled his wife tight against his side and draped an arm around her shoulder.

Others heard the far-off sound, and the crowd's excited chatter faded with an unnatural abruptness. Anxious eyes turned skyward.

Chapter Seventeen

Chapman heard the sound, too. It was a familiar sound, one that sent a sinking sensation through the pit of his stomach. "Oh, God, no," he whispered to himself. "Not now."

He sprinted toward the front porch. Laura Malek and her grandfather were still standing there, waiting nervously with the two aliens until their ship arrived. "How soon until your ship lands?" Chapman said in an ominous voice.

"A few minutes, no more." Aayshen stiffened and clutched his pulse gun tighter. Even from a distance he could sense Chapman's anxiety.

"What's wrong?" Laura pressed close against Aayshen.

The sound grew closer. "We have company. It's probably General Moss, my superior." Chapman tilted his head and glanced up at the eastern sky.

"Don't do anything. Just stay where you are and let me try to handle this." Navigation lights winking in a steady rhythm, a helicopter suddenly appeared and nosed its way through the darkness at treetop level.

The rotor noise increased to a deafening roar as a Blackhawk helicopter swept over the house and began descending, hovering for a moment before it settled into the undulating half-moon of grass stretching between the driveway and road.

Crouching low against a whirlwind of grit and pine straw caught in the rotor wash, Sheriff Rankin ran to Chapman's side. "Who's on board the helicopter, Colonel?" he yelled above the noise. "Some military bigwig?"

Chapman felt ill. Just five more minutes and it would have all been over. "I guess you could say that," he shouted back. Forcing his feet to move, Chapman walked slowly up the driveway. Rankin tagged along behind him, clutching the brim of his hat to keep it from becoming airborne.

The crowd cheered wildly as the helicopter's rear door slid open and General Moss leaped out, flanked by eight grim-faced NSA agents carrying Uzis. The rotors still spinning above him, Rufus Moss paused for a moment and glanced around incredulously, his angry eyes shifting back and forth across the chaotic scene. What the hell was going on here? There were civilians everywhere, at least two hundred gathered along the fence beside the road, including a bunch of teenage cheerleaders who were wiggling and shaking pom-poms while they screamed some kind of chant he couldn't quite hear.

As the rotor noise faded to a high-pitched

whine, he marched down the driveway toward Chapman with the agents in tow. He ground to a furious stop and pinned Chapman with a withering glare. "You better have a damn good explanation for all of this, Colonel." He could hear every word of the cheerleader's chant now, and wasn't amused.

Chapman stiffened slightly, his only visible reaction to the General's rage. "The situation hasn't gone exactly according to plan, General."

Moss glanced at the mob of civilians, then back at Chapman in disbelief. Hadn't gone exactly according to plan? "I'm going to nail your ass to the nearest wall, Chapman." His craggy face turned a hot shade of scarlet. "And when I'm finished with you, I'm going to file so many charges against you that you'll wish you'd never been born."

A fine mist of spittle sprayed across Chapman and Rankin's faces. Chapman ignored it, while Rankin wiped at his cheek with a sleeve.

"*Where* are the EBEs, Colonel?" Moss nearly shouted.

"On the porch."

"What?" The general gaped at Chapman; then his gaze jerked to the house and the knot of people clustered on the front porch. He felt his neck hair rise. They were just standing there, two of them, one tall and blond, the other . . . "Oh, my, God." The aliens were just standing around in the open, in plain view of several hundred slack-mouthed civilians.

Moss rounded on the tubby man dressed in a gray sheriff's uniform and jerked a thumb toward the mass of humanity crowded along the road. "This is a classified operation, Sheriff. Get those bumpkins out of here right now, or you can kiss your job and pension good-bye!"

Unruffled, Bob Rankin flashed him an amiable smile and glanced at the gold stars pinned to the man's shoulders. A two-star general, no less, in Escatawpa. "I don't take kindly to threats . . . General. Neither do the folks who live around here." His smile turned cold. "And judging by what happened here a while ago, neither do the aliens you're so hot to get your hands on. You try to force the issue again and a lot of people are going to get hurt."

Moss stared at him, speechless. A hick sheriff had dared to threaten *him*. He wheeled toward Chapman, a muscle in his jaw twitching spasmodically. "Chapman, I'm giving you five minutes to clear those civilians out of here and take those EBEs into custody. Five minutes, you understand?"

Chapman steeled himself inwardly. No doubt about it, he was going to spend the rest of his life in a military prison. "I'm sorry, General, but I can't do that. I've already given the extraterrestrials my word that we would allow them to leave unmolested."

"You *what*?" Moss felt his blood pressure rising.

"Sir," Chapman grated, eying the NSA goons with distaste, "any chance we might have had of capturing them peacefully was lost the moment you sent your own people into the field without my knowledge. Your top-guns here tried to take them into custody in a public bar and botched things up big-time." Chapman's lips thinned, and his voice turned icy. "You tried to do an end run around me so you'd be a hero in the Pentagon, but it backfired. You lost the element of surprise for us, and have only yourself to blame for the results"—he waved a hand toward the road—"and the presence of all these civilians."

The general's face turned a dark, unhealthy shade of red.

"It's too late, General," Chapman went on. "We've already lost this one. I determined on my own initiative that it would be in the nation's best interest to allow the EBEs to leave before the situation escalates any further. I've given them my word that we wouldn't try to stop them." Chapman exchanged a tense look with Sheriff Rankin, then gritted his teeth and waited to see what Moss would do.

"You," Moss snapped, and pointed to the NSA agent closest to him. "Take Colonel Chapman into custody. He is relieved of duty pending court-martial proceedings."

As the barrel of an Uzi swung in his direction, Chapman touched his mike switch and whispered a single word into the tactical channel. "I'm sorry it came to this, General," he said calmly.

Chapman's men suddenly pivoted, half dropping to one knee, the others standing, legs splayed in a defensive stance. Weapons rose to shoulder level.

"No," Moss whispered. A vein bulged in his forehead and his blood went cold. Chapman's team had turned and pointed their guns in his direction.

"Don't force me, General," Chapman told him quietly.

There was a furtive, scuffling sound in the grass and several metallic clicks. Moss knew instinctively what the sounds represented. Behind him, the National Security agents he'd brought along had dropped to the ground and readied their guns, but theirs were aimed at Chapman and his men.

"You do this, Colonel, and you'll spend the rest of your life in prison."

Chapman smiled thinly. "Probably. But that doesn't change the fact that I made a promise and I'm going to see it through. You can court-martial me tomorrow."

"You're bluffing, Lem," Moss said, trying a different tact. "Be reasonable. Your men wouldn't dare open fire. That's treason."

"You want to find out?"

A cold gust of damp Gulf wind suddenly snatched at their hair and clothes. Treetops shifted uneasily, then bent and swayed as the gust turned into a strong gale. Chapman covered his eyes with the back of an arm as a torrent of dust, pine straw, and decaying leaves became airborne, whipping around the yard at hurricane speed. The hair along the nape of his neck suddenly tingled and stood on end, as if the air around him had become electrically charged. His nose wrinkled. There was a strange smell in the air, too, an acrid scent that reminded him of ozone.

He lifted his gaze upwards and stared at the sky, the unexpected wind tearing at his hair and clothes. Chapman's eyes widened, and a slow, comprehending smile spread across his tense features.

Sheriff Rankin's jaw drooped as he followed the direction of Chapman's gaze. "God in heaven, would you look at that."

Grinning foolishly, Chapman continued to stare

at the huge object blotting out the night sky above them. Static discharge arced and danced across the darkness like thin streamers of blue lightning.

A woman's high-pitched scream echoed from somewhere. More screams followed, both male and female, as fear took firm root along Kali Oka Road. The crowd began to scatter, trampling and fighting each other as they scrambled for cover behind trees and cars. A section of the white rail fence collapsed under the weight of the mob pressing against it. Unsure which way to run, a large group of terrified onlookers spilled across the yard, barreling this way and that to dodge a painful barrage of pine cones and flying beer cans transformed into missiles by the howling wind. Several soldiers joined the melee, racing first in one direction, then the other, their eyes lifting in terror to the thing descending from the sky. Someone near the road let loose with a shotgun and blasted a shower of bark from a pine tree.

The NSA agent guarding Chapman bolted into the darkness as a wild-eyed woman lurched past them, hair streaming behind her, screaming in fear. For a spilt second her glazed eyes met Chapman's, and he realized it was Bobbi-Jean Cooner, the cashier from the grocery store. Another woman and two men raced after her, shouting for her to stop.

The wind and noise died abruptly and a thick, unnatural silence fell across the Mississippi landscape. Soldiers and civilians alike froze like a herd of deer startled by the sharp glare of headlights. No one moved. The sudden absence of sound was even more terrifying than the eerie wind.

General Moss stared raptly at the sky, his expression unreadable. This was the moment the military had dreaded and feared for more years than he cared to count. The moment when his country had to stand firm and tough in the face of superior forces, put on a display of offensive strength and resolve strong enough to convince an alien invasion force that the United States would forever remain inviolate.

"I see it but I still don't believe it," Rankin said, eyes fastened on the thing hovering silently above them.

"Oh, it's real, all right," Chapman whispered, gazing upwards in awe. The alien spacecraft was at least a hundred yards long, about the length of a football field, and shaped like some huge grace-ful bird with sleek curving wings. The hovering ship didn't emit the slightest sound, or refract any light, as though the dark metallic skin absorbed all traces of light and noise. Chapman shook his head in wonder. The ship was immense, beyond his wildest imaginings. "They said a 'shuttle' was coming for them."

"God in heaven," Rankin said again. "If that's a shuttle, I hate to think what the mother ship looks like."

"Yeah." Chapman swallowed down the lump of fear clinging to the side of his throat. He'd been right to guarantee the aliens safe passage. Earth wasn't ready for contact with beings capable of building such a craft. The mother ship Rahs com-manded might be miles long for all he knew. Miles long and bristling with weaponry.

He turned to Moss, shaken by the thought that at this very moment such a craft might be orbiting high above the Earth. "Do you understand now,

General?" he said darkly. "These people are hundreds of years ahead of us, maybe thousands! We're *not* their equals. Contact would be dangerous."

Moss didn't answer, didn't move, but his face and eyes were lit by an emotion that was all too visible. His weatherworn features were twisted with hatred and burning envy, an irrational, xenophobic hatred for the aliens and envy of what they possessed.

Chapman wanted to grab him by the collar and throttle him within an inch of his life, wipe that look of utter loathing from the general's face. The urge was compelling, but in the end he simply shook his head and walked down the driveway to finish what he'd started.

"It's time," Aayshen whispered into her hair. He held her close against him, rocking gently, his hands locked tight against her spine.

Laura glanced up at his chiseled face, but his eyes were opaque, unreadable. "I know," she answered quietly. She buried her face against his chest, the cold metal armor slick and hard beneath her tear-stained cheek. There was nothing more to say, nothing left but this one last moment together. The ache in her heart was like an open wound.

He pulled away from her slowly, his pale eyes tracing over her delicate, heart-shaped features, committing them to memory one by one. The memories would be his constant companions in the years to come, mind-wraiths who'd live within him until the end of his days, sweet reminders of what could have been—might have been. But how could mere memories stem the flood of desire that raged through his veins even now? She was in his blood, a part of him that he would soon lose forever. Two halves that would never be whole again.

Aayshen wanted to scream, bunch his fists and howl his rage at an unfeeling universe and the fickleness of the Fates. Instead, he did what was expected of him, what he had to do.

He turned away, the rage and grief sliding quietly away to burrow within the darkest recesses of his mind.

"Good-bye, Laura," Drallondryn said, his yellow eyes large and luminous with sympathy.

Laura dipped her head slightly and hugged her arms around her chest as Drallondryn slipped past her and followed Aayshen into the yard. She watched in silence as they walked toward the hovering ship, her heart adrift within a black sea of despair. A long slit of golden light appeared in the ship's dark belly, widening slowly until the light became a passageway and a metal ramp descended. Drallondryn moved up the ramp and disappeared inside.

She felt Garner's reassuring presence beside her, the papery touch of his ancient skin as he sought and found her hand. Bryan's eyes were on her, questioning, but she had no answers now, nothing to give. She was empty.

Aayshen paused in the swath of light to say his farewells to Colonel Chapman, their bodies silhouetted by a golden, unearthly glow. The Air Force officer extended his hand tentatively, and Aayshen clasped it, bridging the yawning chasm between human and alien for a single moment in time.

A tiny circle of red light appeared in the wash of gold, danced atop Aayshen's shoulders, then darted across his head and neck, flitting around like a ruby-colored insect searching for a place to sting. The circle of red stilled, and a sensation akin to dread uncoiled and trembled inside Laura's stomach.

A staccato popping sound suddenly rent the night, an explosion of noise that sent people scurrying for bushes and trees.

Shock dulled Aayshen's eyes. For a split second of time his pale, puzzled gaze locked with Chapman's, voicing a silent question. He took a single tottering step, the muscles in his legs and arms numb and strangely heavy. His vision swam, and the pulse gun slipped from his grip. Then the ground rose to meet him and the world went black.

Laura's mouth opened, but no sound emerged. Her scream was silent, a grief-filled shriek only she could hear.

Nausea rose in Chapman's throat as he stared down at the fallen alien with wide, shocked eyes. Madness. The whole world had gone insane. He staggered toward Rahs, his horrified gaze intent on the reddish-blue blood pooling in the grass beneath the alien's neck. He fell to his knees and began hunting for signs of life as a telltale circle of red began dancing a graceful ballet across the unconscious alien's forehead. Chapman wheeled around, frantically searching the surrounding darkness for the sniper who had Rahs in the crosshairs of a laser sight. "Don't do it!" Chapman screamed.

"Stay out of this, Chapman!" General Moss

yelled. "We've gotta show them we aren't scared . . . gotta show these creatures that they're messing with the United States of America, by God!" Moss squinted into the laser sight and centered his aim, targeting the bridge of bone between the alien's eyes. "I'm going to send them a message they won't soon forget!" His finger brushed the trigger, tightening.

"Noooo!" Laura screamed. She leaped down the porch steps and started running.

Chapman didn't think; he just reacted, hurling his body atop Aayshen's instinctively. A single shot cracked across the darkness, then another. The Air Force officer's body jerked and went limp.

Laura stumbled and fell, blinded by tears of rage and grief. Sobbing, she crawled on her hands and knees to Aayshen's side, her hands trembling violently as she touched cold fingers to his neck and face and lips. Her fingers came away warm and sticky-wet, stained bluish red with Aayshen's blood. Laura choked down a tortured sob and gently rolled Colonel Chapman's limp body off Aayshen's chest, their blood mingling together on her shuddering hands.

A soft sighlike moan escaped Chapman's lips, the only sign that he was still alive. But Aayshen still hadn't moved, and she couldn't find a pulse-point to tell if he was dead or alive.

"Drallondryn!" she screamed, glancing around desperately. "Help him!" The ship still hovered above them, but the ramp had ascended in tandem with the sound of gunfire, and Drallondryn was inside.

Rage such as she'd never known rose in Laura's throat like the acid taste of bile. "Why?" she railed, anger flaring hot and bright in her voice and eyes. "He never did anything to you! He never did anything to anyone!" The grief and rage grew inside her, dark embers fanned by the flames of raw emotion. Deep sobs wracked her body as she lay down atop Aayshen's chest and covered his head with her arms.

"Get out of my line of fire, lady!" General Moss yelled, trying to find a clear target in the rifle sight. More red circles flitted across the woman's back and arms as several of the NSA agents took aim.

Sheriff Rankin ran towards the general to kick the gun out of his hands, but a burly agent grabbed him by the arms to stop him. He wrestled to free himself, but the agent was bigger and much stronger. "You murdering bastard!" Rankin yelled at Moss. "You shot them down like dogs!"

Garner watched in growing horror as his granddaughter began shielding Aayshen's body with her own. He shoved the front door open and pushed Bryan inside. "Go hide in your closet and don't come out until I tell you to. You hear me, boy? Your momma's gotten herself in a heap of trouble and I'm going out there to help."

The child looked back at him with wide, frightened eyes. "I'm scared, Grampa."

"Me too. Go on and do what I told you. Your momma's gonna be all right. I promise." Bryan nodded shakily, then disappeared inside. Garner took a deep, steadying breath and climbed down the porch steps, his wobbly gait gaining momentum as he walked across the yard. No one tried to stop him. They didn't even seem to notice him until he was just a few yards shy of Laura's side and it was too late to stop him. They probably didn't consider him much of a threat. Garner smiled grimly to himself, the faint glimmer of a plan taking form in his head. His footsteps became stronger, more certain, his mind and senses keener. In fact, he couldn't remember feeling this focused since the war and the beaches of Normandy. The old, familiar zing was back in his blood, and it felt good. Right.

He came to a wobbly stop at Laura's side, feigning a look of old-man confusion he didn't feel as he glanced around in bewilderment.

"Get out of the way!" Moss shouted from the darkness. "Both of you! Or I'll order my men to fire!"

"Laura," Garner said softly, "look at me."

She lifted her tear-stained face from Aayshen's chest, her dark eyes dull and lifeless.

"Is he alive?" Garner prodded. "Answer me, girl, is he still alive?"

She blinked several times; then the tears began again. "I think so." Her voice cracked and rose, edged with hysteria. "I felt his chest rising a few seconds ago, but I don't know what to do, Grampa. I just don't know what to do!"

"Shhh. Lower your voice so those soldier boys can't hear. He's breathing, that's what matters. And we're not going to let them shoot him again, but you have to get a grip on yourself. Now look at the ground on Aayshen's right side. Do it real slow so nobody sees what you're doing."

Her gaze shifted slowly, and her heart stilled. Aayshen's rifle was lying there. Instinctively she understood what her grandfather had in mind. She gave him a small, tight-lipped smile, a sudden surge of hope shining fever-bright in her eyes.

"You think you can figure out how to use it?" Laura whispered.

"We'll see soon enough." His shoulders lifted in a fatalistic shrug. "I saw him shoot it a while ago. I think I can do it. When I say go, you pretend like you're going to get up, then grab the rifle and toss it to me."

Their eyes met for a long second. "I love you, Grampa."

He smiled back, then extended a blue-veined hand as if he were going to help her rise. "Go."

The heavy pulse gun slid smoothly into Garner's waiting hands and his gnarled fingers settled over what he hoped were the firing controls. "All right you back-stabbing sons of bitches!" he yelled at the soldiers. "The odds have evened up!" He pointed the pulse gun menacingly. "Drop your guns and hit the dirt, or I'll melt your cowardly butts!"

General Moss swore under his breath. "Put that thing down before you get hurt, old man!" The stupid fool was just as likely to incinerate himself as anyone else. "You don't know what you're fooling with."

"Like hell I don't!" Garner pressed a button, and a bolt of blue lanced across the darkness like a thin line of horizontal lightning. The Blackhawk helicopter exploded into flame, the fireball licking the dark belly of the spaceship poised above. "I meant what I said, mister. Put your guns down or there's going to be hell to pay. I'm not gonna stand here and watch you murder any man in cold blood."

Moss stared at the flaming remains of his helicopter in disbelief, then turned back to the old fool who'd blown it to kingdom come. Fear and loathing twisted across his craggy features. "That's not a *man* lying there, you stupid old fool! It's an alien . . . a thing! We've got to kill it. We've got to show them we're willing to fight before it's too late!"

Garner's mouth curled downward in a grimace. "He's a man all right, more of a man than you'll ever be." A thin cheer of approval echoed from somewhere on Kali Oka Road. The cheer bolstered Garner's confidence. What he and Laura were doing was right and decent, the honorable thing to do. And there were others out there in the night who thought as they did, fellow Southerners who still possessed a shred of decency.

Without a trace of shame, Garner decided to exploit that sense of moralistic outrage to their advantage. "Are you people gonna let them do this?" he yelled at the listeners, his angry gaze burning holes in the darkness surrounding him. "You gonna let these Yankee bastards just walk in here and shoot this fellow down like he was some cur dog? They shot his ship down, for God's sake. He had to land here. Nobody gave him a choice about it. Now these Washington people wanna charge in here and either take him prisoner or kill him. Who gave them that right?"

His impassioned voice took on a silky preacher's tone, evoking guilt and indignation. "This is Mississippi, not Moscow or Havana! Let's show the federal government that they can't run over us anymore. This is our town, our state. They work for us, not the other way around! Get out here and help me show these Washington pinheads that we won't take their crap anymore!" His voice climbed another octave, and he lifted an imploring hand. "Help me, for God's sake. All that boy wants to do is go home."

Seconds passed with no response; then a lone figure appeared from behind a tree. Another crawled from beneath a bush and began walking in Garner's direction. Carrie Cooner crept out of the camellia hedge she'd been hiding in, brushed the leaves from her jeans and trod toward the human barrier forming in front of Laura. Her husband waddled after her, trailed more slowly by a bleary-eyed Bobbie-Jean, who staggered along behind him. Ricky cast a frightened glance upwards, then slunk deeper within the leafy bowels of a massive camellia bush.

"Where we going?" Bobbie-Jean said in a beer-drenched slur, wavering slightly as she stumbled on a tree root.

"Just shut up and come on," Carrie told her.. "We're gonna help Miz Malek."

Singly, then by twos and threes, others emerged from their hiding places, gaining strength and confidence as their numbers grew. Several men brought along their shotguns, their sun-weathered faces set in hard, determined lines.

Carrie edged up beside Garner and gave him a nervous look out of the corner of her eye. She'd never seen the old man like this. He looked stronger, younger by a good ten years or so, a determined man in charge of his own fate. "I always knew you were a crazy old coot," Carrie whispered to him. "But tonight takes the cake."

"So what if I am?" Garner laughed quietly. "I haven't felt this good in years."

More people joined the barricade of bodies,

forming a strong wall of outraged humanity between General Moss and his prey. Six of Chapman's men threw down their guns and joined the line, as well as several deputies.

As their numbers swelled, Garner lifted his chin in defiance and glared at the general and his measly little group of men. His thin arthritic fingers tightened around the pulse gun. "The worm has turned, General." Garner cackled gleefully. "So why don't you and your boys just pack up and head for home. You're not wanted here."

The crowd tittered in nervous approval, and General Moss's face flushed to a deep, purplish red. Humiliation washed over him in long, shuddering waves, and his hands and legs trembled with righteous fury. Nobody made a fool out of him. Nobody. "You rednecks have thirty seconds to get out of the way," he screamed in a voice bristling with indignation, "or my men will open fire!"

His only answer was a quiet shifting of bodies. Shoulders brushed as the locals locked arms, their faces cold and rigid with an ageless determination. Rebellion burned in their defiant eyes. The cause no longer mattered. They were Mississippians, and they were battling the federal government, just as their ancestors had over a century before. A woman somewhere along the line began singing an off-key rendition of "Onward Christian Soldiers" in a high-pitched, screechy voice. Others joined in.

"Ten seconds!" Moss shouted over the singers.

The remainder of Chapman's men threw down their guns in disgust and folded their arms. The NSA agents exchanged nervous, frightened glances, unwilling to obey the order to fire on civilians, but uncertain of what they should do.

Muttering under his breath, the agent holding Sheriff Rankin's arms suddenly released his grip and backed away. "This is nuts!" the agent hissed in his ear. "I don't want any part of it!" He handed Rankin back his gun and walked away, still muttering.

Bob Rankin lifted a bushy brow and glanced around, deciding this must all be some kind of fever-dream. Aliens from outer space. Soldiers. A crazed general. People he knew and saw every day standing in a line singing hymns, preparing to fight the Civil War all over again. Over what? His gaze was drawn upward, to the stadium-sized spaceship just hanging there some 30 feet above the top of his head. The ship was still dark and silent, ominously so.

He shook his graying head slowly, wondering if he had somehow been cast for a bit part in some loony movie and nobody had told him. Crazy. The whole world had gone nuts, and he with it. Rankin glanced down at the pistol in his hand and pursed his lips. Somebody had to put an end to the madness, and he guessed it was him. Rankin turned the pistol in his hand until the butt faced outward; then he crept up behind General Moss and whacked him across the back of his skull with the heavy pistol.

Moss crumpled to the ground in a boneless heap.

"Yeah." Rankin glanced at his gun, the unconscious general, and shook his head, amazed that it had been so easy. "Okay, people!" he shouted, trying to sound like it had all been in a day's work. "The war's over. There isn't going to be any more shooting in my jurisdiction. You hear me? The next person who shoots a gun will have to deal with me."

The line of locals cheered and broke ranks, but the sounds they made were halfhearted at best. Soldiers and civilians alike began milling around uncertainly, casting nervous glances at the ship hovering silently above them. It wasn't over yet, and they all knew it.

Rankin prodded the unconscious general with the toe of his boot as a deputy raced up behind him. "Arrogant prick," the sheriff mumbled.

"Sheriff," the young deputy said, his eyes shifting upwards, "what do we do now?"

"First thing you do"—Rankin jerked a thumb toward the body lying on the ground—"is cuff that piece of trash."

The deputy's jaw went slack. "Sir?"

"You heard me. Cuff him and throw him in the back of my car. General or not, I'm taking him in."

The jaw dropped further. "On what charge?"

Rankin shrugged and walked away. "I'll think of something," he called over his shoulder.

Two black-clad soldiers dropped to the ground beside Chapman, checked his vital signs, then scooped up their fallen colonel and whisked him away.

Laura watched them go, feeling the uneven rise and fall of Aayshen's chest beneath the palm of her hand. His breathing had become more erratic in the last few minutes, more uncertain, as if had struggled mightily but was slowly losing the war. She cradled his head in her lap protectively and rocked back and forth, unmindful of the blood seeping through the legs of her jeans.

Fresh tears slipped down her cheeks. Dozens of people had begun to mill and shuffle around, gawking, staring at her and Aayshen like they were some sort of hideous specimens in a reptile zoo. She hated their probing looks and incredulous stares. "What are you looking at!" Laura cried out in anger. She smoothed a strand of silver-white hair away from his face. "Just leave him be."

Garner and Carrie exchanged a worried glance and crouched down beside her. "How is he?" Garner asked.

Her rocking slowed and she looked at Garner through a salty haze of tears. "I don't know. He needs help, and I don't know what to do."

Garner glared at the spaceship hanging above them. Why didn't they come out and help? Anger got the better of him, and he picked up a pine cone and hurled it at the spaceship. The cone bounced off ungiving metal and fell back to the earth. "I know you're in there, cat!" he yelled at the ship. "Get you're scrawny ass out here and help."

The slit of light appeared again, as if in answer to Garner's plea. A ramp slid out of nothingness and slowly descended. A shower of pale gold light spilled across the grass and trees, sparkling in the darkness like a million fireflies.

"Hold on, Aayshen," Laura whispered to his still form. She stroked his hair and forehead with the back of a hand. "Help's coming."

No one panicked this time. The crowd simply stared in mute wonder as the ramp touched ground and a dozen dark shapes appeared in the light, streaming down the ramp in columns of two with Drallondryn at their head. Their dark suits

Jan Zimlich

and helmets gleamed dully in the shower of golden light.

The press of humanity parted silently to let the armored aliens pass. Since Drallondryn was the only one not wearing a helmet, a hundred pair of eyes watched the Kri's every move, fascinated with his catlike visage. An undercurrent of emotion seemed to reverberate through the air, but it wasn't fear or hatred, or even apprehension. Something more akin to morbid curiosity, with a little awe thrown in for good measure, as though they had all been witnesses to a particularly gory traffic accident and didn't know how to react.

Garner and Laura both glared accusingly as the Kri approached.

"Where the hell have you been?" Garner snapped, his wizened features taut with anger.

Drallondryn sighed and dropped to his knees beside Aayshen, studied the jagged puncture wound near the base of Aayshen's neck, then extracted a cylinder-shaped tool from a pouch strapped to his waist. "The wound is serious, but not life-threatening to a Savanian," Drallondryn told them matter-of-factly. "There are no major organs in that area of his neck."

Laura half sobbed, half cried in relief.

There was a small, sighlike expulsion of air as the device hissed against his neck. "I have given him an injection of stimulants and cellular regenerators to enhance healing."

Aayshen stirred slightly, much to Laura's relief. His fingers and mouth twitched, and his head moved a few inches to the side.

As Drallondryn sprayed some sort of meshlike substance over Aayshen's wound, Laura lifted her tear-dampened face and stared hard at the Kri. He'd never answered Garner's question. "You left him out here, Drallondryn," she said in a cold, reproachful voice. "Why didn't you help him sooner?"

His yellow gaze caught and held hers, his vertically slanted pupils dilating slightly in the hazy light. "At what price, Laura? A hundred of your people? A hundred of ours? Your entire world for the sake of a single being?" He smiled gently, like an overly patient adult to a backward child. "Aayshen Rahs is a Savanian warrior, trained to serve and die. As a conditioned officer and a starship commander, he is of great value to us, but if the Fates had chosen this moment to cut the thread of his life, there would have been no hue and cry to avenge his death, because to serve and die is his fate, his only fate. Intervention is not our way. We merely watched and waited until your people resolved their conflict, then came to reclaim what was ours, living or dead."

Laura stared at the Kri, rendered speechless by his indifference, until a hot blaze of anger overrode her disbelief. What if they hadn't resolved "their conflict," as he called it? Would they have just left Aayshen to die here, alone on an alien world? Her mouth tensed, and her eyes glittered darkly from anger and the salt of unshed tears. "The Fates," she hissed at Drallondryn, her voice rising and falling with the force of her emotions. "I'm sick to death of hearing about your precious Fates, that what you are and whatever happens was meant to be! It's just an excuse . . . an easy rationalization you've created to hide the truth! There are no Fates, no outside force that decides

347

how and when your people live and die! It's a lie you use to convince yourselves that your miserable lives have some purpose, some kind of meaning, because deep down you know that you've lost the ability to use your free will, thrown away your right to exist as individuals. For all your high and mighty technology, you're nothing but cold-hearted machines!"

She grew quiet for a moment, her fingers gently moving over the cool planes of Aayshen's face, touching, memorizing. When she spoke again, her voice had softened to a dreamy whisper, but the anger still flamed in her dark eyes. "Aayshen was beginning to understand what living in your society cost him, beginning to realize that our way is better, for all its problems. For better or worse we determine our own futures, decide what we want out of life and go get it. We make our own fate."

Her anger flagged, replaced by disgust and a kind of sad resignation, and with those emotions came something new, a faint glimmer of realization that suddenly crystalized in her mind. For a single space of time, she stared at the Kri in mute wonder; then her mouth twitched and she laughed in disbelief.

Garner and Carrie exchanged looks of concern, afraid she had taken leave of her senses. Drallondryn just stared in amazement.

"Oh, this is choice!" Laura's laughter began turning into tears. "All that noble-sounding crap about humans not being ready for contact with your people is only part of the truth, isn't it, Drallondryn?" She wiped at her tears with the back of a sleeve and giggled uncontrollably. "You're just as scared of us as we are of you! Your people don't want contact with us because they know *we'll* contaminate them! Can't have those backward little humans upsetting the galactic applecart with their old-fashioned beliefs about freedom and individual choice. Some of your people might begin to get ideas, decide they like our way better. They might even show a little gumption and tell your society to go to hell. That's the real truth, isn't it, Drallondryn? Contact is just as dangerous for you as it is for us."

The Kri broke eye contact, squirming beneath the strength and conviction of her words and watchful stare. "Our ways are different than yours, Laura. You cannot begin to understand."

"Different, yes, but not better." She saw that clearly now. "As for understanding, I don't think I want to anymore." Laura glanced downward to find Aayshen staring up at her, his pain-filled eyes burning into her with a soul-deep intensity. Her heart lurched, and she bit back a new rush of tears welling in the corners of her eyes. Tears of joy mingled with grief. He was alive, and he was leaving. A tremulous smile lifted the edges of her mouth.

His lips parted slightly, more a grimace than a smile. "I've been listening . . . I heard what you said to Drallondryn, Laura." He lifted a hand to touch an errant tendril of her blond-red hair. "You were right . . . dangerous . . . for both our peoples." His fingertip brushed her temple and for a timeless second, their minds merged together, creating a sweet explosion of desire and love that flared like a star going nova.

The heady sensation passed, and Laura's lids

fluttered open. Their eyes locked, earthy brown and cool, alien blue. A universe of emotions flowed between them, a lifetime of joy and anguish and rapture compressed into a single second of time. Words weren't necessary. There was nothing further to be said.

At a nod from Drallondryn, a Savanian warrior bent low and lifted Aayshen into his massive arms, turned slowly and walked toward the ramp.

Drallondryn stared at Laura for a long moment, a troubled frown rippling across his brow. "I'm truly sorry," he said quietly, and he was, about many things.

"I am, too. More than you'll ever know." She tried to force a farewell smile but found that she couldn't. She felt dead inside, dead and achingly empty. The warrior carrying Aayshen was ascending the ramp, his armor glittering darkly in the firefly light. "But I'm not sorry that he came here. I never will be." The warrior vanished from sight, and with him, her last glimpse of Aayshen. "Tell him that for me, Drallondryn."

The Kri dipped his head slightly, then turned and walked toward the waiting ramp, the line of warriors following behind him single file.

Laura and the townspeople watched in silence as the ramp disappeared, a mixture of emotions passing across their upturned faces. A quickening breeze rose in the still air, then gusted and swirled into a directionless gale, whipping hair and clothes into a tangled frenzy. Many ran from the swirling wind, scrambling for shelter behind trees and cars, but others held their ground, their curious eyes following the alien spacecraft as it silently rose into the enveloping darkness.

Not Quite Paradise

Her face tilted toward the ship and the distant stars, Laura simply stared, oblivious to the howl of the wind and everything around her.

"Tell him I'll never forget," she whispered to the stars.

Epilogue

Cicadas called from the boughs of fragrant pines, their rhythmic drones rising to a high-pitched screech, then drifting into a silent pause. The thick, earthy scents of honeysuckle, dew-drenched loam, and summer grass hung in the moist Gulf air. Spring had died half-born, and the warm May night was filled with the hot breath and pregnant smells of a Southern summer.

Laura stood on the crest of the levee, her bare feet planted firmly in the fertile soil, and tilted her face toward the distant stars, wondering, as always, which of those cold glints of light was his. At times like these, when she stood alone in the dark and stared at the starlit heavens, she could almost feel him, almost hear him, as if he were somewhere near, calling out to her.

The vivid dreams were even stranger, more disquieting, as if he were there with her, deep within her mind, making love to her in ways she had never imagined. Even after all these months, the erotic dreams were still so real that upon awakening in her lonely bed, she wasn't truly sure that she'd been dreaming at all.

A shudder of desire and longing coursed through her body, and she hugged her arms to her chest to stave off a sudden chill. She was losing touch with reality, going mad by slow degrees. Ever since that night in January, time had seemed suspended, the days blending into endless weeks, the weeks drifting into months, all without meaning or end. She felt as though life itself had paused, and she was eagerly awaiting a sign, a signal of some kind to take another breath and continue her life.

She dragged the heels of her hands across tired eyes and rubbed at the ache in her temples, a deep gnawing pain that grew stronger as the days crept by. Four months had passed since that night, yet when she closed her lids, the memories still flared sharp and bright, unblemished by the haze of time. She remembered it all, his face, his wintry eyes, every look and quiet glance, remembered everything with a preternatural clarity that was frightening in itself.

The summer grass felt damp and cool against the soles of her feet as she climbed down the bank of the levee and continued her nightly walk, a compulsive ritual she'd begun months before. First the river and levee, then the majestic oak where they'd picnicked that chilly day, then a stroll down the long rows of pecan trees now thick and green with leaves. She felt closest to him there, as though his spirit somehow haunted the grove of trees where they'd first made love.

Stop it! she raged at herself. Stop thinking about him. There were no spirits or haunted trees, no dream visitors in the dead of night. An anxious frown rippled across her forehead. If she didn't leave here soon, to escape the constant flood of memories, she really would go mad.

She needed to get away from Mississippi, move on and try to build a new life for herself, Bryan, and Garner. She had to find a quiet little place to settle where no one knew her face or name, no one stared or whispered: an anonymous little corner of the world where Escatawpa was just a word.

There was nothing to stop her from leaving anymore. The nursery stood dark and empty, the plants and equipment now residing in the little row of greenhouses Carrie had built in her backyard. The stock of plants and a year's wages had been her farewell gift to Carrie, enough to help get her own nursery started and go into business for herself. They'd said their good-byes to each other a week ago, shared a few tears and vowed to write, but Laura knew it would be a while before she let anyone know where she had gone. She needed a little breathing space, time alone to mold a new life for her family without the old one intruding.

Laura sighed and shook her head. So why hadn't she left yet? The little U-haul trailer she'd rented was mostly packed, half-filled with bags and boxes stuffed with toys, clothes, and an occasional keepsake. And she had money, too, lots of it, more than enough to make a clean start. "Compensation for her inconvenience," they'd called it, but it was hush money all the same.

Her mouth curled downward in a disgusted grimace. The government had purchased her property for ten times the asking price, but no amount of money could ever compensate for the hell they'd put her family through.

Two terrifying weeks spent as government prisoners on some sort of military base in the middle of a desert. Nevada maybe, or California. She wasn't sure, and no one would tell her where they were. Two long weeks of endless medical tests, interrogations, and isolation from the outside world, all under the watchful eyes of stiff-faced scientists and gun-carrying guards.

Once she'd caught a glimpse of Colonel Chapman at the end of an antiseptic corridor. Their eyes met, and before she was whisked away, he gave her a slight smile and lifted a hand in silent acknowledgment. But when she'd asked to speak with him, she was told that he'd been transferred to a base overseas. No one would tell her anything else. But at least she knew he was alive. Somewhere.

A few days after that encounter they'd suddenly been released, flown back to Mississippi and handed a bill of sale to her property and a huge government check. No apologies or explanations, just terse instructions that she had six months to vacate the property, and a warning that she faced prosecution and a federal prison if she ever breathed a word about what had occurred.

Who were they afraid she'd talk to? Laura almost laughed aloud. During her absence, the media had swarmed across southern Mississippi like a plague of nosy locusts, spewing a constant stream of supposed eyewitness accounts of what had happened that night to every corner of a disbelieving America. A fanatical few believed, but the vast majority had simply laughed and wondered how a bunch of drunken rednecks could have possibly mistaken a crashed military helicopter for a UFO. The supermarket tabloids were still having a field day, and Mississippi was once again the butt-end of a thousand jokes. The witnesses themselves, even Carrie and Sheriff Rankin, had responded to the ridicule by erecting a wall of stoic Southern silence. Among the Mississippians, the subject was now taboo, just another embarrassing incident they would rather forget, a tall tale that would soon fade into local myth.

Laura paused for a moment and stared at the star-spattered sky. Sometimes she wished she could forget, put aside the grief and sadness that had shadowed her life since the night Aayshen left. But she couldn't forget him, and never would. She realized that now. No matter where she finally went, or what she did, Aayshen would always be with her. It wasn't her memories or the quiet Mississippi landscape that bound her to him, or kept him alive inside her dreams. They were linked to each other, hearts, minds and souls forever intertwined.

But if it wasn't the memories or a simple matter of geography, why couldn't she summon the courage to just pick up and leave? It would only take an hour or so to finish loading the last of the boxes, pile the cat and her family into the car and then be on her way. Tonight, if she wanted. Bryan and Garner had been ready for days. What was she waiting for? Why had her mind kept whispering not yet ... not yet, each time she'd given thought to leaving?

Laura turned suddenly, searching the darkness with curious eyes. Why did she have the strange feeling that the agonizing wait was finally coming to an end?

Her thoughts still sliding back and forth between the present and the past, she started walking toward the pecan grove. A sense of urgency seemed to vibrate in the humid air, pushing her onward. Her footsteps quickened.

Treetops shifted and sighed in the warm night-wind, and the chorus of cicadas began their summer song once again. Just as she had on a hundred other nights, she stopped beneath a familiar tree and stared upwards through the thick canopy of leaves, catching quick glimpses of the stars and swollen moon through a thin veil of low-scudding clouds. She'd looked up through these same branches, seen the same starry sky with Aayshen all those months ago.

She closed her eyes and remembered, reliving every moment of that winter night in exquisite detail. She could still feel his gentle fingers sliding across her skin, the sensation of floating on a current of air, still hear her own moan of pleasure as he'd entered her body and mind. This was the place she felt closest to him, the reason for her nightly vigil.

This was the place, her mind whispered, where he would come to her again.

A shadow stirred among the trees, moving slowly, inexorably across the darkened grove. Her heartbeat thrummed in her ears. Moonlight stabbed through the blanket of leaves, and the

357

shadow turned a ghostly silver-white. The thick summer grass bent and rustled as he drew nearer. Laura squeezed her lids shut, not daring to hope, frightened that it was just a dream.

Laura, the mind-voice murmured. His fingers twined through her silky hair, and he pressed his lips to her temple in a feathery kiss.

Her lids drifted open. She could feel his breath fanning her face, feel his strong fingers moving through her hair. She gazed up at his pale face in wonder. This was no dream-wraith, no figment dredged from her imagination. He was real.

"Dreams and memories were not enough," Aayshen said huskily. "Without you I was dead inside." A shy, almost hesitant expression crept across his sculpted face. "I have decided to make my own fate . . . whatever it may be."

"Oh, God." Tears of joy trembled on her dark lashes. "I've missed you so." Her arms slid up and around his neck, and she held him close. She was whole again, whole and more alive than she'd been since the night he left four months before. "I couldn't bear to leave here . . . couldn't go on with my life until I knew for sure." The tears spilled down her cheeks as she buried her face against his chest. "A voice kept whispering to me, telling me to wait, but I wasn't certain . . . I was scared it was just my imagination."

"It wasn't your imagination." His arms tightened around her, and he breathed in the heady scent of her hair and salty skin. "I didn't know if you would understand my message, but I had to try. I wanted you to wait for me, to stay here until I had time to make my way back to you again."

Laura lifted her head and stared at him in wonder, her fingers brushing gently across the face she thought she would never see again. The bond between them was even stronger than she had imagined, a link so deep and powerful that she had instinctively understood his silent plea and remained in Mississippi to await his return.

She touched his cheek, the chiseled line of his jaw, inwardly rejoicing that he'd chosen to come back to her, but at the same time her heart ached with the knowledge that the decision had cost him so much. He'd given up everything, his people, his culture, the only way of life he'd ever known, just to be with her. "I hoped, oh, God, I hoped, but I never dared dream that you'd actually be able to come back," she said in a trembly voice. "How, Aayshen? How did you manage it?"

He brushed an errant curl away from her face. "Once I made the decision, I simply resigned my command and left before anyone thought to stop me," he explained quietly. "Drallondryn helped me. I could not have made the arrangements without him."

Her eyes widened, and she stared at him in astonishment. "Drallondryn? I can't believe it. Why would he help you?"

The ghost of a smile played around the edges of Aayshen's mouth. "He said if you asked why, for me to tell you that he wanted to prove he was not the 'coldhearted machine' you thought him to be."

She smiled softly, remembering the heated words she'd spoken the night they left. The gentle Kri had taken them to heart. A shadow of worry suddenly moved through her eyes. "What will happen to him now, Aayshen?"

He drew her close against his chest and folded

Jan Zimlich

his arms around her. "He's decided to go home to Kri . . . to write a book about Earth and its people. Whatever the consequences, Drallondryn has chosen to make his own fate . . . just as I have."

For the first time in Aayshen's life, the future stretched before him like a dark, empty road, one with hidden twists and turns that would take him in directions he had never imagined, never considered before. The thought of walking down that darkened path filled him with trepidation, as well as a deep sense of wonder and excitement that made him want to plunge headlong into the future and never look back. "I don't know what the future holds for us, Laura, but I want to spend it with you and your family . . . if you'll have me."

She drew his lips to hers and sealed her fate with a kiss that left them both breathless with desire. "Together . . ." she murmured against him. "We'll make that future together, Aayshen."

His cerulean eyes glittered like quicksilver in the starlight. "Life could be difficult, Laura. They might search for us, your people as well as mine. This is not a decision to be made lightly."

"There's no decision to make." Crying softly, she threw herself inside the warm circle of his waiting arms. "We'll leave here tonight. The four of us will just disappear." The soaring mountains and deep forests of Oregon beckoned, the frozen, empty wilds of the Canadian Northwest. "No one will ever find us."

Her pulse quickened as his eager lips and fingertips glided over her face and arms, caressing, touching and exploring her yielding flesh. She wound her arms around his back, imprisoning herself inside his warm embrace. Their eyes locked, and she saw infinity in the pale depths of his fathomless gaze.

This was the place where her life would begin again. . . .

An Angel's Touch

Where angels go, love is sure to follow.

Time Heals by Susan Collier. Tired of her nagging relatives, Maeve Fredrickson asks for the impossible: to be a thousand miles and a hundred years away from them. Then a heavenly being grants her wish, and she awakens in frontier Montana. Saved from the wilderness by a handsome widower, Maeve loses her heart to her rescuer—and her temper over the antics of his three less-than-angelic children. As her angel prods her to fight for Seth, Maeve can only pray for the strength to claim a love made in paradise.

__52030-3 $4.99 US/$5.99 CAN

Longer Than Forever by Bronwyn Wolfe. Patrick is in trouble, alone in turn-of-the-century Chicago, and unjustly jailed with little hope for survival. Then the honey-haired beauty comes to him, as if she has heard his prayers. Lauren has all but given up on finding true love when she feels the green-eyed stranger's call—summoning her across boundaries of time and space to join him in a struggle against all odds; uniting them in a love that will last longer than forever.

__52042-7 $5.99 US/$7.99 CAN

Dorchester Publishing Co., Inc.
65 Commerce Road
Stamford, CT 06902

Please add $1.75 for shipping and handling for the first book and $.50 for each book thereafter. NY, NYC, PA and CT residents, please add appropriate sales tax. No cash, stamps, or C.O.D.s. All orders shipped within 6 weeks via postal service book rate. Canadian orders require $2.00 extra postage and must be paid in U.S. dollars through a U.S. banking facility.

Name_____
Address_____
City _____ State _____Zip_____
I have enclosed $_____in payment for the checked book(s).
Payment <u>must</u> accompany all orders.☐ Please send a free catalog.